THE LEGENDS OF LYNQUEST

SEARCH FOR GREATNESS &
SECRET OF THE CHILD &
TALE OF TWO FACES

WRITTEN
BY

B·F· HESS

ILLUSTRATED BY ALLISON ELROD

ISBN: 1481964534
ISBN 13: 9781481964531

Library of Congress Control Number: 2013910292
CreateSpace Independent Publishing Platform
North Charleston, South Carolina

DEDICATIONS

To my beloved Holly, who is my sunshine, my wellspring
of optimism, and my endless source of goodwill. Also to
the late, great Larry Pontius, whose strong spirit lives on
in his written works. Special thanks to all my family and
friends who continue to support my endeavors. No finer
treasure can a man have, than the support of those he loves.

THE LEGENDS OF LYNQUEST

SEARCH FOR GREATNESS

CHAPTER ONE

THE RUN DOWN

How did I ever get into this predicament? Thought Tobias as he ran down the road leading from the glen. He ran as fast as he could, trying to stay one step ahead of his pursuers. Out of breath, he quickly crossed the road and scampered up the hillside to hide behind a small bush at the top of the hill that provided some refuge from sight. A moment or two passed before the silhouettes of four young boys could be seen walking the road that came from town.

"Where are you, you little runt?" he heard one of them yell.

"Tobi, you pipsqueak, when we find you, you're going to get such a beating!" another yelled.

The small boy sank back behind the bush. He recognized one of the voices. It was Scott Henry, the biggest boy at his school. There was nothing but terror awaiting anyone who had fallen victim to his violent disposition. He heard Scott's voice again.

"You and Tom climb that hill and see if the little runt is hiding up there."

The panic-stricken boy scoured the area with his eyes, looking for another place to hide. Down the road a short distance was a small bridge that crossed Black Water Stream. It was called 'Black Water' because of the thick black mud that lined its bottom. The boy raced down the back side of the hill and sped down the road, looking over his shoulder every once in a while to check and see if they had come around the bend in the road yet. He slid down the slope and into the deep mud of the stream. The cold water rose to his waist, causing his feet and legs to go numb.

Motionless, he peered over the bridge at the hill above the road. The two boys that had climbed the hill searched all the bushes and trees, while the other two boys still walked the road, laughing and joking about what they were going to do to him once they had found him. As the two boys on the road neared the bridge, Tobias panicked. He had to do something. If he stayed where he was, he would be found. He thought about hiding under the bridge, but in order to do that he would have to get completely wet. The bridge was low to the water and there was no way under except to submerge himself completely. He took a deep breath and sank beneath the water. When he rose again under the bridge, he found himself draped in spiderwebs. He wanted to scream, but the boys had reached the bridge and were standing directly over him.

"Where are you, you little scab?" Scott sounded furious.

"Ya know, Scott," the other voice said. "We could probably look all day and never find him out here."

The small boy saw the figures of the two boys through the slender cracks between the planks of the bridge. The cold water began to take its toll on his body and he tried to keep from shivering. By now, the two that had been searching the hill had joined their friends at the bridge.

"Come on, Scott. I'm not going to spend all day looking for the squirt."

"Yeah, besides, he's got to go home sometime. We'll just wait until he comes to school, then we'll pound him into the ground."

"Yeah, I guess you're right. It will only be harder on him when we do catch up with him," Scott replied, laughing.

"Yeah, yeah, yeah," they all clamored back.

They started to walk back to town, chattering and laughing among themselves. Tobias waited awhile before emerging from the water. When he did, he brushed the spiderwebs from his face and slumped down on the muddy bank of the stream. He clutched himself tightly with his arms and shivered violently as he watched the boys disappear around the bend of the road.

As he sat there, he became aware of a sound being carried on the breeze. It was the sound of a woman's voice whispering something ever so softly. "Tobiasssss," said the voice. "Sssseed of Malcolm, wearer of the face of sorrows, born beneath a troubled crown." Tobias looked around, but saw nothing but leaves dancing across the ground as a whirlwind swept them along. He imagined the leaves whispering to him as they scraped along the ground; that is, until he felt cold fingers caress his face, quickening the chill that now took over his body. Goose bumps quickly rose and the hair on the back of his neck stood on end as a wave of dread passed through him. *Truly*, he thought, *something ominous is overshadowing my life.*

He looked around and shook off the feeling as best he could, then stood up, crossed the bridge, and followed the road away from town. He didn't feel like going home. He wondered if he ever could. Instead, he headed for a place on the highest hill that overlooked his house and the sleepy little town of Summers Glen. He retreated here when he needed to be alone or wanted to read a good book without interruption. It was also where he did his best thinking. It was a small clearing, nestled in the center of some enormous rocks that jutted out of the side of the hill.

As he climbed between two of the large rocks that kept his secret place hidden, he was startled by the figure of an old man resting against one of the boulders.

"Ah, you must be Tobi," the old man said.

"Tobias," said the boy.

"Well, Tobias, you look a tad damp for a sunny day such as today."

"That's not funny. I'm cold, too."

"I'm sorry, lad. I did not mean to insult you," said the old man. "Come closer and I will make a fire for you."

Tobias hesitated, not sure what to expect from the stranger. As the man gathered wood and dry grass for the fire, Tobias stood there quaking in his shoes, trembling from head to toe.

"Don't just stand there, lad, give me a hand."

Tobias moved to a pile of wood the old man had stacked at one side of the clearing. One by one, he handed the man the branches, stretching out his arm so he didn't have to get too close.

"Come now, boy, I'm not going to bite you." The old man took out a fair-sized pouch and retrieved two stones of flint from its depths. He struck them together over some dry grass, they released a spark, and smoke began to rise. Tobias watched as the smoke formed a column. The old man blew on the tiny embers and flames began to grow. The pillar of smoke twirled as it ascended into the sky. Their attention fixed on the rising smoke as something strange began to take shape in its midst.

A woman's face clearly formed in the swirling gray. Tobias's face grew grim when the woman whispered his name.

"Tobiasss...the calling has begun..."

The old man, too, saw the face, but quickly dismissed it by waving his hand through the smoke, saying, "Now, I'll have none of your nonsense today." Dumbfounded by the sight, Tobias just stared at the stranger in bewilderment.

It wasn't long before they had a nice raging fire. Moving away from the fire, the old man said, "I am warm enough as it is, so if you don't mind, I will sit over here."

That suited Tobias just fine. He stood as close to the fire as he could without burning himself. Holding his hands out over the flames, he rubbed them together and stared at the archaic man. He was dressed in tattered clothes and wore a pair of small slippers that were made of extremely thin leather. Wrinkles lined his face and a deep scar tracked under his right eye. His long, stringy white hair hung down over his face, partially hiding the wild look of his steel gray eyes. An impish grin seemed to be a permanent fixture upon his face. Tobias said nothing. He fixed a worried stare on the odd character.

The fire snapped and popped, calling Tobias to gaze into its dancing flames. He wanted to look away, but the elf-like man presented such a strange fascination, that Tobias could not break his stare. The man reached into his bedroll and pulled out a long slender box. He opened it and carefully lifted out a pipe of the same dimensions. Filling it with the tobacco he had in the pouch, he lit it, drew a long breath of smoke, and released it into the air. The scent of jasmine mixed with just a touch of cinnamon wafted across to Tobias. It was an enchanting smell, and soon left Tobias feeling more at ease with his company.

"So, what did those boys want with you?" the man asked cautiously.

"Nothing. They didn't want anything," Tobias said sharply.

"Nothing, eh? I have never seen anyone"—the old man paused to puff on his pipe—"run from nothing before. How do you expect to become a great leader of men if—" The old man stopped short and cast a bewildering glance at Tobias as he puffed on his pipe lightly to keep it lit, and then continued. "Well, it's not how your father would have handled it, anyway."

"How do know my father?" asked Tobias.

"I have been in service to your family for a very long time," he said, pointing at Tobias with the end of his pipe. "Do you know those boys?"

"I don't want to talk about it," Tobias snapped.

"You don't want to talk? Then perhaps you would rather listen." The old man's deep, gruff voice was full of mystery. "Well, young Tobias, I have a tale for you, a story so old that few men alive have heard it, and fewer still know it completely. Tell me, Tobias, have you ever heard of Lynquest the Great?"

"You mean the old storyteller? But those stories are just fairy tales," said Tobias sarcastically.

"Most say they are, but I say they're not. They're as real as you or me, and what's more, I know for a fact that Lynquest still lives." The old man's eyes opened wide when the words left his lips.

"Don't be daft," Tobias snapped. "That would make him almost a thousand years old."

"Yes, lad, that it does, but that is not what makes Lynquest great."

"Why is Lynquest called great, anyway? I mean, what makes him so special?" Tobias asked, questioning the old man's sanity.

"Well, to be sure, lad, Lynquest wasn't always so great. He was a boy much like yourself."

CHAPTER TWO

DRAGON'S TALE

He had twelve years behind him as the youngest son of a tanner in the town of Eadenburrow at the foot of Abiding Mountain. Now, Lynquest had two brothers, Robert and John, both of whom were much older and larger than him. Robert and John were known throughout the town for their strength and power. They once pulled a fully loaded hay wagon out of a mud pit by themselves. Few people even knew they had a younger brother. To make matters worse, poor Lynquest had the misfortune of having the first name of Tiny. His father gave him the name at birth when he held his tiny baby boy for the first time.

Tiny was every bit the craftsman in making saddles that his brothers were, but, being the youngest, he was forced to do the tasks of tanning which his brothers hated. Tasks like fetching the hides from the butcher in town, then scraping, cleaning, and salting them before soaking them in the tanning solution. He also had to dry and stretch them on the frames and then lubricate them with fat to make fine leather. His brothers, on the other hand, had the prestigious job of taking the leather and turning it into fine equestrian goods of all kinds.

One morning, young Lynquest was taking the wagon into town to purchase more hides, when he noticed a strange white cloud encircling the mountain like a wreath. The wind blew the tapered ends of the cloud, yet the cloud remained constant. The summit rose out of the billowing haze like some ancient monolith, keeping watch over the surrounding hills.

Day after day, he noticed the cloud never changed its size, nor did it move from its position on the mountain, and it started to make him wonder what could cause such a thing. Some days, he would notice the ground rumbling softly beneath his feet, adding to his growing curiosity about the mountain. Then one day, he decided to finish his chores early and make the long walk up the mountain in search of the source of the strange rumbling. As he neared the cloud, he was taken aback by the overwhelming smell of rotten eggs. He entered the cloak of white with a sense of foreboding, but being a curious sort, he kept going. He slowly made his way through the thick haze to the back side of the mountain. The once faint rumbling of the ground grew louder and stronger with each of his carefully placed steps. Clinging to the steep slope of the mountainside, he soon stumbled upon the entrance of an enormous cave, which he felt sure was the source of the putrid smoke.

Covering his face with his right hand, he entered slowly, moving his left hand along the wall to guide his way into the depths of the cavern. The rumbling noise from the cave slowly turned to a long, deep moan, separated by a strange gurgling, as if the mountain itself was lamenting over some great illness. Tiny followed the wall carefully for some time until he reached the back of the cave, or so he thought. But when he placed his hands on the wall, it suddenly moved away from him! *This can't be*, he thought to himself, so he took a few more steps and placed his hands on the wall again. It felt cold and clammy, not at all like the side wall, which was cold, but dry and crumbly. He felt along the back wall slowly. It felt like an enormous stone that had been sculpted and polished until it was smooth. He pounded on it with his fist and it moved again, this time with a jerk.

"Go away," a deep voice grumbled. "I am in no condition to kill today, so go, and think yourself fortunate."

Tiny froze. Petrified, he stepped back and collected his thoughts. He listened to the gurgling sound closely and recognized that who, or whatever it was, was very ill. *Hack, hack, hack*, the deep voice began to cough. A huge billow of white smoke burst forth from the depths of the cave. The ground trembled underfoot, and dirt from the ceiling rained down on Tiny's head. He braced himself against the wall to keep from falling over. The ground settled under his feet, giving him back his stability.

"You shouldn't cough so hard," Tiny squeaked. "The mountain may come down on you."

"Mmm, it matters not," said the voice softly. "I am all but dead anyway."

"It sounds like you are terribly ill," said Tiny.

"Not ill," the voice answered. "Wounded."

"Wounded?" Tiny asked, startled by the answer.

"Yes! Now go, before I decide there should be two deaths in this cave. Leave now and you may yet live."

"But what if I could help you?" Tiny asked.

"I doubt you could," said the voice.

"Show me the wound and I will try," said Tiny. He stepped toward the voice and felt along the smooth surface of what he now knew was not the back wall. He kept searching with his hands until he came to an object sticking out. It was cold and hard like steel, and shaped like the hilt of a sword.

"It feels like a sword," observed Tiny.

"It is," answered the voice. "It is the reason for my pain. Please pull it out."

"If I pull it out now, you may bleed to death. I will go get something to bind the wound. I will be back shortly," said Tiny. He quickly rushed out of the cave and down the mountain.

Once he had reached his home, he set about the task of gathering together the things he would need. He took the small handcart that belonged to his father and filled it with firewood, a large iron cooking pot, and a satchel full of old linens. He also took the largest skin he could find and filled it with water. After adding a flint stone and a container of camphor oil that his father used on the horses' wounds, he took hold of the cart's handle and started back up the mountain. The heavy load made the trip difficult, but he persevered until he reached the cave. Quietly, he rolled the handcart into the cave and stacked the wood on the ground, preparing to make a fire.

He placed the pot over the wood and filled it with the water. He gathered dry grass from the mountainside and spread it on the wood around the pot. Kneeling down with the flint and rock in his hands, he began striking them together. *Chick, chick, chick.* The sparks shattered the murky darkness of the cave.

"What now?" the voice groaned. "Can I not suffer in silence?"

"I have brought something to bandage your wound," Tiny said. After a spark caught the dry grass, he gently blew on it until a bright blue-orange flame arose. Tiny waited in silence until the flames engulfed the pot and the water began to boil. As the fire grew, it shed light on the back of the cave. The faint outline of the sword could be seen protruding out of the far wall, and for the first time, Tiny watched as a steady stream of blood flowed from the wound. He moved closer to the sword and peered at it through the haze. The metal shone red by the light of the fire, and on the hilt of the sword was the image of a serpent's tongue. Tiny reached for the handle slowly.

"Now, this is going to hurt, but it has to be done," he said, trembling.

"Then do it," answered the voice sternly.

Tiny clasped the sword in both hands, placed his foot against the wall, and, in one stroke, pulled it from the wound. Such a roar of pain soared out of the murky depths of the cave that the mountain shook to its core. Dirt and rocks rained down once more. Tiny fell to the ground, still clutching the sword in both hands. When the dust cleared, the fire still glowed, though it had dimmed a little. Tiny regained his feet and looked at the wound. It was bleeding much worse than he had thought it would.

"I am going to have to burn the wound to stop the bleeding," he said. "However, if you let out another yell like that, we will both be dead, trapped under this mountain," he added.

"Would it not be easier just to kill me?" asked the voice.

"Maybe," said Tiny. "But I cannot just let you die. You're losing a lot of blood. If I don't close the wound, you will die."

Tiny wiped the blade of the sword clean and washed it in the boiling water. He then placed it on the fire and fanned the flames until the blade radiated with a wild red light of its own. Lifting the blade from the fire, he returned to the wound.

"Now, remember, you must try to keep your tongue or this is all in vain," said Tiny.

"I will try," answered the voice.

"For both our sakes, I hope you do," Tiny said. Then he raised the fiery sword to the wound. "Here it comes." He thrust the sword back into the hole from whence it came.

A low rumble in the cave grew louder as the sword remained in the wound. "Rrrrrr..." Tiny only held the sword in place for a moment, then pulled it out and ran from the cave.

The rumble gave way to a roar that rocked the mountain. "Rrrrrraaaaaaaah!" Tiny fell to his knees on the mountainside and waited to see if the cave would still be there. The ground settled once more, and Tiny returned to the cave to find it still intact. He entered slowly. There was only the sound of heavy breathing, and with every breath the smoke got thicker. The fire had gone out, smothered by falling dirt. Tiny found the container of camphor oil and the linens on the ground, and dusted them off as best he could. He felt along the walls until he found the wound. He very carefully spread the oil on the injury. When he touched it, the wall flinched, yet no sounds came from within. Tiny packed the puncture by soaking the linens in the warm water and laying them across it.

"I will leave you now, but I will return to check on you tomorrow," said Tiny. Silence settled in the cave, except for the heavy breathing. Tiny took his father's cart and started home.

That night at dinner, his father questioned him about the missing items.

"I noticed a few things missing around the house today," he said. Robert and John began smiling at the thought of Tiny's impending trouble. "I have already asked your brothers and they had no idea," he added.

"That's no surprise," Tiny retorted.

"Shut up, you little runt," John said, lacking any wit for a clever retort.

"Quiet, John," his father said sharply. Then, turning to Tiny, he asked, "Did you take them, son? I want to know." The room fell silent for a moment.

Tiny hated to lie. It was something his brothers were constantly accusing him of and he never wanted to prove them right. He knew his father was a compassionate man and probably wouldn't have minded him taking the things if it was to help someone else. So he answered, "Yes, I took them to do a favor for someone. I will return them when I am finished, Father. I promise."

"See, I told you, Father. He stole them," said Robert.

"I did not," said Tiny. "I only borrowed them."

"You did, too," accused Robert. "You took them without asking and that's the same as stealing, you little thief."

"That is enough!" his father shouted. "Now, Tiny has given me his word that he will return them and that is good enough for me. I don't want to hear another word on the matter." The room fell silent and they finished their dinner.

The next morning, Tiny rose early and reloaded the handcart with wood. He refilled the skin with water and made his way back up the mountain. Every morning and every night for five days, he kept watch over the mysterious voice, making sure the wound was kept clean and the linens were replaced. Every day he sped through his chores, and every day he walked the long path up the mountain. Finally, on the sixth day, when he awoke and looked out at the mountain standing in the distance, he saw that the thick white smoke had been replaced by a pale white haze. He gathered his things as before and started out for the mountain, a tired but determined boy. As he neared the mouth of the cave, he heard no sound at all.

He stood in front of the cave and stared into the black emptiness of the enormous hole. The smoke that came from the darkness wasn't as thick as before. The smell was strong, but not nearly as strong as it was on previous days. He slowly entered the cave, but when he reached the iron pot he had left, he found that it had been turned upside down. Tiny dropped the skin full of water he was carrying and knelt down to see what had happened.

At the sound of the skin falling, the voice spoke from the depths of the mountain. "So, you have returned."

"The water," Tiny said. "Someone has poured it all out."

"It was I," said the voice. "I no longer had use for it. Just as I no longer have use for you."

"But I thought we could be friends," Tiny said as he picked up the iron pot.

"Now, about your death," the voice said.

"My death?" He quietly started to back out of the cave, clutching the pot as he did so.

"Yes," said the voice. "Did you think I would forget? I have an excellent memory, as did my father, and his father before him." Tiny had backed out of the cave completely and was preparing to run. "We dragons never forget," rumbled the voice.

"D-d-dragon?" said Tiny.

"Yes, a dragon," the voice bellowed, as the immense head of the beast burst forth from the mouth of the cave.

Tiny wanted to run, but his legs trembled beneath him. He couldn't take his eyes off the creature. The horrendous head of the dragon was almost as large as the cave entrance itself. It was dark green, with the face of a lion, and a bone-white mane encircled its head. Two horns that looked like polished brass protruded from the top of its head. Its solid gold eyes shimmered with slivers of black onyx in the centers.

"I did not forget the way you disturbed my rest and how you persistently returned to my cave again and again." The dragon flashed its long white teeth and glared at the helpless boy. "But I won't forget the great care you took in healing my infirmity. Dragons are ill-tempered by nature, yet we can also be very grateful."

It was only then that Tiny realized he wasn't going to be eaten. The toothy display upon the dragon's face was an attempt at a smile. Tiny stood motionless. His lower lip began to tremble. He tried hard to think of something to say, but couldn't.

"Speak up, boy. Don't just stand there gawking. What are you staring at, anyway? Is there someone stuck between my teeth?"

"What?" said Tiny, stepping backward.

"Dragons are not without a good sense of humor," he said, laughing. "At least this one's not," he added. "What is your name, boy?"

"Tiny," he said timidly.

"Fitting name for one of your stature. I am Subakai, an eastern dragon of wisdom. I had already traveled a long way, injured, when I took refuge in this mountain. You needn't fear me, young human. I will do you no harm. Because of your steadfast devotion to my well-being, I will break a long-standing rule, and for the first time in my two thousand years I will call a human 'friend.'"

"Two thousand years? You're ancient," said Tiny.

"Not really," said Subakai. "We dragons live to be much, much older."

"Do you breathe fire?" asked Tiny, still marveling over the immense size of the creature's head.

"Not yet," he said. "I have not yet earned my fire."

"Earned your fire? I thought all dragons were born knowing how to breathe fire," said Tiny.

"Not all dragons. As a dragon of wisdom, I must earn my fire by searching the world over for the seed of wisdom that will carry me into adulthood."

"But I saw smoke," said Tiny. "That's what led me to you."

"I have smoke, but I have not yet achieved my fire." To demonstrate this, the dragon drew a deep breath, opened its enormous mouth, and let go a huge cloud of smoke that enveloped Tiny, leaving him wheezing from the smell.

"Please," said Tiny, coughing, "if you don't mind...I can't breathe." He quickly moved out of the cloud, away from the cave, clasping his chest as he cleared his lungs.

Seeing that Tiny had moved away from the entrance, the dragon said, "Ah, I haven't been out of this cave in weeks. I must get out and stretch."

Tiny, who was still bent over clutching his breast, looked up as the dragon began to emerge from the cave. The dragon's long snakelike body was interrupted by only two pairs of short stocky legs. The first pair, set only a small distance below the head, was so far apart from the second pair that its belly dragged the ground. It looked as if a long green wall had gotten up and walked away. Two long plates of armor protected its back, and its tail was almost twice as long as its body. A long ridge of sharp spines ran the length of its back, and a flat plate the size of a small shield crested the tip of its tail. The dragon raised its head and front legs into the air. Its massive jaws opened wide, while its claws stretched out, grasping at the air. Suddenly, the two plates on its back rose up like two great coffin lids that opened in opposite directions and became the largest set of scaly wings he had ever seen. The dragon spread them wide before Tiny, as if it was showing them off. They rose before his eyes like two colossal sails of a ship, blocking out the morning sun and leaving Tiny standing in the shadow.

"You can fly?" asked Tiny.

"Of course," said the dragon. "How did you think I arrived here, by boat?"

"Have you ever...I mean, would you ever consider..." Tiny stammered a little, not knowing how to ask his question.

"Ah, you want to take a trip, don't you?" surmised the dragon as he peered down at the small boy.

"Just a short trip," said Tiny. "I have never flown before and this might be my only chance."

"Well then, we had better make it a good journey." The dragon lowered his head to the ground and said, "You may use my mane to climb on top of my head."

Tiny approached the dragon and took hold of a fistful of the thick white hair. Before he pulled on the tresses, he stopped and asked, "This won't hurt you, will it?"

"No," said the dragon, "the hair grows from the armor around my head. It won't hurt at all."

So Tiny took another handful of the mane and began to climb atop the serpent's head.

Once on top, he sat between the two shiny horns and wrapped his arms around each one. He almost lost his stomach when the dragon raised its head into the air. The dragon leaned forward and began to thrust its wings to the ground. A cloud of dust burst forth from the ground, and dry grasses on the slope of the mountain started dancing under the force of the wind of the dragon's thrusts. Slowly, the great leviathan rose into the air.

With each movement of its wings, its body twisted and turned like a ribbon in the wind. Up, up, up they rose, until the very peak of the mountain stood far beneath them. Tiny's hands began to sweat as the tremendous height dazzled his eyes. They swooped and climbed into the clouds, then dove again, emerging above Tiny's house. He saw his broth-

ers, like two small insects, marveling at the strange bird that soared above their heads. Quickly, they ascended back into the clouds. The cold, moist air rushed past Tiny's face. His clothes were soon made damp by the clouds' moisture, and little drops of water began to form on his face and hands.

Holding on was difficult, but out of sheer fear Tiny clung to the beast's horns with the strength of a lion. Tiny could only see the thick white haze of the cloud before him, when suddenly it opened up into a world that he had never seen before. It was as if a giant veil had dropped to reveal a scenic cloudscape so beautiful that it almost hurt his eyes to look upon it. There before him, in the nakedness of the sun, was a whole world, complete with towering mountains and deep chasms, all of which were made from the tops of the billowy white clouds.

Tiny looked over his shoulder. The serpent's tail slithered through the clouds like a snake in water. The bright mist moved with every bend and twist of his tail. The two of them frolicked among the clouds for a while, and then descended back to earth, resting on a hilltop far from any town. The dragon rested his head upon the ground to make it easier for Tiny to climb down. Tiny's feet gently settled on the ground and he regained his balance. He trembled, alive with excitement and curiosity. He sat on the ground next to the horrendous head of the beast, fell back into its full, soft mane, and exclaimed with a sigh, "That was amazing!"

A moment or two passed as Tiny stared up at the sky, and then a question popped into his head.

"Su...Su...," Tiny stuttered, as he tried to repeat the dragon's name.

"Subakai," said the dragon.

"Subakai?" Tiny said inquisitively.

"Yes, my diminutive friend," answered Subakai.

"How did you get wounded?" Tiny asked carefully.

"It was in the prodigious caves of the Thundering Mountains. I had sought to rest there for a while, for my search had made me weary. I stumbled upon a great door deep within the caves. It was lit by two urns of fire, one on either side. I was trying to read the inscription on the door, when a strange knight in blood red armor stepped out of the shadows brandishing his sword. His helmet covered his face completely, so I could not tell you what he looked like.

"He fought like a demon. At one point, he leapt upon my back and thrust his sword into my side. I rose up and crushed him against the ceiling of the cave, an act that would have killed an ordinary man, but he kept coming. I swung around and struck him with my tail again and again, but each time he would jump to his feet and make another attempt at reaching his sword still buried in my side. I finally decided that I could not wear him down, and if he ever retrieved his sword, it would spell the end of me.

"I fled the caves and traveled until I reached your mountain. I have been searching for my seed of wisdom for many years, and in my travels I have seen many things, but I have never seen a human fight like that. It was as if he could not be killed."

"So, you have been traveling for some time, then?" Tiny asked.

"I have," the dragon replied.

"What kinds of things have you seen?"

"I have seen the emerald green cliffs standing at the edge of the Black Sea of Sorrow. I have seen the glistening silver walls of the Valley of the Sun at twilight. I have watched as ships laden with treasure and men racing to their deaths followed the enchanted sound of the siren's song at the Sea of Fear. I have smelled the mysterious blossoms on the Island of Panthallimos which inspires everlasting love."

As he spoke, a strange sensation overcame Tiny and he was filled to completeness. He became aware of the greatness of the world and longed to find his destiny. It was as if he was a small piece of a very large puzzle, and he yearned to find his place of importance, his path to greatness. He snuggled back into the dragon's soft mane and said, "Tell me more about these things."

"Which ones?" Subakai asked.

"The flowers," said Tiny. "Tell me more about the mysterious flowers that inspire everlasting love."

"The story tells of the two tribes that lived on opposite sides of the island. They were at war with each other for many years. One day, a young man had spotted a young woman picking wildflowers on the slopes of Mount Ashor. Every day, he would return to the same place to find her doing the same thing. She would pick only the fragrant purple blossoms. So he gathered as many as he could carry and waited for her to arrive the following day. She did, and they fell deeply in love. But she was from the warring tribe on the other side of the island and they could not be married.

"One night, the men of his village raided the other tribe and the young woman was killed. The young man watched from a distance as the girl's family buried her on the slopes of the mountain. He took the seeds of the flower she loved so much and spread them over the entire hillside where she was buried. It is said that he watered them every day with his tears. If they are picked and given as a gift of love, then that love will never die."

"That's beautiful," said Tiny. "I wish I could travel."

"Perhaps you will someday," Subakai said.

"Will you stay with me? You can live on Abiding Mountain and I can visit you," urged Tiny.

"I do not think I can. I still have not finished my quest for the seed. But I will come and visit you from time to time. Just look for smoke upon the mountain and you will know that I am there."

Tiny felt good that he had found a new friend. He gazed into the clouded sky and listened to the slow rhythm of Subakai's breathing. As he did, the strenuous schedule of the previous five days and the excitement of the morning's adventure caught up with him, and he drifted off to sleep.

He was awakened by a loud crack of thunder and a sudden downpour. It was almost dark and Tiny had slept the entire day. He leapt to his feet and said, "Oh no, it's late. I've got to get home. My father is going to kill me."

Subakai called out, "Climb on. I will take you home straightaway.'"

Tiny climbed on top of Subakai's head and they sped through the driving rain and wind, back to the mountain cave. Tiny gathered his father's things and raced down the mountainside, yelling, "Good-bye. I will come and visit you again as soon as I can."

When he arrived home, his father was standing outside, calling his name. Tiny was out of breath and saw his father's look of disappointment.

"I am sorry, Father. I hope you are not too angry with me."

"Well, I am not pleased. Dinner is going to be late because of you, and I had to split your chores up between your two brothers," his father said loudly.

"Look," said Tiny, "I have brought your things back."

"Good, leave them here and go clean up. You can put them away after dinner."

Tiny went straight inside and changed out of his wet clothes, washed his hands, and waited quietly at the table for dinner.

At dinner, his brothers were suspiciously quiet. They glared across the table at him in silence. Tiny knew he would have to deal with them sometime. He knew there would be a price to pay for making them do his chores.

"So, where were you today, Tiny?" his father asked. "What was so important that you had to miss doing your part around here?"

Robert and John snickered when they saw Tiny struggling to find an answer.

"I was visiting a sick friend and I just lost track of time," Tiny said finally.

"A whole day?" Robert questioned fiercely.

"He is lying, Father," said John. "He stayed away on purpose so he would not have to do any work."

"I did not," retorted Tiny. "Anyway, my friend is better now, so I will stay home tomorrow and make sure everything is done."

"You better, you lazy worm, or we will squash you like the bug you are."

"Stop it!" their father yelled. Robert and John fell back into silence and fumed as they sent icy-cold stares from beneath their lowered brows across the table to Tiny. "If I had known it was going to cause this much trouble, I would not have asked."

The room dipped into silence and the sounds of chiming silverware emphasized the lack of conversation. John drew his mug to his mouth and guzzled down some ale. Then, setting the mug firmly back on the table, he wiped the excess ale from his lips with his hand and said, "Me and Robert saw a strange bird today, flying over the house."

"That's right," Robert added. "It had one long tail feather that moved like the tail of a kite."

"It was a dragon," said Tiny.

Suddenly, all motion stopped. His father and brothers looked at him as if his face had just fallen off. His brothers burst out in laughter.

"A dragon?" said John.

"Where did you get that?" asked Robert. "You have been daydreaming too much and you finally snapped."

"Well...I mean...it could have been, couldn't it?" said Tiny, trying to recover his dignity. "What I meant was, it could have been anything." His words were muted by the laughter. Even his father looked at him as if he had just been named the court jester. "I am finished with my dinner now, Father. Can I be excused?" Tiny just wanted to disappear.

"Yes, son," his father said, smiling, "you may go."

Tiny took care of his dishes and slipped outside to escape the laughter. Once outside, he gathered together his father's things in the handcart and slowly towed it around the house to the barn. The ground was soft and muddy, which made the pulling hard. He made sure to avoid the large puddle that always formed next to the barn after rainstorms. Once he entered the barn, he set about the task of putting every item in its place. The large iron pot he placed in the corner. The large water skin he hung on the peg by the door, and the handcart he leaned against the far wall. When he turned to leave, he found Robert and John standing in the doorway.

"We have come to get paid for doing your chores," said Robert.

"I don't have any money," said Tiny apprehensively.

"We don't want money. You see, we have been working so hard today, thanks to you, that we now want to have some fun."

Tiny tried to make a break for the gap between the two young men, but John stuck his leg out and tripped him, causing Tiny to fall headlong, face-first onto the muddy ground.

"So, you thought you saw a dragon, eh, runt?" said Robert. "The only dragon you're going to see will be a draggin' through the mud." Then his brothers each grabbed a leg and dragged Tiny across the muddy ground to the large puddle that lay beside the barn.

"Come on, guys, I just got cleaned up," said Tiny, attempting to talk his way out of his predicament. His two brothers lifted him high into the air by his feet, then, taking hold of his arms as well, they swung him to and fro. Once, twice...

"Come on, guys. You don't want to do this!"

On the third swing, they released Tiny into the air, hurling him face-first into the deep pool of mud. *Splash!* He landed flat on his stomach. He lay motionless at first; then, pushing his hands deep into the mud, he peeled his face from the cold sludge. Rolling over, he sat up and tried to wipe the mud from his eyes.

"You just remember this the next time you decide to disappear," said John.

"Yeah," added Robert, "if we have to do your work one more time, you would be smarter to stay missing." His two brothers turned their backs on him and walked back to the house laughing.

Tiny sat there, embarrassed and frustrated. He tried to think of a way to explain this to his father. He stood up and slowly made his way to the horses' watering trough where he washed his face and hands. Making his way back to the house, he opened the door and called for his father.

"Good grief!" his father exclaimed, when he saw Tiny standing in the doorway. "What happened to you?"

"I slipped and fell into the mud," said Tiny, as he stared past his father at his two older brothers, who tried to look busy.

"Wait here a moment while I get you a clean set of clothes," said his father. He left and then returned with some dry clothes, a towel, and a blanket. "Here, go wash yourself in the river and clean out those muddy clothes."

Tiny made the short journey across the road and down the hillside to the river. It was late in the evening and the moonlight shone on the slow-moving water. Before cleaning himself, he sat upon a rock and stared at the glistening water, at how it moved so gracefully downstream. Once again, his mind was filled with the stories told to him by his dragon friend. Once again, he was filled with the longing for unseen places and challenging adventures. *Somewhere out there,* he thought, *there is a place where the routine stops and life begins.* He felt sure that this river would lead him to that place.

At that moment, he made a decision to follow the river, his river to life, to wherever it might lead. His brothers would always be older than him and he could not bear the thought of spending the rest of his young adult life catering to them. He pondered the question of leaving home and all that it meant while he was cleaning up. The water was cold, but with all he had on his mind, it did not seem to matter.

After wringing out his wet clothes, he tied them into a bundle. Wrapping the blanket around himself, he snatched up the bundle of wet clothes and started back to the house. He walked slowly, for he truly did not want to return, but he knew leaving home would be a journey he would have to prepare for. Once at home, he hung the wet clothes on the front porch rail and went directly to bed, without saying so much as good night to anyone.

The next morning dawned early, as usual, and Tiny was up and about his duties, cleaning the house, feeding and watering the horses, and preparing the leather for his brothers. But this time, before taking the leather into the workshop, he cut thin strips off the length of each hide. He hid these long strands of leather in a sack in the barn. Each time he had to prepare the skins for his father's shop, he would do the same thing.

It was several weeks later when he finally had enough leather strands to fulfill his plans. He took his father's ax and went to a grove of trees, where he cut down six trees of medium size and stripped them of their limbs. One by one, he dragged them to a place at the edge of the river that was well hidden from the road by shrubs. He then took his sack full of leather cords and lashed the logs together, making a raft. He covered it up with branches, leaves, and dry grass so it couldn't be seen, and left it there.

The next day, he finished his household chores early and started up the path that led to the mountain. He had thought about his dragon friend many times in the previous weeks, but his brothers were watching him closely and he didn't want them finding out his plans. At first he thought his friend might have moved on, but that thin white haze still encircled the mountain, making him anxious to reach the cave. When he did, he was happy to hear the snoring of his monstrous friend.

He called out softly, "Subakai, are you in here? It is I, Tiny. I need to talk to you."

The snoring stopped and the sound of movement could be heard inside the cave. Slowly, Subakai's head emerged from the cave. His eyes of gold squinted as the sunlight hit his face.

"Well, well," said Subakai, "I haven't seen you for almost four weeks."

"It has been five weeks, actually," said Tiny.

"So, to what do I owe this honor?" Subakai asked.

"I have come to say good-bye. I am leaving home."

"Leaving home? But where will you go?" Subakai asked.

"The city of Salizar lies three days down the river from here. Maybe I will find greatness there," Tiny said with hope-filled eyes. "I just know that as long as I stay here, I will never be anything but a servant for my brothers' dirty work."

"Silly man-child," said Subakai. "Greatness is not found. It is uncovered. You are already great. The world just does not know it yet. I have seen the greatness in you. You need not have to leave to become what you already are, but I would be doing the world a great injustice by not allowing them the chance to see for themselves the miracle that is Tiny Lynquest."

"You are too kind, my friend," said Tiny. "I will miss you."

"And I you," said Subakai.

"Will I ever see you again?" Tiny asked.

"I do not know," Subakai answered. "But it is the time of sowing for the farmers and the days are growing long. I will return every year at this time until my quest is over. Perhaps we will meet again. If you should ever return home, look for the smoke on the mountain and I shall be waiting."

Tiny reached out, sinking his arms deep into Subakai's thick white mane, hugging him as tightly as he could. He wiped the tears from his eyes with the long white hair, and pulled a thick lock of it from the dragon's neck.

"I shall keep this always to remind me of you," said Tiny.

He turned away and headed back down the mountain. Subakai rested his head upon the ground and watched as the boy descended the mountain, still clutching the lock of long white hair tightly in his little fist.

When Tiny arrived home, it was business as usual. He ate dinner that night and went straight to bed. This time, he made sure he bid everyone a good night. Though he could no longer stay, he did not want to leave on bad terms. Late that night, he wrote a letter by candlelight explaining everything. He left it on his unused bed for his father to find the next morning.

Quietly, he slipped into the kitchen and took the loaf of bread that had been baked that afternoon. He wrapped it in a towel and placed it, along with the lock of Subakai's mane, in the sack he had used for his strips of leather. After this, he silently sneaked out to his father's smokehouse and took a large portion of the dried beef that was hanging there. He placed this into his sack as well.

Then, looking back at the house standing in the moonlight, he gave himself one last chance to change his mind. It seemed so peaceful at night, with the soft sound of the crickets chirping their incantations. He almost changed his mind, but the cool night air brushed his cheeks and awakened his sense of adventure once more.

He turned again to the river at the bottom of the hill. Its slow-moving water sauntered effortlessly downstream, and with it flew Tiny's dreams. Like moonbeams on the surface of the water, so easily broken by a ripple but always returning, so, too, the thoughts of a better life dogged him relentlessly.

He shook off the sleepy daze which had crept up on him, slung the sack over his right shoulder, and sped off down the hill to his waiting raft. He uncovered it and turned it corner to corner until he had moved it the short distance to the water's edge. Searching the surrounding bushes, he found a long branch that was relatively straight. He broke it free of the bush and stripped it of its leaves and twigs. Then he climbed aboard his craft and used the branch to set himself adrift.

Soon, he was as the water itself, set in motion by some unseen force and driven toward his destiny. It was a three-day journey to the city of Salizar, but Tiny took his time, stopping to talk to the people he met along the river. He was anxious to get to the city, but somehow it didn't seem to matter if he wasted a little time along the way.

Halfway through the first day, Tiny began to get hungry, so he rummaged through the sack he had brought. To his surprise, he pulled out the thick white lock of Subakai's mane. He had forgotten he had put it in the sack. He held it in his hands for a moment and ran his fingers through the silky white strands. Then he braided them into a long belt and tied it around his waist. The strands were extremely strong and made a fine belt.

On his fourth day on the water, he came to a fork in the river. A wide canal had been made in the left bank of the river. Tiny didn't know which way to go. He knew the river led directly to the city, but he had never heard of a detour. So rather than get lost, he decided to stay on the course he was on. It was only a short distance further that he realized he had made a grave mistake. The calm waters gave way to wild rapids and surging currents. Frantically, he tried to steer his small raft in the direction of the shore, but it was drawn into the strong currents of the fast-moving water. Huge rocks jutted out of the now foamy white river. He thought to himself, *Well, welcome to your first adventure, Tiny*, as he used his branch to push away from oncoming boulders. Suddenly, his branch snapped against the rock and the corner of his raft smashed into the stone, causing it to spin beneath his feet. He fell face down on the logs and clung to the leather bindings.

Unaware of the direction he was going, the raft suddenly fell away beneath his body, and for a moment he was weightless as he and the raft dropped into the frothy white foam. The raft landed with a *crack* on an enormous boulder; the water-soaked lashings broke loose and his well-crafted raft fell apart under his outstretched body. He was sucked downstream under the torrent of rushing water, and was struggling to get to the surface, when a log that had been caught between two rocks became dislodged and the current hurled it toward him, striking him on the head. His unconscious body floated downstream.

"My story would end here, if not for his good fort—"

"Tobias! Tobias!"

"My mother!" Tobias shrieked. "It must be dinnertime," he said as he came to his senses. Tobias looked around and realized the once raging fire was reduced to a smoldering pile of embers, and the sun had begun its descent in the western sky.

The old man plucked the pipe from his lips, turned it over, and tapped it against a rock, saying, "Well then, I guess that will be enough for today."

"But what happened to Tiny? How did he survive?" Tobias asked in excitement.

"Now, now, I will finish the story tomorrow, if you return. For now, you had better go. Your mother will get worried."

Tobias turned to leave the rocky fortress, but before stepping between the two large rocks that sheltered the clearing, he stopped and looked back at the old man. The stranger smiled and nodded slightly as a gesture to promise he would be there when Tobias came back. Tobias climbed through the rocks and started down the gently sloping hillside that led to his house.

His mother, still waiting to greet him at the back door, let out a loud exclamation. "Heavens to pigsty! Where have you been? You're covered in mud."

It was true. Though his clothes had long since dried, they were still caked with a thick coat of the black mud that lined the bottom of the creek. Tobias just looked up at his mother, smiled, and shrugged his shoulders.

"Well, you cannot eat dinner like that. Quickly, go inside and clean up before dinner."

Tobias swept past her in the doorway without saying a word. He cleaned up and changed his clothes as fast as he could.

That night at dinner his father asked him about school. "Are those boys still bothering you?"

"No, Dad, it's all right. They don't mean anything by it," Tobias answered.

"Maybe I should have a talk with your teacher," said his mother.

"No!" Tobias said sharply. "It's all right. I will handle it, Mother."

"OK," said his father, "but if it happens again I am going to talk to their parents."

"It won't happen again. I promise," said Tobias. After that, nothing else was said about the matter.

CHAPTER THREE

MYSTERY CHILD

The next day dawned worrisomely for Tobias. It was a school day and he knew what awaited him there. He couldn't avoid it. He had to go. On top of that, the promise he had made the night before to his father weighed heavily on his mind. If he didn't do something about Scott and his cronies, his father would, and that would make his life unbearable. Tobias decided to leave for school early to avoid meeting up with the unfortunate ones. He left so early, in fact, that he had to wait for the teacher, Mr. Belgard, to come and unlock the schoolhouse door. Once inside, he sat at the front of the class, which he later realized was a poor choice for a seat. He was forced to endure pieces of chalk being bounced off the back of his head by the hard-luck gang sitting behind him. At recess, he stayed inside the schoolhouse and did his work. It was the only time that he wasn't being bothered. As the day wore on, he became increasingly worried. *What will I do when class is dismissed?* he thought. *How can I get away if they are closer to the door than I am?*

"Sally, will you come and demonstrate this math problem on the board?" Mr. Belgard asked.

Suddenly, Tobias's attention was drawn to the front of the classroom. Sally sat two seats behind him. In order to reach the front of the classroom, she would have to pass him in the aisle. *If I could just get Mr. Belgard to hold me after class*, he thought. So, as Sally moved quickly to the front of the classroom, Tobias stuck his foot out into the aisle. Sally's face took on a stunned look as her feet floundered beneath her. She struggled to regain her balance, but it was too late. The chalk she was clasping went flying as her body hit the floor with a thud. She lifted her now red face and glared at Tobias.

"You did that on purpose," she said fiercely. "Did you see that, Mr. Belgard? Tobias tripped me."

"Tobias, I want to see you after class," Mr. Belgard said in an ominous voice.

The class was abuzz with *ohs* and whispering. Someone in the back of the room said "Now he's going to get it." Tobias sat quietly and waited for three o'clock. Finally, the inevitable had arrived. The teacher looked up from the reading lesson for the day, checked his pocket watch, and then, turning, looked Tobias right in the eye and said, "Class dismissed."

The schoolhouse erupted with commotion as the other students gathered their things and prepared to go home. Tobias remained motionless, staring at his folded hands on top of his desk. The room fell silent as the last of the children exited through the door.

Mr. Belgard rose from his chair and slowly approached Tobias. He had in his hands the ruler of wrath that was used to cure children of their disruptive behavior. He tapped the end of it on Tobias's desk.

"Tobias," he said in a soft, but stern, voice. "I want you to tell me what came over you. You are generally one of my better students." Mr. Belgard waited in silence for an answer.

Without looking up, Tobias said, "I cannot say, sir."

"Do you mean you don't know, or you won't tell me?" he asked.

"I just cannot say, sir. I'm sorry," Tobias repeated.

"Well, I can't have you disrupting my class, now can I?"

"No, sir," Tobias answered politely.

"So what do you recommend as a punishment, Tobias?"

"I'm sure I do not know, sir."

Mr. Belgard twisted the ruler impatiently in his hands as he thought. "Well, it was your first offense," he said. "Promise me it will not happen again and I will let you off with a warning, and you can clean the chalkboard for a week."

"Yes, sir. Thank you, sir. It won't happen again. You have my word," Tobias said with great relief.

"But," the teacher snapped loudly, "if it does happen again, I will be forced to use this." He waved the ruler in Tobias's face.

"Yes, sir. I understand, sir," Tobias said, as he bound his books together with a string. He looked over his shoulder at the empty street outside the schoolhouse.

"You are dismissed, Tobias," the teacher said.

"Yes, sir. Thank you, sir," Tobias answered, but he hesitated in leaving the classroom.

"What is the matter with you, boy? I said you are dismissed. Now go!" Mr. Belgard's voice rang out in the empty room. Like a shot, Tobias leapt to his feet, snatched up his books, and raced out the door.

From the moment his feet hit the street, he knew he was in trouble. One of the boys yelled, "There he goes! Get him!" They had been waiting for him outside the schoolhouse and now were running toward him from both sides of the street. Tobias managed to get ahead of them a little when a wagon full of vegetables stopped in front of the boys. He sped down the street and ducked into the alley next to Shuler's grocery store. He went straight to the back door of the store, and, taking a deep breath, he plucked the cap from his head, opened the door, and stepped inside. Old Man Shuler was stocking shelves when the sound of the door startled him.

"Tobi," he said cheerfully, "you gave me a start, young man. Haven't you ever heard of knocking?"

Tobias said, "Sorry, sir. I did not mean to scare you, but I just came to see if you needed any help today."

"Not today, Tobi. I just finished storing all of Mrs. Henderson's preserves. Try again on Tuesday. I'm expecting a shipment of melons from Sloan's farm I could sure use your help with."

"Oh, well," Tobias said in disappointment, "I guess I will see you Tuesday, then. I'll just go out the front door."

"All right, Tobi. You take care now." Mr. Shuler went back to what he was doing as Tobias moved toward the front of the store.

He stood at the front door and peered through the large plate glass window of Mr. Shuler's store. Tobias could see Scott and his friends searching the alley next to the store.

As he stared through the glass, he noticed something strange about his reflection. The scene of the boys searching the alley faded into the background as he focused on his own image in the glass. It was his own face, but older somehow. His skin was bone white and chiseled into a hardened expression, as if made of stone. His own eyes looked deep, hollow, and full of rage and madness.

He felt his face with his fingers. *It feels like my skin*, he thought. *What is happening to me?* Something truly dark and insidious lay behind the face he saw. If only he had time to examine it closer, but as he was pondering his reflection, one of the boys spotted him standing at the window.

"Look, there he is! He's hiding inside Shuler's store!" shouted Tom.

Tobias bolted through the front door of the store.

"Aha!" Scott yelled. "This way! Come on, he is getting away!"

Tobias once again ran for his life. He raced down the walkway and ran square into a woman carrying a basket full of dried flowers. The basket took flight and the flowers were scattered about the ground.

"My goodness!" the woman exclaimed.

"I'm sorry, ma'am," Tobias said. He stopped momentarily to help pick up the flowers, but when he looked over his shoulder to see Scott and Tom closing in on him, he dropped the flowers and took off down the street. He turned a corner into another alley, only to find it was a dead end. Scott and Tom had turned the corner and were standing at the entrance to the alley, laughing.

"Now we got you, you little toad," said Scott.

Tobias backed up against the wooden fence and prepared to climb it, but then he heard voices coming from the other side of the fence.

"Did you get him, Scott?" one of the voices called out.

"Yeah, come on. You don't want to miss the whuppin of a lifetime," Scott called back.

Seconds later, two boys scampered over the fence and dropped to the ground. It was Bill Hunter and Todd Foreman. Neither one was as big as Scott, but definitely not anyone he would want to meet in a hidden alleyway. Tobias moved cautiously away from the fence and up against the wall of the hardware store. There were some crates stacked against the wall that Tobias tried to lean into. As the boys gathered around, Bill moved in to strike, but Scott put his hand out.

"Wait," he said, "the first hit is mine." Scott drew his fist back and hurled it into Tobias's chest. The air left his body with the force of the blow and Tobias clasped his chest, gasping for breath. "That's what you get for snitching on us to Old Man Shuler," Scott said with a twisted grin on his face. "You knew you had it comin'."

"Now we're gonna finish you off," said Bill, and they all began laughing. In a moment, their wicked laughter died and they stood dumbfounded, staring at something on top of the crate above Tobias's head.

"Hey! How did you get up there?" Todd asked.

"I didn't see him come in. Who is he?" asked Tom.

"Who cares," said Scott. "We'll get him, too."

Tobias slowly looked up at the top of the crates. There, standing motionless, was a small boy of nine or ten. He wore a suit of leather and a shiny black cape that was obviously many sizes too big for him. The cape had a hood that was draped down the boy's back. His right hand seemed to be clutching something, which he nervously twisted in the palm of his hand. His face looked stern and serious, undaunted by the boys.

"Well, what are you waiting for?" Scott yelled. "Get up there and get him!" he said, slapping Tom on the back of the head.

"All right, all right," Tom snapped back reluctantly. He moved toward the crates and prepared to climb them.

The small boy raised his right hand in the air and pitched the object he was holding to the ground. It exploded with a *crack!* and an enormous blue cloud filled the air. Confusion reigned among the boys and they yelled.

"What happened?"

"Where did he go?"

"Do you see him?"

"I can't see anything!"

The small boy leaped down beside Tobias and said, "Let's go."

"But how?" Tobias asked. "They're still in our way."

"Leave that to me," said the boy.

He then reached back and pulled the hood over his head, and suddenly he was gone. Tobias watched in amazement as the blue cloud started to clear. Bill, who had been standing in the gap between the fence and the other boys, quite clumsily fell flat on his face.

"Ow!" Bill hollered, cradling his leg. "Someone tripped me."

Tobias felt a hand catch hold of his arm. It was the boy; he had reappeared.

"Quickly," he said, "let's go while he is still down."

"But surely they will see us leaving," Tobias said.

"They cannot see us, they can only hear us. So say nothing."

The boy carefully stepped over Bill, who was still holding his shin, but when Tobias moved to step over the downed boy, he began to stand up. Tobias took advantage of the situation and kicked Bill firmly in the ribs, and down he went again, holding his side this time.

Meanwhile, the other boys searched frantically around the alley for the two missing youths as the strange boy led Tobias out, still holding him by the arm.

"They didn't see us," Tobias said. "How is that possible?"

"I cannot say," said the boy. "Now, you need to hurry home. There is someone waiting for you."

Tobias looked down at the ground, trying to think of whom the boy could possibly mean. Then it dawned on him. "The old man," he said out loud.

The boy let go of his arm. Tobias turned toward him to thank him, but he had vanished. Tobias stood in confusion for a moment, trying to understand what had just happened. His thoughts returned to the boys in the alley, and he realized that they would be emerging soon in a very unhappy state. He took off for home. Tobias looked back just long enough to see Scott, Tom, and Todd helping Bill limp home.

At home, Tobias didn't even stop to greet his mother. He put his books away and marched straight out the back door. He climbed the hill in search of the old man he had met the previous day.

CHAPTER FOUR

PUT TO THE TEST

Tobias found the man nestled in the rocky crag, just as he did the day before. The old man was on his knees, hunched over a large mat. He had before him three small tin bowls, each with a different colored powder in it, a stone grinding bowl with a grinder in it, a scale for measuring out portions, and three acorns that had been hollowed out. He was using a paper funnel to sift a strange mixture of these powders into the hollow acorns.

"What are you doing?" Tobias asked.

"Huh? Oh, it is you, young Tobias. I will be with you in a moment," said the old man. "Come for the rest of the story, have you?"

"I have something to tell you," Tobias said anxiously. "I met the strangest boy today. He had on a black cape and—"

"A boy, you say?" asked the old man.

"Yes, yes," Tobias said impatiently. "And he saved me from Scott and the others."

"How old did you say this boy was?"

"I didn't," said Tobias. "But he could have been nine or ten."

The old man finished what he was doing and put his things away. "Nine or ten, aye. Yes, yes, I know the boy you speak of."

"You do? Great," said Tobias. "I did not get a chance to thank him, so if you know him, maybe I could—"

"So, did you come for the rest of the story or not?" the old man snapped, as he leaned back on a rock and reached for his pipe.

"Yes, but—"

"Good, then sit and be quiet while I try to remember where we were."

"You had just gotten to the part where Tiny had drowned in the river."

"He did not drown," said the old man. "If he had drowned, the story would be over. No, he was only knocked senseless."

When he awoke, he found himself in strange surroundings. He was in an enormous room that was decorated with the finest tapestries and curtains. His clothes had been changed as well. He was wearing a long nightshirt with cuffs and a collar of frilly lace. The bed he was lying on was larger than his entire room back home, and it was covered in the finest linens. It wasn't until he heard the sound of someone snoring that he realized he was not alone.

There was an odd-looking man asleep in a tall-backed chair in the corner of the room. He wore a long flowing robe made of a deep purple cloth that glistened in the light. A cord of gold was tied around his waist. The man had almost no hair to speak of, except a thin line of black hair that encircled his head like a wreath. There was a ring of gold in each of the man's ears, and an extremely long thin mustache had been twisted and tied to the rings on either side of his head.

Tiny moved to sit up at the edge of the bed, but when he did, he discovered that a string had been tied to his toe. The other end of the string was tied to the strange man's thumb. With a tug of the string, the man awoke.

With an amazed look on his face, he said, "Well, you did survive."

"Where am I?" Tiny asked. "And who are you?"

"I am Barnabus. I have been charged with watching over you until your recovery—or your demise. We really did not know which way you would go."

Tiny untied the string from his toe and tried again to sit up on the side of the bed. The room began to spin when he did, so he lay back down.

"Perhaps you are still weak from starvation. You have been asleep for almost eight days."

Barnabus walked to the door and called for a page. "Bring some hot broth and bread immediately." The page ran off in a flash. "Now," he said, turning back to Tiny, "who are you, and how did you wind up in the river?"

"My name is Tiny Lynquest. I am a leather crafter from the town of Eadenburrow, a few days north of Salizar. I was on my way to Salizar to make a life for myself in the city when I got caught in the rapids."

"Yes, and you are to be congratulated, young man. You are one of the few to survive the rapids."

Just then, the page returned with the food. He promptly placed the tray on the table beside the bed, laid out the napkin and silverware as if he were serving royalty, and, without saying a word, turned and left the room. Tiny looked down at the tray: it was beef barley and vegetable soup with a large portion of bread. As the smell wafted up to his eager nose he realized how hungry he was. Tiny ravenously devoured the meal, since he hadn't eaten in days.

"Well, I must say," remarked Barnabus with a smile, "a healthy appetite is a good sign that one is getting better."

When Tiny had almost finished his meal, the page returned and whispered something to the odd gentleman. The two conversed quietly so that Tiny could not hear. As they spoke, they looked curiously at the boy eating his food. Then all at once, the conversation broke and the page abruptly left the room. Tiny was beginning to feel a little awkward.

"The page will retrieve your clothes. I took the liberty of having them laundered."

"Laundered?" Tiny asked in a confused voice.

"I had them cleaned," Barnabus answered plainly. "His Highness, King Standforth, will be requesting an audience with you."

"The king!" exclaimed Tiny.

"Oh, that is right, you do not know where you are. You are one tremendously fortunate young man. Not only did you survive the river, but you had the outrageous good fortune to be found by a personal guard to His Highness, the Prince of Millstaff. The prince, in his capacity for kindness, brought you with him to Ironcrest Castle. He makes the journey twice a year."

The page entered the room swiftly once more, carrying Tiny's clothes. He placed them on the bed and turned to gather the now empty dishes in an orderly fashion on the tray. Before leaving the room, he stopped momentarily to tell Barnabus something. Barnabus nodded and said, "We will be there within the hour." Tiny tried standing again. This time he felt much better; a little weak, perhaps, but steady.

"I see you are feeling better," said Barnabus. "Good, get dressed. We have an audience with the king within the hour."

Tiny reached for his clothes, but something was different. "Hey, these aren't my clothes!" he said with surprise.

"Yes," replied Barnabus, "your clothes are not appropriate for an audience with His Majesty, so while you were unconscious I had you measured and this suit was made. You were to either meet the king in it or be buried in it. We did not know which. I pride myself on being ready for every contingency."

The suit was made of a fine cloth and obviously made for formal wear. The thought that the clothes were made with his funeral in mind only added to the discomfort of the fit. But, he wore them without complaint, so as not to upset his host.

"There," said Barnabus, as he straightened the lace collar around Tiny's neck. "That should do nicely, don't you think?" Tiny just stood there looking uncomfortable. "Now, if you will follow me, the king will be expecting us."

Barnabus led him through a maze of corridors, walking rather briskly. He gave Tiny a short lecture on how to greet the king. "When greeting the king," he said, "one must stand up straight and bow with his eyes to the floor. Speak only when spoken to, and always finish your sentence with 'Your Highness.' Do not fidget or stammer when you talk. Speak clearly and always use good grammar. Do not slouch, and for goodness' sake, don't do anything embarrassingly common, like scratch yourself." Tiny listened in quiet desperation as he struggled to keep up with the fast pace in which Barnabus walked.

They arrived at a set of vast doors with two guards posted. Barnabus took one last look at Tiny as he stood before the doors. "Shoulders back," he said firmly, and then he reached out and lifted Tiny's chin up slightly. "Stay here and do not move," he said, as he vanished beyond the doors. Only a moment or two had passed before his return, and the doors swung wide open. Tiny was taken aback by the size of the great hall and the detail in which it was furnished. The towering marble pillars that lined the walls, the tremendously high ceiling, and the beautiful tapestries all added to Tiny's growing feelings of inadequacy. There was a rug that seemed to be woven from spun gold and crimson cloth that stretched the length of the hall.

"Well, what are you waiting for?" Barnabus snapped.

Tiny shook off the daze and followed Barnabus across the outstretched rug. Ahead of them sat the king, neatly perched on his throne, complete with crown, scepter, and the entire assembly of advisers. Barnabus leaned close to him and whispered, "Let me do all the talking," as Tiny drew near to the throne.

"Good afternoon, Your Highness. I have brought him as you requested. His name is Tiny Lynquest and he is from the town of Eadenburrow, three days north of our fair city."

The king looked Tiny over carefully and asked in a deep, serious voice, "How old are you, boy?"

"He says he is—"

"Silence, Barnabus!" the king yelled, as he slammed the butt of his scepter down on a large brass plate on the floor, apparently put there for that purpose.

Tiny's chin began to tremble. "I am twelve years of age, Your Highness," he said in a shaky voice.

"And your parents know of your absence?" the king asked.

Tiny recalled the letter he had left for his father. *Surely, he has found and read the letter by now,* he thought. "Yes, Your Highness. My mother died when I was born and my father is aware of my absence."

"Did he approve of your leaving at such an early age?"

Tiny paused for a moment. He didn't want to lie, but if he told the truth, he might be sent back home. It was during this pause that he noticed a young lady standing to the right of the king. She had been watching his answers with a strange intensity and seemed to be hanging on his every word. Tiny reluctantly gave in to the truth.

"I did not ask him for permission, Your Highness."

At these words, the young lady smiled a sweet smile and nodded gently.

"Do you mean to say you ran away?" asked the king.

"I did, Your Highness," Tiny replied in embarrassment, lowering his eyes to the floor.

"So, I should send you back to face your father, then."

"Oh no, Your Highness. That would only make matters worse. I mean, I can't go back, Your Highness."

"Then I shall send a message to your father."

"If it pleases Your Highness, I would like to write the letter myself. I had every intention of keeping in touch with my father once I had reached the city."

"Then what am I to do with you?" the king asked. "I cannot turn you loose in the city. There is no end to the trouble a boy of your age could get into." Just then, the young lady leaned in and whispered something in the king's ear. The king stared at Tiny a moment before asking, "Have you any talents?"

"He is the son of a ta—"

"I am speaking to the boy, Barnabus!" the king snapped, slamming his scepter to the floor. "You will have to forgive Barnabus. He is an excellent adviser, but sometimes a little too zealous in his duties," said the king calmly.

"I am a tanner and saddle maker by trade, Your Highness. My family has made tack for many generations."

"Barnabus," said the king.

"Yes, Your Highness?" answered Barnabus.

"Who makes the tack for the royal stables?"

"A most reputable vendor in the city, sire," Barnabus answered.

"Yes, we shall see. I will give you a fortnight in which to create a saddle. If you can better the best saddle of the vendors in the city, then you shall stay as the saddler to the royal stables. If you cannot, then I will send you home to your father under an armed guard."

"As you wish, Your Highness," Tiny said as he bowed respectfully.

"Barnabus shall purchase all the necessary tools and materials you will need for the task." Turning to Barnabus, he said, "Barnabus, see to it."

"Yes, Your Highness. I will see to it right away," Barnabus replied with a bow. Turning to Tiny, he said, "Come with me."

Tiny bid the king and all his assembly a good day and followed Barnabus through the castle, across the gardens, and to a small room adjacent to the stables. There, he made a list of all the things he would need and gave it to Barnabus.

"These are your quarters while you are with us. I should not see you anywhere but here or in the stables. The servants eat in the kitchen. You can find it by following the path that leads behind the garden. Breakfast is at first bell, lunch at second, and dinner is, of course, at third. Miss them and you do not eat." With that, he bid Tiny good-bye and closed the door behind him.

Tiny looked about the room. It was a modest room at best, with a table, two chairs, and a bed in the corner. Upon the bed, neatly folded, were his clothes, his shoes placed carefully beside them. Among the folded clothes was the belt he had made from Subakai's mane. He quickly climbed out of the stuffy clothes he was wearing and put on his comfortable leather suit. It felt good to be himself again.

The third bell rang from somewhere outside the palace walls, so Tiny hurried down the path to the kitchen. He felt a little awkward at first, but none of the other servants seemed to notice him. He ate his dinner in silence and returned to his quarters. He went to sleep that night wondering what else could possibly happen to him on his quest for greatness.

The next morning at first bell, Tiny awoke and quickly made his way to breakfast. It was just before sunrise, and the dark shadow of night had begun its retreat in the eastern sky, giving way to the pale blue light of dawn. The morning was fresh and full of awakening possibilities. Tiny felt charged with the excitement that comes from the unexpectedness of a good challenge. He couldn't wait to start working on the king's saddle.

Upon his return to his room, he found all the items that he had requested for the saddle. The tanned leather was draped over one of the chairs, and all the tools were laid out on the table. He went to work straightaway, working through most of his meals and late into the nights. He finished the saddle in just under a week.

Now it was time to decorate it. He knew it had to be more beautiful than any saddle ever seen. *But how?* he thought. *What to carve into the leather? And how can I decorate it when I have no cloth to decorate it with?* Dusk had given way to night and fatigue settled on Tiny, so he sat on the edge of the bed and pondered the problem awhile.

He tried to think of the most beautiful thing he had ever seen, but being from the small town of Eadenburrow, he hadn't seen very much. He thought of Abiding Mountain in the morning. Then his thoughts turned to Subakai and his eyes of black and gold. Tiny began playing with the tassel at the end of his long white belt. The shiny white hair glistened in the candlelight like gossamer strands of ivory. Suddenly, it became clear to him what he was going to have to do to decorate the saddle. He took off his belt and started to carefully unbraid it.

The following day began like all the rest. The first bell rang, and Tiny resumed his work on the saddle. But shortly after the first bell, a knock came on the door. Tiny covered the saddle with his blanket and opened the door. To his amazement, he found a servant bearing his breakfast. Lunch and dinner were also delivered, and each time Tiny would cover the saddle, so that no one could see his work until it was finished. For the remainder of the two weeks, his meals were brought to his room. Though he didn't know why, he sure enjoyed the convenience.

On the twelfth day, he completed his task. He kept it covered and awaited his audience with the king. On the fourteenth day, he rose at the chime of the breakfast bell and dressed once more in the clothes he was given on his first day at Ironcrest Castle. A servant brought his breakfast as usual, but Tiny was too nervous to eat. Several hours passed before Barnabus arrived to escort him to the great hall.

Once they had reached the great hall, he was told to wait at the back of the room until he was called for. So he waited, with his saddle neatly bundled up in his blanket.

"Call the saddle maker from the city!" the king shouted.

A man entered the hall through the giant doors carrying a bundle. He walked briskly up to the king and laid it at his feet. Pulling at the covering, he stepped backward. The entire assembly sighed at the sight of the saddle. It was made of lightly tanned leather and had red velvet and purple cloth lining the seat. It had carvings of the royal crest on each side.

"A beautiful work indeed," said the king. "And now the boy." The king waved Tiny forward with his hand.

Tiny sped forward and placed his bundle beside the other saddle. He drew a deep breath and pulled the covering away.

The assemblage of the hall fell silent. Tiny's nervousness grew as the silence thickened. The afternoon sun streamed through the windows and struck the saddle with a brilliance that even Tiny could not believe. Tiny had made intricate carvings of two great dragons on the saddle, highlighting all the features of the dragons with the shiny white strands of Subakai's mane. The almost black leather set off the pearly white hair. Every piece of leather had some small design. The seat was of soft, light brown suede, outlined in white. The horn was polished brass, and engraved upon it was a picture of the king's royal crest. All in all, the brilliance of the saddle seemed to glow with a light all its own.

The king stared at the saddle as if he could not believe his eyes. Then, placing a hand on Tiny's shoulder, he said, "Young man, it can well be said that you have earned your place in this kingdom." Tiny had never felt prouder than he did at that moment. "My boy, you will serve this kingdom well as the saddler to the royal stables." Tiny bowed low before the king.

King Standforth returned to his throne. Turning to the young lady who was once again standing close to his side, he said, "This is my daughter, Princess Aleana." Tiny bowed low before the princess. "And this is your savior, Prince Aaron, from the kingdom of Millstaff. It was he who plucked you from the river and brought you here."

Tiny again bowed deeply, and said, "I am forever in your debt, Your Highness."

The prince smiled and said, "Not at all. Perhaps you can return the favor someday."

The king proceeded to introduce Tiny to all the officials in the palace, and in turn Tiny bowed to them all. His back was sore when he returned to his room. After dinner, he found that only a few strands were left from Subakai's mane. He carefully braided them and wore them about his neck.

In the months that followed, he enjoyed his service to the king. He wrote to his father many times, and though he spoke of doing well, he never told him of his service to the king. Tiny had managed to convince the king that he would do better to buy his tanned leather from a small tanner in Eadenburrow. He had said, "It would be better quality leather at a better price, even if you do have to transport it."

Several months had passed, when one day as he was working in his shop, there was a knock on the door. He opened the door to find the princess and two of her royal guards.

"Your Highness! I am deeply honored by your visit," said Tiny nervously. "I hope that all is well."

"You can dispense with all the formalities, Tiny. Is it all right if I call you by your first name?" the princess asked plainly.

"Most certainly," replied Tiny. "Won't you and your guards come in?"

"Actually, I came to ask your advice on a certain matter. Will you walk with me?"

"As you wish, Your Highness," said Tiny.

The princess turned to her guards and said, "You may follow, but not closely." The two guards lingered awhile before following them through the garden at a distance.

She led him down a path and through a small gate. From there the path wandered through a rose garden with towering arches covered with vines of roses. The sight took his breath away. The path opened up in a large area that was hedged on all sides by tall shrubs.

A variety of trees filled the area, and the songs of a thousand birds fell like the fruit of each tree.

"This is my favorite place to come and think," she said. "Father has collected birds from all around the world for me."

"But why don't they fly away?" asked Tiny.

"Their wings have been clipped," she said. Just then, a pale white dove with a copper breast swooped down and landed upon the princess's shoulder. "All except this one," she added, smiling. "Him, I raised from a hatchling. I call him Hermes, after the ancient god of flight. Hermes always seems to find me, no matter where I am in the palace."

"He is beautiful, Your Highness," said Tiny.

"Go ahead," she said, "pet him."

Tiny reached to pet the bird, but it ruffled its feathers and flapped its wings. "I don't think he likes me," said Tiny.

"Nonsense," said the princess. "Hermes likes whomever I like. Here, try again. This time move a little slower." Tiny reached out again slowly, and stroked the crown of the bird's head. "See! You two were meant to be friends."

"That is nice, Princess, but I do not see why you have brought me here," said Tiny.

"I brought you here to talk to you about a matter of some delicacy, and we will not be interrupted here."

"What seems to be troubling you, and how can I help?" asked Tiny.

"It is about the prince of Millstaff. As you may have heard, he comes to court me twice a year. He has been doing so for some time now. I have grown very fond of him and he has asked for my hand. But, I am not one to make a hasty decision. So, I have come to ask your advice."

"But what does a leather worker know of love? I craft saddles and bridles, Your Highness, not marriages. Surely, there is someone in your father's household better suited for this task."

"I have been watching you closely since you arrived at the palace. It was I who ordered the servants to bring your meals to your room. I came to you, Tiny, because I have observed that you are an honest, hardworking soul. I watched you carefully as you answered my father's questions. You could have lied to my father about your leaving home, but you did not. I admire that. It is true, my father has people required to give me advice, and so they do. They give me his advice. My father has more than my happiness to think about. He arranged the match to gain a powerful alliance with the king of Millstaff. I refuse to be another victim of politics. I do not wish to marry a man, prince or not, who does not return my love. How can I know that his affections are not some political game?"

"I see," said Tiny. "Hmm…perhaps a quest is in order."

"A quest?" asked the princess.

"Yes, Your Highness. An old and wise friend once told me of a purple blossom that grows on the slopes of Mount Ashor on the island of Panthallimos. This rare flower is said to have the power to inspire everlasting love. The journey is long and perilous, but anyone willing to take such a journey must be driven by true love."

"Yes, truly these are wise words," the princess said, smiling. "I will know if his love is true. Tell me, young Lynquest, how does one so young know the world so well?"

"Not I, Your Highness. It is my friend who knows so much of the world."

"Someday I must meet this friend of yours, Tiny."

"Perhaps someday you will, Your Highness, perhaps someday."

The princess bid him a good afternoon and returned to her guards smiling. She told her father of her request before she would consent to marry, and the king promptly sent a letter to the kingdom of Millstaff. To the surprise and delight of the princess, the prince embarked on the quest immediately. It would be two years before he would return. In that time, the princess sought Tiny's friendship to help cheer herself until his return. Tiny grew very fond of the princess. As time went on, he developed a devotion to her that surpassed even that of the king.

Upon the return of the prince, there was a parade and people celebrated in the streets. When the prince reached Ironcrest Castle, Tiny was summoned to the great hall once more.

When he arrived, the king shouted, "Who invited the royal saddler?" *BAM!* The king slammed his scepter down on the brass plate.

"I did, Father," said Aleana.

"May I ask why a saddler should be present at the engagement of my daughter?"

"I felt he should be here. It was on his advice that I required the quest before my marriage."

Just as the king was about to speak, a page entered through the great doors and called out, "His Highness, Prince of Millstaff, Prince Aaron!"

At that moment, the prince entered the hall, clutching a large bouquet of big purple flowers. Though the flowers had been picked, their beauty had not faded, nor had they wilted. Prince Aaron approached the throne where the princess was standing. He knelt down on one knee and placed the flowers at her feet. Then, reaching out, he took her by the hand and said, "I know why you requested the flowers, Princess. As heaven is my witness, you already had my undying love. But as I am a slave to my heart and my heart belongs to you, I have done your bidding." He then kissed her hand and rose to his feet. Turning to the page, he clapped his hands twice and the page flung wide the big doors. A long line of servants, twenty-five in all, began entering the room; each one was carrying a large basket of the fragrant purple flowers. One by one they laid the flowers at the feet of the princess and departed from the room. The air grew thick with the sweet fragrance.

After the last of the servants left, the princess summoned Tiny closer to the throne. Tiny approached the throne and stood beside the prince.

"Prince Aaron, I give you Tiny Lynquest. You saved his life two years ago and he has proven himself invaluable to the Crown. It was on his advice that I sent you on the quest, and only now, after you have proven your love, will I consent to marriage."

The prince turned to Tiny and bowed to him. Tiny felt a little awkward, so he bowed in return.

"Sir," said the prince, "now I am indebted to you. For, I have saved your life, but you have given me my reason to live. No finer queen will there ever be."

Tiny smiled at the prince and said, "I agree entirely, Your Highness. Yours will be a happy household."

"Well, young Lynquest, it appears that you have proven yourself a good and worthy servant," bellowed the king. "What shall be your reward?" Then, after pausing a moment, the king said, "I know! You shall have your choice of steeds from the royal stables."

"Your Highness, I am speechless," said Tiny. "I am not worthy of such a prize."

"Nonsense," said the king, "if I said it, then it shall be so!" He slammed the scepter down.

"As you wish, Your Highness," said Tiny respectfully.

The king had many horses from which to choose. This made the decision a difficult one. Tiny finally settled on a beautiful black-and-white stallion that was like himself, small but full of spirit. He gave it the name of Reckless, because of the way it pranced around the yard, careless and clumsy. Now that Tiny had his own horse, he was free to travel the countryside and see more of the city. From then on, Tiny spent most of his free time wandering the streets of Salizar and talking to the merchants.

CHAPTER FIVE

A DARK KNIGHT

As late summer arrived, the citizens prepared for the weeklong festival of the harvest. It was a time when they celebrated the year's good fortune and food. Tiny loved this time of the year because it gave him a chance to see people at their best. Everyone seemed so generous and compassionate toward their fellow man. Street performers, jugglers, knife throwers, and all manner of dancers exhibited their skills; there was even a man doing magic and telling stories.

Tiny grew particularly interested in him because of the man's skin; it was as dark as a walnut. Tufts of spongy gray hair covered his head and he had eyes as black as coal. His voice had been made rough by the passing of time. He wore clothing of the most vibrant colors. He was obviously a man of the world. Tiny watched as he amazed the children with tricks of magic and tales of great adventure.

After a full day of celebration, Tiny went back to where the odd storyteller had been performing, but he was gone. As Tiny was returning to the palace, he caught a glimpse of someone disappearing into Ironcrest Woods. As there was still time before nightfall, Tiny decided to investigate. He followed the mysterious figure into the woods. He trailed him as quietly as he could, until the person stopped at a place obviously prepared as a campsite. Tiny crept closer to see if he could get a better look at the person's face, but as he neared the stranger, a piercing screech came from above him and gave his position away.

"Who is there?" the stranger said, spinning around.

Tiny froze. He wasn't sure if the man saw him or not.

"*Manobo, chea o so guy!*" said the stranger.

Suddenly, a bird attacked Tiny, swooping and clawing at his head. He leaped from the bushes, flailing his arms in the air, trying to wave off the bird. The stranger burst out laughing. Tiny looked up. The bird stopped its attack and rested upon the man's arm.

"That's not funny. I could have been hurt!" said Tiny.

"Impossible," said the man. "I did not tell him to hurt you. I only told him to flush you out, and here you are," the stranger said, chuckling.

"You're the magician that was performing at the festival," said Tiny.

"Yes," said the man. "My name is Lucias Merriweather. I am not a magician by trade, but it helps me survive. What might your name be?"

"My name is Tiny. I work for His Majesty, King Standforth, as a saddler to the royal stables."

"Well, such an honor for someone so young, and bold too, for to follow a stranger into the woods is an awfully brave thing to do. Well, Tiny, are you hungry?"

"It is against the king's law to hunt on his land, you know," said Tiny.

"I am not hunting on the king's land. I only stay here," said Lucias. Then, turning to the bird, he said, "Manobo, *kongy ono gonnie*," and it took flight.

"But how do you live?" asked Tiny.

"I perform in the city for the little money I have, and nature provides the rest. Come sit with me and we will talk," said Lucias, as he began making a fire.

"Aren't you afraid I may tell the king you are staying in his woods?"

"No," said Lucias. "It does not matter if you tell. They will never find me."

"But I found you," said Tiny.

"Yes, but you were lucky," replied Lucias.

Tiny sat on the ground next to the fire. "What do you do, then?" asked Tiny.

"What do you mean?" asked Lucias.

"You said you were not a magician. Well then, what are you?"

"I am a knight."

"A knight?" said Tiny. "You do not look like any knight I have ever seen."

"It is true, I am not a knight of this kingdom, but I am a knight nevertheless. I am a knight of Bonangi. My queen's kingdom, the kingdom of Kongwana, is at the other end of the earth to the south."

"But you speak my language so well," said Tiny.

"I have visited and at times lived in Salizar throughout my life. I am the last of a noble knighthood sworn to guard and protect the secrets of Bonangi."

"What is this Bonangi?" asked Tiny.

"I am sorry," said Lucias. "Did you say you were hungry or not? I have some bread here, if you are." He reached for a satchel and pulled out a small loaf of bread. He broke it in half and handed one to Tiny. Tiny was about to refuse it when Lucias said, "You know, in my country it is an insult to refuse your host's offer of food." Tiny reached out and took the bread. Just as he did, the carcass of a rabbit fell out of the sky and landed right in front of Lucias. Tiny looked up to see a falcon landing in a nearby tree. "Ah, dinner is here," said Lucias.

"I thought you said you were not hunting in the king's woods," said Tiny sharply.

"I did," said Lucias. "I am not hunting. Is it my fault he likes sharing his dinner with me? You see," he explained, as he prepared the meat, "Manobo and I have struck a bargain. He likes his meat cooked and I hate to hunt. This way, we both get what we want."

"How long have you had him as a pet?" Tiny asked.

"He is not a pet. He is a friend, a companion. Manobo has been with me since I was young. He protects me from spies like you."

"I was not spying!" Tiny exclaimed.

"Then why were you following me?" asked Lucias.

"I was just curious, that is all," replied Tiny. He looked around at the darkening woods. The sun began to set and the shadows grew thick and long across the forest floor. "Why do you stay out here? Don't you have enough money to stay in the city?" asked Tiny.

"I like it out here. There is strength out here in the silence of nature. Here, a man's thoughts can grow strong and tall like trees and his spirit is at peace. Besides, strangers are not always welcome in the city. Especially one so easily noticed as I."

"What do you mean?" asked Tiny.

"I mean, there are many who fear people with dark skin such as mine. There are even some who hate us, just because they do not understand our ways," said Lucias.

"But, you do not seem scary to me," replied Tiny.

"That is because you have conquered your fear of strangers. Your name betrays you, Tiny, for there is much about you that is grand and wonderful," said Lucias. "Your name means small, but I see around your neck a thin braid of dragon's mane and you live as a servant to the king. I have seen you riding through the city on a horse of fine breeding and you have a character as strong as nature's own. No, if you ask me, you are anything but tiny."

Tiny watched as the campfire lighted the man's face. His features were aged and chiseled by time, but life still shone brightly through his eyes and he had a compassionate way about him that made Tiny feel at ease. They finished eating and Lucias walked Tiny to the edge of the woods. He waved good-bye and disappeared into the darkness.

Every day at the festival, Tiny would watch Lucias perform for the children, and each evening he would search Ironcrest Woods. Each time he would find Lucias camping in a different spot. On the evening of the last day of the festival, Tiny found Lucias in yet another location. This time, he was by a stream. Tiny brought dried meat for Manobo and a big pheasant for the two of them.

"I brought dinner tonight," said Tiny, as he threw the dried meat to Manobo. The bird caught it without hesitation and began devouring it.

"Ah, you found me again," said Lucias.

"Yes," said Tiny, "I am getting quite good at it."

"Good, good," said Lucias, "I enjoy your company. Come, sit, and I will cook that bird of yours."

They ate their fill while Lucias told one of his wild tales. After they finished, Tiny asked, "Now that the festival is over, what will you do? Where will you go?"

"I don't know," said Lucias. "I may stay here for a while. There is something about this place that interests me."

"What is it like being a knight?" Tiny asked. "I mean, it must be a wonderful life, full of adventure."

"It is, at times," said Lucias, "and other times, it can be very lonely and dull. It is something I cannot easily explain. It is something you have to live to understand. I know, I will teach you, if you truly wish to know."

"I do! I do!" answered Tiny in excitement.

From that point on, whenever Tiny went to visit Lucias, he would teach him something about his knighthood. He taught him how to track animals without being noticed, how to sword fight while balancing on a fallen log, how to hide yourself among things of nature, how to store smoke in an empty acorn shell, and how to use illusion to trick your enemies...but most of all, he taught Tiny to use his wit instead of his muscle. "A man is only as weak as his mind," he would say. "Your wit is like a sword, keep it sharp and it will serve you well."

Tiny would practice sneaking up on Manobo without being seen. He found that sword fighting on a fallen log was painful, as his body kept finding the ground repeatedly, but he was relentless in his studies. He took great care in mixing the powders just right, in order to make the strange blue smoke, and the acorn shell had to be hollowed out so thin that it would break when it hit the ground. Lucias taught him to find the truth in every situation, and that to be a knight, one must always be true to the Crown and to the cause for which he fights and lives.

Over time, they became great friends. Lucias spoke of Bonangi many times, and Tiny would listen intently and try to understand, but he always ended with the question, "But what is Bonangi?"

Finally, Lucias said, "Bonangi has the power to bind all men together as one heart in wisdom, strength, compassion, and truth, or in confusion, ignorance, fear, and hatred. It is the spirit that moves all people in one direction or the other, drawing them closer together in understanding, or pulling them apart in prejudice."

Tiny still felt like his question had not been answered, but he did not press the issue any further.

CHAPTER SIX

THE DRAGON DANCE

Four years had passed since he first arrived at the palace, and Tiny was no longer a boy, but a young man. He had become quite popular with all the servants and guards at the palace, and was also well-known in the city for his kind ways. It was in the early spring of the fourth year that a letter arrived at the palace which disturbed the king, so much so that he refused to eat. One week after its arrival, the princess came to Tiny with the problem.

"I am truly worried, Tiny," she said. "My father won't eat and he hasn't slept in three days. The content of the letter has him deeply vexed. I have never seen him this way."

"May I ask, what was in the letter that would trouble him so?" asked Tiny.

"The letter is from a sorcerer. He is demanding that my father hand over his scepter to a knight that he has sent. If Father does not comply, then the sorcerer will destroy the city."

"How can one knight destroy a whole city?" asked Tiny.

"This knight rides a great dragon," said the princess, "and he consumes everything by fire."

Tiny remained silent and thought about the problem as he rolled the thin braid of Subakai's mane between his fingers.

"Father has already sent his army against the knight, but I'm afraid they are not faring very well," she added.

"Perhaps what the king needs is a dragon himself," said Tiny. "I have a friend that may be able to help, but I must return home first. I cannot promise he will help, but if you send a messenger with me, I will send news as soon as I find out."

"A messenger will not be fast enough. Take Hermes," she said.

"Hermes?" asked Tiny.

"Yes, my dove. He will find me no matter where I am."

"Tell the king not to give up hope. I will fight this knight myself if I have to."

The princess went to her father immediately and a cage was acquired for the bird, which was placed inside and covered.

Tiny left that night and rode hard for three days. On the evening of the third day, Tiny could see the silhouette of his old house standing in the shadow of Abiding Mountain. The thought of seeing his father again filled him with great joy—and a little fear. What would he say to him? How did he feel about Tiny leaving? Could he ever forgive him? These questions had plagued Tiny for years, and now he was going to find out the answers to them, like it or not.

He searched the mountain for any signs of smoke to tell him that his dragon friend was waiting, but there were none, only the large, dark mountain standing in the distance and the figures of two men standing outside his father's house. They were his brothers. When they realized it was Tiny riding up the road, they called out to their father.

"Hey, Pa, the runt found his way home!" yelled Robert.

"Pa, the squirt finally came home," said John.

Tiny heard them calling him names just like they used to do. This brought a smile to his face. "It's nice to know some things haven't changed," he said to himself. Tiny had always suspected that his brothers didn't really hate him; they just enjoyed giving him a hard time.

At the sound of his sons' voices, their father stormed out of the house. Tiny was dismounting when his father marched up and spun him around.

"I can explain!" said Tiny, but before he could get another word out, his father threw his arms around Tiny and squeezed the wind out of him.

"Goodness, it's good to have you home again," his father said. Tiny sank into his father's crushing arms. Any thoughts of his father being angry with him took flight, and for a moment he just enjoyed his father's affections. "Take care of your brother's horse," his father told Robert and John.

Tiny smiled and handed the reins of his horse to John, who took the horse to the barn for food and water, muttering all the way.

"Come inside and we'll talk, son. Robert, go and prepare Tiny's room for the night," said his father.

"It's his room, let him do it himself," said Robert.

"Just do it!" demanded his father.

Robert sauntered off, grumbling as he went.

"Tell me, son, how is the city? Is it big? What do you do there? Tell me everything. I want to hear all about it," said his father.

Therefore, Tiny told him about the river ride and how he arrived at the palace. He told of how he was commissioned to make saddles for the king, and that he was in service to the king at that moment, though he did not say what for. He told him it was a personal matter for the king.

"It's doesn't matter what brought you home," said his father. "What matters is that you are here."

At that moment, Tiny's brothers stumbled into the room. "We are finished doing what you said, Father. Is the squirt staying more than one night?" asked John with a slight smile.

"Guess what?" said Robert to Tiny. "We have been making leather for the king."

"McCain asked for our leather personally," said John.

His father looked at Tiny with a raised eyebrow to see if he was going to tell them that he was the reason they were making leather for the king. Tiny knew they couldn't stand the thought of tanning the leather he made the king's saddles from, so he just smiled and said, "Really? That's great. I always thought you made the best leather."

"Are you hungry?" asked Tiny's father. "I will make dinner, and we will eat and talk about all the things that have happened in your absence."

Robert and John did most of the talking, and a little arguing. Tiny just listened.

After dinner, Tiny drew his father aside and told him privately that he could only stay a few days. "The task I am on for the king is a very dangerous one and I don't know if I will return."

"I see," said his father. "Then I have something for you."

He left the room for a moment and returned with a small wooden box. He took a key which he had strung around his neck and unlocked it. Opening the lid, he retrieved a dagger of unusual beauty. It was two hands long and made of silver. It had an emerald embedded in the hilt on either side, and the blade was long and slender.

"It belonged to your grandfather, on your mother's side. When your mother passed away, she left it to you. Now that you are a man, it is yours. May it protect you on your quest."

Tiny picked it up. "I don't know what to say," said Tiny.

"Your grandfather was quite a fighter. You have the same spirit, son, strong and full of life. I am proud of you."

Tiny tucked the knife among his things and, bidding his father a good night, turned in for the evening.

The following day dawned cold, but clear. Tiny watched for the smoke on the mountain, but there was none. Every morning he would awake in anticipation of renewing Subakai's friendship, but each day the mountainside stood out clear, without so much as a small cloud anywhere. After four days, no sign of Subakai's presence was found. Tiny was beginning to get discouraged. *Maybe Subakai has moved on,* he thought. *Maybe he has forgotten.*

Tiny took several trips up the mountain, only to find an empty cave and a sword stuck in the ground at the entrance. It was the sword that Tiny had pulled from Subakai's side. Tiny plucked it from the ground and ran his hand along the rusty blade. *I could use this,* he thought. *Now, if only Subakai were here. I have already stayed away from the palace too long.*

He took the sword back to his father's house and cleaned and sharpened the blade. The fifth day passed with still no sign, then the sixth, and the seventh. Tiny wrote a letter to the king on the evening of the seventh day, stating that he would not be able to help vanquish the knight. He rolled it into a tiny scroll and sealed it with a drop of wax. He held the letter until morning.

He rose early the next morning with an overwhelming sense of disappointment. Tiny readied the message to be sent, but just as he was about to release the bird, he looked up at the mountain and beheld the most beautiful white cloud encircling it like a wreath. Tiny placed the bird back into its cage and stared up at the mountainside with joy.

"What's the matter, son?" asked his father.

"The cloud," said Tiny.

"Yes," said his father, "it appears every year about this time."

Tiny set out to climb the mountain once more. This time, when he arrived at the top, he found his old friend resting just inside the cave.

"Subakai," Tiny called out timidly. "It is I, Tiny. I have returned."

Tiny stood in front of the cave and listened. There was something moving in the cave. Just like before, the immense head of his friend emerged from the cave.

"Tiny!" said Subakai. "It is you!"

Tiny ran forward and squeezed Subakai tightly, burying his face in the thick white mane. His arms could scarcely reach halfway around the beast's neck.

"Your size is always a surprise to me," said Tiny.

"My size?" said Subakai. "It seems to me you have grown yourself."

"True," said Tiny, "I have grown some, but I am still small for my age."

"Still, you are a grand sight for these gold eyes," said Subakai.

"Unfortunately, I have come to ask a favor of you, my giant friend."

"If I can help, I will," said Subakai. "What troubles you?"

"I have done well for myself, Subakai. I am in service to the King of Ironcrest, and I have come on his behalf to ask you to help me vanquish a knight that has come against the kingdom."

"Only one knight and you need my help?"

"This knight rides a dragon of great strength," said Tiny.

"Ah, and you feel that one good dragon deserves another," said Subakai.

"I will understand if you do not wish to help. I know how you feel about humans."

"I have found that not all humans are bad, thanks to you. I will do as you ask, but I will deal only with you."

"I am indebted to you, my friend," said Tiny.

"As I am to you," replied Subakai.

"I will return as soon as I can and we will fly to the city under cover of night. Until then, rest. It is most certain that we will both need it."

Tiny hurried back down the mountain and quickly wrote a new letter, sealed it, and attached it to the dove. *All hope for Salizar rests on those tiny wings*, he thought, as he released the bird into the air and it took flight. "Go," he said softly, "and make your namesake proud."

Tiny readied his things and said good-bye to his father and brothers.

"This time you have my blessing," said his father. "Take good care of yourself."

"I will try, Father," said Tiny. Then, turning to his brothers, he said, "Though you have always treated me poorly, I want you to know, I have always cared for you and looked up to you both. I hope life treats you well."

Robert and John were struck dumb by this, but as he turned away, John said, "I'm gonna miss ya, runt."

Tiny treasured those words, because he knew it caused him great discomfort to say. "I will send for my horse later," said Tiny, and he marched off toward the mountain.

At that point, Robert turned John and said, "Where does he think he is going? The city is in the other direction."

Tiny traveled the path he had followed so many times before. At the top, he sat and watched the sunset in the west and wondered if he would ever see another.

When night had fallen, Subakai emerged from the cave and said, "Come, young man, the time is nigh and the stars are calling our name."

Tiny rose to his feet and climbed atop Subakai's massive head. Subakai climbed to the side of the mountain, which had a sheer cliff face, spread his wings, and lunged off. His wings cut through the cold night air as they soared above the town. The stars beamed brightly, and Tiny could see his father's house for what he thought was the last time. They followed the reflection of the moon on the river until they arrived at the woods just beyond the castle. Subakai landed in a small clearing amid the trees. Tiny climbed down from Subakai's head and nestled himself into his soft white mane. They slept until morning and had their dreams of flight.

At first light, Tiny awoke and wiped the sleep from his eyes. "The king will be waiting to see me," he said. "You'd better wait here. I will come for you when the time is right." He then disappeared into the woods.

When he arrived at the palace, the king was notified of his arrival and sent for Tiny immediately. This time, Tiny was summoned to his private chambers. A guard showed him to the king's quarters. As he entered the room, the door was shut behind him. The king stood at the window, looking out over his kingdom and wringing his hands. Barnabus was trying to persuade the king to eat, to no avail.

"Please, Your Highness, you must keep up your strength," said Barnabus.

"I will have nothing until this matter is safely behind us!" said the king.

"Your Highness, I have come straightaway," said Tiny.

The king spun around and said, "Tiny! I am glad you are here. I received your letter, but it's too late, I'm afraid. That cursed knight will descend on the city tomorrow at noon. My army has failed and lies in utter ruin. The knight comes to claim the scepter tomorrow, and to make matters worse, I no longer have the scepter."

"What!" exclaimed Tiny.

"It was stolen last night while I slept," said the king.

"The shadow of a dragon was seen flying over the castle last night, sire. Perhaps the knight has the scepter already," said Barnabus.

"Then why did we receive the letter of our impending doom this morning?" asked the king.

"The shadow your men saw last night was me," said Tiny.

"You!" exclaimed Barnabus.

"Yes," said Tiny. "I flew on the head of a dragon last night."

"You what?" said the king.

"You have a pet dragon?" asked Barnabus.

"Not a pet," said Tiny, "a friend. And I have persuaded him to help us in our plight. But he will only deal with me."

"I must say, a dragon would make a worthy adversary for another dragon," said the king.

"You're not serious, Your Highness," said Barnabus. "Can one really trust a dragon?"

"With my life!" said Tiny angrily.

"A better question would be, do we have a choice?" asked the king.

"Have you forgotten, Your Highness, that only a knight of the realm can champion your kingdom?" asked Barnabus.

"Then I shall knight him," said the king.

"But, but," stammered Barnabus.

"But nothing!" shouted the king. "Bring me a sword!"

A sword was brought in, and Tiny knelt down and lowered his head. The king took the sword and knighted him right there on the spot.

Tiny looked up and said, "I will give my life for you and your kingdom, sire."

"Let us hope you don't have to, Tiny," answered the king.

When Tiny left the palace, he was truly excited. He was a knight, just like Lucias. He searched the woods for Lucias to tell him the good news, but when he finally stumbled on the campsite, Lucias was packing his things as if he was going somewhere in a hurry.

"Lucias," Tiny cried, "you will never guess what has happened! I have been made a knight."

"Have you really? That's nice," he said as he packed. His departure seemed urgent.

"Are you going somewhere?" asked Tiny.

"I have a pressing matter elsewhere," said Lucias.

"Will I see you again?"

"It's possible, I guess," said Lucias.

"Here, let me help you," said Tiny, as he bent over to pick up Lucias's shiny black cloak.

"No!" snapped Lucias. "I will get that." As he tried to pull it from Tiny's hands, something fell out. It was the scepter.

"It was you," Tiny growled. "You stole the scepter."

"No, wait!" Lucias yelled. "You don't understand."

"All that talk about truth and honor, and you are nothing more than a thief."

"Yes, I did steal it, but not for its worth. If you will just listen—"

"I have listened to you long enough," snapped Tiny. "You know I must return the scepter to my king."

"You will have to kill me first," said Lucias.

"Then so be it," said Tiny, and they both drew their swords.

Tiny lunged forward, clashing swords with Lucias. He returned the blow with a thrust of his own, which Tiny deflected. The sound of clanging swords broke the stillness of the woods. To and fro they moved across the small clearing, dodging each other's advances. Tiny narrowly escaped a blow to the head when Lucias backed him against a tree, but he spun around and met Lucias with a thrust to the side. Lucias dodged his thrust, but it tore his shirt under the arm.

"This is one of my best shirts," said Lucias. "Your fighting has greatly improved."

"I have only just begun," said Tiny, and they continued to thrust and parry.

Then suddenly, Lucias advanced with such force that Tiny could not hold him back. As Tiny stepped backward, frantically blocking every blow Lucias made, he tripped over the scepter that was lying on the ground and fell into a hollow at the base of a large tree. Lucias raised his sword high and came down with such force that it loosed Tiny's sword from his hand and sent it soaring a good distance away. Lucias placed the tip of his sword on Tiny's chest above his heart and pressed ever so lightly. Tiny cringed at the thought of being run through.

"Now," said Lucias, "will you listen, or shall I kill you?"

"It seems I have no choice," said Tiny.

"I told you, Tiny, that I was a knight of Bonangi," said Lucias.

"So you say," answered Tiny, still staring at the blade resting on his chest.

"Well, meet Bonangi," said Lucias, as he bent over and picked up the scepter. "Look at it, Tiny. It was for this that I was born. I have spent my entire life waiting for this very day. In my kingdom, many, many years ago, long before I was born, there lived a great spiritual leader among my people. My kingdom had been at war for many years, and this leader grew weary of the way men treated each other. So he disappeared for five years into the mountains. Many thought he had died, but he returned, carrying the scepter. Look at it closely, Tiny."

Tiny gazed up at the scepter. It was a strangely shaped thing. It had a long square shaft, as long as a man's arm, and was twisted to a point. A solid opal sphere, twice the size of Tiny's fist, sat atop the shaft. Out of that sphere rose a hand made with great detail. Every crease, every nail was formed to perfection, and upon the index finger of the hand sat a ring bearing the largest white diamond he had ever seen. The entire scepter was made of pure gold, and a band of ivory encircled the opal sphere. It was a magnificent sight. Tiny had seen it many times while it was in the king's possession, but never had he noticed the great care with which it had been crafted.

"You see the ring?" asked Lucias. "In the beginning there were four rings. This is the ring of wisdom. It is the key to true wisdom. You see, the man who created Bonangi sought to impart man's best qualities to the scepter, so he crafted the rings and searched for the spells that would unlock these qualities in man: the qualities of wisdom, strength, compassion, and truth. The sovereign who possesses the scepter with all four rings has the power to unite all people as one heart in peace.

"Unfortunately, there are other qualities in man's heart that are not so admirable. Qualities like fear, greed, hatred, and corruption. These are kept alive by the spirit called Salina. She is the reason the rings were secretly hidden throughout the world. She is the one we knights truly fight. She lives deep within the netherworld and casts her spells of illusion, causing men to fear and hate their fellow man. She feeds off these emotions and grows stronger by their presence.

"Every thousand years a doorway opens between her world and ours. It is the only time when she can get the scepter. That time is now. She has between the first and second full moon of spring. There are only two more days until the second full moon. If I can keep the scepter until then, the world will be safe from her madness for another thousand years."

"But if the king doesn't turn over the scepter to a foreign knight, he will destroy the city of Salizar by dragon fire," said Tiny. "I cannot let that happen."

"No, don't you see?" said Lucias. "The knight is working for her. He will turn the scepter over to her and the whole world will be at war."

"No, you are wrong," said Tiny. "The knight is working for a wizard."

"A wizard?" asked Lucias.

"That is how the letters have been signed," said Tiny.

"That can't be so. It is a lie designed to throw me off the track. Somehow she is behind all this."

"Either way, I mustn't return to the king without the scepter," said Tiny. "So if you're going to kill me, you had better do it."

"There is only one way I can let you have the scepter."

"What is that?" asked Tiny.

"You must become a knight of Bonangi. I will have to perform the ceremony myself."

"I will do whatever it takes," said Tiny.

Lucias slowly lifted his sword from Tiny's chest and sheathed it. He then took the scepter and stuck it into the ground. He found four large stones and placed them across from each other so that they formed a square, with the scepter at one corner.

"Take off your shirt," said Lucias.

"Why?" asked Tiny.

"It is part of the ceremony," Lucias answered. So Tiny took off his shirt. "Now, sit here," said Lucias, pointing at the stone opposite the scepter. Tiny took his place at the stone.

Lucias drew lines in the soil, connecting the stones in a square. Then he drew lines from each stone to the stone across from it, so that there was a cross in the center of the square. Lucias lit a fire in the center of the square and placed a small pot of water on the flames to boil. He then took out a small satchel and retrieved four small tins from it. Opening them, he set them around Tiny. They were canisters of paint: white, red, black, and yellow. Lucias took them and painted Tiny's face, neck, back, chest, and arms; even his fingers were painted four different colors.

"You mustn't wash this off until morning," said Lucias. "Tomorrow, when you awake, go to the river and bathe. Wash the colors off completely, or they will become permanent."

Lucias rose to his feet, grabbed a small sack from among his things, and paced around the square, chanting in his native tongue. At each stone, he would reach into the sack and cast a handful of something into the fire. The flames would surge skyward, and the strange smell of jasmine and cinnamon filled the air. The first time the flames leaped into the air it startled Tiny, but Lucias didn't stop. Around the square he went. Once, twice, three times. By the time he had gone around four times, the smell began to overwhelm Tiny and he could feel himself slipping into a trance. His eyes were open, but it seemed like a dream. Lucias stopped at the scepter and knelt down behind it.

"Look at it, Tiny," he said. "Gaze into the palm of the hand."

Tiny suddenly found that his eyes were drawn to the center of the hand on the scepter. A dim light flickered in the palm of the hand. This light grew brighter and brighter, until its brilliance outshone that of the fire. Tiny's eyes opened wide, yet he could not look away.

"Now, speak," said Lucias.

Tiny began to speak, though he did not know where the words came from:

> *Foolish man has lost his sight,*
> *Four rings a hand to make it right.*
> *The wisdom stone a diamond white,*
> *The gift of wisdom's brightest light.*
> *The tigereye, though small in size,*
> *The gift of truth will fill their eyes.*
> *The Mater's heart, a serpent's tooth,*
> *A ruby stone, the gift of youth.*
> *The stone of strength, black and old,*
> *Will wake the dead, though bones lie cold.*

"Now," said Lucias, "let's see what tomorrow holds for you." He plucked the scepter from the ground, and with the palm still glowing, he touched it to the boiling water. The water lay still, as smooth as glass, then Lucias gazed into the pot and began to chant:

> *Dragon's dance, the siren sings,*
> *A knight will come on crested wings.*
> *He breathes no breath, with hollow eyes,*
> *The dance of death as dragons fly.*
> *Riddle me a mystery.*
> *The oaken wizard, a bluff I see.*
> *Can ancient wood, a simple tree,*
> *Beckon bones to battle thee?*

Suddenly, a wave of terror swept across Lucias's face. Dumbfounded, he stood in silence for a moment. He turned his eyes to the ground as he tried to cope with whatever it was he had seen. He then shook off the pervasive thought and turned his attention back to Tiny. Meanwhile, Tiny, still in a trance, sat in silence.

"Remember," said Lucias softly, then he lightly touched Tiny on the head with the scepter, and Tiny fell fast asleep.

Morning came quickly and Tiny awoke alone. Lucias had packed all his things and left. Tiny sat up and looked around. Lucias was nowhere in sight. The scepter was stuck in the ground in the place where Tiny had sat the night before. The fire's embers were cold and the woods were damp with the morning dew. Tiny stood and found his shirt. He then pulled the scepter from the ground and started the short walk to the river. Once there, he placed the scepter in a spot where he could keep an eye on it while he bathed. The water was ice-cold, but refreshing. He used a rough stone to scrape the paint from his skin. *What a strange life I have*, he thought, as he scraped his back against a fallen tree to get the paint off. Once he had washed thoroughly, he dressed himself, collected his prize, and started back to the castle.

The king was amazed to see Tiny return with the scepter. Filled with queries, he began to question Tiny.

"Was it the knight? Where did you find him? Did you kill him?"

"No, Your Highness," Tiny answered. "It was not the knight you seek. I found him in the woods preparing to leave the kingdom."

"Should I send guards to scour the woods?" asked the king.

"No, Your Highness, that won't be necessary. He is no longer a threat to the safety of the scepter."

"Good!" said the king firmly. "Now, we must get you ready for your battle, Tiny. We only have until noon. Barnabus will lead you to the armory where you may pick from any armor or weapons we may have."

Barnabus led Tiny through the castle once more, this time without saying a word. The two of them walked down a darkened corridor that led to the guards' quarters. Just beyond that point, they approached a door where a guard was posted. Barnabus motioned to the guard to unlock the door. The guard plucked the keys from his belt and opened the door. Barnabus escorted Tiny inside and said, "Choose your weapons, Sir Lynquest." Tiny could tell that the words did not sit well with Barnabus, but he did not care.

He looked about the room carefully. It was a large room with two doors. Both were kept locked and guarded. There were weapons and armor of all shapes and sizes. There were maces and lances, battle axes and hammers, shields and swords, chest plates and helmets. Tiny tried on a suit of armor, but found that it was too heavy. He tried on a helmet, but he couldn't see very well. Next, he thought he might be able to use a lance, but when he picked one up, he found it too hard to keep the point in the air.

"Perhaps if I had some time to practice," he said, smiling.

Barnabus just rolled his eyes and shook his head in disapproval. After sorting through the entire armory, Tiny finally decided that the only weapon that served him well was his own sword and a small bronze shield he found among the armor.

Clasping the shield in his left hand, he turned to Barnabus and said, "Well, I guess this will do."

"That's all?" exclaimed Barnabus. "A small bronze shield and a sword?"

"I have my grandfather's dagger, too," said Tiny.

Barnabus shook his head again and mumbled to himself, "It's hopeless. I might as well start packing my things." Louder, he said sarcastically, "Oh, well, you're the knight. You should know best."

They returned to the king, who at the time was busy staving off his daughter's demands to eat. "My dear child, I cannot eat," he said. "I am much too nervous. My army lies in ruin and my entire kingdom rests on the shoulders of a sixteen-year-old boy. How on earth could I possibly eat now?"

Tiny overheard this as they approached the king's chamber, and it bothered him that the king still thought of him as a boy. *Boy or man*, he thought, *someone has to stand up to this threat*. And he felt sure that he was that someone.

As they entered the room, the king realized that Tiny might have overheard his comment.

"Lynquest," said the king, "are you ready?"

"Yes, sire," answered Tiny.

"But where is your armor? Where are all your weapons?"

"I only have need of this shield and my sword, sire."

"But, how can you defeat the knight without weapons?" asked the king in frustration.

"I don't plan to out-battle the knight, Your Highness, but to outwit him. My greatest weapon, sire, is not my sword. Even a boy of sixteen knows that life's battles are not fought on the ground or in the air, but in the mind. And that is where I shall beat him."

"Well said, Lynquest," said the king. "I am sorry I doubted you. Go, vanquish the scourge, and I shall grant you a portion of my kingdom."

"I would rather have your respect, sire," replied Tiny.

"I tell you, you shall have much more," said the king.

With that, Tiny left the king's chamber, bound for the clearing where Subakai awaited.

The day was perfect, warm, but not hot. There was not a cloud to be seen anywhere in the sky. Subakai was growing restless when Tiny returned.

"I was beginning to think you might not return," said Subakai.

"I am sorry, my friend, if I made you wait, but I had to make sure that all was in order before I came," said Tiny.

"I understand," said Subakai.

"Well, the sun is high and I think it is time," said Tiny.

Subakai rested his head upon the ground and Tiny climbed on top. He settled in between Subakai's two large horns. He drew his sword once Subakai had taken to the air. They soared above the city. As their shadow passed over the ground, people scattered like insects. Tiny searched the horizon until he saw a speck in the distance. He watched as the spot grew larger and larger, until he realized that it was the opposing dragon.

"There he is!" he shouted to Subakai. "Quickly, we mustn't let him reach the city. We must fight him over the countryside."

All the subjects at the palace watched from their vantage points as Tiny raced to meet his fate. Tiny's heart pounded wildly and his hands began to sweat. He trained his eye on the rider of the dragon: a knight in a strange suit of armor. It was a crimson suit, almost bloodred.

"It's him!" cried Subakai.

"Who?" asked Tiny.

"The knight who left his sword in my side. The sword you hold in your hand. Now I will have my revenge!" roared Subakai, as he launched his snakelike body through the air.

The foreboding dragon belched fire into the air as he drew nearer to Tiny and Subakai. Tiny's hair whipped about his face and his grip on Subakai's horns tightened. The opposing dragon was of immense size. It had one great eye and two horns that stuck out straight forward like a bull's. It was a dark gray color and had a bloodred mane that ran the length of its back. It wasn't as long and as slender as Subakai, but it was well armored with tough dragon scales.

The rider perched between the great dragon's wings, holding a lance poised to strike Tiny down. As they drew near, Tiny readied his shield to deflect the blow. The dragons collided with amazing force, their talons flailing in the air. Subakai stuck the opposing dragon in the eye with the large plate at the end of his tail. The rider's lance struck Tiny's shield. The force of the blow almost knocked him from his perch, but he tried to cut the lance in two with his sword.

The two dragons broke off their battle and separated, only to turn and attack again. This time, Subakai twisted his long body and clamped the dissenting dragon's jaws shut with his hind legs. The rider's lance succeeded in knocking Tiny off Subakai's head, but he managed to lock his right arm around one of Subakai's horns. The lance remained between the two great horns atop Subakai's head. Subakai twisted his neck down and to the left, snapping the lance in two.

Then the ruthless dragon raised his enormous hind claw and tore at Subakai's breast. The two great leviathans once again broke their struggle and retreated to open air.

Tiny retook his place atop Subakai's head and started to plan his next attack, when he saw something that caused his heart to sink in his chest. They had turned to face their opponents, when suddenly the dragon changed color. It was no longer dark gray, but sky blue. It had changed its color to match the sky and now it couldn't be seen at all. Only the rider could be seen, riding on a crest of air.

How can we fight what we cannot see? thought Tiny. "Try to hide in the sun!" he yelled. The red knight raced toward them. "Now!" screamed Tiny.

Subakai burst toward the sun, but it did no good. The now invisible dragon moved with him and caught him around the neck with its massive jaws. Tiny looked back and could see the light blue dragon's head. He took his sword and struck the dragon's nose several times. Subakai writhed in pain. Finally, Tiny struck the dragon next to its eye and it loosened its grip on Subakai's neck. Subakai quickly twisted away and broke for freedom. The two dragons circled in the sky, each looking for a way to attack. Tiny thought about how he was able to see the dragon against Subakai's dark green body and it gave him an idea.

"Breathe, Subakai!" he yelled.

"But I haven't any fire," screamed Subakai.

"I know. It's not fire we need. Now breathe!"

Subakai took a deep, deep breath and filled the sky with his thick white smoke, creating an enormous cloud around them.

"Now climb above the cloud," said Tiny.

The two rose rapidly above the enormous white cloud. Suddenly, the red knight raced toward the cloud, and for a brief moment the silhouette of the light blue dragon appeared against the pure white smoke.

"There, see him?" shouted Tiny. "Quickly, Subakai, before he disappears into the cloud."

Subakai dove for the dragon's tail and caught it close to the end between his teeth. The dragon, feeling the pain of Subakai's grip, turned back to its original dark gray. It turned to face its captor and drew a deep breath, preparing to engulf them in flames. Subakai quickly wrapped his long tail once, twice, three times around the dragon's neck and tightened his grip until the dragon's breath was cut off. Head to tail and claw to claw, the two leviathans wrestled in mid-flight. Tiny took the opportunity to leap from Subakai's head onto the opposing dragon's back.

Using the dragon's bloodred mane, he made his way up to where the knight sat. The two dragons pitched to and fro as each one struggled to gain dominance. Tiny reached the knight and drew his sword. He thrust the blade through the knight's back, but to his amazement, the knight only spun around and swung at him with a mace. Tiny struck again, this time connecting with the rider's head. The knight's helmet flew off his head and tumbled through the open air.

Tiny stood speechless, startled by the two sunken eyes of a man long dead. The knight was not a man at all, but a collection of bones brought to life by some strange magic. Tiny was so taken aback by the sight that he was nearly hit by the knight's return blow.

As the two clashed weapons, Tiny noticed a thin silver chain with a ring strung on it dangling around the specter's neck. The band of the ring was thick and gold, with a large black stone set in it.

Once he had seen the ring, he knew what had to be done. Tiny released the dragon's mane that was keeping him steady, raised his shield, and threw himself against the knight's weapon. The mace collided with his shield and the force of Tiny's body sent the skeleton reeling. At that moment, Tiny reached out and snatched the silver chain from the rider's neck. The knight dropped his weapon and plummeted to the earth. Tiny victoriously held the silver chain in his hand. Just then, the dragon pitched to the left and Tiny lost his balance. He dropped his sword and began to slide off the dragon's back.

Reaching to his belt, he pulled out his grandfather's dagger and plunged it into the dragon's side. It lodged deep between two plates, and the dragon twitched and squirmed in agony.

Subakai held fast to the dragon's tail and throat as Tiny dangled, clinging to the dagger. He dropped his shield and struggled desperately to regain his place on the dragon's back. He had put the silver necklace in his mouth to give himself a free hand. He then reached for the bloodred mane once again and caught a clump of it tightly in his fist.

Once he had a firm grip on the mane, he pulled the blade from the dragon's side and tucked it back into his belt. The dragon's wings began to slow their rhythm as it struggled to breathe. Tiny knew he hadn't much time.

He pulled himself atop the beast and made his way down the tail. As he reached Subakai's head, the other dragon's tail still between his teeth, the great gray dragon's body went limp. Tiny leaped back on top of Subakai as he released the dragon's limp body. The dragon fell to the earth, causing a great crash when it landed among the trees of the forest.

Tiny pulled the necklace from his mouth and gazed at the ring upon the chain. *The stone of strength, black and old, will wake the dead, though bones lie cold.* The words haunted him. He had recovered the ring of strength. He clutched it tightly in his hand as Subakai wafted gracefully to the ground.

They landed close to where the dragon fell, but once again it was nowhere in sight.

"Gone?" said Tiny inquisitively. "But how? I saw you kill him. I saw him fall."

Nevertheless, the dragon's body was not there. The knight, on the other hand, was a pile of broken bones and armor. Even the skull which had struck fear into Tiny's heart lay shattered on the ground. Tiny found the sword he had used to battle the knight, the same sword that had been buried deep in Subakai's side. Tiny treasured this sword. It was a symbol of their friendship. The people of the city, who had been watching the sky, rushed to greet Tiny and Subakai. They brought food for the dragon and tended to his wounds.

There was a great celebration that day that lasted far into the night. Subakai had his fill of the city's hospitality and then retreated to the solitude of the clearing in the woods to rest. Tiny was taken to the king on the shoulders of the crowd. The king awaited his arrival on the balcony overlooking the courtyard that was packed to overflowing with a joyous crowd. The air was thick with the sounds of jubilance until the king began to speak.

"We truly owe a debt of gratitude to our beloved Tiny Lynquest. He is surely a man among men. I have commissioned a medal to be made in his honor, and that this day every year shall be celebrated as the great day of dragons."

The crowd exploded in excitement and began to cheer, "Tiny! Tiny! Tiny!"

Tiny was truly overwhelmed. The party took to the streets as butchers, bakers, and merchants opened their shops to the hungry mob. Food and drink of all kinds were brought before Tiny. He ate until he couldn't eat another bite and then quietly disappeared into the crowded streets. He slipped away into the woods and joined Subakai in the clearing. He sat on the ground next to the tired dragon and said, "Subakai?"

"Yes, my friend," answered Subakai.

"I would like to thank you for all you have done. They are calling me a hero, but I couldn't have done it at all without you. Thank you."

"Think of it no more," said Subakai. "I was merely helping someone who once saved my life."

"I don't blame you for coming out here," commented Tiny. "At least it's quiet."

"I am only good around one human, and that human is you," said Subakai.

Tiny smiled and leaned back against his dragon friend. Staring up at the night sky, he drifted off to sleep.

The following morning, he woke at dawn. A strong western breeze was blowing and the sky was filling with clouds.

"Looks like we're in for a storm," said Tiny.

"Yes, it doesn't look good," answered Subakai.

"I thank you again," said Tiny. "I know you are eager to continue your search for wisdom, so if you want to leave, I will understand."

"What will you do now?" asked Subakai.

"Well, there is still the matter of the sorcerer. I will have to do something about that, but you don't have to go. You have done enough," said Tiny.

"I will not leave until I know you are safe," replied Subakai. "Go and see your king, and I will await your decision."

CHAPTER SEVEN

SORCERESS OF EVIL

So Tiny embarked for the palace once more. When he arrived, he was pleased to see the king eating a hearty meal.

"Tiny!" exclaimed the king. "Come join me." Then he motioned to a servant to bring another setting.

Barnabus was nervously trying to discuss the matter of the wizard with the king. "But, Your Highness, we are not out of danger yet. There is still this sorcerer we must deal with. He will be far more dangerous than the knight."

"This much is true," said Tiny. "I outsmarted the knight, but even I am not sure I can outwit a sorcerer."

"And what about the dragon?" added Barnabus. "We still don't know whether you were successful in killing it or not."

"Yes, Your Highness," replied Tiny, "there is much left to be done."

The king's face grew serious and he set down his fork. "Then it looks like I have no choice," he said. "I must give you the greatest weapon that my kingdom possesses to battle this wizard."

"Your Highness, NO!" said Barnabus.

"We have no choice, Barnabus. If Tiny fails, we will have to turn it over anyway."

"But the scepter has been in your family for hundreds of years," argued Barnabus.

"I know, but it is the only way," said the king. He then lifted the scepter from his lap and gazed at its beauty as if he were looking at it for the last time. He handed it to Tiny and said, "Please, bring it back to me safely."

Tiny took the scepter from the king. "I don't understand," said Tiny. "How can a scepter be a weapon?"

"You will," answered the king. "In times of great trouble, it has been the source of tremendous wisdom. Use it wisely and it will carry you to victory."

"But how shall I find this wizard?" asked Tiny.

"One of our scouts has found something lying several days to the east, a strange structure that hasn't been there before. It lies in a place known as the Forest of Bones."

"I don't like the sound of that," said Tiny.

"An ominous name, to be sure," said Barnabus. "But how will you get there?"

"Subakai has agreed to go with me. He can travel much faster than horses. I will leave immediately," said Tiny.

"Go, and our hearts go with you," said the king.

Tiny left the king's chamber, and made his way down the grand staircase. He found his way back to the armory, where he acquired a quiver in which to keep the scepter. Once outside, he followed the path that led through the garden, but before he reached the gate, the princess called to him to stop. She had been weeping, for her eyes were red and weary. She said nothing, only clasped his arm tightly and kissed his cheek. Then she returned to the garden fountain in silence. Tiny was stunned, but, lacking anything to say, he turned and left the garden quietly.

When he approached Subakai, the dragon woke with a start.

"You startled me," said Subakai.

"I am sorry, my friend," said Tiny.

"So, what was their decision?"

"I must go and vanquish this sorcerer before he rises against the kingdom."

"A sorcerer is a challenging adversary, my friend. You will need an ally."

"Then you will come?" asked Tiny hopefully.

"It is as I said. I will not leave until I know you are safe."

"Good. I had hoped you would come." Then Tiny hugged his large friend.

As he did, the scepter that was nestled in the quiver on Tiny's back touched Subakai gently. The great dragon smiled an awkward but genuine smile and said, "Thank you, Tiny."

"For what?" Tiny inquired. "I haven't done anything."

"You have done more than you know."

Tiny smiled and shrugged his shoulders, then once again climbed on top of Subakai's head.

By now, the sky had grown thick with dark clouds and the wind raged through the trees.

"Go east," said Tiny, "to a place called the Forest of Bones."

"I know of this place," said Subakai. "We will have to go with great speed. It is a long way from here."

They rose into the air as Subakai beat his wings toward the ground. Soon they were soaring over the city, and people everywhere came out to watch as the two disappeared on the horizon. Hours went by as they flew against the wind. The clouds stirred about in the sky like some primeval soup. Finally they reached a place of rolling hills. At the top of the highest hill was a bluff that towered above the area. There on the bluff stood an enormous ball that looked as if it was made of dark blue glass. Within the ball stood the sorcerer, a man of great height; as tall as a house he stood, robed all in white. His face was as pale as milk and his hair and hands were a strange green hue.

"We are here," said Subakai as he circled in the sky.

The sorcerer turned his face to the sky and waved his long green hands about violently. Suddenly, lightning struck all around them. One bolt struck Subakai's wing, causing him to falter in midair. His wings went limp, and he rolled over and began falling.

"Subakai!" yelled Tiny as he fell forward, clinging to Subakai's horns.

Subakai regained his balance, but the scepter was hurled to the ground. It landed on the ground, just at the base of the bluff.

"Quickly," said Tiny, "we must reach the scepter before he does."

Subakai swooped to the ground and landed next to the scepter. The sorcerer glared viciously at Tiny and motioned to the ground with his hands. Tiny jumped down from Subakai and stepped toward the scepter, but as he did, he felt something crawling up his legs. He looked down to see vines winding their way up his legs, holding him fast where he stood. He looked at the scepter only a few steps further away.

He drew his sword and began hacking at the vines, but as he cut them, more grew. He fell to the ground in the direction of the scepter and reached for it. He stretched his arm as far as he could. His fingers could just reach the hand on the scepter. As he touched the hand, he got a surprise. It suddenly grasped his with a firm grip. Tiny raised it into the air in amazement. The scepter was now a sword.

The long shaft of the scepter had become a fine double-edged blade. Its weight, too, seemed to be far lighter and more manageable. Tiny wielded it as if it were part of his own arm. He struck the vines with the scepter, and they released his legs and retreated into the ground. The wizard, having seen that Tiny was free, again motioned to the ground with his lanky fingers. Tiny took another step toward the wizard, but the ground beneath his feet grew soft and he began to sink.

"Help!" he yelled as he sank into the soil. He tried to pull his feet out, but it was too late. Still clutching the scepter, he grabbed at the ground around him, but nothing seemed to work. "Subakai! Help me!" he screamed, as his head disappeared into the dark brown soil.

Subakai quickly spun around and plunged his tail into the ground. Down, down he reached with his long tail, searching the murky soil for any sign of Tiny's body. Finally, a look of relief came over Subakai's face as he lifted his tail out of the ground, with Tiny clinging to it. He set Tiny down on solid ground. Tiny shook the dirt from his hair and glared up at the wizard.

The wizard was furious. He began to roll his hands one over the other. Faster and faster he rolled, until a ball of light began to glow in the space between his hands. He caught this ball up in one hand and cast it to the ground at Tiny's feet.

The ground cracked and two mounds rose before Tiny. Soon, the bone-white face of a skeleton in full battle armor and brandishing a sword arose before Tiny from the first mound, while the other mound produced a skeleton armed with a battle-ax. They lashed out at Tiny; the sound of metal on metal reverberated as the scepter deflected the blows of the skeletons' attack. Tiny marveled at how the scepter responded with lightning speed— as if it had a mind of its own. He struck one of the skeletons through the chest. The skeleton's weapons and armor fell to the ground, and it turned its face and hands to the sky and stood as motionless as a statue.

Suddenly, two more mounds appeared behind the motionless skeleton. Tiny struck down the second skeleton, only to see two more take its place. Every time he vanquished one, two more appeared. Soon, both he and Subakai were surrounded by an army of the undead. Subakai encircled Tiny with his long body and swept the skeletons away with his tail, but they only returned.

"I cannot hold them back!" he yelled.

Tiny quickly pulled the black ring from a pouch tucked beneath his belt. He slipped it on his finger and said, "Then let them come."

Subakai opened his body to the battling horde and Tiny sprang into the midst of the army. He struck this skeleton and that one, then another and another. Each time the result was the same. The skeleton would stand motionless with its face and hands turned to the sky as two more took its place. Subakai would beat them back with his tail and his head, but they would just return.

Out of frustration, he drew a great breath and opened his tremendous jaws. An enormous ball of fire burst forth from his throat, spun through the air, and exploded into the wall of bony warriors. They burst into flames. Their armor dropped to the ground and again they turned their faces and hands to the sky.

"Subakai!" Tiny shouted. "You have fire!"

Seeing his warriors in flames, the sorcerer turned his attention to the sky. Again, without a word, he motioned to the clouds and down came the rain; with such force that Tiny could hardly see. Flashes of lightning lit the thick black sky; booming thunder rocked the area. Skeletons, engulfed in flames, surrounded Tiny, but he felt no heat. The skeletons' weapons struck his body again and again, but somehow he bore no wounds. He slowly fought his way through the thickening horde until he reached the base of the bluff. He turned his eyes to the sorcerer, while Subakai set the warriors on flames by the dozen.

Lightning struck at the moment he reached the sorcerer and Tiny saw a figure standing beside the wizard. It was Lucias, and he struck at the bubble with his sword, to no avail.

"Lucias!" Tiny called out. "Catch!"

He then swung the scepter sword around and around and released it, sending it soaring above the battle. It landed at Lucias's feet, and he quickly picked it up. Lucias held the sword high in the air as the sorcerer stared at him with a face of terror. Lucias struck the ball with one mighty blow. It exploded with tremendous force, throwing Lucias backward to the ground. The rain suddenly stopped and the warriors froze in their tracks. Tiny watched as the clouds broke and light fell on the bluff and the skeletons' upturned faces. The sorcerer turned his panic-stricken face to the sky.

Tiny watched the wizard grow, tall and strong. His hands reached for the sky as his green fingers stretched to meet the sunlight. Even the ends of his hair were pulled upward toward the heavens. His feet seemed to sink into the soil under the weight of his size. His face grew long, distorted, until it no longer looked like a face. Tiny watched in amazement as he realized he was no longer looking at a sorcerer, but a tree; a large white oak standing on the bluff. The skeletons, extinguished by the rain, had turned into maple, birch, and elm trees. Consumed by the fire, they now stood around him like statues of smoldering coal.

Tiny ran to his friend, calling out, "Lucias, are you all right?"

Lucias got to his feet, still clutching the scepter tightly in his hands. "It was an illusion!" he yelled back.

"What was?" asked Tiny.

"The sorcerer, the skeletons," replied Lucias. "It was all an illusion."

Tiny looked around and realized it was a grove of trees that he had been battling, and the wizard was a huge oak standing on a bluff alone. *The oaken wizard, a bluff I see. Can ancient wood, a simple tree, beckon bones to battle thee?* The words echoed through Tiny's head as he recalled the riddle.

As Tiny drew near to the top of the bluff, the sound of a woman's laughter broke the silence. He stopped and looked around. A doorway of brilliant light appeared between him and Lucias; a light so bright streamed out the door that Tiny had to hold his hands up to block the glare. A woman of unusual beauty appeared in the doorway, laughing with wicked intent.

"Lucias, you old fool," she said, "I knew you would bring the scepter to me."

"Salina!" Lucias cried. "It's not yours yet, witch."

"And Tiny," she said, turning her attention to him "I have to admit, I underestimated you. A mistake I shall never make again."

Tiny squinted against the light just to get a glimpse of the raven-haired beauty.

"You bested my knight and conquered my wizard, but I still have my pet. Camille!" she called out. "Fetch me the scepter!"

A freak windstorm arose; the trees waved to and fro and dust clouded the air.

"The dragon!" screamed Tiny. "Lucias, look out!"

But it was too late. The large gray dragon appeared out of nowhere over Lucias and snatched him up in its massive claw.

"Nooo!" Tiny howled.

The dragon raised Lucias into the air. Lucias squirmed as the dragon tightened its grip. Just then, a large bird swooped out of the sky and attacked the dragon's face and eye. It was Manobo, attempting to rescue his lifelong friend.

"Tiny," called Lucias with a strained breath. "It's time for you to have this." And he slung the scepter to the ground.

Tiny ran to the scepter and swept it up in his hands. He spun around and faced Salina, shouting, "Release him, or I will kill you now!"

"Go ahead, boy," Salina said. "I dare you."

Tiny ran to the doorway and swung the scepter sword. The blade passed right through the witch. Tiny staggered backward. "What?" he exclaimed.

"Ha, ha, ha," she laughed. "Foolish boy. You didn't think you could kill me, did you? Ha, ha, ha, ha! I have been the source of human misery since the beginning of time. I am immortal!"

"Let me," cried Subakai, as he took to the air.

"NO!" screamed Tiny. "You may hurt Lucias." Tiny looked to the western horizon. "Look, witch," he said. "The sun is setting. Soon you will have to return to your dark world without the scepter."

"Yes, perhaps," she said, "but Lucias is the last Bonangi knight and soon he will be dead. I will merely wait for you to die and return in another thousand years. I have all eternity, foolish mortal."

"Release Lucias, or I swear I will hunt you down, no matter where you hide," said Tiny.

"Very well, child. Camille! You heard the boy, drop him."

"No!" screamed Tiny.

The dragon tightened its grip once more and the sound of crushing bones met Tiny's ears.

"Aaaahhhggg!" cried Lucias. Then the dragon loosened its grip and Lucias plummeted to the ground.

Tiny raced to his side. He slowly rolled him over and Lucias smiled a feeble smile as blood trickled from his mouth.

"You wretched woman," scowled Tiny. "So help me, I will see you suffer for this."

"Not for a thousand years!" she yelled. "Not for a thousand years!" Her laughter echoed across the hills as the last light of day disappeared.

Then suddenly, the dragon was gone and Tiny was left alone with his dying friend. Manobo landed on the ground beside Lucias and nervously looked him over. Tiny knelt and propped Lucias's head upon his lap.

"Lucias, it's ok. I have the stone of strength. You won't die," he said, as he slipped the ring from his finger.

"No," said Lucias in a shallow voice. "It must not be used for selfish reasons."

"But you're dying," said Tiny. "Let me save you."

"No, some things are greater than I. Listen," he gasped. "Listen to me. You are the last Bonangi knight. You must succeed. If it is a thousand years she wants, then a thousand years she shall have."

"What are you talking about?"

"Search for the remaining stones. They"—he moaned as he clutched Tiny's hand—"they will restore the balance in the spirit. Look for the heart first, it will give you time."

"But, I can't do it alone," said Tiny.

"You must," answered Lucias. "The world's fate depends on it." Then Lucias turned his eyes to the sky. "Look," he said, as he stared up at the bright full moon, "the moon is smiling on me. Don't cry for me," he said softly. "I have been faithful to my quest. It was for this reason I was born. It is only just that I die on this night. Let me..." He took a short breath.

"Hold it one more time?" Tiny finished for him, as he laid the scepter on Lucias's chest.

Lucias clasped the scepter with both hands and smiled. "Don't worry," he said, "I will always be with you." With that, the final breath left his body as the expressionless stare of death came over his face.

Tiny held Lucias's head in his arms and began weeping uncontrollably, saying, "No, Lucias, no."

Subakai touched down lightly next to them. "Who was he?" he asked softly.

"A noble man," answered Tiny. "A very noble man."

Tiny and Subakai took Lucias's body and buried it in a secret place far from anywhere. He laid a stone to mark the spot and carved Lucias's name into it. Manobo watched nearby as Tiny placed the body and mourned his dear friend. Manobo would never leave that spot, as if some extraordinary loyalty kept him there. Tiny stayed all through the night until the morning. Then he and Subakai returned to the palace.

Tiny found the king ruling from the great hall once more. A look of full and complete joy came over his face when he saw Tiny enter the room. The princess ran to greet Tiny, enveloped him in a grand hug, and kissed him on the forehead.

"Princess Aleana!" said Barnabus in exasperation.

"It's ok, my daughter. We are all happy to see our Lynquest again."

Tiny stood still with an awkward look on his face. He didn't know how to respond to the princess's admiration. She loosened her grip on him and he approached the throne, clutching the scepter tightly in his hands. He laid it down upon the king's lap, took two steps backward, and knelt down on one knee with his face to the floor.

"Get up, Lynquest," said the king. "It is I who should be kneeling to you. You have accomplished a great task, one that no other could accomplish. For this, I hereby decree that in my kingdom you shall no longer be known as Tiny. From now on, everyone shall call you Lynquest the Great."

Tiny stood without expression.

"What is the matter, Lynquest? You should be happy. You vanquished the wizard."

"Yes, Your Highness," Tiny answered. "But it came at an awful price."

"What do you mean?" asked the king.

"Part of me died out there. Perhaps it was my youth. At any rate, I don't think I will ever see the world the same way again. I guess you could say I did an awful lot of growing in a very short time."

"I understand, Lynquest. Is there anything we can do?"

"I must return to my father's house to reassure him of my safety."

"Yes, yes, by all means, go and set your things in order."

Tiny smiled at the king, bowed, and then he turned and bowed to the princess before leaving.

CHAPTER EIGHT

Triumphant Return

He returned to Subakai, who took him back to Abiding Mountain. The two of them watched the sun sink slowly in the sky as they talked about the future.

"So, I guess you will be returning home now, huh?" Tiny asked.

"Yes. Thanks to you, I can finally go home," answered Subakai.

"Me? What did I do?" asked Tiny.

"You gave me the seed I was searching for."

"I did?"

"Yes, you did," replied Subakai.

"I don't recall giving you anything," said Tiny curiously.

"Silly human, the seed of wisdom isn't a *thing*. It is words to remember in times of great trial."

"And what might those words be?" asked Tiny.

"You showed me that true wisdom is like a good friend you always want by your side whenever there is trouble. And real wisdom is in knowing who to turn to in time of need."

Tiny smiled a big smile and nestled his head deep into Subakai's mane. After the sun had set, Tiny bid his friend a fond last good-bye. He ran his fingers through his thick white mane and patted him on the muzzle.

"I hope our paths cross again someday," said Tiny.

"As do I," said Subakai. "Ours is truly a rare and beautiful friendship. Go in peace, and perhaps I will look for you someday."

"That would be nice," said Tiny. "But I have much to do before Salina's return. Who knows what lies ahead? I will leave this here," he said, sticking his sword in the ground. "And I will return to this spot whenever I am at my father's house."

He said good-bye and hugged the great dragon one last time before starting down the mountain toward his father's house. When he arrived, he found that all the people of Eadenburrow had congregated there. There was food and ale. Laughter and song filled the evening air. To reach the house, he had to weave his way through the crowd. It was as if everyone in the valley had come to see his father.

"To Tiny!" someone yelled.

"To Tiny!" the crowd answered.

The sound of tankards clanking filled the house. Then Robert stood on a chair with his mug raised high and shouted, "To my baby brother, the dragon slayer!"

The whole house roared with laughter, and again came the sound of clanking as the toast was confirmed. Robert looked down from his lofty position and Tiny's eyes met his. A wave of excitement rushed across Robert's face as he leapt down from the chair and snapped Tiny up in a crushing embrace. Ale sloshed from Robert's mug over Tiny's right shoulder and down his chest. Robert stepped back, brushed the ale from Tiny's chest, and looked at him like he hadn't seen him in years.

"Who would ever have believed it?" said Robert. "Ladies and gentlemen," he said loudly, "I give you my brother, the dragon killer!"

The crowd showered him with applause, and countless hands stretched from the crowd to pat him on the back and head.

"Where is Father?" asked Tiny loudly.

"He is in the kitchen," Robert answered. "Here, I'll take you to him."

Turning to the crowd, he shouted, "Make way, clear a path, knight of the realm coming through," as he pushed people back. Once they reached the kitchen, Tiny saw his father still preparing food for the throng of people.

"Tiny!" he shouted. He stopped what he was doing and caught Tiny up in a warm embrace.

It feels good to be home, Tiny thought, as he sank into his father's arms. "Where did they all come from?" asked Tiny.

"They came from the surrounding glens. You're a hero, Tiny," said his father. "The news of your victory traveled up the river from Salizar and they came from everywhere to see if they could find you."

"Hey!" said a voice from the crowd. "Let's hear the story!" It was his brother John, urging the crowd to near riot to hear the story of the dragon. So Tiny made his way to the table and climbed on top.

"All right, all right," he said. "Calm down and I will tell you how it all started."

"And so began Tiny Lynquest's days as a storyteller." The old man nodded to Tobias. "He would return to the palace and serve the king, leaving from time to time to continue his quest for the remaining two stones. He outlived the king and loyally served the princess after him. Throughout all that time he was known as Lynquest the Great. But there were times when he grew weary of the search and would return to the place where Lucias was buried. It reminded him of what true greatness is. For you see, Tobias, to risk your life for those you love is one thing, but to die for those who not only did not know you, but did not accept you—therein lies true greatness." The frail old man rested back against the rock and pulled his pipe from between his teeth. "And that is how he became known as Lynquest the Great."

CHAPTER NINE

A CLEAN SWEEP

Tobias sat mesmerized by the old man's story. "So what happened to him? Where is he now? And did he ever find the other two rings?" Tobias asked eagerly.

"Ah," said the old man, "that is another story altogether. It's getting late and your mother will soon be calling you for supper."

"Tobias," his mother's voice faintly rang out over the hillside. The old man smiled a big smile and blew a puff of smoke.

"But, but, I want to hear more," said Tobias. "What happened to the princess, and how could Lynquest possibly be alive after all this time?"

"Now, now," the old man retorted, "you've heard enough for one day. You have heard more than anyone. Now be off with you, before your mother gets worried."

"Will you be here tomorrow?" asked Tobias.

"I'll make no promises," he said. "At my age, I never know if I can keep them. So for now, I will just say good night."

"But I don't know your name," said Tobias, as he turned to climb out of the rocky fortress.

"That's right, you don't," said the old man. "But someday you will."

"You're him, aren't you? You're Lynquest."

The odd old man smiled an impish grin and his steel gray eyes flickered with delight as he puffed on his slender pipe.

"Tobias!" His mother called again. "It's supper time!"

Tobias took one last look at the man withered by time. He knew he would not see him again for a long time, if ever, and he wanted to remember him. He wasn't sure if he believed the old man's story, but it didn't matter. It was still a great story. The archaic man waved him off with his pipe and Tobias started down the hill to his house.

The next morning Tobias was up early. He sped through breakfast and got ready for school. Before leaving for school, he went out the back door and climbed the hill to the rocky crag which hid the old man. He climbed between the rocks and into the small clearing, but the old man and all his belongings were gone. There were only three small acorn shells left next to where the fire had been. Tobias picked them up and looked at them in his hand. They were the shells that had been hollowed out. They were filled with something now because they were heavier. Tobias suddenly remembered that the old man had filled the acorn shells with strange powder. He said that Lucias taught Lynquest how to hide blue smoke in the husks of acorns. *If that old man was Lynquest, then these are filled with blue smoke,* he thought.

As he stood there pondering this, an idea came to him. He carefully put the acorn shells in his pocket and started back home. He found his mother's broom and took it back up the hill. He hid the broom behind the largest boulder and started off to school.

That afternoon, after school had let out, he made sure the boys saw him leave. They quickly pursued him, running as fast as they could, but Tobias had a good head start. He ran down the road that led out of town, around the bend, and down the road to the bridge at Black Water Creek. At the bridge, he waited until Scott and his gang came around the bend.

"There he goes!" shouted Tom.

"Quick, you and Bill cross the creek here and try to cut him off, while me and Todd take the bridge," said Scott.

"But we'll get all muddy," protested Tom.

"Just do it!" Scott yelled.

So Tom and Bill scampered down the slope and waded into the creek. The thick black mud hampered their crossing, and Tobias easily passed them as they reached the other side. Tobias ran as fast as his short legs would carry him, down the road and up the side of the hill to the rocky outcrop. He made sure the boys saw him climb over the rocks into the middle of his stony fortress, but because of his small size, he could squeeze between the rocks on the other side without being seen. He found his mother's broom and quickly climbed to the top of the tallest rock, making sure he was not seen.

"He went in there," said Bill. "He's hiding in those rocks."

"We've got him now," said Scott. "You two go around to the other side, and we'll climb in on this side and trap him in the middle," he said to the two muddy boys, Bill and Tom. As the boys climbed over the rock, they didn't notice Tobias, who was lying flat on the top of the tallest rock, so as not to be seen.

"He's not here," said Tom in bewilderment. The four boys stood around in a circle in the midst of the small clearing, puzzled by Tobias's disappearance. Tobias knew it was now or never. He jumped to his feet, pulled the acorn shells from his pocket, and hurled them to the ground in the center of the four boys. The shells exploded with a *crack!* and huge plumes of blue smoke rose out of the stony pit.

"Oh no," said Bill. "Not again."

Tobias leaped into the middle of the blue smoke, clenching the broom handle tightly in both hands. Then, as if he was battling an army, he began to swing it this way and that. He swung it high. *Smack!*

"Ow, my nose!" a boy yelled.

He swung it low. *Crack!*

"Ow, my leg!" screamed Scott.

The smoke kept the boys in constant confusion as Tobias dealt blow after crushing blow.

"Hey! Ow! Stop!" they screamed.

Snap! Pop! Pow! went the stick.

"I'm getting out of here!" yelled one.

"Me, too!" said another.

"Yeah," said Todd, holding his nose. "If you want him so bad, Scott, get him yourself!"

"No, wait!" yelled Scott. "Don't leave me. My leg is hurt."

The three boys helped Scott climb out of the rocky crag and down the hill. Tobias stepped out of the now thinning smoke and climbed back on top of the tallest rock. Staring down at the boys, nursing their wounds and helping Scott limp back to town, he called out to them.

"You boys better never try that again, or you'll get the same. Do you hear me?"

Scott glanced back momentarily with a worried look on his face. Tobias knew then that he wouldn't have any more trouble from them. Tobias then had a strange notion that someone was watching him.

He turned to face the top of the hill, and there, at the peak, was the young boy that had helped him in town. A dark cloud in the distance overshadowed the boy, and Tobias heard that strange whisper once again ringing in his ears. "Time...time...time...will make you mine," the mysterious voice echoed. A chill ran down his back as he recalled the reflection he had seen in the glass. The thought was unsettling, but then again, he thought, *if time is what it takes to understand, then I still have time to grow.*

Tobias waved to the boy, who stood motionless, his long black cape blowing in the wind. The boy smiled; a faintly familiar smile that puzzled Tobias. He called to the boy, but got no answer.

Tobias turned away for only a moment and the boy was gone. Not so much as a footprint was left behind to show that he had even been there at all. Though Tobias would ponder the question of the child's identity many times, it would be years before he would finally know who he was, and it would take even longer to discover the origins of the haunting whispers that called him to a dark, foreboding, and uncertain fate.

THE LEGENDS OF LYNQUEST

SECRET OF THE CHILD

CHAPTER ONE

OVERSEERS OF DESTINY

Somewhere on a hilltop overlooking a small glen far, far away from the city of Salizar, the immense figure of a dragon and its rider floated silently to the ground.

A boy of nine or ten slid from his vantage point atop the beast's head and his feet quietly touched the ground. They both watched in silence as a man chopped wood near a farmhouse below. The sun was setting rapidly in the west and the man hastened through his task, unaware he was being watched by the dragon and his rider.

"Is that the boy you spoke of?" asked the dragon.

"Yes," said the boy. "He is not a child anymore. I stood right where I am now eighteen years ago and watched him defeat his childhood bullies."

"He has become quite a man," said the dragon, as he watched the man make quick work of the firewood.

"That he has, Subakai," said the boy. "Tobias has become a good strong man. One fit to be king."

At that moment, a small girl rushed out of the farmhouse, calling out as she ran, "Father! Father!"

The boy looked into the dragon's eyes and said, "But she will become greater still. She will become a seer of enormous power, a queen who will heal the world of a great madness and unite all the provinces into one mighty country." The dragon and the boy listened intently to what the little girl had to say.

"Father, Mother said you should hurry and wash up. Supper is almost ready!"

Her father stopped chopping for a moment, smiled at his little girl, and arched his back to stretch his muscles. "Oh!" he said loudly as he stretched. "I finished just in time, ha ha." Then he buried the ax head deep into the chopping block. "How is my precious Emily tonight?" he asked as he took her by the hands.

"I'm so excited, Father. Lynquest the storyteller is coming to our town tonight and I can't wait," she said, bubbling over with enthusiasm.

"Good, good," said her father. Then he gently swung her around by her hands. She touched down lightly right in front of him.

Then, stepping on both of his feet, she said, "Come on, let's go wash up for supper."

Holding hands, they trotted off toward the house, laughing and giggling all the way.

Back on the hilltop, the boy turned to his dragon friend and said, "Well, they seem like a happy sort."

"They most certainly do," answered the dragon. "Are you sure that the girl is capable of defeating Salina and sealing the door to the netherworld? She is so young, it is hard to tell."

"I am sure of it," said the boy. "True, she has some growing up to do, but in ten years, she will be a force to be reckoned with."

"If it is as you say," said the dragon, "then you will need my help."

"Subakai," said the boy, smiling, "I have been your friend for almost a thousand years. And in all that time, I have had need of your help more times than I care to remember. Why should this be any different?" The boy stroked the dragon's thick mane and smiled gratefully. "Well, I guess I should be going," said the boy. "I have a story to tell."

"What story will it be this time?" asked the dragon.

"I have decided it will be Sebastian's tale of Malice and Avarice and the sacred ruby," answered the boy.

"Aren't you afraid they will know your secret?" asked the dragon.

"They love the stories, but they do not believe them," said the boy. "Emily is different, though. She will know it is true. Her heart will tell her it is so."

"I will be waiting for your return," said the dragon. "If I am not here, you know how to contact me."

"I have your horn right here," said the boy, as he clutched a piece of the great dragon's horn tied to a leather strap slung over his shoulder. The boy then turned toward town and started off down the hill, his black cape whipping and dancing in the evening breeze.

CHAPTER TWO

TRICK OF THE HEART

At last, supper was done and the dishes were all put away. The time had come for them to get ready for their evening in town. Emily scurried through the house, frantic with antici- pation as she searched for her hat and scarf. Her parents had been talking about his arrival for weeks and she didn't even know who he was. She heard them talking in the next room as they got ready for their trip to town.

"He must be ancient by now," said Emily's father.

"I was only fifteen when he last came to our village," said her mother.

"I was only eleven," said her father. "And he was an old man, even then."

"His stories are always so exciting," said her mother. "I wonder what it is going to be about this time."

"I don't know," her father answered. "I've already heard the one about his dragon friend and his service to the king. I hope it's a story I have never heard before."

After listening to her parents' staged conversation, Emily grabbed her hat and scarf, finished dressing, and waited for her parents at the front door. "Well, I'm ready!" she said in a loud voice, hoping to urge her parents along.

Her mother promptly came out of the bedroom and put on her gloves. "Did you dress warm?" she asked. "You know it's going to be cold tonight and I don't want you getting sick."

"Yes, Mother," Emily answered in a frustrated voice.

Emily's father had been out in the barn hitching the horses to the wagon, and had brought it around to the front of the house. Jumping down from the wagon, he stepped in- side and said excitedly, "The horses are ready and adventure is high, so let's be on our way!"

He reached down, swept Emily up into his arms, and whisked her away to the waiting wagon. He then helped his wife into the wagon and wrapped them both in a big, thick woolen blanket. He turned and sat down, snatched up the reins in one hand, snapped them on the horses' backs sharply, and exclaimed, "We're off!"

The sun had almost completely set by the time they reached town. A crowd gathered in the village square around a raging fire. The tall flames danced and popped over a bed of timbers the width of a large wagon wheel. It was a cold autumn evening, and Emily was delighting in watching her breath turn white as it hit the crisp night air. She heard someone call out her father's name.

"Tobias! Tobias Miller!" A man stepped through the crowd with his hand extended.

"Scott? Scott Henry?" asked her father.

"In the flesh," the man answered as he shook her father's hand.

"Well, it's been years, Scott. How's that leg?" asked her father.

"Oh, it lets me know when the weather is changing."

"I still feel kind of bad about that," said her father.

"You shouldn't," said Scott. "I deserved it. I was a bully. I had it coming. Ha, you sure surprised us that day, I'll tell you."

A sudden hush fell over the crowd. The silence drew her father's attention away from his conversation. Someone whispered, "He's here, he's here." The words echoed through the waiting crowd. A small boy pushed his way through the crowd and stood next to Emily. She watched as he took something from his pocket. It was an acorn shell. He glanced at Emily and smiled in a mischievous fashion as he held the acorn shell in his outstretched hand. He chuckled with delight, and then he tossed it into the fire.

It exploded with an enormous *crack!* and the confused gathering of people lurched backward to escape the blast. A large pillar of strange blue smoke rose out of the fire. Emily turned to the boy to ask why, but he had vanished into the crowd. She searched the audience from where she stood, trying to find the boy's face among the many people that were there. Not finding him, she turned her attention back to the strange smoke rising from the flames.

As it cleared, there stood the figure of a man within the pillar of smoke. The man showed no sign of urgency when he stepped from the fire, his clothes completely untouched by the flames. He had his face to the ground, but she could see his long, stringy white hair and shiny black cape, which he wore over the most ragged old clothes.

When the man looked up, she saw his badly weathered face and a deep scar under his right eye. At first, the old man fascinated Emily, but as she looked into his steel gray eyes, she realized he was staring directly at her. Emily sank back into the security of her father's warm embrace, and for a moment, she hid her face in the folds of the thick wool blanket.

The moments passed like hours as she waited for the first words to be spoken. A small child broke the silence, but was quickly shushed by his mother. Just when she felt the silence was too much, he began to speak in a low, soft voice.

"I was just a lad of seventeen when I began my quest for the gem known as the Heart of Mater." His gruff voice rumbled with mystery. His audience was held spellbound as he introduced himself. "My name is Tiny Lynquest, and this is my tale. Little did I know, when I started my search, that it would take me almost twenty years to find the ruby, and the rest of my life to understand its powers. If I had known then what I know now, I would have probably just stayed home."

The crowd erupted with laughter at the sound of such a notion.

Tiny paused a moment to let the crowd settle and then he looked around. When the last voice had succumbed to the thickening silence, he raised an eyebrow for dramatic affect and continued in a deep, mysterious voice, his steel gray eyes beaming with intensity.

CHAPTER THREE

BAZAAR WOMAN

After searching for so many years, I myself began to doubt the stories of the stone. It was among my journeys to the city of Kautchitzar that my traveling companion, Shamus Bogbottom, and I found an old fortune-teller. Now, Shamus was not known for his manners. He was a temperamental dwarf who always spoke his mind, even at the worst possible moments. But as a traveling companion, I found him to be truly reliable and a constant source of entertainment. All in all, he was the smallest giant I have ever known.

It was he who led me to the woman who started it all. I was walking through the city bazaar, when I felt Shamus's small hand tug at my sleeve. "This way!" he said in excitement. "I think I have found someone who can help us in our quest." He dragged me through the crowded streets, pushing and shoving as he went. 'Come on. Get out of the way!' he shouted at the slow-moving people. "Move it, you cows!" he barked.

"Still making friends, I see," I said, smiling as he tugged on my arm.

Then I heard a shrill voice call out. "Lynquest! Lynquest the Great!"

I turned to find a shriveled-up old hag of a woman, with only a tooth or two in her entire head. She was hunched over and bony, with one arm hanging lower than the other. The shawl draped across her slender shoulders hung all the way down to her knobby knees, and a hairy mole to the left of her nose seemed to hang there like a period at the end of a very ugly sentence.

"Lynquest the Great, you are, are you? Lynquest the Great? But my eyes deceive me, that can't be right, as I stand here, bewildered and all. Can anything great come from someone so small?"

"Not me, you old hag!" snapped Shamus. "Him!" he said, pointing to me.

"Shamus!" I barked sharply. "Please forgive my friend. He is sometimes short in more ways than one. I am Tiny Lynquest," I said, introducing myself.

"No matter," she said. "Tiny or short. The measure's the same when you're both the same sort."

In indignation, Shamus replied, "What say you, old hag?"

"Old hag, says you, old hag? I know what you seek, I do, I do. Help you, I can, this is for sure, but once more *old hag* and I say no more. My name is Croisha, Croisha the cruel. Call me a hag and I'll make you a fool."

"We're sorry if we have offended you," I said, glaring at Shamus. "Please. You said you had news for me."

"Have news for you, have news, yes, yes, but I can't tell you here. Someone may hear, may hear, I fear."

The strange woman grabbed me by the arm and dragged me down several alleys while Shamus followed as best he could, weaving and bobbing through the crowded streets, shouting at the people as he went.

We came to a doorway with some narrow stairs just inside. We ascended the stairs and entered a small but comfortable living chamber. In the center of the room was a large square table with a map of the entire country carved in the top of it. On the wall opposite the door hung a beautiful tapestry with the images of an eagle and a panther.

In a corner of the room, I noticed a tall, oval-shaped, full-length mirror. I can't quite say why, but it made me feel uneasy, as if it were more a window than a mirror. I remember thinking, *What is a woman with an obvious beauty handicap doing with a full-length mirror? The view doesn't get any better the more you see of it.*

On the wall to my left was a shelf with a conspicuous collection of shoes of all types and sizes. Next to each pair was a personal item or a piece of jewelry. Lying beside the first pair was a silver ring with an extraordinary emerald in it. The second pair had a charm of some sort on a gold chain. Thirteen pairs in all I counted and each had some article of personal value next to it. The old woman noticed me staring at the shoes.

"Number fourteen, you are. Thirteen before have tried and died, tried and died. Hee, hee, hee," she cackled.

"Died! Of what?" asked Shamus.

"Don't know, says I. I've never gone. I have a desire to keep living on."

For the first time, I was beginning to get truly nervous, and she knew it.

"Lost your stomach, have you?" she asked.

"No!" I snapped. "Now, say your piece, woman, and let us be on our way."

"Ah, but first you must give me something, something of worth. Hopefully something you've had since your birth."

I reached to my belt and took out the dagger my father had given to me as a boy. "Take good care of it," I said. "I will be back to reclaim it."

"One more thing I need from you. I need your shoes, your shoes will do," said the hag.

"My shoes? But what will I wear?" I asked.

As the words left my lips, she turned and retrieved a small wooden box from under the table. Shamus's eyes lit up with mischievous delight.

Opening the box, she took out two small slippers made from some strange kind of hide. Being a tanner in my youth, I had seen shoes made from all kinds of skins, but these shoes did not look like any animal hide I had ever seen. I shuddered at the thought that they might be made from a hide closer to my own.

She handed them to me.

"These?" I exclaimed. "Paper soles would put more space between my feet and the ground."

"Don't be deceived, says I. Protect you, they will, from fire, from ice. They'll keep your feet warm, and what is twice as nice, they leave no tracks, no tracks, says I. Speed you on your way, they will, when the sun is high."

"Are you sure they will fit? They look too small," I said.

"Try them on and you will see, they fit, they do, fit perfectly," she cackled with delight.

I slipped them on my feet, and to my amazement, they did fit perfectly. In fact, they were the most comfortable shoes I had ever worn. I was about to compliment her on the fit, when I began to feel my toes tingle, then the bottoms of my feet, and then my ankles.

"Hey!" I yelled. "I can't feel my feet."

"Ha, ha, ha," she laughed. "Get used to them, you should. You have no choice. They won't come off, so save your voice."

"You sure have a strange sense of humor, old woman," remarked Shamus.

Laughing and shaking her head, she placed my shoes on the shelf with the rest. Turning to me again, she said, as she pointed a boney finger at the map on the table, "Now, the heart you seek, it lies nor'west, nor'west is true. Eldabron Pass will lead you to. Lead you, lead you to Ring of Stone, where glaciers old have made their home. Where caverns cold, deep and blue, give way to jungle thick, no path cut through. An ancient city awaits you there. Venture in if you dare. This is where your search begins. The Heart of Mater lies within."

While she was speaking, I glanced at Shamus, who was strangely preoccupied with the objects that were left in the wooden box.

The box that once held the shoes was left open on the table. In it were two velvet pouches of miniature size. I watched as Shamus did something that froze me in my tracks. While the woman's attention was still focused on the map, he carefully plucked one of the velvet pouches from the box and slid it into his pocket. Then he quietly closed the box.

I shot a menacing look his way, but he just smiled back at me and casually drifted toward the door. I realized that it wouldn't be long before she discovered the missing item, so I moved closer to the door as well.

After the woman finished talking, she turned to me again and said, "You must go now, go now, you must. The day is gone, it's almost dusk." Walking me to the door, she told me a riddle I was to solve during my journey:

A door, a key, to a hidden lair, look beneath the only stair.

Before we left, I realized that I hadn't paid her, so I turned and asked, "But why have you done all this?" Her reply was stranger still. It puzzled me for a long time.

She said, "Work is long and life so short, a woman's got to have some sport, hee, hee, hee," she cackled. With that, she closed the door, still squawking heartily to herself.

I must say, it gave me a rather uneasy feeling. Shamus remarked under his breath, "That's one strange witch."

As we walked back to where my horse was tethered, I asked rather sarcastically, "When did you become a thief?"

"I'm not a thief!" exclaimed Shamus. "I just figured that if you want your grandfather's dagger back, we had better have something to trade for it. I don't trust that witch."

"Neither do I, Shamus. Neither do I," I said plainly.

We made our way back to the bazaar where I had left my horse tied. The sun was setting and the bazaar had long since closed for the night, but as we mounted my horse, the shrill voice of a woman could be heard screaming in the distance.

"Thief, you are! Scoundrel, I say! I will get you for this, yes, yes, you will pay!"

Shamus, being as short as he was, stood on the back of my horse waving the velvet pouch in the air, shouting, "Who's laughing now, old hag?"

"Shamus," I said, "I'm surprised at you. I thought you were a ladies' man."

"That was a lady?" he asked, laughing. "Actually," he added, "I do rather fancy the plain ones. The pretty ones leave you."

"The plain ones can leave you, too," I retorted.

"Yeah, but who cares!" he said, chuckling. "Besides," he added, "it's a long way from plain to downright ugly." Still snickering, he wrapped his short arms around my neck as we rode off.

I simply said, "Shamus, you're incorrigible."

We rode straight to the inn to collect our things. I knew that Eldabron Pass was impassable during the winter. It was late autumn, and still a three-week ride through the pass to the town of Forest Glen.

We rode all that night and into the evening of the following day, when I decided we needed to get some sleep. We made a fire in a clearing not too far from the trail. There, we ate our dinner and prepared for a good night's rest, but when I fell asleep, I was beset by a most disturbing dream.

My dream that night was lucid. I wandered in the woods aimlessly through a thick fog that rolled along the ground. There was only silence as I moved through the woods. When I approached a clearing, the fog rolled back to reveal a small pool of calm dark water. There was nothing to disturb the reflection of the trees against the endless sky, not even a ripple. Yet, an image, as faint as a spider's web at first, grew clearer as the sky grew darker.

It was the hag. She was leaning over her map, chanting, "Yes, yes, sleep at night. We travel better on the moonless night."

Suddenly, darkness fell all about me. I strained to see something, anything, but couldn't. I stood in silence for a moment and listened. Straining at the void, I began to hear the rhythmic trod of an animal of great size running. As it ran, a low rumble came from the darkness, and I heard the paws of the great creature beating the ground as it drew closer and closer.

I squinted into the darkness in the direction of the sound, and after a moment, I saw two tiny lights dancing in the black. The louder the beast's steps became, the brighter the lights grew. The once low rumble became a loud roar. Only then did I realize that it was a cat of enormous size. The air grew thick with the sound of the great cat's footsteps, and I saw the outline of a massive panther as black as a moonless midnight. With eyes of fire and fangs like sabers, the great cat turned loose its claws and lunged at me.

I awoke with my heart in my throat, beating frantically. I sat up and placed my trembling hands over my face. Whispers from the twilight of slumber filled the air about my head. "Sleep, sleep, the night is deep. Darkness feeds the cat that creeps." The words sent chills through me.

I rubbed my eyes and looked around to assure myself it was only a dream. The dawn surrounded me and the embers of last evening's fire smoldered in the pit. A small white plume of smoke rose into the crisp morning air and the smell of the campfire moved through me.

Shamus was bundled up in the saddle blanket with his head on the saddle, still snoring away.

A deep breath of cool morning air gave me back my sense of reality. I pondered the dream for a moment, but its meaning escaped me. The only thing I did understand was that we should no longer rest at night out in the open. I made a conscious decision to sleep only during the day, and only for a few hours at a time; a point that Shamus would find completely to his disliking.

After extinguishing the fire, I woke Shamus, packed my things, and prepared for the rest of what would end up being a very long journey.

CHAPTER FOUR

A NARROW PASSAGE

Traveling was good for a fortnight and a half, but as we reached the foothills of the Eldabron Mountains a cold rain began to fall. Fortunately for us, there was a small town nestled in the foothills called Highborn. We boarded my horse at the stables, and then treated ourselves to dinner. Afterward, I acquired a room for myself at the inn.

Shamus was busy entertaining himself with the tavern maids. Last I had seen, the women in the tavern had surrounded him as he danced on a table. How he loved the attention. I left him to his foolishness and went to my room for an early night. I finally got a good night's sleep.

The next morning dawned cold and the rain had turned to snow overnight. There was already enough snow to cover my horse's hooves, and I knew if we didn't hurry, we wouldn't make it through the pass. I quickly gathered my things together and set out to find Shamus.

I found him sleeping off the evening's frivolities in a rocking chair in front of the tavern's fireplace. He was bundled in a thick wool blanket. The fire had long gone out, and one of the ladies, no doubt, had wrapped him in the blanket like one would a child. I remember thinking to myself, *You know, there are times when being a dwarf is not such a bad thing.* He looked peaceful, and I almost hated to wake him, but our need for haste was such that I nudged his shoulder and peeled the blanket off him like a second skin.

"Hey," he grumbled, "I wasn't done with that."

"Yes, you were," I said plainly. "The rain has turned to snow, and if we don't leave now, we won't make it through the pass."

His eyes slowly crept open, and he peered up at me through the haze of his ale-induced slumber, he asked, "Now?"

"Yes, now. Right now!" I barked.

"Ok, ok," he snapped. "Let me find my hat."

He looked around in the dim morning light and snatched up his hat from the floor next to his rocker. He beat the dust off it and placed it firmly on his head of thinning strawberry blond hair. Looking up at me, he said angrily, "Well? Let's go!"

We saddled up my horse in the heavily falling snow and headed out for the Eldabron Pass. By noon, when we reached the pass, the snow still fell hard. It had accumulated to just below my horse's shins, which made traveling increasingly difficult.

I gazed at the pass for a moment, and even in the near-whiteout conditions, I knew it was treacherous. There was a narrow trail, perhaps only wide enough for my horse. It ran between a cliff face on the right and a deep chasm on the left. I knew my horse would spook easily if he saw the great height, so I dismounted, reached into my saddlebag, and retrieved a set of blinders.

"What are those for?" asked Shamus, still huddled on the back of the horse.

"I don't think Reckless likes heights," I said. "So, I will need to lead him from here."

"Reckless? Couldn't you have named him something else?" he complained.

I placed them over the horse's eyes and began leading him up the trail. Near the top, the wind howled. My thickest coat did little to protect me from the bitter cold. Shamus had wrapped himself in my bedroll and was hunched over in the saddle, holding his hat on his head.

As we drew near to the highest point of the trail, my breathing became shallow and my limbs began to ache. My body felt like that of an old, old man. I took short breaks to rest as we approached the top of the pass. It was becoming increasingly hard to concentrate on anything. Oddly enough, my feet felt perfectly warm and comfortable, but I knew we had to get off that mountain.

We plodded along slowly, with each step taken being shorter than the last. Finally, I could step no more. I saw the summit in the distance, but failed to summon the strength to go on. Shamus, knowing I was faltering, looked down from his perch atop the horse. He smiled a gentle smile as if he understood, then he began to sing. He sang as if it were a warm summer's day.

There was something in the conviction of his song—something so carefree, so full of life—that I began to regain my courage. I tugged on the reins of my horse and began to sing along. It was an old song I had learned as a boy. Somehow, singing it kept my mind off the bitter cold. So, there we were, two fools railing at the storm with song.

Oh, dear sweet Maggie, ne'er do well, far and away the village belle.
She couldn't sing to save her life, but could dance away a summer's night.
She took up with a captain man, who stole her heart, then took her hand.
But all the time that they were wed, he begged her not to sing in bed.
Hey, Maggie, ho, Maggie, I love ya, don't you know, Maggie?
But save the singin' for the birds, your dancin' feet say more than words.
Things turned bad when they put to sea, for the captain man and Maggie McCree.

Her dancin' made the mast to swing, but men jumped ship when she'd go to sing.
The sailor men would cheer her on, with flute and lyre and sailor song.
Singing, poor young Maggie can't sing a note, but her dancin' surely rocks the boat.
Dear sweet Maggie Mae McCree, won't you please save a dance for me?
Hey, Maggie, ho, Maggie, we love ya, don't you know, Maggie?
Heaven has its fill of song, dancers too know right from wrong.
Hey, Maggie, ho, Maggie, we love ya, don't you know, Maggie?
But save the singin' for the birds, your dancin' feet say more than words.

The song made me feel better, but it also reminded me just how much I missed the warmth of home. My thoughts drifted to all the lavish comforts of Ironcrest Castle, of King Standforth and Princess Aleana and even stuffy old Barnabus, and left me longing for home.

We reached the summit in almost blizzard conditions. I could barely see the trail in front of me, so I hugged the cliff face and began my slow, careful descent. Halfway down, the wind had subsided some and I saw the tree line of a very dense forest.

Shamus's eyes lit up when he saw the trees. "Look!" he exclaimed as he pointed. "Thank the powers that be. We're not far from Forest Glen now!"

I guess even his hearty soul had grown weary of these conditions.

It was only a matter of time before we reached the edge of a very dark, old forest. The trees towered over us like giant spires holding up the sky. I had to strain my eyes to see the top of even one of the mammoth trees.

Once inside the forest, the traveling became easier since there wasn't as much snow on the ground. The trees' enormous boughs covered the trail, providing some shelter from the falling snow.

Shaking the snow and ice off myself, I took the blinders off Reckless, and then Shamus and I rode the rest of the way into Forest Glen, a town of fair size nestled deep in the woods. Forest Glen was a quaint northern town steeped in mysticism, with legends about the giant woods that surround it having circulated since antiquity. I had once heard a story of a magus that lived in Forest Glen. There were rumors that this man knew more about the Ring of Stone than anyone, so once we had reached the town, we sought him out.

We started our search at the local tavern, because if anyone knew how to find someone, it was a tavern-keep. The tavern was but a stone's throw away from the stables, which only added to the charm of the town. When Shamus and I entered the tavern and approached the bar, the tender had his back to us and was busy polishing tankards.

"Excuse me," I said politely.

The man turned to face me. I was about to ask him about the magus, when Shamus barked out, "How about some warm ale to warm my bones?"

The man stood for a moment with a puzzled look on his face. "Here now, how did you do that?" asked the tender in bewilderment.

"Do what?" I asked plainly.

"I heard a voice, but your lips didn't move. I could have sworn your shoes asked for some warm ale," said the tender.

"Down here, you great oaf!" snapped Shamus.

The tavern-keep leaned forward and peered down at my little friend.

"Am I going to get that drink, or what?" Shamus barked, as he glared up at the man. "Oh, never mind. I'll get it myself," he said in disgust.

Shamus proceeded to pull himself up onto a bar stool and then stepped on top of the bar. The tavern-keep watched in astonishment as the audacious little man snatched up one of his polished tankards, walked the full length of the bar, and tapped the keg at its end. He then took a big gulp of ale, wiped his mouth with his sleeve, looked back at me, and said, "Pay the man, Tiny."

The tavern-keep spoke up. "Here now, someone your size shouldn't be calling anyone tiny."

"It's his name, you dolt! His name is Tiny Lynquest. You know? Surely, you've heard of Lynquest the Great!" Shamus was furious.

"Why, I ought to ring your little neck!" exclaimed the tavern-keep.

"Never mind him," I said quickly. "As a child, he was dropped on his head." I glared at Shamus, who just smiled as he casually swilled his ale.

"They should have finished the job," grumbled the tavern-keep.

"Here, this is for the drink," I said, handing him some coins.

"Did the two of you just come through the pass?" he asked.

"Yep," I replied.

"In this weather?" he asked. "You'd both have to be crazy to try that on a day like to-day," he said in amazement.

"Yeah, well, here we are," I said plainly.

"Well, you'll be the last ones this year, I suspect," he remarked.

"Hey," I said, "while I have you here, maybe you can help me find someone."

"Maybe," he said. "It depends. Who are you looking for?"

"An old magus," I answered. "I heard he lived in this town."

"You must be speaking of Malyki," he said. "He doesn't live in town, but outside town, a little ways into the woods to the north. He lives in an old shack out there."

I thanked him and paid for the information. Shamus finished his drink and we went back outside. We retrieved my horse and started out for the north side of town.

CHAPTER FIVE

Shadow in the Woods

A short distance from town there stood a shack set back a ways from the path. It looked a little run-down, but all in all, not a bad place to live. Shamus and I dismounted and tied Reckless to a tree. We then walked up to the door and knocked. A gray-haired old man with a long white beard that was parted down the middle answered the door. He leaned on a walking stick. His face was weathered by time, but displayed a gentle smile.

"Yes, what can I do for you two young men?" he asked politely.

"Is this the home of Malyki, the magus?" I asked.

"Yes, it is. I am he," he answered.

"My name is Tiny Lynqu—"

"Lynquest!" he exclaimed, cutting me short. "Not Lynquest the adventurer?"

"The same," I said, smiling. "And this is Shamus."

"Shamus Bogbottom," said Shamus as he tipped his hat slightly. "I'm from the tribe of Gibbons in the highlands of Lochlorna."

"Well, Shamus from Lochlorna, come in, do come in," the old man said with excitement. "I have long wondered if adventurers such as you would have use of the services of an old magus like myself," he said, closing the door behind us. "So, what brings you hither?"

"The Ring of Stone," I said. "I have heard it said that no one knows more about the Ring of Stone than you."

"It is true," he said, smiling. "I have lived my whole life in the shadow of the mountain known as the Ring of Stone."

"Don't you mean 'mountains'?" I asked.

"No," he said. "I mean 'mountain.' You see," he continued, "it was once a great volcano thousands of years ago. Then it lost the very top of its peak in a violent eruption, leaving a massive crater in the center. As the years went by, the volcano fell dormant and its crater became a fertile valley. Only I know the way into the valley."

He was a kindly old man and I soon felt at ease in his company. The shack he lived in looked much better on the inside than it did on the outside. I looked around the room. Malyki seemed to be an immaculate housekeeper, as everything in his house was neat and in order. There was a single plate with a knife, fork, and cup on a small table. A nice fire was heating a big black pot that was hanging in the fireplace. Being that I was chilled from our journey, I drew near to the fire and began warming my hands.

"Ah, cold, are you? I suspect you're hungry as well," said Malyki, as he went to the cupboard to fetch more settings for the table. Shamus's eyes lit up like those of a dog anticipating a bone. "Now, you must have dinner with me," Malyki added.

"Well, I won't insult you by saying no," said Shamus.

Malyki smiled wide. Shamus had made himself right at home. He swaggered over to a large sack of grain that was lying on the floor next to the wall, plopped his bottom down and stretched out. This was an act which Malyki seemed to find amusing.

"Good, good. I have more than I would eat in a week, anyway."

As he readied the table, I gazed into the fire. After watching the flames dance for a moment, a question dawned on me.

"If you're the only one who knows the way into the valley, why haven't you told anyone?" I asked.

"Oh, there have been others whom I have told, to be sure, but they have never returned. After a while, I grew tired of sending them to their deaths, so whenever someone comes around these days, I say nothing. It's better for them that I don't," the old man answered kindly.

"And yet, you're willing to help us. Why?" I asked.

"The stories," he said. "I have heard the many stories that are circulated about you. Never have I heard so much about one man. I felt there must be something special about you. Besides, I would not help you at all if it were not for him."

"Him? Him who?" I asked.

"The Ancient One," he said plainly. "He has lived in the valley for hundreds of years. He is trapped there. I have been to the valley myself, many times, but could not help him. My last hope lies with you."

A moment of awkward silence followed, as neither of us knew what to say. Eventually, he burst out, "All right, then, it's ready, time to eat. If you could be so kind as to bring me the pot that is on the fire, I will dish it out."

Shamus quickly jumped to his feet and approached the table, rubbing his stomach. His eyes were alight with the prospect of a free meal. He snatched up a fork and began nervously tapping the table with it.

Malyki chuckled with delight. He seemed to get some amusement from Shamus's rude and somewhat quirky behavior. I took the cloth that hung on the mantel, folded it several times, and used it to grab the handle of the big pot. I took it to Malyki and held it steady as he spooned out the contents into the three waiting bowls. I didn't know what it was, but after an early morning and a hard day's journey, I was famished.

"What is it?" I asked. "It smells heavenly."

"Rabbit stew," he answered. "It's my own recipe."

Breaking a loaf of bread, he placed a piece on each plate, and we all sat down and commenced eating. Shamus tore into his bread with ravenous speed and began dunking it into the bowl with his fingers. After shoveling a forkful of the stew into his mouth, he then stuffed the bread in after, making a horrific gurgling sound as he did.

"Shamus!" I said in disgust.

"What?" he shrugged with his mouth full.

Malyki laughed. "I simply must hear how this charming fellow became your traveling companion," remarked Malyki.

"Well," I started, "it all began one fine summer day on one of my earlier quests for the Heart of Mater. I was riding through the fields and fjords in the countryside of Glockenshire, when I heard the sound of sheep bleating in the distance. I rode down into the valley a little ways and saw a flock of sheep being routed by a mountain lion. Well, I looked around for a shepherd and saw Shamus behind a large boulder, relieving himself—"

"I was not!" Shamus interrupted loudly. "I told you. I was lacing up my shoe! You never tell this story right."

"Well, whatever the case," I said, continuing my story, "I watched as Shamus sprang out from behind the enormous rock, snatched up his crook, and began chasing the lion down."

At this, Malyki raised his eyebrows in amazement.

"It wasn't until the mountain lion noticed him that he realized he was in danger of being eaten himself. I guess the lion figured he was easier to catch. Shamus ran for his life back to the huge boulder. In one move, he used his crook to propel himself to the top of that rock. I was astonished. The mountain lion leaped toward the top of the boulder, but Shamus beat him back with his staff. Finally, the lion took hold of the staff with its teeth and pulled it out his hands. It fell to the ground. The big cat then crouched low, preparing to pounce on poor Shamus. That's when I grabbed my timber ax and hurled it at the lion, striking it on the head. It fell to the ground momentarily. Long enough—"

"Long enough," said Shamus, interrupting again, "for me to jump down, grab the ax, and sever the cat's head." He said this with great satisfaction. "Then that crotchety old codger Kroner came out. It was his sheep I was guarding. He came out complaining in that grumbling, crass voice of his. Blah, blah, blah, lazy. Blah, blah, blah, good-for-nothing halfling. Halfling! Can you believe that? He called me a halfling!" said Shamus in disgust.

"I tried to explain to Kroner that Shamus saved his sheep. Of course, it was by offering himself as bait," I said, snickering.

"That's right," Shamus proclaimed. "Halfling! That's not a name you call a full-grown man."

"What would you call yourself?" asked Malyki, holding back laughter.

Shamus answered in one word. "Unique," he said, jutting his chest out.

"That you are, Shamus. That you are," said Malyki, laughing.

We continued eating and talking, until our hearts were lightened and our stomachs were full.

After we had finished, I scooted my chair back, patted my stomach, and remarked, "That was the finest meal I have had in quite a while."

Shamus leaned back in his chair, lovingly rubbed his belly, and released a loud belch.

"Shamus!" I said. "Have you no shame?"

"What?" he asked crassly. "You know, in some parts of the world, that's a compliment to the cook."

"Yes, I know. And you would be oh so gracious if we were actually in those parts of the world!" I retorted.

Malyki burst out laughing.

"What I am trying to say is that was truly a fine meal," said Shamus.

"Thank you," Malyki said, smiling with great pride. Once the table had been cleared, he sat back down, pulled on both parts of his long flowing beard, and said, "Now, I must tell you how you can find your way into the valley. First, you go straight north until you are out of the forest. At that point, you will see the Ring of Stone Mountain standing in the distance. On the side of the mountain that faces west, there are two cliffs that face each other. From a distance they look like one cliff. Don't be fooled. Behind these cliffs, on the slope of the mountain, there is a glacier. At the base of the glacier, partly hidden by the cliffs, is an ice cave. If you follow this cave, it will lead you to a tunnel that continues through the mountainside."

I pondered what the old woman had said to me. *Lead you, lead you to Ring of Stone, where glaciers old have made their home. Where caverns cold, deep and blue, give way to jungle thick, no path cut through.* Suddenly, I realized something, and in the moment's excitement, I burst out, "So that's what she meant."

"She who?" asked Malyki.

"Oh, some old woman I met when I was in Kautchitzar. She told me this in a rhyme, but I didn't understand it until now."

As I said this, Shamus leaned back in his chair a little to give his well-rounded stomach some room. Placing his hand in his pocket, he discovered the velvet pouch he had taken from the old woman. He took it out of his pocket and said, "As a matter of fact, I took this from her when we left."

"Let me see that," said Malyki.

Shamus handed it to him; he placed it on the table and opened it up, and began to peel the pouch back to reveal its contents. It was a small figure of an eagle carved out of cherrywood, perched on a pedestal with its wings outstretched. Malyki turned it over to reveal strange symbols carved on the bottom. He then stood up and crossed the room to a bookshelf that stood against the far wall. He examined the collection and plucked out one book. He then returned to the table, opened the book, and quickly thumbed through the pages. My eyes followed his bony index finger as it lightly skimmed a page and then came to a stop.

"Here it is," he said. "It reads: *Sentinel*."

"What does that mean?" asked Shamus.

"It means guardian or protector." He read on for a moment, and then added, "Apparently, if you had a map and placed this figure on it, a great eagle would appear and do your bidding." He gently closed the book, put the figurine back into its velvet pouch, handed it to me, and said, "You will want to hold on to this, it may be of use."

I took the pouch and placed it in my pocket. We spoke briefly of its powers. One subject led to another, and somehow the conversation turned to the stories that have circulated about my name. After dispelling some of the legends about me that were untrue, I found it was getting close to dusk, so I thanked Malyki for his hospitality and told him that we should get back to town to prepare for the next day's travels.

"Shamus," I said, "it's time to go."

I knew that his absence usually meant mischief, so I looked around the room. To my surprise, he had curled up on that sack of grain and fallen fast asleep. I snickered to myself when I heard him snoring up a storm.

"Shall I wake him?" I asked.

"Don't bother," answered Malyki. "He is fine just where his is. You can collect him in the morning."

"I suppose he'll be all right, as long as you don't mind," I said.

"Not at all," said Malyki. "Actually, I kind of like the repugnant little fellow."

"He does grow on you, if you let him," I said. "Like a wart," I quipped.

We both chuckled quietly, and then he said plainly, "I am but a solitary old man living in an isolated part of the world. It did me good to have some company."

His remark left me with the feeling that he was a lonely old man in need of a friend.

As I stood in the doorway, Malyki looked past me to my horse tied outside. "There is one more thing," he said. "You will have to exchange your horse for a sled and a team of dogs. You can't reach the valley on horseback."

"This should be interesting," I said. "I've never driven a team of dogs before."

"It takes some getting used to," he replied.

I bid him a good night, mounted my horse, and quietly rode the distance back to town. The full moon shone down and the stars beamed brightly through the treetops, but the evening had an eerie calm about it.

I returned to Forest Glen, got a room at the Woods Hollow Inn, and turned in for the night. With a full stomach and a hard journey behind me, sleep came quickly.

The next day, I awoke in the early hours of the morning. The sun had not risen yet, but I knew it would not be long before it did. I gathered my things and went to the stables. The man who ran the stables had a team of seven dogs and a sled. I knew Malyki was right; I couldn't make the journey through the deep snow on horseback. So I offered my horse in trade for the dog team and sled. At first he was against the arrangement, but after I promised to give him several gold coins upon my return, he agreed. I also added that he had my horse in case I didn't return. He laughed and said, "I'm not worried, the dogs are trained to return without a driver." I quickly packed the sled and was on my way.

After leaving town, I arrived at Malyki's run-down old shack. I smiled when I thought of the kindly old man's hospitality. As I tied the dog team outside, I noticed strange tracks in the snow that circled the house. I drew closer and bent over to examine the tracks. They were the paw prints of an enormous cat, pressed deep into the snow. I followed them as they circled Malyki's house three times and then disappeared into the woods. Suddenly, I remembered the dream I had had on the road. I began to get the uneasy feeling that I was in great danger.

Hastened by the unsettling dream, I looked around the woods. The air was calm. The dogs were restless, looking about and sniffing the air. That is when I heard it, a faint whisper hanging on the dormant breeze. "Shhhaaammmuuusss."

The great boughs of the trees swayed back and forth as if there was a mighty wind, but it was still as calm as death. The witch's words danced around me in every direction like sprites frolicking through the woods.

> *Little thief, little thief, one so bold,*
> *With every breath you're growing cold.*
> *Eyes milk white and fevered skin,*
> *This is how you'll meet your end.*

"Shamus!" I exclaimed. I bolted for Malyki's shack and began beating on the door.

Malyki flung it open wide and said, "Come, come quickly. It's your friend. He's under a spell. It's the hag. She's chanting her incantation even now." Malyki raced to his bookshelf and frantically plucked books from it, then snatched ingredients out of the cupboards. "I must prepare a counterspell at once, or he will die."

My eyes fell upon my little friend, who was curled up into a ball on the floor, trembling violently. I knelt down and took him by the shoulders. "Wake up!" I said, shaking him. "Wake up!"

"It's no use," said Malyki. "The witch has him. Quickly, put him on the bed."

I picked him up off the floor and placed him gently on the bed. "His skin is on fire," I said. "But look at his breath."

As Shamus trembled, puffs of shallow breath flowed from his body as if he was freezing to death. His eyes, wide open, wild, and as milky white as the driven snow, stared as though he was caught in a trance.

"His lips are moving," I said.

His chin quivered violently and he whispered, "Beware, midnight stalks you. You must run. You…must…runnnn." His final word fell from his mouth with his fading breath.

"Go!" snapped Malyki. "You are of no use here. I will save your friend, but you must go. Your life is in danger as well."

I rose and bolted toward the door, but something held me back. Looking back at Shamus, I said, "But I could—"

"Go!" barked Malyki.

Overwhelmed with the feeling of helplessness, I reached for the door. "I will return as soon as I can," I replied.

"Yes, yes," said Malyki plainly. "I know it's difficult, but you must trust me."

I acknowledged his promise before I quietly left him to his craft. Once outside, I mounted my sled and urged the dogs into the north woods. As I made my way through the woods, I felt a presence watching me from a distance. I clasped the whip in my right hand and, in a stern but quiet voice, ordered, "Let's go, mutts, hyah."' The dogs quickened their pace.

Above the sound of the dogs' panting, I heard the rustling of movement in the woods behind me. I looked over my left shoulder and caught a glimpse of a pair of eyes shining from behind a tree. Like two flames, they burned the image of that horrible cat into my mind.

I raised the whip into the air, tightened my grip on the sled, and cracked the whip over the dogs' heads. The dogs immediately broke into a fast run. With shrieks and yells, I hastened them on. Whatever it was, it was at full gallop behind me. I heard it crashing through the woods as it grew closer with every heavy stride.

With the tree line up ahead, I feverishly whipped the air above the dogs' heads. *Crack! Crack! Crack!* The whip echoed my urgency. The dogs were at a full gallop and still the beast gained ground. We broke through the tree line and into the deep, fluffy snow. With leaps and bounds the dogs carried me beyond the shadows of the woods and into the brilliance of the glistening white sunlit hillside. Realizing that I was too heavy and the snow too deep for the dogs to carry me any faster, I leapt from the sled.

With whip still in hand, I turned to my pursuer just as it reached the edge of the trees. Cracking the whip repeatedly, I tried to discourage it, to no avail. It only charged the edge of the shadows, and then paced back and forth, roaring with rage. Its vague shape, the form of a great black cat, bore down on the edge of the forest shadows, but went no further. Its eyes burned like white-hot embers. When it roared, its fangs looked like two daggers, eager for the kill. Though the beast railed at me from the edge of the shadows, it did not pursue. I puzzled at this for a moment, as it occurred to me that, for some reason, I was beyond its reach. There I stood, dumbfounded, knee deep in the brilliant white snow with whip in hand, while my dog team hastened onward across the sunlit slope. They were already halfway across the snowbound plane when I suddenly realized it and called out, "Hey! Whoa! Stop! Halt! Stop, you stupid mutts!" I left the great cat pacing in the shadows and pursued my escaping dog team.

CHAPTER SIX

VALLEY OF VOICES

Leaving the apparition pacing in the shadows, I followed after my team of wayward dogs. Eventually, I found myself with feet firmly planted on the runners of the sled, urging the dogs on.

Half the day had passed and I was nearing the west side of the mountain. Just as Malyki had said, I saw two cliffs facing each other. Nestled behind these cliffs was an ice cave, just as I had been told. I released the dogs from their harnesses and turned them loose. *The man may get his dogs back*, I thought, *but the sled might come in handy*.

I drew near to the cave and carefully stepped inside. The walls, ceiling, and floor looked like pale blue glass. The floor sloped up, and I wondered how I was ever going to climb it. A breeze—cold, like one would expect from an ice cave, but slightly warm, or temperate, like one would feel in late spring—caressed my face as I scaled the cave floor.

A fair distance onto the glacier, the ice gave way to mountain and the passage grew narrow. At one point, the passage was so narrow that my first thought was that I wished I hadn't eaten so well at Malyki's house. I squeezed through, and soon I neared the other end of the cave. By now the breeze was no longer temperate, but downright hot!

I stood at the end of the cave and saw the whole valley stretched out before me. The cave had opened out onto a bluff high above the valley floor, which was completely consumed by dense jungle. A pyramid rose in the center of the valley, and another odd-looking building was carved into the face of the mountain on the north side.

A cascading waterfall seemed to pour out of solid rock on the east wall, and a strange man-made pool lay between the pyramid and the north wall. It looked like an enormous coliseum overrun by nature. Caves and hollows riddled the inside walls of the valley, but this was the only tunnel that went all the way through the mountain.

I started my descent down the steep slope and into the valley. When I had reached the bottom, I realized that it was not going to be easy moving through the thick jungle. At times, it was so thick that the sunlight couldn't penetrate the trees to reach the ground. My movement through the undergrowth was hampered because I didn't have a sword, or even my dagger, to cut a path. I wondered what dangers I might find at any moment.

Once I passed the pyramid, I turned north toward the pool. As I neared the clearing there, I could hear two distinctly different voices talking to each other.

"I wonder where the boy is today," said the first voice.

"You don't think he is around here, do you?" asked the second. "He might try to steal my beautiful gold."

"Shut up, you twit! That's all you think about, your precious little treasure. I want to be rid of the rotten little toad once and for all." The first voice grew loud with anger.

"Maybe the boy's got treasure of his own. If we could find him, you could kill him and I could have his gold," the second voice said.

As I listened, something snapped in the dense foliage to my right. I quickly remembered the cat and felt my heart sink in my chest. Motionless, I prepared for the worst. *Perhaps the owners of the voices could help me*, I thought.

I took a deep breath, but before I could make a noise, a young boy of about nine or so darted out of the bushes and clapped his hand over my mouth. His face was dirty and his clothing was not much more than a tattered loincloth. His skin was rough and tanned, and his long black hair hung over his face.

Motioning for me to be silent, he tugged at my arm so I would bend over enough for him to whisper in my ear. He drew near and delicately whispered, "Don't…say…anything. Just follow me." Pulling on my arm again, he led me back into the jungle. As we left the clearing, I heard the voices ranting.

"What's that? I heard something," said the first voice.

"It's the boy," said the second.

"Come," said the first. "Let's find him and gorge ourselves on his flesh."

At these words, the boy quickened his steps through the jungle, still dragging me along. He pulled me back past the pyramid and then turned right to reach the stream. We followed it for a bit, and then crossed to a point where the jungle grew thicker with branches, vines, leaves, and briars that we had to climb through. Finally, we arrived at a hidden cave in the wall of the mountain. He pulled me inside and motioned for me to be silent once more. He then listened for a moment at the mouth of the cave as we tried to catch our breath. Then he turned to me and said, "I believe it's all right to speak now. Who are you, and why have you come to the valley?"

CHAPTER SEVEN

THE ANCIENT ONE

"My name is Tiny Lynquest, and I am searching for the Ancient One," I said.

"And what do you want with the Ancient One?" he asked.

"I have been told that he is trapped in this valley and I wish to help him find his way out," I answered.

"You have been misinformed, young man. He is not trapped here. He stays of his own free will, so you can go home now, before you get yourself killed," he said in an irritated voice.

"But I am sure Malyki told me—"

"Malyki!" he said, cutting me short. "You have spoken with Malyki?"

"Yes! He seemed to think I could help the Ancient One," I exclaimed. "Besides, I'm not leaving without the heart."

"Aha!" he said wildly. "You would claim to help the Ancient One, but really you seek the Heart of Mater."

"I came for both, but if the Ancient One doesn't need my help, I will still seek the Heart of Mater," I said.

"Perhaps the Ancient One can help you. How long have you had those shoes?" he asked.

"Not long," I answered. "I got them from an old woman several weeks ago."

"A woman in Kautchitzar?" he inquired.

"Yes. But how did you know?" I asked in amazement.

"You have more to worry about than finding the Heart of Mater," he replied.

"What do you mean?" I asked.

"There is a great cat stalking you. It is drawn to the wearer of those shoes," he said.

"I have seen it," I said.

"You have? Well, you are more fortunate than most," he said with surprise. "Where did you see it last, and when?"

"This morning it chased me through the woods north of Forest Glen, about a half day's travel from here," I answered.

"You have one thing in your favor," he said.

"What's that?" I asked.

"It is going to be a full moon tonight. The shadow panther cannot travel in bright light. It can only leap from shadow to shadow during the day," he said.

"That's why it didn't follow me past the forest!" I exclaimed. "There weren't shadows in the bright snow."

"Good. That will give us time to prepare," he said.

"Prepare, how?" I asked.

"We will need to gather much firewood and move to a cave high above the valley floor, away from the shadows of the trees, preferably on the south wall of the valley. It is a sheer wall and thus no outcrops to create shadows. It is also well lit by the midday sun. It's not a solution, but it should give us time to think of something."

The boy seemed to be determined to keep me out of harm's way and I was in no position to argue. Before we left the shelter of that cave, he told me to stay close and to be as quiet as possible. We spent most of that afternoon gathering firewood and storing it in a cave he had selected high on the southernmost wall. It was near the place where the stream disappeared under the mountain.

Late that afternoon, he told me that I had better stay in the cave until he returned, saying not to build a fire until he got back. I was not used to taking orders from a child, but I thought I would humor him until I could determine where to find the Ancient One. When he finally returned later that day, he carried a bow, two large birds, and a sack. He said nothing as he set about the task of making a fire.

"I could have done that for you," I said.

"Look," he said. "There are many things about this valley that you don't understand yet. I will tell you in due time, but for now, you can put your skills to work plucking these birds."

I took the birds from him, sat down on a ledge overlooking the valley, and started plucking. He made the fire in the back of the cave, then took the birds and placed them over the fire to cook. As we waited, we sat opposite each other across the fire, not saying a word. Tension mounted as a conversation seemed unavoidable.

I looked over at him and said, "So, you know Malyki, then?"

"He used to visit me when he was younger and could make the trip," he said, stirring the coals as he spoke.

"When he was younger?" I asked in doubt. I couldn't take it any longer. I lashed out, saying, "Who are you, boy, and where is the Ancient One? Are you going to lead me to him or not?"

"If you had your wits about you, you would already know that I am the Ancient One!" he snapped loudly.

"Wait a minute…you? You couldn't be any older than nine or ten years old at the most. How could you have known Malyki when he was young, and how could you have known about the shadow cat, the shoes, or the old woman, unless you had seen—" I stopped cold.

With a face twisted by outrage, he stared back at me. "I have seen too much!" he railed.

"Just how old are you?" I asked.

"Old enough to know when someone is being rude!" he snapped.

I fell silent out of embarrassment. We ate, not uttering a word, and then bedded down for the night.

CHAPTER EIGHT

THE PLAN

The next day, I made a formal apology to him. "I…I…I'm sorry if I insulted you last night. I didn't mean to show any disrespect," I said awkwardly.

He turned to me, smiling with some embarrassment, and said, "I am sorry, too, young man. After all these years alone, I am afraid I am not very good with other people."

"Please allow me to start over," I said, holding out my hand.

He took my hand and shook it firmly. "All right," he said. "But from now on, you listen to me, ok? I have seen far too many adventurers like you go to their graves because they would not listen to a child."

I looked him square in the eye and said, "Deal! Now, how about showing me around this valley of yours?"

"Good idea. Maybe we can find something to use against that menacing shadow panther. First, we must stop by my hidden cave to pick up some things."

We put out the fire and moved to the mouth of the cave.

Then, turning to me, he said, "Once we are down in the valley, you must keep your voice down. They don't know you are here and I would like to keep it that way—for a while at least."

He turned and started down the mountain, with me right behind him. Moving through the jungle, we made as little noise as possible. There was something out there that he seemed determined to avoid, and I was not anxious to find out why. We reached the stream and crossed into the thick tangle of vines and briars that concealed his cave.

Once we had climbed through the briars for a second time, I asked, "Why don't you cut yourself a path through all that?"

"Surely you jest," he said. "That would lead Malice and Avarice right to my door."

I didn't understand his explanation, but didn't question it.

He rummaged through his things and produced a sword and a small ax, both of which were sharpened to perfection.

"We will need these," he said, handing me the ax. "Where would you like to start?"

"Well," I said thoughtfully, "that pyramid in the center of the valley seems interesting enough."

"Good," he agreed, "we will start at the beginning."

Taking a torch from the wall, he laid it on a pile of dry grass on the floor of the cave, and using a flint, he made quick work of lighting it. He snatched up the torch and extinguished the flames on the floor of the cave before we left. He held the torch overhead in one hand and the sword in the other, and he quietly led me through the jungle toward the pyramid, which lay at the heart of the valley.

When we reached the entrance to the pyramid, he looked up through the trees and said quietly but distinctly, "The sun is almost at its highest point. The two brothers will sleep through the heat of the day. It should be safe to talk now."

Though I was unsure of who he was talking about when he said the two brothers, I resigned myself to the thought that whoever they were, they were one of the many things about the valley that I would find out in due time. I simply nodded in agreement.

We entered the pyramid, and he began to tell me of the ancient civilization that had made the valley their home many hundreds of years before. He told me they used to worship the sun and the moon. The pyramid was where they had offered sacrifices to the sun god.

As we walked, I noticed the walls, ceiling, and floor were covered with carvings and writing. We walked through a narrow pass that sloped up to the top of the pyramid. Once at the top, we stood in a round chamber with a hole in the center of the ceiling, through which I could see the pale blue of the infinite sky. When we entered, the light from the torch immediately reflected off every wall.

"What is this stuff?" I asked, touching one of the walls. "It looks like a looking glass."

"It is white gold that has been polished until it shines like a looking glass," he answered.

As I turned to view the entire room, I tripped over something large sticking out of the middle of the floor. I tumbled backward right onto my backside. "How clumsy of me," I said, as I stood up and dusted myself off. I immediately turned to see what it was I had fallen over. There, in the middle of the room, was a diamond the size of a small boulder.

"Good grief," I said. "Is that what I think it is?"

"Yes," he replied, laughing. "It is a diamond."

Boy, was that an understatement! It was the largest diamond I had ever seen, and it was set in polished gold as well. It shone with a brilliance to match the sun. Light began to fill the room as I gazed at the monstrous gem.

I thought to myself, *it's a good thing Shamus didn't come. He probably would have hurt himself trying to get that thing out of the floor.*

"It is almost midday. We have to leave the chamber quickly," he said.

The light had begun to creep down the right-hand wall when we started for the door. It hadn't even reached the diamond yet and the temperature in the room had risen considerably. We made it halfway down the passage and stopped. We walked far enough that we left the entrance to the chamber behind us, and yet, I felt the intense heat radiating from the room, though it lasted only a short while.

I noticed the markings on the wall again and was intrigued. So, I asked him what they were.

"It is a calendar," he said. "That is how I knew it was going to be a full moon last night. The ancients followed the heavens closely and kept track of the stars. This calendar records all the events that occur in the skies, past and future, until a point when the scribe for some reason simply stopped writing."

I have always been a curious sort, so I asked, "So, where is today on this calendar?"

He took two steps down the passage. Staring at the wall, he raised his finger and said, "Here it is. Here is the full moon of last night and—oh, look! There is going to be an eclipse on the day after tomorrow."

"What?" I exclaimed. The thought of the eclipse settled in my mind like a seed in fertile soil. I knew I could use it against the panther, but I didn't know how.

"Yes, see, right here," he said, moving his finger to that point on the wall. "Is that important?" he asked.

"It could be," I said. "But I don't know how yet."

I struggled with the thought for a moment, then shrugged my shoulders and prepared to leave the pyramid. We made our way back outside and through the dense jungle, our path made difficult by the thick foliage. As we walked, I gazed up at the glimmering light dancing around the leaves at the top of the trees.

Then I stopped for a moment and looked back at the pyramid. That simple seed began to take root and an idea came to me. The boy noticed I was no longer following him, so he stopped and looked back.

"What is wrong?" he asked.

"I think I have figured out how to deal with the panther, dangerous though it may be," I said, still puzzling.

"How?" he asked.

"Well, you said the panther could not exist in a well-lit place," I said.

"He cannot," the boy replied.

"Then it is just a matter of trapping him in a room full of light," I said with satisfaction.

"Ah," he said. "You plan on somehow trapping it in the pyramid's chamber."

"Exactly," I said. "Since the cat only stalks at night, if I can get it to chase me during the eclipse, I can lead it to the chamber."

"Then what?" he asked.

"Then I merely wait for it to follow me into the chamber and somehow keep it there until the room fills with light."

"But you will cook!" he exclaimed.

"Not if I am quick," I said.

"That is an awfully risky plan," he said.

"Do you have a better one?" I asked.

He shrugged his shoulders and said, "I guess you really have no choice, do you?"

"My point exactly," I said. I told him my plan in detail, and then we set out for the south end of the valley.

He took me to a place directly south of the pyramid, where the trees were thinner and the sun shone through them to the ground below. The Ancient One climbed into the trees and began to clear the top branches away, while I started clearing a path back to the pyramid.

It was a simple plan, really. We would clear a small opening in the trees and a path that I could follow as the panther chased me. I would wait in the clearing in the sun until the eclipse, at which point I would run for my life.

Using the rest of the afternoon, I worked my way back to the pyramid entrance clearing every branch, rock, stick, and pebble away from the path. I didn't want anything in my way when I was running.

As evening grew closer, I was dragging off the branches that had fallen as the Ancient One cut the treetops. Once again, I heard the voices in the jungle and the sound of large branches snapping. I looked up into the trees to see if he had heard them, too. He had stopped cutting and was perched among the branches, motionless and listening.

I moved closer to the pyramid, crouched down and peered around the east wall. Emerging from the north jungle were the heads and enormous spread hoods of two gigantic snakes. I could see them for the first time. They towered high above the dense foliage of the jungle, moving toward us. One of the snakes had a scar on his lip like someone had hit him with a sword.

I looked back at the boy hanging in the trees and realized he was in harm's way. The serpents were sure to find him there, dangling in the trees, so I gathered all the rocks I could find and quickly ran around the other side of the pyramid. When the serpents neared the pyramid from the north, I hurled the first stone. It landed behind the snakes to the left.

"What was that?" one of them asked.

"What was what?" said the other.

"I heard something—it's the boy. He is going to reach the stone. He's going to reach my riches," said the snake with the scar.

"Calm down, Avarice, my brother. As of yet, I have not heard anything," the second retorted.

I threw another stone, this time a little further into the north jungle.

"I heard something that time," said the second serpent.

"See, I told you. Now let us hurry. Quick, before he reaches our cave," said the first.

"Relax, brother," said the second. "He may enter the cave, but he will never leave."

As they turned back toward the direction they had come, the second began to call out to what it thought was the boy.

"Is that you, boy? You can't hide forever. I am a patient serpent. I know it is just a matter of time before you slip up. I have waited so long to taste your flesh. I hope you're not too tough. It would be such a disappointment." He laughed as the two disappeared into the jungle.

I quickly returned to my friend, who I had left hanging in the trees. I found him with his feet already firmly on the ground.

He approached me and said, "Thank you. It is quite possible that your quick thinking has just saved my life."

I smiled and said, "Don't mention it. I hate snakes anyway, especially really large ones that talk of eating people." After that, we retired quietly to the safety of our cave on the southernmost wall.

Later that evening, as he sat across the cave from me, I noticed him staring at me.

"What's the matter?" I asked, trying to get at his thoughts.

"I know you seek the Heart of Mater. What I do not know is what you need it for," he said, pondering my intentions.

"Well, I suppose if you really must know," I said with reservations.

"Humor me," he said.

"Well, it's kind of complicated," I said. "I am a knight of Bonangi. It is a secret knighthood sworn to protect a sacred scepter. The scepter bears the form of a great hand. At its origin, the hand wore four rings. The Heart of Mater is one of those rings. I have already acquired two of the rings. I have only the heart and the Eye of Truth to collect. When I was sixteen, my mentor, a noble knight by the name of Lucias Merriweather, used his dying breath to set me on the quest to reunite the sacred rings with the scepter. I am to find the domain of the evil siren Salina and forever seal the door that leads to her realm. I have one thousand years before that doorway opens up, or Salina's evil will infect the hearts of all mankind. Lucias believed that the heart would give me time to find the Eye of Truth and the one who could use the scepter, a true heir of Millstaff, one who has yet to be born."

"It is true," he said. "The Heart of Mater will give you time. It will give you all the time you never wanted." He lowered his eyes to the ground. "Time is a funny thing," he added. "Even if you have an endless supply of it, you cannot take back the time you have spent, or undo the things you have done."

This thought seemed to sting him a little, so I did not pry into it any further.

"Well," I said, "even if I retrieve the heart, my quest has still just begun."

He gave a nod and we settled in for a long night of listening to the sounds of the jungle.

CHAPTER NINE

TO KILL A SHADOW

The next morning, I sat on the ledge at the entrance to our cave and gazed out over the valley. I noticed that, though the sun was up, there was no light shining on the valley floor. The sun had yet to rise above the high walls of the canyon. I heard the boy approaching me from behind, so I turned and asked, "Are there no sunrises in the valley?"

"No," he said plainly. "Or sunsets either. In order to have things such as these, you must have a horizon. Here in the valley we have only walls." He gave a great sigh and added, "Oh, what I wouldn't give for a truly spectacular sunset. It has been so long."

The sun crept down the west wall of the canyon and gave off enough light so one could see the tops of the trees. A flock of birds took flight, squawking and screeching as they hit the air.

"I wonder what caused that," I mused.

"The serpents are searching for me," he explained. "They do so throughout each night, until the heat of the next day."

"That's why you made the fire so far back in the cave, and why you didn't light it until after dark, to hide the smoke."

"Now you know why I did not cut a path through the jungle that covers my cave," he said. Scratching his head, he added, "Actually, the valley would not be a bad place to live if it were not for those cursed snakes. Yes, I have learned to hate those two." Anger began to seep into his voice as he went on. "Those overgrown maggots have made my existence in this valley an eternal hell. I would gladly give you the Heart of Mater if I thought you could help me kill that abomination."

"Why don't you leave?" I asked. "You have eternal youth."

He grew silent. Turning away, he said, "I have been here too long. I would not know how to go back."

I could see that he was hurt by something I had said, so I didn't say any more.

As the day went on, the valley heated up. The snakes' movements in the valley grew silent, so we decided to resume work on the clearing we had started the day before. As we worked, I searched for any traces of the panther's presence in the valley. I thought perhaps I would find a paw print or claw mark on a tree that would tell me if the cat had made its way into the valley yet. There were no traces of the panther, but I knew it was just a matter of time before I had all the proof I needed. We finished the work on the clearing early, so we spent the rest of the afternoon hunting for dinner. That night we ate our dinner after dark, as usual, but as we ate, a great roar rose up from the depths of the canyon. We both stopped eating and listened.

"It's the panther," I said nervously. "It's in the valley."

"It will be searching for you tonight," he said. "We must keep the fire bright for you. It may find the cave, but if the fire is bright, it will not be able to enter. There is another drawback to all this," he added.

"And what's that?" I asked.

"The serpents now know I am not alone," he replied.

I stood up and quickly placed more wood on the fire. It wasn't long before the entire chamber at the back of the cave was full of light. To take my mind off the fact that death was stalking me, I asked him to tell me the legend of the heart.

"Well," he began, "the legend tells of a boy lost in the labyrinth of caves within the mountain. While he was lost, the boy found the stone resting on a sacred shrine among the many caves and chambers that honeycomb the north wall. Two days later, the boy emerged from the cave, tired and thirsty. He drank from the sacred pool that lies before the temple of the moon. Still clutching the stone in his hand, he then washed it in the pool. One of the tribal elders saw the boy drinking from the pool, and took him to the priestess of the temple and chastised him. The stone was taken from him. The years went by, but the child never grew any older. The people of the valley became frightened of him and cast him out. Over time, the number of people living in the valley became too great, and they began to starve. The tribal elders decided to leave their precious valley, but before they did, the priestesses of both temples placed a curse upon a serpent's egg to protect the valley from outsiders. The legend goes on to say the boy returned to the valley to reclaim the stone, but the serpents found him before he could reach it."

"Where is the heart now?" I asked.

"It is said that the priestess of the moon hid the stone in a secret chamber behind the temple," he said.

"But the temple is carved into the face of the mountain," I said.

"Exactly," he said. "I never found the entrance behind the temple. When I came, I found a map of the labyrinth that also leads to the chamber, painted on the wall inside one of the many cave homes."

"So you have reached the stone," I said.

"Yes," he said. "But before I could take it, the two brothers returned and I ran. I barely escaped with my life. I have tried many times over the years to retrieve the heart, but the serpents are too zealous in their vigil to watch over the stone. Besides, the entrance to the labyrinth is also the serpent's lair."

"Why didn't the priestess get any younger when she touched the stone?" I asked.

"The secret to the power of the stone is in the pool," he answered. "You must drink from the pool before touching it." By the time he had finished his story, it was late, so I added more wood to the fire and prepared to go to sleep.

"Well, good night, ah...hey, you know, I don't know your name," I said.

"That is right, you don't," he answered. "And neither do I."

"You don't know your own name?" I asked in disbelief.

"Living alone for so long, I have not had use for a name. I have long since forgotten it," he said.

"Well, that won't do." I pondered this for a moment, and then I said, "How about Sebastian Andrews?" I turned to see him glaring back at me.

"If you cannot kill that panther, I may not need a name," he said sharply. "Now go to sleep. The eclipse is tomorrow and you will need your rest. I will stay up and keep the fire bright."

The next morning, I awoke to find him sitting on the ledge at the mouth of the cave. As I approached him, he turned to me with his finger to his lips, motioning for me to be quiet. Kneeling down, I looked over the edge. The serpents were carefully searching the jungle beneath our cave. Apparently, the panther had led them to the jungle below it. Leaning in to me, the boy whispered, "They might be stupid, but they have excellent hearing."

Still looking down, I could see the heads of both great snakes, although only one tail did I see, slithering through the jungle. Back and forth they went, side by side, retracing their path. As they did, they called out to the boy.

"Man-child, we know you are here somewhere. You know we will eventually find you," said the serpent with the scar.

"That one with scar is named Avarice," the boy whispered to me.

"We know you are not alone, boy," said the other.

"And that one is Malice," he said, pointing.

"Surrender the stranger to us and we will show you mercy," said Avarice.

"Yes," Malice added. "We will give you the heart."

I looked to see if he was taking any of this seriously. The boy whispered, "Watch this."

Then, cupping his hands over his mouth, he said in a distant voice, "You fools couldn't find your own tail."

"Fools, are we?" cried out Avarice. "When I find you, child, I will pierce you with my fangs and watch you bleed to death. Then I will eat you and make a nest out of your bones."

Malice was more cunning. He called out to the boy, saying, "Tell me, boy, is it good to have company again? Do you misss your family?" The words slithered up from the jungle.

"A word of advice, child," said Avarice. "Don't get too attached to the stranger. He will be dead in a few days."

"And you will be all alone again." Malice chuckled to himself.

"Just you and usss," said Avarice.

The thought of being alone with them must have been too much for the boy to take. He scrambled around looking for rocks to throw at them. He quickly gathered some up and hurled them at the serpents. The first few fell short of the snakes, but the fourth one found its mark, hitting Malice on the snout.

As the serpents turned to look in our direction, I quickly grabbed the boy, throwing him to the ground and pinning him there. Holding his arms to his sides in a tight hug, I whispered, "It's all right, it's all right. Let it go." The boy squirmed and wriggled in my arms, but I held him fast. Still trying to calm him down, I said, "I give you my word, I will not go after the heart by myself. I will not leave you alone with those things."

At that, he stopped struggling. I loosened my grip on the boy and took him back into the cave. He looked inconsolable. Filled with rage, his face was caught in an expression somewhere between anger and deep sorrow. I thought for a moment he was going to cry, but nothing happened.

The snakes were left to argue over which direction the stones were thrown from. The boy sulked about the cave the rest of that morning.

It wasn't long before the sun was high in the sky and I knew it was time to face the panther. I turned to the boy and asked, "Are you coming with me?"

He looked up at me, his face made weary from rage at the serpents' teasing. "I cannot," he said. "I just could not stand to—" He stopped and lowered his head.

"I understand," I said. He had seen enough.

As I turned to leave the cave, he said in a somber voice, "You know there is no hope of your keeping that promise you made."

"Oh yes, there is," I said. "Hope is all I have. It is also all I have ever needed." Then I turned and descended the mountain.

The first thing I noticed when my foot touched the jungle floor was the deadly silence. I moved through the jungle slowly, snapping twigs and rustling bushes, trying to get the cat's attention. Halfway to the clearing, I was beginning to think my plan wasn't going to work, when I heard a large snap behind me. Startled, I looked down at the small, unbroken branch still in my hand. I slowly turned to face my fear and dropped the flimsy branch.

There it was, only it was different somehow. It wasn't nearly as dark as the last time I had seen it, and its eyes looked like two small flames instead of bright burning embers. It panted as it crept toward me.

I quickened my steps through the jungle, but the cat kept pace close behind. Its movements were slow and steady as it trod methodically in my direction. I easily reached the clearing before the cat. Standing in the middle of my bright circle of light, I waited for the panther to appear. I heard its heavy panting and rhythmic footsteps as it neared the clearing.

Slowly, it emerged at the edge of the clearing. It began to pace the boundary of the shadows, searching for a way to reach me. Nervously, I kept a good distance from all the sides of the clearing and sharply watched the edges of my circle of light for any changes in brightness. The shadow-line began to grow hazy as the eclipse slowly consumed the sun.

With the onset of impending darkness, the cat seemed to almost double in size and intensity. It became darker than darkness magnified, and its eyes became again the hellish fires that sent waves of fear rushing through my body.

As my sanctuary of light disappeared beneath my feet, the panther crouched low, drew back its ears, snarled, and began to claw the ground. I knew then it was time to run.

I broke from my clearing with all the strength I could muster. The cat lunged forward and quickly closed the gap. Suddenly, my feet began to burn and almost seemed to quicken their pace by themselves. I ran faster than I ever thought possible. I had gained some distance on the cat by the time I reached the entrance to the pyramid.

I looked back and saw its eyes—like two knives slicing through a cloak of black, they split the darkness. I hurtled up the long dark corridor until I reached the chamber at the top. I turned back and once again waited for those burning eyes to appear. I moved backward until I reached the wall opposite the door. I could distinguish the faint outline of the cat's face in the utter darkness; its eyes glowed with a wild light.

Thinking it had me trapped, the menacing black apparition slowly entered the room. It crouched and lunged for me. I tried to leap out of the way, but a massive claw caught my right shoulder, laying it open. Helpless, I lay there, clasping my arm, when the cat turned again and lunged a second time.

As its feet left the ground, a beam of light from the sun splintered the darkness. It struck the diamond in the center of the room. The room filled with light, catching the panther in midair and holding it there. Like some strange ornament, it hung there as I watched the sunlight dissolve its edges, breaking it into thousands of tiny pieces. The room began to heat up fast, so I jumped to my feet and scrambled out of the chamber, leaving the panther to hang in the brilliant sunlight.

I made my way down to the entrance of the pyramid, then turned and gazed back up the passage toward the chamber. While I was watching to see if the cat would emerge from the room, I felt something grab my left shoulder. It almost prompted me to start running again, but when I turned around, I found the boy standing there.

"You came!" I exclaimed happily.

"Yeah, well, I had to find out whether or not I had a name," he said, smiling.

We waited until the heat of the chamber subsided, and then we made our way up the passage and back into the chamber. He had brought a torch, and when we entered, we found nothing but an empty room. The panther had completely vanished, leaving no trace that it had ever existed. I took a deep breath and gave a sigh of relief as we left the chamber.

Standing at the base of the pyramid, I was feeling mighty cocky, so I threw my arm around the boy's shoulder and said, "Yes, I think Sebastian Andrews will do nicely."

We laughed for a little while as I told him of my fear and then we started back to the cave. Once there, he applied some strange paste to my shoulder. It was light brown in color and had the texture of oatmeal, but that is where the similarities ended. Whatever it was, it stunk like a pigsty in summer, but it stopped the pain. He then bandaged it with a piece of banana leaf and some braided palm fronds. I reminded him that he hadn't had much sleep the night before, so I recommended that he rest while I searched for dinner. Feeling the wear of the day's excitement, he reluctantly agreed. I picked up the bow and quiver of arrows, and once again headed out.

Almost as an afterthought, he said, "Oh, by the way, in case you get any foolish notion that the arrows will be useful against the serpents, they won't. They have no effect on it. The serpents' scales are too thick."

"Don't worry, my friend," I said. "I will be back before the cool of the evening."

"See that you are," he replied.

I left the cave and traveled through the jungle very carefully. The serpents were still slumbering in the cool of their lair beside the temple of the moon. I passed the pyramid and reached the clearing in front of that temple. Sebastian must have known I was going to come here. After hearing the legend of the stone, I couldn't help myself.

I stepped into the clearing and approached the pool. The water was a strange bright blue-green color. It was an oddly shaped pool with twelve flat stones around it. Each stone had a different configuration of stars on it.

I knelt down and dipped a hand into the water. It felt warm to the touch. I then dipped both my hands into the water and drew out as much as they could hold. Closing my eyes, I took a mouthful and swallowed. It was sweet and warm, and the warmth moved through me. It was delicious. I drew some more out and drank again, then again. It was wonderful. It was like drinking a daydream. I felt warm, completely satisfied. An overwhelming sense of peace came over me. I stood up and recovered my senses.

Slowly I moved toward the temple. It was a huge structure carved into the north face of the mountain. Two enormous pillars with ornate carvings on them stood at the entrance. The temple itself was built on a mound, so that the ground sloped down toward the pool.

I quietly ascended the mound and entered the temple where I found myself in a great hall, with a high ceiling and walls that were decorated with ornate carvings of women holding hands beneath a crescent moon and stars. There were ornate runes etched into the walls bordering the top and bottom of all four walls; the ancient prayers and incantations of a long-forgotten people, no doubt. The light streaming in the door behind me shone on an ancient stone altar and two figures carved into the farthest wall. I moved toward the altar in order to take a closer look.

The altar was carved out of one piece of solid granite. It stood about a hand's width from the northern wall of the temple. The wall behind the altar had the images of two large crescent moons, with the face of a woman carved into each one.

There were two figures that were statues of women. They were at least twice my height, and each held a crescent moon in her hands high above her head. They were set a few paces away from the ends of the altar and were turned in such a way that they looked directly at each other across the altar.

A cool breeze wafted through the doorway and I knew it wouldn't be long before evening, so I left my search of the temple for another day. The sun was just starting to drop behind the western wall of the canyon when I arrived back at the cave. Sebastian was once again perched on the ledge overlooking the valley.

As I approached carrying two small rabbits, he said, smiling, "So, you made it back."

"Was there any doubt?" I asked, laughing.

"Well, most would not have, but I am coming to realize that you are not like the rest," he said. He took the rabbits from me and went back inside the cave to prepare them.

"I can help you with that," I said.

"Nonsense," he said. "The valley is my home and you are my guest." As he prepared the food, he asked, "So, what did you think of the pool?"

"Is there nothing you don't know?" I replied.

He smiled and said, "I knew that after you heard the legend, you would be curious. So, what did you think?"

"It was strange and wonderful," I said. "So warm and sweet, I almost couldn't stop myself from drinking."

"How much did you drink?" he asked.

"Three handfuls," I answered.

"Hmm, you will dream hard tonight," he said, smiling.

"What do you mean?" I asked in excitement.

"I call that pool, the pool of imagination," he said. "For when you drink of it, it will give you great and sometimes terrible dreams."

The sun had gone down, so I made the fire in the usual place and he put the rabbits on to cook. While they were cooking, I said, "I went to the temple, too, you know."

"Naturally," he said. "And what did you think of it?"

"It was spectacular. It must have been a marvel to watch them build such a place, although I didn't see any door leading behind the temple," I said.

"It must be hidden," he said.

"Yes, but where? There is no place inside the temple to hide a door," I replied in a puzzled voice. "Wait! The old woman told me a riddle before I left her. I was supposed to solve it on my journey."

"What was it?" he asked.

"I don't know if I can remember it now," I said. "Let me see...*a door, a key, to a hidden lair, look beneath the only stair.*"

"But there are no stairs in this valley," he said.

"Are you sure?" I asked.

"Positive. I have been all over this valley and there is not so much as a single step any-where," he said, frustrated that I would even question him.

For some reason, my thoughts kept returning to the temple and the statues in it. "Those are interesting statues inside the temple," I said.

"What do you mean?" he asked.

"I mean, it's unusual for the statues to be facing each other like that, isn't it?" I asked in return.

"I would not think so," he said. "They have been staring at each other that way for hundreds of years."

"Wait! The statues!" I said in excitement.

"What about the statues?" he asked.

"Don't you see?" I asked. "It's not *stair* as in step. It's *stare* as in 'to look.' *Look beneath the only stare* means that we should be looking somewhere behind or underneath the altar in the temple."

"So? If a door is there, that altar is too heavy for the two of us to move," he said.

"Maybe, but maybe not," I said. "If we use a small tree trunk stripped it of its branches, we might be able to slip it behind and pry the altar away from the wall."

"I am not sure," he said. "It sounds too risky. Even if you find the door and locate the chamber, the serpents would be on you in a heartbeat."

"You have a point. I will have to give it some more thought." After that, I spent the rest of dinner in quiet contemplation.

Once dinner was over, I sat back against the wall of the cave and watched as Sebastian slowly stirred the coals of the fire with a stick.

"Sebastian," I said.

"Yes," he answered.

"When you spoke of the snakes earlier, why did you call them an abomination?" I asked.

"Because that is what it is," he answered.

"There, you did it again," I said.

"Did what?" he asked.

"You called them an *it*," I said.

"That's what *it* is!" he repeated impatiently.

"But, I saw two snakes this morning in the jungle," I said.

"No, what you saw was two heads of the same serpent," he said in exasperation. Realizing that I hadn't comprehended this fact until now, he went on. "When the priest-esses put their curse on the serpent's egg, it changed. The priestess of the sun put a curse of hatred, so the serpent would be compelled to kill all newcomers in the valley. The priestess of the moon put a curse of greed on the egg, so that it would stay in the valley, protecting the sacred articles of both the temple and the pyramid. There are also some riches stored in the labyrinth."

"Oh, that's why you call them *Malice* and *Avarice*," I said, finally understanding. "So, there is really only one snake that we have to contend with. That's even better."

"Believe me, that is enough," he replied. "We have only the bow and arrows and a sword to use against it, and the arrows will not work. That has been my problem."

"Yes, that is a problem that is going to take some imagination to solve," I said.

I was beginning to feel sleepy, so I found a comfortable place next to the fire to lie down. Turning to Sebastian, I bid him a good night and closed my eyes.

CHAPTER TEN

CAPTURE THE HEART

I found myself in front of the pool at midday under a bright, hot sun. I faced the north wall of the canyon with the temple of the moon in front of me to my right. To my left was the gaping entrance to the serpent's lair. I gazed into the cave, but it only gave up darkness and a strange rushing sound, as if something was being dragged through the dirt.

As the sound began to get louder, I realized it was the serpent nearing the entrance of the cave from the inside. I tried to run, but couldn't lift my feet. I was frozen in my tracks. The serpent appeared at the entrance of the cave. Both Malice's and Avarice's eyes lit up with delight when they saw me standing there. Frantically, I struggled to move my feet, but couldn't.

The brothers said nothing as they drew closer, baring their fangs and hissing as they came. I cried out, "Sebastian! Sebastian, help me!" But there was no answer. I kept thinking to myself, *This can't be happening, it's too hot, they should be in their cave.*

Closer they came, their heads bobbing and weaving. Just as they got within striking distance, a great shadow passed overhead, far too fast to be a cloud. I peered into the sky, but whatever it was, was hidden by the sun.

Suddenly, one of the snake's heads rose up, preparing to strike me down. As it did, a loud screech came from above the snake's heads. The two brothers looked up as an enormous eagle dropped out of the sky, landing on the serpent. Talons and beak flashing, it tore into the serpent with a fury. With the flapping of its enormous wings and its beak pulling at the snake's flesh, the bird was a well-matched rival for the massive snake.

The snake twisted and turned as it struggled to break free of the bird's claws. The two wrestled fiercely, and as they did, moved closer to me. The snake's tail, twisting and twirling, struck me, knocking me to the ground. I suddenly realized that I was about to be consumed in the battle of the two creatures. I started screaming, "Sebastian! Sebastian! Sebastian!"

I woke to Sebastian shaking me harshly and saying, "Wake up. Tiny, wake up! It is only a dream."

My eyes popped open and I focused on his youthful face, drew a deep breath, and said, "You weren't kidding when you said that I would dream hard."

He laughed and shook his head, saying, "It is almost dawn. Are you going back to sleep?"

"Are you joking? I don't think I can after that." I said, still catching my breath.

"So, tell me about your dream," he said.

I recounted my dream to him, and when I was done, I reached into my pocket and pulled out the velvet pouch that Shamus had taken from the old woman.

"What is that?" Sebastian asked.

I took the figure out of the pouch and said, "It's something given to me by a friend." My thoughts turned to Shamus and his frail state when I saw him last. I continued, saying, "Malyki said it was a sentinel or protector and that it has magical properties. It was in the box that the shoes came from, with another velvet pouch just like it."

"Do you know how to use it?" he asked.

"Malyki told me how to use it," I said. Holding it in my hand, I felt a strange bond with the bird. Maybe it was the dream, but I began to see a way to deal with that serpent. "You know, I believe we can use this against that snake," I said. I told him what I had in mind, and we spent the better part of that morning formulating a plan.

After we had worked out all the details, Sebastian walked over and picked up the sack he had brought to the cave on my first night in the valley. Reaching into it, he pulled out a large key. It was as long as my forearm and had an odd-shaped handle at one end.

"Here," he said. "I found this in the temple when I first arrived in the valley."

I took the key and examined it. It was made of solid bronze and was very heavy. It had ornate carvings of the sun, moon, and stars on it. "You keep it for now," I said, handing it back to him.

He took the key and placed it back into the sack. He snatched up his sword and began sharpening it with a stone, which he had also retrieved from the sack. As he did this, a wicked little grin came across his face.

I stood at the entrance of the cave and once again gazed out over the valley. I watched as the serpent wandered aimlessly through the jungle, hurling accusations and abuses at the boy. I was certain Sebastian could hear them. I looked back at him. The expression on his face was becoming more serious with every word that rose up from the valley. The stone grazed across the silvery edge of the sword, making a high-pitched *zing* as it repeatedly left the tip of the blade. The sound seemed to give him great pleasure.

"Are they always like that?" I asked.

"Like what?" he replied.

"So vocal in their search for you," I answered.

"Yes. Every morning for as long as I can remember, I have woken to the sound of their voices antagonizing me," he said, still sharpening his blade.

"That must be hard to deal with," I said.

He stopped caressing the blade with the stone for a moment and looked directly into my eyes. Still wearing that somber expression, he said, "You have no idea." Then he returned his attention to the edge of his blade.

That afternoon, when the serpent had retired for the day, I asked Sebastian for the key, which I tucked under my belt. I then grabbed the ax and the torch we had used in the pyramid. Sebastian took his sword, slipped into a leather sheath, and tied it to his side with a leather cord. I checked my pocket to make sure I still had the velvet pouch containing the sentinel.

We then descended into the valley and found a grove of ironwood trees. We selected the appropriate tree, cut it down, and stripped it of all its branches. After carrying it inside the temple, I went outside and grabbed two handfuls of sand, and spread it in front of the altar. Taking the tree trunk, we placed the small end of it behind the altar and began to pry it away from the wall.

At first, I didn't think it was going to move, but then it budged just a little. I took a deep breath, placed my heels against the north wall, and pushed with all my might. Sebastian's face turned red from the strain as we pushed together.

Slowly, the massive altar moved on the sandy floor. We gradually moved it far enough away from the wall so that a small door made of solid gold could be seen in the floor. I took the key from my belt and inserted it into the colossal keyhole.

I was just about to turn it when Sebastian said, "Wait, the serpent might be just on the other side of this door." I nodded and we went back outside to start the second part of our plan.

Sebastian set about drawing a map on the ground using a stick, while I tried to light the torch. Once lit, I took it and placed it next to the altar. I then returned to Sebastian, who was just putting the finishing touches on his drawing.

"Is that it?" I asked, looking at his drawing.

"I think so," he answered.

"Are you sure that's the whole valley?" I asked again.

"Just a moment," he said, and he double-checked. "Yes, that is it. That is the entire valley," he said, reassuring me.

"OK," I said, kneeling down. "Now, remember, I need you to lure the serpent here, next to the pool." I drew the snake on the map.

"Yes, I understand," he said in a nervous voice.

I took the figure of the bird out of the velvet pouch, and then, looking into Sebastian's eyes, I asked, "Are you ready for this?"

Without saying a word, he nodded and went to take his place at the entrance to the serpent's cave.

I watched as he slowly approached the cave. Once he was standing at its mouth, he leaned in and said in a quivering voice, "Malice, Avarice, I am out here. Why do you not come and get me?"

He looked at me where I was crouched down over the map he had drawn. I motioned to Sebastian with my hands to continue. He turned his attention back to the cave.

Taking a deep breath to fortify his courage, a stern look of determination settled across his face. He leaned in once more and yelled, without any hesitation in his voice, "Are you in there, worm? Can you hear me? Come out and meet your end! It is time for you to die! Come out! Come out here and fight me like the worm you are!"

He waited for a moment to see if there was any noise rising from the cave. A faint sound of arguing voices rose from deep within the labyrinth.

Sebastian called out again. "Did you hear me, serpent? I am calling you out here to end this! Come and face your doom!"

Again he fell silent and listened. There were no voices this time, but I could hear the sound I had heard in my dream. It was the sound of something being dragged through the dirt. Only this time it was much swifter than in my dream. I knew the serpent was moving rapidly through the cave toward the entrance.

I motioned for him to back away from the cave. No sooner had he taken his third step backward, when the two great heads of the snake broke free of the darkness within the cave. They emerged with such force that Sebastian fell backward to the ground. Immediately, the serpent's hoods spread wide, casting their shadow on the ground where Sebastian lay. He jumped up and pulled his sword from its sheath. Using the blade, he caught the intense sunlight and shined it into the serpent's eyes. The serpent cringed with pain as the bright light struck their eyes.

"What is the matter, Malice? Can you not see well?" Sebastian taunted. "Perhaps you are getting old," he said.

"Child, when I am done with you, you will be begging for death to come," the serpent answered.

Just then, Avarice came down on Sebastian with fangs drawn, but Sebastian was too quick. He struck the snake across the snout with the razor-edged sword. The snake quickly drew back, shaking its head violently, as the wound began to bleed.

Sebastian took several steps backward in the direction of the pool.

"Where are you going, man-child?" Malice asked. "The fun has just begun."

"Yes, child," Avarice chimed in, "I want to reunite you with your long-dead family." They began to cackle to themselves.

"It is a shame, really," said Malice. "I am almost going to miss you while I am digesting your flesh."

As he said this, the serpent's tail moved around to one side, curling and twisting as it neared Sebastian's legs. Sebastian spun around and swung at the tail. *Whoosh!* The sword swept past the tail, slicing off the very tip of it.

"Ha, ha," Sebastian laughed, "a souvenir. I shall keep that piece of your tail long after I have killed you both!"

The snake's heads were bobbing and weaving with anger. Their eyes filled with rage, as they looked for a way to strike Sebastian without suffering another wound. Sebastian steadily moved backward as the serpent moved in on him, striking as it came. Their fangs shone in the sun like four arched sabers, and each time Sebastian's sword connected with one, a *ping* rang out.

Finally, the serpent had moved far enough into the clearing. So, I focused on the map and placed the figure of the bird on the drawing of the snake that I had made in the dirt. I turned my eyes toward the sky and searched for any sign of the sentinel. Several moments passed and nothing happened. I was beginning to think I had just sent Sebastian to his grave, when out of the sky there came a bird as great in size as the snake itself. It swooped low and landed directly on the serpent, sinking its talons deep into Avarice's back, below the hood. Beating Malice's head down with its wing, the eagle caught hold of Avarice's head with its beak and started thrashing it about.

Sebastian was quickly forgotten in the mêlée, so he turned to me. I shouted, "Now!" and we both raced to the temple.

Once inside, we quickly moved to the small gold door. I reached down and turned the key. It rotated with very little effort. Using the handle of the key, I pulled, but the door was too heavy for me to lift. Sebastian grabbed hold of the key and we pulled together. The door slowly opened, creaking as it did. We gently leaned the door against the back of the altar. I then snatched up the torch and peered down into the hole we had just uncovered.

It was a small hole, only a little wider than my shoulders. There were indentations on one side, obviously foot, and handholds carved into the solid rock. I descended first, holding the torch high above my head. At the bottom, the path opened out into a wider passage, long and dark. I waited for Sebastian to emerge from the tiny hole and then we moved together. Not knowing if or when the serpent would return, we moved as swiftly as we could.

We came to a fork where the passage split in two different directions. I stood for a moment wondering which one to take, left or right. One would lead to the chamber with the heart and the other, no doubt, would eventually lead back outside to the serpent.

I started toward the passage on the left, but as I did, Sebastian said, "No, it is the other one."

"Are you sure?" I asked.

"Trust me," he said, pushing me in the opposite direction with one hand.

We followed the passage he chose as it led us down an incline, deep into the bowels of the mountain. Suddenly, the passage opened up into a vast chamber with a shallow pool. In the center of the pool was a mound of earth, and from it, a small sapling with full white blossoms grew in the darkness. There, among its many branches, hung the ruby that I sought. It was in the shape of a heart and was set in a ring that hung on a chain of the finest gold. The bloodred gem caught the light from the torch as I approached it, turning the snow-white blossoms bloodred.

I took out the velvet pouch, which was now empty, and opened it. Placing it under the ruby, I very carefully slipped it over the gem and untangled the gold chain from the small tree's branches.

Turning to Sebastian, I said excitedly, "I've got it," but Sebastian wasn't there. I looked around the room and found him in a corner, staring down at the floor. I crossed the room to see what he was looking at. Next to the wall were the remains of yet another unfortunate adventurer. With a broken leg and two broken ribs, he obviously had made it down into the chamber, but died before reaching the stone.

I noticed that he didn't have a torch, so he probably didn't even know he had found what he was looking for. He was leaning up against the wall, still clutching a spear that he might have leaned on as he descended the passageway.

As I looked at Sebastian's face, I saw that he wasn't looking at the bones of the dead man at all. He was staring intently at the large spear the dead man was holding. It had a long, square, needlelike head made of solid bronze, as big around as my finger and as long as my arm. It tapered down to such a fine point that it left no illusions about its ability to penetrate that snake's thick hide. The jagged edges of all four corners of the square needle also meant that once it had found its mark, it was not likely to be pulled out easily.

A wicked smile and a devious look came over Sebastian's face as he bent to pick up the spear.

Looking back at him, I said, "I got the stone. Now can we get out of here?"

"Certainly," he replied, and we started for the passage.

Before leaving, I raised my torch high and took one last look around. I wanted to remember this moment for the rest of my life.

Sebastian and I ascended the passage, each of us clasping his prize. He with his spear and I with my stone, we headed back for the temple. I reached the small hole by which we had found our way down into the catacombs and quickly climbed up into the temple.

As I crossed toward the door, I could see the serpent down by the pool. The giant bird was gone, and one of the serpent's heads lay dead at the waterside. The other was drinking from the pool, and it suddenly turned and saw me moving through the temple. It rushed to the entrance, dragging the limp head of its brother along the way. It reached the doorway before me, trapping me inside.

"Youuuu! You sent the great bird that killed my brother," the serpent howled at me. "You are a dead man," it said, blocking the entrance. I tried to use my torch to get it to back away from the door, but it wouldn't budge. The doorway was too narrow for the snake to enter, so I was safe for the moment. Still, I could not stay in this temple forever. I had to leave sometime, and the wretched snake wasn't showing any sign of backing down. I turned to Sebastian for some idea of what to do, but once again, he was gone.

"What's the matter, stranger? Has the boy deserted you?" the serpent taunted me. "Looks like you are going to die alone, like all the rest," he said, glaring at me with those cold gray eyes.

"No! You are going to die, Malice, like your brother," said a voice from behind the serpent.

The snake's eyes opened wide as he realized the voice was behind him. It was Sebastian. He had followed the other passage that led outside and was standing directly behind the serpent. As the snake turned to face the boy, Sebastian cried out, "Die, you tempest from hell!" and hurled the spear at the snake. It pierced Malice through the hood below the head.

The snake cringed and shrieked as its body began twisting and twirling, writhing in pain. Head over tail, the great serpent rolled down the slope on which the temple was built, moving closer and closer to Sebastian as he did. Sebastian stood motionless with his hands behind him. Just as the snake reached the boy, it righted itself, raised its head high in the air, and came back down with its fangs out stretched.

"Sebastian!" I cried out.

The serpent's body jolted backward in pain, went rigid, and then collapsed to the ground. I ran to see if Sebastian was all right. I found him staring down at Malice in silence. He fell on his knees before the body of the great snake. He bowed his head and covered his face with his hands.

I looked at the serpent. Sebastian's sword was buried to the hilt in the viper's flesh. He had pierced it through the throat and skull, pinning its mouth closed, leaving his blade sticking out between the serpent's eyes.

At first I thought he had been wounded, so I asked, "What is the matter? Are you all right?" He remained motionless. "Are you hurt?" I demanded.

Raising his head and hands to the sky, he cried out, laughing, "Finally! Finally silence!" The whole valley echoed his words, causing flocks of birds to take flight. The entire canyon seemed to breathe a great sigh of relief. Turning to me, he asked, "So, tell me, have you ever eaten snake before?"

That night we made our fire right there next to the pool, without fear of reprisal. I myself was not too fond of the idea of having snake for dinner, but, not wanting to ruin his moment of glory, I ate. Sebastian seemed to be enjoying himself as he tore into the meat with a ravenous appetite.

"Done already?" he asked. "Do you want some more? There is plenty here," he said, laughing as he looked toward the carcass of the great snake.

"No, I am quite full, thank you," I replied, holding my stomach for effect.

After dinner, I took the velvet pouch, opened it, and let the contents slip out onto the ground. Very carefully, I picked up the gold chain and gazed at the ruby in the light of the fire. It was a beautiful gem, the size of a chestnut, and the light shone through the bloodred stone, causing it to glow. It was a prize in itself. Even without the powers it held, I would have risked my life to reach it.

I looked over at Sebastian, who was still enjoying the last bits of dinner. I knew I shouldn't ask this question, but I felt compelled to know, so I said, "Sebastian?"

"Yes, my friend?" he answered.

"How long have you been in this valley?" I asked.

He paused from eating for a moment, and then threw the last bits of his dinner into the fire. He moved to the edge of the pool, knelt down and gazed into the water at his reflection in silence.

Regretting my question, I tried to retract it by saying, "I know I shouldn't have asked that. I'm sorry. Just forget it and I won't say another word."

"No, it is all right," he said. "If anyone deserves to hear the whole story, it is you." He turned to me with a somber face and began his tale. "I was already an old man of sixty-five when I came to the valley. I had crossed an ocean and two continents to get here. Back then, there were fewer people who knew about the stone, so I was one of the first to come.

"When I arrived, I spent a week or two observing the serpent unnoticed. I learned its habits, when it hunted and when it slept. My plan was simplicity at its finest. I would wait until nightfall, while the serpent hunted, then sneak into the cave and search for the stone.

"Unfortunately, I didn't take into consideration the size and depth of the labyrinth. It took me all night, and still I had not found the chamber with the stone. My torch was getting small and I knew the serpent would be returning, so I started looking for a way out. It was in the search for daylight that I stumbled across the heart hanging in the sapling.

"As I touched it, it changed me into the child you see now. But before I could even wrap my fingers around the stone, I felt something grab hold of my leg. It was the serpent's tail. It had found me and wrapped its tail around my leg, pulling me to the ground and halfway across the chamber.

"Using what I had left of my torch, I singed the serpent's tail, causing it to release my leg. I jumped to my feet and we faced off. The snake entered the room and, using its body, surrounded the small tree in the center. I fled for my life, running aimlessly through the catacombs, until my torch finally went out. Somehow, I managed to find daylight without the cursed snake finding me.

"At first, I was delighted with my youthful appearance, but as the years went on, I realized that I was not getting any older. The stone had not given me a second chance at life; it gave me an eternity as a child. Strangely enough, though my appearance was that of a child of nine or ten, inside I felt no different. Inside, I was still sixty-five, and was tired of the years that went on endlessly."

Sebastian turned his back to me and faced the pool once more.

"Eight hundred years I have been in this valley. Eight hundred years I have watched them come in search of what I had already obtained, only to watch them wind up as food for that cursed snake. None would listen to me. None would hear me.

"And me? I would have given my life to reach the stone and return to my family across the sea. I would give anything to undo the things I have done—to relive my life, as a man should, through the songs and games of his grandchildren, to see the light that shines from the faces of my grandchildren when they smile and to find my youth in their laughter."

At those words, I saw the strain on his face as he fought back the emotion, saying, "No one told me. How was I to know that I would be sacrificing everything? I sacrificed my family, my home, my life, only to be trapped in the body of a child forever. Now, my family has all passed away, my children and grandchildren, until there is nothing left for me to return to. Yes, I was a vain and foolish man eight hundred years ago when I came to this valley. I paid the ultimate price to learn the secret of the heart."

I looked at the boy hunched over the pool, gazing at his reflection in the water, and for the first time, he looked ancient to me. For the first time, I could see beyond the child, into the soul of the man that lay within.

"I meant what I said, you know," he said to me.

"What was that?" I asked.

"You can keep the Heart of Mater. I have what I want, the solitude of the valley. I will ask you one small favor, though," he said.

"What's that?" I asked again.

"Let me touch the stone one last time," he said. "I want to return to the man I was and live out the remainder of my years here in seclusion."

"Why don't you return with me?" I asked.

"There is nothing for me out there," he answered. "All that I knew is gone and I am too old to start over. Just let me die among the ruins and bones like all the others in the valley."

"No!" I exclaimed. "Leave the valley to the dead and come with me. There is a man out there who cared enough to send me to help you. That is the only reason Malyki sent me at all." Then, holding out the stone by the chain, I said, "Come, touch the heart and live out the rest of your life in the house of Malyki. He sent me to retrieve you and I dare not return without you."

Turning to face me, he said, smiling, "You are a compassionate soul, Lynquest. Truly, the Heart of Mater has found a good home in your hands."

Walking over to where I sat, he took hold of the stone. His hand began to quiver, then his arm, and finally his whole body began to convulse violently. A strange wind blew about him like a whirlwind of time and the years were laid upon his body like so many coats of paint. The water in the pool began to boil and bubble and a bright blue-green light erupted from it, filling the sky.

The image of a woman appeared in the light. She had long flowing hair, with two braids pulled tight in a wreath around her head. Her face was weathered but gentle, like that of a kindly matriarch from a common memory. Compassionate blue eyes looked down upon Sebastian with an expression of mercy, and she began to speak.

"You have learned well the lesson of the stone. True youth is found within. Now, depart and share this knowledge as a child of time." The image faded with the dying of the strange blue-green light.

I turned my eyes back to Sebastian, who had let go of the stone and was on all fours, steadying himself on the ground. The body of a frail old man emerged. It was hard to believe at first that this was the same person, but as he looked up, I stared into his eyes. He smiled the same friendly smile I had seen at the pyramid the day we defeated the panther. I dropped the stone to the ground and clasped his arm, helping him to his feet.

Once standing, he bent over and picked up the heart by the chain. Smiling, he said, "Here, you dropped this."

Carefully, I placed it back into the velvet pouch. I pulled the drawstring closed and put the pouch into my shirt pocket.

"This calls for some music," he said, as he reached for the sack that he had retrieved from our cave. Searching through it, he pulled out a small wooden flute, which he placed to his lips and began blowing gently. The most enchanting song filled the air as I leaned back against a rock and gazed into the starlit sky.

We spent the night beneath the stars, enjoying the freedom that came with our victory over the serpent. That night, I dreamt of only peaceful things, such as home, the castle Ironcrest, and of my promise to my long-dead mentor, Lucias.

The next day, we slept until the sun had cleared the canyon wall. We discussed plans for the day and made up our minds that, since the snake was no longer a threat, we would explore the cave. He made another torch and lit it. I carried the sack and a large stick, which I dragged across the ground as we moved through the many passages of the cave.

Many hours passed as we moved from chamber to chamber, looking for the one that the serpent had called home. Finally, we came upon a passage that was much wider than the rest. It sloped uphill and opened into an enormous room. There was a pile of bones up against one wall. Some of them were whole, some of them were broken into fragments, and some were ground into a fine white powder.

"He was not kidding," Sebastian said. "He really did make a nest of his victim's bones."

In the back of the chamber was a smaller room, filled with treasure of all kinds. There were hundreds of gold coins, goblets studded with gems, bowls, and lamps made of the finest white and yellow gold. There were weapons, too. Swords with great gems set in the handles, beautiful shields studded with diamonds, and armor of all kinds. I bent over and picked up seven pieces of gold and put them into my pocket.

"Is that all you want?" asked Sebastian.

"No," I said, "that's all I need."

We then commenced filling his sack with treasures until I thought we couldn't carry it back. I wrapped my belt around the large stick and tied it to the handle of a shield. We then placed the sack on the shield and dragged it behind us. We followed the line that I had drawn in the sand as we explored and easily found our way out. Once outside, I looked to the sky and saw that the sun was nearing the western wall. If we were to make it to Malyki's house before dark, I knew we had to hurry.

CHAPTER ELEVEN

NEW BEGINNINGS

We gathered up our few belongings and departed for the cave. As Sebastian crossed in front of the pool, I saw him bend over and pick something up. It was the serpent's tail. He looked at me and said, "I will be taking this for sure."

His complete self-contentment made me laugh. Sebastian then pulled his sword from the serpent's skull and we headed off toward the cave across the stream. This time, he cut a path through the dense jungle that covered his cave.

"We will need some blankets or furs to keep us warm once we are outside the valley," I said.

We entered the cave and went straight to a pile of furs that he had collected from other adventurers and stored in the corner. We took the furs and tied them together, making a hammock of sorts. Tying both ends to a long pole, we filled our hammock with all his belongings, including the sack of gold. But, when we tried to pick it up, the pole snapped in two.

"It's too heavy," I said. "We will have to leave some gold."

We went back to the pool and set two goblets and two bowls in the place where we had camped the night before. They sat there as a monument to the last night we had spent in the valley. I then went into the temple and retrieved the small ironwood tree we had used to move the altar. Bringing it outside, we tied our hammock to it, hoisted it onto our shoulders, and headed out toward the western wall.

The sun had already dropped behind the wall by the time we reached the tunnel that led out of the valley. Moving through the cave was difficult with our large package. At times we were forced to set it on the ground and drag it through the narrow pass between the rocks. Once the rocks gave way to ice, however, the traveling became all too easy. We merely placed our bundle on the icy ground, straddled it, and slid along the floor of the glacial cave.

Like two children sledding on an icy slope, we raced through the cave over bumps and dips. We bounced until we reached the bottom, where the bundle stopped short, throwing us into the deep, fluffy snow. We landed face-first, side by side in the frigid white powder.

"Are you ok?" I asked, laughing.

"Ok? I am fantastic! I cannot remember when I have had so much fun," he said, brushing the snow off himself.

Suddenly, his laughter fell silent, as he looked out over the horizon. Looking up, I beheld what had struck him dumb. The sky was adorned with all the hues of red, orange, and pink. It was a striking sunset, and nature had on all her colors. It was if she had been waiting for this day to show off the fullness of her beauty.

The clouds hung like fiery mountains in the sky against the purple backdrop of the distant Eldabron Mountains. It was almost too much to behold. I realized at that moment, I had never really appreciated any sunset as much as I did that one.

Sebastian's face held no expression, but his mouth hung open as the miraculous view filled his eyes. I watched in silence as one small tear rolled down his cheek and fell to the frozen ground. I remember feeling ashamed of how I had always taken my freedom for granted. I swore that I would never forget how precious each day really is.

Leaving Sebastian alone with his thoughts, I started packing our things onto the sled I had left by the mouth of the ice cave. Sebastian said nothing when he turned toward me. It was at that moment, when my back was turned, that I felt something cold and squishy hit the back of my head and slide down my neck.

Sebastian burst out laughing. "Oh, is that how it is, is it?" I said, taking up a handful of snow. I ducked behind the sled and threw a fast ball of snow at him, striking him right in the chest. He fell backward to the ground as if he had been hurt, rolled over, jumped to his feet, and threw another snowball at me. We frolicked for some time, then collapsed in the snow, laughing to the sky. There was a moment of silence as we huffed and puffed in the cold evening air.

"I hate to be a spoilsport, but if we don't get started back, we won't reach Malyki's house before morning," I said, catching my breath.

"Well, we best be going, then," he said with a chuckle. We both turned our attention to the packing of the sled.

Once packed, I handed him the whip and said, "Get on the sled. I will pull, as long as you promise not to use that whip." I then picked up the dogs' harnesses, still hitched to the front of the sled.

He laughed and said, "Then, mush, you!" and we started out across the snowbound slopes.

"I'm afraid the dogs were much better at this," I said, laughing at myself. "But we will get there all the same."

The journey across the outer slopes of the Ring of Stone took all night. The heavy load meant, at times, we both had to pull, and at other times we both enjoyed a fine sled ride down some of the steeper hills.

It was dawn by the time we reached Malyki's shack nestled in the woods. Smoke curled from the chimney and there was a light in the window. I pondered the health of my friend and traveling companion, Shamus. News of his demise would surely be a sour note upon my heart. Then, I saw the faint figure of a short, stout person moving on the front porch of Malyki's quaint little shack. It was Shamus! His arms were full of firewood and he stood motionless, staring in our direction.

Suddenly, he threw the wood to the ground and began to call out. "Malyki! Malyki, they are back! They are back!" he cheered. Running as fast as his short legs could carry him, he called out to me, "Tiny! Tiny, is that you?"

"Yes," I answered. "I am ok, but I could use some help!" I said as I plodded along, pulling the sled behind.

Shamus ran up and threw his arms around me, nearly knocking me to the ground.

"Easy, easy! Not so hard," I exclaimed. "I have been walking all night."

"Gosh, it's good to see you," he said. "I was starting to get worried."

"You, worried?" I asked sarcastically.

He dismissed my sarcasm with a wave of his hand, and then said, "Here, let me help you with that." I was surprised at his eagerness to help.

He took hold of the harness and began to pull. Sebastian just smiled at the sight of our reunion. Moments later, we were all inside Malyki's house enjoying the warmth of the fire and a bowl of porridge. Malyki was delighted to see his old friend again, even though he didn't recognize his aged face.

The four of us talked late into the afternoon about the valley, the panther, and our victory over Malice and Avarice. Malyki told me how he labored for two days and nights before the spell on Shamus could be broken. Before nightfall, I finally took the sled back and acquired my horse, Reckless. Even he seemed happy to see me again.

Shamus and I stayed on at the house of Malyki for several weeks, and in that time, I noticed a change in Shamus. Not a big one, but a subtle change in his temperament. On occasion, he even used the words *please* and *thank you*, something that was truly un-Shamus-like.

Sebastian never once missed watching a sunset from the foothills of the Eldabron Mountains. Every day, he would take his flute into the town of Forest Glen and play for the children while they danced and sang. On one occasion, Shamus joined in with the children's merriment, and I remarked to Malyki that Shamus seemed different somehow.

He smiled slightly and confessed to adding a little honeycomb from a forest beehive to the potion with which he healed Shamus. He said it was to sweeten his disposition. I simply said, "Nice touch."

Sebastian stayed in that town, playing games with the children and telling stories to anyone who would listen. And though he had many riches, it was safe to say that the thing he treasured most of all was life itself.

CHAPTER TWELVE

HEART TO HEART

Lynquest turned to the crowd, still hanging on his every word, and said, "So, let it be known that, from that day to this, there has been no one more like a child in his heart than Sebastian Andrews." With that, Lynquest bowed low to the crowd as they applauded his story.

Turning to face Emily, he bowed the deepest of all, and out of his pocket fell a small velvet pouch. It landed at Emily's feet, and she quickly picked it up and handed it back to the kindly old gentleman. As he took it, he bowed low again. This time, as he did, he looked deep into her eyes and smiled a generous smile. He then winked at Emily and whispered, "I shall see you in ten years, Princess." She suddenly remembered the boy who had cast the acorn into the fire and realized it was the same mischievous smile.

As the crowd quieted again, someone yelled out, "What about the old hag, Lynquest?"

"Yeah, yeah," others chimed in. "What about it, Lynquest?" they clamored.

Turning to face the fire, Lynquest lifted his arms high into the air and said, laughing, "Ah, but that is another story entirely." He then threw something into the fire and it exploded into a pillar of blue smoke once more. Stepping into the smoke, he said, "Another time, perhaps, but for now I will bid you all a good night."

When the smoke cleared, he was gone. Emily searched the crowd for him, but he had vanished.

"How did he do that, Father?" Emily asked.

"I don't know," her father answered. "It's just something he does."

By now it was very late, and the once dense crowd of people began to thin as they sought the warmth of their homes. "Come on, Emily. It's very late and we have to get you into bed," said her mother as they walked back to their wagon.

Emily was anything but tired. She climbed aboard the wagon and nestled up against her mother for warmth. Her father climbed up, sat down, and shook the reins. The horses started out down the long road that led out of town. Once outside town, they came upon a young boy walking along the side of the road. As they passed him, Emily looked at the boy's face. He smiled back at Emily and waved.

"It's him!" Emily shouted. "It's Lynquest!"

"Don't be silly," her mother said. "That was just a boy."

"But the stone, he has the Heart of Mater. He can change," said Emily, clasping her mother's arm.

Her father burst out laughing and her mother said, "That's just a story, dear. That's what he does. He tells stories. But they are only stories, after all."

Emily wanted to tell them about the velvet pouch and the child she saw before Lynquest appeared, but she knew they wouldn't believe her, so she quietly sank back into the warmth of her mother's arms.

Once at home, Emily quickly put on her nightclothes and hopped into bed. Her father came in and sat down on the bed next to her. Emily sat up and asked, "Father, do you really think it happened?"

"Oh, I don't know honey-B. There are a lot of strange things in this world, but none are stranger than that old man, that's for sure," he answered. Brushing the hair from Emily's face, he kissed her forehead and said, "When I was a boy, I met the old man and he told me a story. He was as old then as he is now."

"Really?" asked Emily. "Will you tell it to me?"

"Yes, yes," he answered. "Someday I will. Now go to sleep."

A drowsy feeling started to settle in as Emily yawned and snuggled deep into her warm bed. As she drifted off to sleep, she smiled a subtle but confident smile, for she knew that, ruby or not, she would never grow old knowing the secret of the child.

Emily dreamt that night of the old man; of her father and a scepter and a promise unfulfilled. Never in her wildest dreams could she have known that Lynquest's greatest adventure was yet to come, and she would be the key to it all.

THE LEGENDS OF LYNQUEST

TALE OF TWO FACES

CHAPTER ONE

THE GATHERING

In their seventh year, on the day of reckoning—a day held in honor of the end of the Great War—hundreds of children from the city of Salizar and the surrounding countryside assembled in the grand corridor that led to the great hall. An invitation would arrive for each child two weeks after his or her seventh birthday, to attend an audience with the queen on the day of reckoning. No child knew the reason for this audience, only that the queen requested it.

On this particular day of reckoning, some of the children whispered and giggled in the vast echoing chamber of the grand corridor. Two guards stood staunchly before two massive doors; the doors of the great hall that lead to the throne room of the queen. The guards' faces were stern and unchanged by the children's quiet taunting.

Suddenly, one of the gigantic dark wood doors creaked open and a portly gentleman squeezed through. He whispered into one of the guard's ears, to which the guard gave a stern nod, and then returned to his motionless stance. The portly little man then turned and addressed the children.

"Eh-hmm." He cleared his throat. The children fell silent. "My name is Bartholomew Featherbee. You can call me Mr. Featherbee. Now, I don't need to remind you children that this is an audience with the queen. Certain behavior is expected. Any foolishness will not be tolerated and will be dealt with immediately. You shall all enter the room quietly and in rows of four. You will sit where I seat you and will not touch anything. If on the off chance you are asked a question, you will be required to stand and address the queen as Your Highness. It is usually customary to give a slight bow before answering, like thus." Mr. Featherbee placed his hands behind him and bent his balding head toward the crowd of children.

Immediately, laughter rang out from the children and echoed throughout the halls of the palace.

The fat little man stood up straight, glaring at the children, then turned to the guard at his right, saying, "Once, just once, I would like them not to laugh when I do that." He then shook his head and mumbled, "Every year it's the same thing—ha, ha, ha, hee, hee, hee," and he disappeared behind the massive door.

Only a moment or two passed before a gentle rap came at the door. The guards, standing opposite each other, both reached out a hand and swung the doors wide open. Mr. Featherbee stood in the middle of the giant doorway, facing the children with one finger over his mouth. He urged the children to be silent, and then, stepping to the right side of the doorway, he raised his arms.

"You may form a line here," he said, directing the children in front of him.

Once a line was formed, he simply stepped to his left and repeated the motion. At the completion of the fourth line, he spun on his heels and took his place at the front of the parade of children. Without a word, he clicked his heels twice and the guards ushered the children into the room with a wave of their hands. Featherbee stepped briskly in front as they all entered the great hall together. He led them across the glistening marble floor toward a throne of pure gold perched on a platform of white alabaster.

There, a vast carpet with the image of the great battle between this nation, Salucia, and the nation of Kongwana, to the south, stretched out in all directions at the foot of the throne. In the center of the massive carpet was the likeness of the royal scepter. Its long, square shaft was twisted to a point. The sphere at the top of the shaft had a hand that bore four rings. Clutched in the hand was a single rose colored red with a purple hue.

The children marveled and mumbled as they entered the room. Mr. Featherbee began seating the children in a half circle in front of the golden throne, starting on the left and working his way across the room. Once he had completed the task, he turned to the nearest guard and, with a face as serious as a funeral, said, "Tell the queen the children are ready." Then he took his place before the assembly.

Several long moments passed and the gaggle of children began to get restless, whispering and giggling among themselves. Suddenly, a wave of silence fell over the group as they watched a little old lady quietly enter the room. She was finely dressed and wore a stately crown of jewels upon her head. Cradled in her right arm was the royal scepter of Salizar, complete with the four legendary rings of old.

Quietly and without any fanfare, the elegant old matriarch crossed the great hall, ascended to the throne, and took her place as head of state. She then peered out across the room full of young faces as if she were a woman at the market selecting a ripe melon. "No," she said. "No, these won't do at all. Bartholomew!" she said stoutly.

"Yes, my Queen?" asked Mr. Featherbee as he approached the throne.

"I don't like the look of them. Take them away, away with the lot of them!" she snapped.

Featherbee motioned to the guards to gather up the children. The children murmured in fear and began to huddle together, unsure of their fate. The guards drew nearer and nearer, grasping their swords as they came. Just as they were but a few steps away, the queen's eyes fell upon one child seated in the front row; a frail little girl who was clutched something in her hand. It was a single red rose.

Once the girl realized the queen was looking at her, she held the rose up, offering it as a gift to the queen. "Wait!" shouted the queen, as she threw her hand in the air. The guards froze where they stood. One particular guard began to snicker to himself.

The queen glanced over at him and her somber face cracked a subtle smile. "I have decided I like this group. I think I will tell them a story instead."

The children released a collective sigh as the guards returned to their posts, laughing to themselves. "It gets them every year," said one guard, chuckling.

The queen turned her attention back to the rose held out by the little girl. Her eyes filled with compassion as she called the child forward with a wave of her hand. The girl approached the throne, still holding the rose before her.

The kindly matriarch gently took the flower from the girl. "What is your name, child?" asked the queen.

"Holly, Your Majesty," answered the little girl, a nervous trill in her voice.

"Thank you for your gracious gift, Holly." The queen gazed at the rose in the morning light of the great hall. "It is a beautiful rose, my dear."

Holly bowed gently and returned to her seat.

"I, as you probably know, am Queen Emily," she said to the crowd of young faces. "I am known as the Queen of the Eternal Rose."

Her eyes fell upon the royal scepter cradled in her arm. The stem of a single red rose veined its way up the length of the scepter and a full beautiful blossom was held in place by the golden hand bearing the four ancient rings of life. The rose glistened with a strange purple hue, as if the ancient rings provided all the rose's needs for life. She swept the delicate petals of the flower with her finger. A look of fondness came across her face. Perhaps a memory of someone dear to her had surfaced in her mind.

Looking into the faces of the silent group of children, she began to speak, loud and clear. "You have been brought here in your seventh year to hear a story. I have chosen your seventh year because it was at this age that I first met the man known as Lynquest the Great. He came as a storyteller to the small village in which I lived. To call him great, in my opinion, is a vast understatement of the truth.

"He was a man who lived for a thousand years and ventured to the four corners of our world to reunite the sacred rings of Bonangi with the royal scepter of my forefathers. I suppose, in hindsight, it is fitting that I have the burden of telling this tale, being that I was the last person to ever see him.

"In the years before the war, times were troubled. The true king had died and a false king had claimed the throne. The only real heir to the throne, an infant boy, had suddenly disappeared without a trace. All this had taken place long before my birth."

CHAPTER TWO

KEY TO THE PAST

As a child growing up, like most of you children, I was consumed by the stories and legends of Lynquest. I knew most of them by heart. That is how I knew him, by the stories my father had told me, but nothing could have prepared me for the real man.

I had seen him once as a child, as I said. He told a story of the ruby on a cold autumn night in my hometown of Summers Glen. My real introduction to him was years later. It was a lifetime ago, and a whole different world. I was different then. I was a girl trapped in a small town far, far away from the pomp and circumstance of Ironcrest Castle.

It was two weeks after my seventeenth birthday. I spent my days working in the store my father had worked in as a boy, but my afternoons were mine to do with what I wanted. Most of the time, I would go to my special place and watch the people of the town go about their business.

On a particular day, as I sat on one of the large boulders that overlooked my house and the town, I saw Old Lady Hanson battling the wind as she hung her laundry out to dry. Mrs. Jennings was busy scolding one of her eight children for playing in the mud. She caught the boy up by his left ear and dragged him inside, ranting about the mess the whole while. Mr. Tommory was watering his horses in a cloud of dust caused by Mrs. Tommory beating her rugs upwind. The sight of Mr. Tommory's frustration with his wife was somewhat amusing. He tried to yell at her, but could only muster a hacking cough. Eventually he gave up and went on with his chores.

It was a lazy sort of day. The clouds in the sky cast their shadows to the ground and moved slowly across the face of the valley. The movement of one particular cloud took me by surprise. It was much too fast to be a cloud and far too big to be a bird. I watched as it swooped across the length of the valley and disappeared beyond the hill behind me.

A moment or two later, I thought I saw something out of the corner of my eye. Turning to look over my left shoulder, I found nothing but empty sky and the distant hill. I glanced around to reassure myself that I was still alone. I found nothing, and turned my attention back to the town. The clouds had moved on and the people of the town were once again bathed in sunlight. It was at that moment that I noticed my own shadow had grown. It appeared to be taller than before. This puzzled me, until I realized that someone had to be standing behind me.

I quickly spun around to find an old man in a dark cape standing on the hill behind me. "Ah!" I shrieked, as I struggled to keep my balance on the rock I was sitting on.

"I am sorry, Princess. I did not mean to startle you," the man said softly.

"Where did you come from?" I asked in frustration.

The man stepped down from the hilltop above me and approached the rock I was sitting on. He was a man that looked older than dirt, with long white hair. He looked familiar, though I could not tell you why. There was a deep scar beneath his right eye and his face was badly weathered by time, but a warm and friendly smile seemed his most prominent feature.

"Where I am from is not nearly as important as why I am here, Princess," he said calmly.

"All right," I said. "Why are you here?"

"I have come to bring you your birthright, Your Highness."

"Would you stop that? I am not your princess," I snapped.

"Oh yes, you are," he retorted. "You have been since the day you were born, Emily Miller. Or should I say Emily of Millstaff?"

"What? You're crazy, old man! My name is Miller, just like my father's," I said, laughing.

"Your father's name wouldn't be Miller if I hadn't brought him to your grandparents when he was an infant," he said, staring up at me.

"So," I scoffed, "you came all the way from Ironcrest Castle to tell me I'm a princess?"

"Yes, Your Highness," he answered plainly.

"What's the matter? Couldn't the kingdom afford to send a younger man?" I asked, snickering.

A big smile came over his face and he burst out laughing. "Good, good," he said. "That is just how I had hoped you would be—painfully honest."

"Well, you have to admit, it sounds a little hard to believe," I said, chuckling under my breath.

"Hard to believe, perhaps, but true nonetheless. Look here, I have brought you a gift." He reached into his breast pocket, pulled out a key, and held it in his outstretched hand.

"A key?" I questioned. "What do I need with a key?"

"Ah, but this is no ordinary key. This is the key to your kingdom. You cannot be a princess without it."

"It looks like an ordinary key to me. A little old, perhaps, but other than that, it is just a key," I said dubiously.

The man turned to look down at the town. "Do you see that dark carriage riding through town?" he asked.

"What, that one?" I said, pointing.

"Yes, that one," he said. "There are two men in that carriage, and soon they will arrive at your house to talk with your father. Why don't you go and see what they want?"

I watched the carriage as it rolled through town and then turned up the road that led to my house. It piqued my interest when I saw the driver jump down and open the door of the carriage. Two men stepped out. I looked at the old man.

He just raised his bushy white eyebrows and smiled. "Well, what are you waiting for?" he said.

I leaped down from my vantage point and started off down the hill to my house.

"Oh, Princess," he called out. I stopped and briefly turned back. "You will need this," he said, tossing me the key. It glistened in the afternoon sun as it flew through the air. I caught it with both hands and sped off down the hill, my dress dragging in the tall grass all the way.

I arrived at the back door just as the gentlemen reached the front. "Goodness, where is the fire?" asked my grandmother, as I rushed past her to reach the door before my father. My efforts were in vain, for my father was already standing in the doorway and addressing the men.

A voice came from beyond the threshold. "Is this the home of one Tobias Miller?"

"Yes, it is. I am Tobias Miller. What can I do for you gentlemen?" asked my father.

"My name is Forrest Greenwald, and this is my esteemed colleague, Eldon Churchill. We have come about a matter most urgent. May we come in?"

"Certainly," said my father, and he swung the door wide open to allow them entry. "Please come in and sit down," said my father. My mother entered the room with a look of concern on her face.

"Thank you, no," said Mr. Greenwald. "I will just say what I have come for. As you may have heard, the dreadful man who called himself our king, King Dorauch, is dead, and fortunately he has left no heir to the throne. So, a massive search has been undertaken to find the true heir to the throne of Ironcrest. I am speaking of the infant child, of course."

"What does that have to do with us?" asked my mother, her voice crackling with concern.

"News of the king's passing had not reached us yet," said my father. "I'm afraid living in such a remote little town has left us out of touch."

"We have come all the way from Ironcrest Castle to answer a letter that arrived shortly after the would-be king's death," said Mr. Churchill.

"Yes, the letter refers to you as the true heir to the crown of Ironcrest," Greenwald added.

"Me?" exclaimed my father with a chuckle. "I'm afraid you've been misled, gentlemen. I am the only son of Thomas and June Miller."

"No, wait!" said my grandmother as she stepped from the kitchen. Silence fell over the room and all eyes turned to her. "I had hoped that I would never have to say these words," she said softly. "But no, son, you are not of my womb."

"What?" remarked my father in astonishment. "I think I had better sit down," he said, bewildered.

"Your father and I had been married and living just outside Salizar for four years when this elderly man came to us, holding you in his arms. This was before we came to this town, you understand? We had tried many times to have children of our own, but it just wasn't to be. Then he brought you to us," she said, looking deep into my father's eyes. "Oh, you were such a beautiful baby. Well, it was like a dream come true, you see. The old man told us that King Dorauch would be searching for you, so we kept you out of sight until we could move to another town. We told everyone you were born on the journey. Once we found Summers Glen, the days turned into months and months turned into years, and now I have this beautiful granddaughter." She lovingly smiled at me while nervously clutching a thin black box.

"What is that in your hands, Grandmama?" I asked.

"Huh?" she said, still lost in the memories. "Oh, this is something the strange old man gave us when he handed us your father. He said to take good care of it until we found the key. We never did find a key to fit it."

My hand, as it rested in my pocket with the key in it, began to sweat. "Grandmama," I said, tightly clutching the key.

"Yes, child," she answered.

"It's funny you should mention...an old man and a key," I stammered.

"Why is that, sweetie?" she asked.

"Because an old man just gave me this," I said, as I held out the key.

The two gentlemen's eyes grew wide as I presented the old-looking key.

"Land sakes," she declared. "Well, it couldn't have been the same old man, honey. This was years ago."

"Well, try the key, Grandmama, let's see if it fits," I said anxiously.

She took the key from my hand and slid it into the keyhole on the front of the box. The eyes of the entire room watched in silent anticipation. It fit perfectly. She turned the lock.

"Come on, Grandmama," I said frantically. "Open it!"

She slowly opened the box. The lid creaked with mystery and suspense. Inside was a single piece of paper, neatly folded and sealed.

Mr. Greenwald reached out his hand. "May I?" he asked politely.

"Please," my grandmother answered. "I don't think I could read it, anyway. My eyes aren't what they used to be."

Mr. Greenwald reached into the box and retrieved the letter. He carefully inspected it, making sure not to damage the wax seal. "Look here!" he exclaimed. "It truly is the royal seal with the Millstaff crest. I have seen His Highness use it many times."

"Should we open it here?" asked Mr. Churchill.

"We must," Greenwald answered. "This is what we came for." Mr. Greenwald's fat little fingers broke the seal and opened the letter. Quickly, he skimmed through the writing, checking the handwriting, the words that were used, and even the ink and paper it was written on. "It is from him," said Greenwald.

"Him who?" asked Mr. Churchill frantically. "The suspense is killing me. For God's sake, just read the letter, Forrest!" he snapped.

"None other than King Malcolm of Millstaff himself. He penned the letter with his own hand. Look, it's signed and stamped with His Majesty's royal ring. It reads:"

Dear Son,

I am sorry that I couldn't be there to watch you grow up.

But, times being what they are, I have had to send you away for your own protection. An imposter has laid siege to the throne and will stop at nothing to ensure that the Millstaff name is lost forever.

I myself have fallen ill and do not have much time left. I have placed you in the capable hands of a loyal subject. He will make sure you have a good home with lots of love. Not even I will know where you are. It is better to keep your identity secret until the appropriate time.

Please forgive me, son, for the course I had to take. My greatest wish is that you should rule with a strong but compassionate hand. I know it is an awful responsibility, but it is my only legacy, and your true birthright.

You have my undying love. Now, take the crown and restore the Millstaff name to its former greatness. To prove that my hand penned this letter, I have stamped it with the royal ring and placed the ring with the letter. Wear it with pride, son: it is the key to your kingdom.

Eternally,

Your father

Malcolm of Millstaff

Immediately, the two gentlemen searched the box for the ring, but found nothing.

"What does all this mean?" asked my mother.

"I suppose…it means you and your family should return with us to Salizar until we can determine who the author of this letter is," said Mr. Churchill.

"Of course, if the ring were there, there would be no doubt as to the letter's authenticity," said Mr. Greenwald plainly.

"Yes, yes," said Mr. Churchill. "You and your family shall be guests of the palace until we can get this whole business sorted out. We will leave the letter in your charge until you have a chance to put your things in order. Mr. Greenwald and I will return in a day, to escort you to the palace."

"Please have your things packed and be ready to go by noon tomorrow," said Mr. Greenwald.

My father just sat there with a blank look on his face. "What's the matter, Father?" I asked. He looked as if he was going to be sick. The two gentlemen just stared at my father like they were waiting for an answer.

"I…I…I," he stammered clumsily. "I don't know what to say. I am at a loss for words."

"You will come with us to Ironcrest Castle, won't you?" asked Mr. Greenwald.

"Yes, yes, of course," he answered. "I just need time to take this all in."

"I wish we could afford you more time, but there are certain factions that would take this opportunity to seize the throne. We should return to the palace as soon as possible," said Mr. Churchill.

"You should tell no one about this matter," said Greenwald firmly. "If you truly are the rightful heir, then no one must know until your coronation."

"True," said Mr. Churchill. "We will have to be very careful not to draw too much attention to our party once we are on the road. If someone asks you, say that you are going to visit family, and leave it at that."

"Just don't say where!" added Mr. Greenwald. "We will leave you for now and return tomorrow. Until then, we bid you a good afternoon."

Mr. Churchill politely bowed his head to my father and mother as he reached for the door. Mr. Greenwald gave my father an awkward look of appreciation as he turned to leave.

I heard the door close behind them, and just like that, we were left in the wake of their strange, life-changing visit. My father stood, looked down at the floor, and shook his head as he moved toward the door.

"Tobias?" my grandmother inquired lovingly.

"No…it's ok, Mother. I just need some time to think," he said, placing a reassuring hand gently on her shoulder as he walked by her.

There was a long, awkward moment of silence after he left the room.

"I suppose he needs some time alone. Maybe I'll start packing," said my mother.

"Here, I'll help," said my grandmother.

That left me standing all alone with my thoughts. I pondered what all this would mean to me. I would be a princess, with servants of my own and ladies-in-waiting to take care of my every need. I have to admit, the idea sounded rather appealing. *Wait a minute*, I thought. *The old man could probably shed some light on the letter.* I scampered through the kitchen and out the back door. I marched up the hillside to the place where I had seen the old man.

There, upon the very rock I had been sitting on, was my father, silently staring out at the town in which he had grown up.

"Are you ok, Papa?" I asked curiously.

"Oh, yes, honey- B. I'll be all right. It's just that all this seems like some cruel joke, that's all. I am a schoolteacher, what do I know about ruling a kingdom?"

"You mean you don't want to be king?" I asked, surprised.

"It's not that," he said. "There is something else that has been bothering me my whole life. Tell me, honey, do you think a person can avoid his destiny?"

"What do you mean, Father? What is it that you want to avoid?"

"There has been something dark that has been overshadowing me since I was a boy. A voice that keeps whispering to me, calling to me," he said.

"What on earth do you mean?" I asked.

"Oh, never mind," he said. "It's probably nothing."

"Don't you think it would be grand to be king?"

"Now, don't misunderstand me," he said, looking down from the rock. "The prospect of being king sounds exciting, but not all things are as good as they sound. There was a time long ago when my thoughts were filled with aspirations of greatness."

"So what happened?" I asked.

"Oh, I don't know, honey- B. Somewhere along the line, I redefined what is truly great. You see, a king makes his mark in the world by making laws and governing his fellow men. When he passes on, he leaves them behind as his gift to the world: to be changed or disobeyed. A teacher, on the other hand, gives his gift to the children, who use this gift for the rest of their lives. After I am gone they will still be using my gifts, as will their children, and their children's children. So you see, you do not have to be a king to touch many lives."

"I never thought of it that way, Father," I said.

"But, on the other hand," he added, "as king, I can improve the learning system throughout the country."

"That's true," I said.

Then he turned to me, smiling, and said, "Nothing really changes for you, does it? You have always been my little princess."

I climbed on top of the rock, sat down next to him, and leaned into him. He wrapped his arm around me and we watched the shimmering sun go down on our little town.

CHAPTER THREE

JOURNEY TO SALIZAR

The following day we rushed around and packed things. We loaded up the wagon and set everything in order. Mr. Williams, next door, promised to watch over things while we were gone.

The two gentlemen arrived promptly at midday, astride two horses preceding the black carriage they had come in the day before. Mr. Greenwald addressed my father as he approached. "Good day, sir. Mr. Churchill and I will ride ahead so as not to draw attention to your carriage." My father agreed cordially and began to load our things onto the carriage. "Would it not be better if I did that for you, sir?" asked Mr. Greenwald politely.

"Thank you, no, that's quite all right," answered my father, smiling.

Mr. Churchill shot a disparaging look at Greenwald. That marked the beginning of an interesting rivalry between the two esteemed colleagues. More and more, I became aware of Greenwald's shameless groveling in my father's presence, a point that was not lost on Mr. Churchill. It seemed that whatever chore my father would undertake, Mr. Greenwald would be there to relieve him of the burden. Even watering the horses appeared to be a task too strenuous for my father, according to Mr. Greenwald. And sure enough, not too far away, Mr. Churchill would be watching, with a puzzled and suspicious look on his face.

This went on for about a week and a half. Then one night, as we camped in the woods not too far off the road, the five of us were just sitting down to eat when Mr. Greenwald approached my mother as she prepared my father's plate.

"I will serve you and your husband, Mrs. Miller, if that is all right with you," he said.

"Oh…I guess that would be all right," she said in a peculiar way.

Greenwald took the tray and transported it to my father as he sat beside the fire. "Here you are, sir, the finest cut of all," he said, holding the tray out to my father.

My father took the tray from him slowly. He didn't quite know what to say.

"Eh-hmm," Mr. Churchill coughed. "Mr. Greenwald," he said in a stern voice, as he smiled to hide his frustration. "Could I have a word with you, please?"

"Certainly, Eldon," Greenwald answered, as he walked to where Churchill was standing, just beyond the trunk that held our kitchenware.

I desperately tried to look like I was searching for something among our things as I listened in on their conversation. "Silverware," I said. "Now, where is that extra silverware?"

"What are you doing?" scowled Mr. Churchill.

"I'm sure I don't know what you mean, Eldon," answered Mr. Greenwald.

"Yes, you do, Forrest. You know very well what I mean. You have been groveling at that man's feet for a week and a half. Explain yourself," said Churchill. His demand was short and to the point.

"I assure you, Eldon, my intentions are noble enough," Greenwald retorted.

"What does that mean?" asked Churchill. "I have known you for over thirty years and I can tell when you are up to something, Forrest Rupert Greenwald."

"Ha, Rupert!" I laughed. I couldn't help myself. *Rupert!* I thought. *And I thought my middle name was bad.* Suddenly, I realized I had exposed my position. I turned to find both of them glaring at me, with eyebrows lowered in a menacing manner. "Ah, there it is," I said, scrambling to find the silverware. I snatched up a soup ladle and nonchalantly walked away.

"We will discuss this matter further over dinner," Churchill barked.

I quickly snatched a plate, gathered all my silverware while still holding the ladle, and tried to find a place to eat close to our escorts, yet far enough away to appear uninterested. I selected a spot at the rear of the carriage in the shadows of the trees that surrounded it. I plopped down on the ground just behind the wheel with a full plate of food and a nosy disposition.

From there, I could hear them just well enough and watch them from between the spokes of the carriage wheel. *This is great!* I thought. *Dinner and a show.* This was probably the most excitement I was going to have on the entire trip. They started whispering to each other, but began to speak louder as they felt no one was listening.

"What is this all about, Forrest?" asked Churchill.

"I was just trying to be polite," answered Greenwald. "I simply thought Mr. Millstaff—"

"Aha!" said Churchill. "You said Millstaff."

"What? No, I didn't," argued Greenwald.

"Oh yes, you did," Churchill objected. "You think he is the heir to the throne."

Greenwald took a deep breath and accepted his defeat. "Well, look at him," he said, gesturing toward my father.

"Yes, Forrest, I see him," said Churchill.

"Well?" said Greenwald. "I know it has been over thirty years, but look. Do you not see the eyes, the strong chin? He even talks like King Malcolm."

Churchill squinted in the direction of my father. "Now that you mention it, he does resemble our good King Malcolm."

"So it is not such a stretch of the imagination, then," said Greenwald.

"Maybe not," said Churchill.

"Well, I have always thought that the position of chief adviser to the king was a most desirable position to hold," said Greenwald with some discomfort.

"Why, Forrest Greenwald, you treacherous little whelp! You know full well that I was to be considered for that position when King Malcolm died," Churchill said with a scowl.

Ooh, this is getting good, I thought to myself.

"Maybe, maybe not," Greenwald scoffed. "Before the good king died, I was the overseer of Ironcrest Castle, the gardens, and the kitchen. Therefore, it stands to reason that I should be considered for the position."

"Ah…but I was his chief diplomat to the northern territories and the clansmen of Lochlorna. I was an important part of the treaty between the tribes," protested Churchill.

"An important part? Ha, ha," Greenwald scoffed. "You held the king's coat as he witnessed the treaty."

Churchill's face turned red with anger. "I signed that treaty as well, you know," Churchill growled.

"That may be so, but we both know that I am the more capable man when it comes to seeing to our new king's needs," snapped Greenwald defiantly.

"Well, we shall see about that!" Churchill barked loudly. He then set his tray on the ground and marched over to where my mother and father were having a peaceful conversation. He took a deep breath and shook off any traces of anger that might be lingering. "Will you or your good lady be having seconds tonight, sir?" he asked with a demeanor that could only be described as aggressive etiquette.

"No…I don't think so, Mr. Churchill. Thank you," replied my father, as he and my mother puzzled over Churchill's sudden interest.

"Please! Call me Eldon. If you should need anything, anything at all, feel free to ask me and I shall fetch it without hesitation."

"Thank you…Eldon? No, we will be just fine," answered my father.

"Why don't you finish your dinner before it gets cold?" asked my mother.

"Very well, sir, madam," he said. Then he gave a slight nod and returned to his seat, glaring at Greenwald with eyes that can only be described as burning coals of rage.

I could not help myself; I began to snicker at the thought of those two disgracing themselves to gain my parents' favor. I watched my mother and father laughing, at our escort's expense, no doubt. Greenwald must have heard me; he shushed Churchill's grumbling and traced the snickering back to me. Glancing up, I found him looking down his nose at me hiding behind the coach.

"Have you heard quite enough, Miss Emily?" he asked with contempt.

"I suppose," I said, still snickering. "I guess I'll eat somewhere else, then, shall I… Rupert?" I took my tray and sat closer to the fire.

Having heard all I needed to, the remainder of the journey would prove to be a trip most entertaining. As far as the actual journey went, I couldn't tell you how long it was.

To my best recollection, there were only two events on the whole trip that were truly noteworthy.

The first happened several weeks into the damp, dreary, endless carriage ride. The jostling of the carriage across the rugged ground made reading rather difficult, but I had finished all the books I had brought for the journey. I lost myself in staring mindlessly at the gloomy gray clouds hanging low above the ground. It was then that I saw it...or maybe I thought I saw it; a green ribbon slithering through the clouds. It dipped below the fluffy gray mist just long enough for me to see it, and then it was gone. Rubbing my eyes, I looked into the mist, but it offered up only the gray haze and the endless road that lay before us.

"Emily!" my mother nagged. "Pull your head back inside this carriage right now, young lady. You're liable to lose it if you're not careful." She always watched my behavior closer than an old schoolmarm.

The second event that I recall took us all by surprise. We were nearing the end of our tiring journey and were approaching a bluff that overlooks the city of Salizar.

Greenwald and Churchill had reached the bluff before us, when suddenly a mighty wind came from out of nowhere and stirred up the dust and leaves into a swirling cloud of confusion. The trees that lined the road swayed violently to and fro in the mighty gale, and the carriage rocked back and forth. The team of horses pulling the carriage was at full run; without warning, they came to a complete halt with a jolt. We were all tossed around inside like thrashing wheat.

The coachman called out, "Easy, now, easy."

An ominous shadow swooped down to the ground.

"Dragon!" the coachman cried out.

The horses reared back and the door to the carriage flew open. My father leaped out to steady the team and nearly got trampled. A great dragon stood between our escorts and us.

Greenwald and Churchill turned back, but were kept at a distance by the flailing of the dragon's long green tail.

"Emily!" my mother cried, as I lurched forward and leaped out of the carriage.

There, atop the dragon's massive head, was the old man I had seen before the beginning of our journey. "It's him!" I yelled to my father. "That's the old man who gave me the key."

The dragon lowered his head to the ground, and the old man slid from his vantage point and approached my father.

Greenwald called out, "What is the meaning of this intrusion? This man is a royal diplomat! You have no right to detain us!"

The old man turned to face them and said, "Silence, you! I would talk with the king!" Calling to the dragon, the stranger said, "Subakai, hold them fast until I say. Tobias!" he called to my father. Then he gestured with his hand for my father to follow and led him to the bluff overlooking the city of Salizar.

I watched nervously from beside the carriage. Greenwald and Churchill raged helplessly against the dragon's aggressive posturing. I could hear them bickering between themselves under their breath over whose responsibility it was to watch the carriage. The serpent gave a blood-chilling roar and both of our escorts pulled their horses back slowly, away from the whiplike tail; a whip, I might add, that had an ominous scaly tuft at the end the size of a small shield.

My father and the old man spoke far enough away that they couldn't be heard, but I could see the strange old man pointing to the city and telling him something. Then he reached into his breast pocket and pulled out an object. It was a ring. The gold gleamed in the fleeting light that shone between the clouds. My father held out his hand and the gentleman placed it in his palm, folding his fingers over it in a fist.

The man looked deep into my father's eyes as he held my father's closed fist in his hands. Then he did something I thought most unusual. He flung his arms around my father and hugged him. He hugged him like he had known him all his life.

Once he had released his embrace, he returned to the dragon, saying, "Come, Subakai. I fear we have overstayed our welcome." The dragon lowered his immense head to the ground and the old man once again took his place between the dragon's two massive horns. "Gentlemen," he said, addressing Churchill and Greenwald, "I bid you a good day."

The dragon lunged forward and charged the bluff with outstretched wings. His huge body dropped below sight for a moment, then soared into the horizon and disappeared in the clouds, leaving us completely bewildered.

Immediately, the two sophisticated gentlemen, Eldon and Rupert, began to quarrel as they quickly dismounted and competed on foot toward my father.

"It was your idea to ride ahead," snapped Greenwald.

"How on earth was I to know that a dragon would fall out of the sky? I mean, really!" shouted Churchill angrily.

"You're the ambassador! Why didn't you talk to it!" argued Greenwald.

"Now you're just being ridiculous," snapped Churchill. "You're the head of the palace. Why didn't you tell it to tend to the gardens?"

"Gentlemen, please!" my father commanded. "I have had quite enough of your childish behavior!"

I ran to see my father as he faced off the two gentlemen. When I got there, Greenwald and Churchill were standing in front of my father, hurling questions at him.

"Who was that man? What did he say?" Churchill demanded.

"What was that he gave you? Where did he say he got it?" Greenwald added. "Did he give his name? Well?" asked Churchill. "Say something, won't you?"

My father stood there, holding the ring in his fingers a moment as we all marveled at the sight. It was the royal signature ring, the one that was missing from the little black box.

"It was him," said my father.

"Him who?" inquired Greenwald.

"It was Lynquest," said my father, puzzled. "He said he had been holding this for me and that he wanted to make sure I was the only one to receive it."

"I wonder what that old storyteller has to do with all this," said Churchill.

"Let me see that," said Greenwald.

My father, being cautious, slipped the ring on his finger and held out his hand. Mr. Greenwald stepped forward, plucked the monocle from his breast pocket and examined the ring up close.

"Hmm," he said curiously.

"Well…what do you think, Forrest?" inquired Churchill.

"Exquisite!" exclaimed Greenwald. "Simply exquisite."

"Yes, yes, but is it real, Forrest?" asked Churchill, fighting back his frustration.

"Well, if one takes into consideration the Millstaff crest on either side—"

"Is it authentic or not, you old twit?" demanded Churchill.

"I say!" Greenwald grumbled. "There's no need for insults."

"Well then?" Churchill gestured with his hands for the answer.

"We will have to examine it more closely, of course, but it certainly looks like it," said Greenwald, nodding.

My father noticed the intrigued look on my face, so he held out the ring for my perusal. It was an enormous old ring studded with gems all along the band. The top was flat and square, with the royal crest carved into it, obviously for stamping documents.

"Imagine that," said Greenwald. "After all these years, the true king has come home, King Tobias of Millstaff."

"Long live the king," added Mr. Churchill. Then they both bowed low before my father with their eyes to the ground.

My father turned to face the bluff. Below lay the city of Salizar, stretched out like a blanket of fireflies in the waning light of dusk, a kingdom awaiting its king.

"Beautiful, isn't it?" asked Churchill.

"Yes, quite beautiful," said my father quietly.

"Salizar alone is not the whole of your empire," said Greenwald. "Dorauch the destroyer, as he had come to be known, conquered many of the surrounding territories in your absence."

"They are part of your domain as well, but there is fighting among the different territories," said Churchill. "It's an enormous responsibility for such a new king."

"I stopped you two from fighting, didn't I?" my father quipped. He gazed a moment or two longer at the city, then turned and went back down the hill to the carriage.

After that, the two gentlemen began calling my mother and father Your Highness and Your Grace. I was no longer Miss Emily, but Princess Emily. A title I felt I could get used to, though it did remind me of that day when this all began.

As I climbed back into the carriage, my eyes were drawn once more to the distant bluff. So many questions, so many possibilities, and somehow, I knew it all had to do with that strange little old man, Tiny Lynquest.

CHAPTER FOUR

STRANGE BEGINNINGS

Once we were settled in the carriage for the remainder of our journey, I watched Churchill quickly pen a letter, which was immediately signed by both gentlemen. My father then sealed the letter, using the ring for the very first time. Greenwald would bear the letter to Ironcrest Castle, while Churchill escorted us to an inn just outside the city for the night.

We were up early the next morning. Churchill had slept in the coach, and he and the coachman had taken turns watching over us. They were both more than a little groggy the next morning and slow to move, but move they did, bright and early.

"We had better be going," said Churchill as he hustled us into the carriage. "There is no telling what kind of greeting we will receive once we're at the palace. We will enter the palace quietly through the garden gate. No one should notice us there." He then said to my father, "I mean no offense, but I still would like to converse with the other advisers, so we can settle this matter before your coronation."

"I understand completely," said my father.

I watched as Churchill mounted his horse and my father climbed back into the coach. The coachman called out, "We'd best be off!" He snapped the reins and yelled to the horses, "Hyah!" The carriage started with a jerk and we were on our way. It wasn't long before we had arrived at the entrance to the city.

Two towers rose high into the air on either side of a massive gate. The walls connected to the towers seemed to go on forever in both directions. *Salizar must be immense*, I marveled to myself. Three guards on either side of the gate paid us no mind as we passed into the city along with a throng of other people; merchants, farmers, and the like.

All manner of life, busy with the business of living, stirred around us as we passed. There were mothers clutching their children by the hand as they sauntered through the city streets choked with merchants selling goods and produce, oxen and sheep, poultry and fish; all this for sale at the going rate of exchange. It was just as one would imagine a normal day would be like in a big city. The restless crowd bustled through the streets, and I, like a spider in the corner of a crowded room, watched as people went about their business, indifferent to our presence.

My attention was caught by a strange disturbance in the street up ahead. The people seemed to be parting right down the middle of the road. I tugged at my father's coat and pointed in the direction of the disturbance. Churchill's face grew very grim at the sight of the commotion as it made its way through the street toward us. The masses fell silent at its approach. To my amazement, I saw a chair riding atop the shoulders of six large men.

"It's the throne," groaned Churchill with great frustration. "No," he added. "It wasn't supposed to be this way."

The procession stopped before our humble carriage, and an ominous character, dressed all in white, stepped forward. The hood of his robe hung loosely about his pale, sickly face. His long white hair hung down like silk. His eyes glowed with a bitter intensity. There was a sinister demeanor to the man. His face seemed to radiate an unnatural light. If I didn't know better, I would have said he was already dead.

Churchill burst through the ranks of the crowd and glared at the apparition that stood before us. "Elexi," he said, grinding his teeth.

The pale specter's mouth formed a subtle, wicked grin as he saw the discontented Churchill. Then he threw his hands in the air and spoke directly to the watching crowd. "Good people of Salizar, the gods of fortune have smiled upon you today! For today, your true king has returned to you. Behold, I give you Tobias of Millstaff, son of Malcolm and true heir to the throne!"

The multitude erupted in commotion. The door to the carriage was flung open, and my father was plucked from his seat and carried above the heads of the mob. Hand-to-hand, they passed him along, chanting "Hail, hail, King Tobias of Millstaff! Long live the King of Salizar!" They all shouted with one voice as they went.

Churchill struggled through the swarm of people, but it was too late. My father was swept away on the shoulders of his newfound fame. He looked back at Mother and me with a look of helpless desperation. He was seated on the throne and handed the royal scepter by the grim-faced man.

Churchill shouted above the din, "I will have words with you, Elexi, just wait! The nobles will hear of this outrage!"

Elexi just smiled and called to the crowd, "Take our new king to the palace. Take him to Ironcrest Castle."

Churchill turned, grabbed the horses' bridles, and led our carriage down a narrow alley. The streets were thick with people hampering our way, but Churchill was undaunted. With a dogged determination he forced his way through the crowd, yelling, "Clear the way! Let us through!"

Finally, the alley opened onto a much wider street with fewer people to bar our way. We followed this street until it led directly to the palace wall, so high that one could scarcely see the tops of the trees on the other side. We followed the wall to the west until we came to a small gate where Greenwald waited. His portly physique and nervous demeanor made him look like a fattened hog standing outside a butcher shop.

As we approached Greenwald, Churchill staggered up. With a red face and out of breath, he stammered, "What…happened? I thought I told you to give the letter to Edmond?"

"I tried," Greenwald retorted. "But Elexi reached me first and seized the letter. He has control of the palace guards. He is up to no good, Eldon, I just know it. What are we going to do?"

"Now calm down, Forrest," said Churchill. "We have to keep a clear head. We shouldn't do anything until we can find out what his plans are. So for now, just agree with whatever he says. Right now we need to talk to the rest of the council."

"That's just the thing," said Greenwald. "They're not here."

"What?" snapped Churchill.

"They're gone. Apparently dismissed by none other than Elexi himself," said Greenwald.

"This is troubling news, Forrest, troubling news indeed. Well, our first priority is to the king and his family, so you take the queen and the princess to their quarters and I shall see to the king—that is, once I find him," said Churchill.

"Very good," Greenwald mumbled.

He opened the door to the carriage and took our hands as we stepped to the ground. He dismissed the coachman and led us through the garden gate. We passed through the gardens and the aviary, entered the palace, and went up to our rooms.

After riding for three weeks in a cramped carriage, it was wonderful to feel the soft, warm goodness of a feather bed. And what a grand bed it was, too, an enormous bed with curtains and a canopy, in a room with a fireplace and a vanity, complete with combs, brushes, and an assortment of perfumes. There was even a balcony overlooking the gardens.

"All this is mine?" I said, as I looked around the room. "I love it!" I exclaimed, and threw myself on the bed.

Greenwald smiled with delight at the sight of me reveling in my new quarters. "I'm glad you approve, Your Highness," he said. "Maribelle will attend you while I see your mother to her quarters."

A heavyset middle-aged woman stepped into the room. "Good afternoon, Your Highness," she said.

"Please," I said, "call me Emily."

"I beg your pardon, Miss, but it is not proper to call you by your first name."

"Why not?" I asked.

"Because it would not be respectful," she said. "Besides, I would get in trouble if anyone heard me."

I looked at Maribelle's face. She had big brown eyes that reminded me of my grandmother. "You have a very kind face, Maribelle," I said.

"It's nice of you to say so, Your Highness," said Maribelle.

"There you go again," I said. "Look, call me Miss Emily, or even Princess, anything but Your Highness. It's a little too proper for me, ok?"

"As you wish, Miss Emily." She smiled gently as the words left her lips.

"I can see we are going to get along swimmingly, Maribelle," I said.

"Yes, Princess, I believe we will," she said. "Shall I see if we can find you something to wear for supper tonight?"

"Yes, Maribelle, that would be nice," I said, trying to sound regal. Having a woman almost three times my age at my beck and call was more than just a little awkward, but she was so sweet and kind, she made me feel right at home.

By this time Churchill had caught up with my father. He and Elexi were in the war room, a large room with three enormous windows that faced east. Except for a big oak table that took up most of the space in the room, it was rather plain. The table had to have been built inside the room, for it was much too large to fit through the doors, even though the doors themselves were large and imposing.

"Yes, I thought I might find you in here, Elexi," said Churchill as he entered. "Planning your attack on another defenseless territory?"

"Eldon!" exclaimed Elexi. "I am surprised at you. You are going to give our new king a bad impression of me."

"Oh really?" mocked Churchill. "I thought I was just being honest. Let's see…the last time I saw you was just after your master, that bloodthirsty Dorauch, passed away. You were busy fleeing the palace with your tail tucked between your legs, weren't you?"

"Yes, it is true," Elexi said with a scowl. "I did leave rather hastily, but then I realized my talents as a chancellor could still be useful to the new king. Besides, I couldn't leave my good friend General Zimond. You remember him, don't you, the head of the royal guard?" His eyes grew wide with the weight of his words.

"Since when did you ever get along with General Zimond?" asked Churchill.

"I guess you could say we finally found common ground." A sinister smile crept onto Elexi's face.

"Why, you little snake!" Churchill blurted out in rage. "If you think I'm going to let you—"

"Gentlemen, please," said my father. "Can we have some semblance of unity here? If I am to be king, I am going to need all the advice I can get, so if you don't mind, let's keep our discussions on the affairs of the country!"

"Very good, sire," Elexi groveled. "Please accept my humblest apologies."

"As you wish," Churchill grumbled.

Churchill approached the table where my father and Elexi were standing, on which was painted the whole known land, conquered and unconquered territories alike.

"As I was saying, sire, this region here has been rebelling against our rule for quite some time," Elexi said, pointing a bony finger to the map. "What shall we do?"

Churchill's eyes floated down to the position on the table just southeast of our grand city, along the coast. "Those are the Auquaterian people, Your Highness," said Churchill. "They were once a proud people—that is, until Dorauch imposed his will on them."

"So theirs was one of the territories that Dorauch conquered?" said my father.

"Yes, sire," answered Elexi.

"Did they have a king of their own?" asked my father.

"Yes, sire, but Dorauch had him slain," Elexi answered rather smugly.

"Then we shall grant them their freedom and restore the rule of that region to the former king's family," said my father quite firmly.

A subtle smirk came across Churchill's face; he knew this would not sit well with Elexi.

"But, but, sire," Elexi stammered. "It will mean losing all those taxes. And the other territories will want their freedom as well."

"Then we shall grant it," said my father.

"What?" Elexi protested. "Surely you jest, sire. This will mean—"

"Look!" snapped my father. "I don't want the blood of Dorauch's rule on my hands! Isn't it better to make allies of the surrounding territories than to try to rule a house that hates you? Yes, it is better to start fresh in the spirit of peace than to continue sowing the seeds of discontent."

"Well spoken, Your Highness," Churchill stated. "Very well spoken indeed."

"No matter," said Elexi. "All this can be discussed in detail after your coronation on Saturday."

"Saturday!" screeched Churchill. "But, that's only two days away."

"Precisely," said Elexi with a devious grin.

"Why so soon?" asked Churchill.

"Well, he is the true heir to the throne, is he not?" Elexi argued. "He has the ring."

"Have you discussed it with the others?" asked Churchill, prying.

"There are no others. I dismissed them all," barked Elexi.

"Under whose authority?" raged Churchill.

"My own!" shouted Elexi. "I was the chief adviser to the most recent king! I was second in command! I felt too many voices might confuse our new king. Besides, Dorauch did well under my tutelage, King Tobias will, too."

"I don't know what you're up to, Elexi, but you won't get away with it. I'll see to that," Churchill sneered.

"Is that a threat, Eldon?" Elexi's eyes gleamed with the prospect of a challenge.

"You had better watch your step. That is all I am saying, because I'll be watching your every move." Churchill marked the moment with his finger in Elexi's face.

Elexi taunted Churchill with a raised eyebrow and a sideways smile. "I wouldn't have it any other way," he remarked.

My father just watched the discourse with a bewildered amusement, as one would do with two arguing children. Churchill, driven to the point of exasperation, bade my father a good afternoon and stormed out of the room in a huff.

Maribelle and I found ourselves with some time on our hands before supper, so she showed me around the palace. It was as beautiful then as it is today; the great halls all adorned with towering columns and lofty ceilings were brightly painted back then with blues and golds, reds and yellows, and of course the draperies all matched the décor. Oh, it was such a sight to behold.

As Maribelle showed me the palace, I noticed an inordinate number of mirrors. There seemed to be at least one in every room; there were two in the war room and four in the throne room. Some were big round mirrors with beveled edges, and others were full-length oval mirrors in ornate frames.

"Why so many mirrors?" I asked.

"They came to the palace sometime after Elexi arrived," said Maribelle. "A gift from some far-off land. Elexi loves them, you know."

"Does he now? I wonder why? They are nice, but still rather plain for a grand palace such as this," I said, as I ogled all the fine paintings and freshly cut flowers.

"Oh yes," she said. "I probably shouldn't say this, but he is really quite vain, you know. I have seen him, many times, standing in front of one of these mirrors talking to himself."

"Ha," I laughed. "I can't imagine him having anything he could possibly be vain about." We both had a good laugh at his expense and then she took me out to see the gardens.

After supper, I retired to my room and watched the onset of night from my window. The lights of Salizar grew brighter and brighter as they danced across the horizon.

The following day was filled with all the pomp and circumstance of learning how to greet visiting dignitaries. I never knew that simple things such as walking, talking, sitting, and dining could be so complicated. The title of Princess had begun to lose its charm. But Maribelle was patient and Greenwald tenacious as we whittled away the hours pacing back and forth improving my royal gait.

Churchill had become a fixed part of Elexi's shadow, who in turn had attached himself to my father's right arm. I chuckled to myself at the heinous display of mistrust between Churchill and the gaunt Elexi. Still, I could see Churchill's concern; there was something truly unsettling about the man.

Father looked more out of place than ever with his two shadows anticipating his every move. Mother fared no better, as she had three ladies-in-waiting. All in all, it must have looked like the circus had come to town and we were training for the main event.

I was so glad to have Maribelle as my tutor. She was as patient as the day was long and we frequently took breaks. On one of the breaks we strolled through the gardens. It seemed the perfect way to relax after one of Greenwald's so-called lessons.

The heart of the garden featured a fountain in a cobblestone courtyard completely covered by wicker arches and vining roses. The light streamed through the white wicker and vines, freckling the granite cobblestones with a soft bright glow. The fountain, a statue of a maiden bathing under the water falling from a golden chalice, with figures of children dancing beneath her, added a soothing sound to the fragrant scent of the pink, white, and red roses.

"I could stay here forever, Maribelle," I said.

"This is one of my favorite places as well, Miss Emily," said Maribelle.

It was then that I noticed a young boy pruning the roses. "Good afternoon," I said as we approached the boy.

"Good afternoon, Princess," he said, turning his youthful face my way. As he did, it suddenly struck me—I had seen him before.

"Don't I know you from somewhere?" I asked.

"Perhaps, Your Highness, but I could not say where," he answered with an impish grin.

"I'm sure of it," I said, probing my memory.

His smile grew wider. He was a small boy, about nine or ten, with steel gray eyes and a smile that reminded me of an elf.

"What's your name?" I asked, still prying.

"Why do you ask, Your Highness? I am just one of the many workers here at Ironcrest Castle," he said. "I work for the groundskeeper, Mr. Hopkins."

"Aren't you a little young to be working at the palace?" I asked.

"No, mum, I am older than I look," he said with a raised eyebrow.

I believe I was making him nervous with my questions. Even Maribelle gave me a look of concern, so I dismissed him, saying, "No matter, I'll remember sooner or later."

I found out from Greenwald only an hour later that the youngest person Mr. Hopkins had hired was twenty-five years old.

This was a minor distraction, due to the fact that my father's coronation was only a day away, and the palace, the court, and indeed, the whole of Salizar, were preparing for the momentous occasion. I had many more lessons to learn before this long day was done.

CHAPTER FIVE

CHANGE OF FACE

On the day of the coronation, the entire palace was up at the first crowing of the cock, preparing for the ceremony. The throne room was adorned with all manner of festive regalia befitting a new king.

Greenwald and Churchill were dressed in their finest clothes and carried themselves in a polished, stately manner. Even Elexi was dressed in formal attire, though his usual white robe still hung on him like a death shroud.

Maribelle laid out the dress I was to wear that day, and Greenwald delivered a wide violet ribbon sash with the letters E. B. M. embroidered in gold across it. "E. B. M.?" said Greenwald curiously. "Hmm, what does the B stand for?" he asked.

"Business," I said sharply. "As in, my own."

"Ah, we shall see," he said with a devious grin. I flashed him a look of contempt before he left the room.

Even before breakfast, my father, my mother, and I were thoroughly bathed, dressed, and groomed to perfection. We were then seated on three thrones that were set before us by eighteen bearers, who hoisted us atop their shoulders, marched into the throne room, and set us in front of the entire assembly—my father in the center, my mother on his right, and me on his left.

We rose to our feet and for three hours we greeted, one by one, every prince, dignitary, or governor that had come to honor my father's ascension to the throne.

It was excruciating!

By the time it was over, my feet felt like I was standing on nails. From the governor of Arabu to the prime minister of Zalcateck, we greeted them all. I had smiled so much that I had a headache from the chin up.

They came bearing gifts of all kinds. The representative of one strange country brought, of all things, a mask of pure white. It was a sinister-looking thing, with deep eyes and a furrowed brow. "How…unique," was all my father could muster when he accepted the gift. Little did I know, then, that that mask would be the object of many sorrows.

As the day wore on, my father gave many speeches, first to the assembly in the throne room, then to the people of Salizar. We stood on a balcony that extended out from the outer wall above the courtyard of the palace.

"Good people of Salizar, as your new king, I will make a solemn promise to you," said my father with outstretched hands. "As your king, I will strive to rule with a compassionate heart. I will strive to temper the rod of judgment with mercy and wisdom. Together we shall make the city of Salizar shine as a star in the heavens. May all other nations look to us for the light of strength and wisdom."

The crowd roared back, cheering, "Long live King Tobias! Long live the house of Millstaff!"

"My friends!" he added. "I promise you, we shall be worthy of the world's admiration!" Again the crowd erupted with cheers of exaltation.

Elexi stepped forward and leaned close my father's ear. I stood near enough to hear him say, "I think that went rather well, wouldn't you say, sire? You have them eating out of your hand."

My father turned to him and said, "I mean it, Elexi. Things are going to change for the better around here."

"Of course, sire, things will change." Elexi's eyes glistened as the words left his lips, then he shrank back into the shadows.

After the speeches, we enjoyed a celebration that lasted into the night: a celebration full of food, dance, and song. My father looked tired, but cheerful. At the evening's end I read the look of relief in my parents' eyes. "Thank goodness that is over with," said my mother, as she shuffled slowly off to her quarters.

It felt good the next day to get into some semi-comfortable clothes and do nothing. My unproductive days consisted of strolls around the grounds and guided excursions into the city, accompanied by Maribelle, of course.

It wasn't until a few days after the coronation that I began to notice strange things occurring at the palace. I was taking my usual midday stroll through the garden when I saw the boy again; he was standing behind an enormous lilac bush. As soon as he noticed me watching him, he took off running.

"Stop!" I yelled. "Please wait!" I tried to pursue him as best I could, but they don't make dresses suitable for running. "Young man, please! I want to talk to you!" I called out, as I struggled to hold the hem of my dress above my knees.

He led me past the aviary, along the eastern wall of the palace, and into the servants' entrance to the kitchen. Determined in my pursuit, I followed. Out of the kitchen, down the corridor, and up the grand stairs he went, with me trailing, out of breath. At the top of the stairs, he bolted to the left across the landing. I caught up to him in the foyer of the war room. There was nowhere he could go. He turned toward me. His face was just as before. That impish grin beamed beneath those steel gray eyes. His clothes were the same except for a long, flowing black cape, the hood of which was draped down his back.

"Why did you run?" I asked, gasping for breath.

He put his finger to his lips and said, "Shhhh." Then he reached back and pulled the hood over his head.

I tried to extend a friendly hand, but as I did, he disappeared; vanished, right before my eyes. I stood there, mouth agape, unsure of what I had just seen. Feeling rather foolish, I looked around dumbfounded, in silence, making sure no one saw me talking to myself. Nothing but the sound of my own racing heart and ragged breathing filled the foyer. I stood for a moment to collect my thoughts, and then I realized there was another sound: the sound of someone's voice. It was faint, but distinct. The sound was coming from the war room.

I quietly moved to the doorway and peeked in. It was Elexi. He stood in front of one of the long oval mirrors. "I must say, you are amazing," he said to his reflection.

I guess he really is vain, I thought to myself.

"Your plan is flawless, Your Worship," he said, still gazing at his image.

Huh, vain and confused, I thought.

"Yes, my Queen. It will be done, just as you command," he added.

"Wow, really confused." I could feel the words slip from my lips. Elexi stopped and looked around. I quickly ducked behind the wall and held my breath. *He heard me. Damn. I wonder if he saw me. I wonder if he'll bother to check.* My mind raced. In a panic, I slipped away as quickly and quietly as I could. Moving rapidly down the stairs, I reached the bottom, turned the corner, and ran squarely into Greenwald.

"My goodness, Princess. Where are you going in such a hurry?" he asked.

"I'm sorry, Rupert. I didn't mean to run you over. Have you seen my father?"

"He is in the throne room, with Eldon, Princess Emily," Greenwald answered with a huff. "I'm on my way there right now to help them catalog the many gifts left by our guests."

"There is something I have to tell him," I said, still panting.

"You look like you have seen a ghost, Princess," he remarked.

"No," I said, "just Elexi."

"That's what I said, a ghost," Greenwald said, chuckling to himself.

"May I join you?" I asked.

"I would be honored, Princess," he said. "So, what is the old codger up to now?" he asked, referring to Elexi.

"Who?" I asked.

"You know. The old ghost, Elexi," he said. "What is he up to now?"

"Oh, nothing, really. Just idle vanity, with his reflection," I said.

"That sounds like Elexi, all right," said Greenwald.

"He is a very, very strange man, Greenwald," I said.

"That, Your Highness, is putting it mildly," he laughed.

As we walked down the great hall, two guards readied themselves for our approach by reaching for the handles of the two massive doors to the throne room. As the doors swung open before us, I saw my father slumped over in his throne, with his chin resting in the palm of his right hand and a bored, far-off look in his eye. He smiled when he saw me enter the room.

"What's wrong, Father?" I asked, kissing him on the cheek.

"Oh, nothing. I'm afraid I don't feel much like a king yet," he mumbled.

Churchill was busy rattling off the gifts and the countries they came from to the royal treasurer. Greenwald went straightaway to pack the fragile ones for storage.

"I thought perhaps we could go for a walk down by the fountain in the gardens," I said.

"That sounds wonderful, honey-B, but I'm afraid I can't just yet. I'm simply too swamped with things to do. Unfortunately, I don't actually get to do them. I just get to oversee them being done. I'm bored to tears," he said, exasperated.

"Papa, I have to tell you something about Elexi," I said softly.

"What about him?" my father asked.

"I saw him talking to his reflection in one of those mirrors," I said.

"So?" he answered. "Vanity isn't against the law, it's just foolish," he said.

"Yeah, but he kept referring to himself as—"

Just then, the doors swung open and in walked Elexi.

"Your Highness!" he said loudly, beaming a shifty smile. "I have been looking all over for you."

"Why should today be any different?" my father responded sarcastically.

Churchill and Greenwald chuckled over that one.

"Sire, you cut me to the quick. I have only concern for your well-being," groveled Elexi.

"I wonder sometimes," said my father.

"Excuse me, Your Highness," said Churchill, "but there is an item missing."

"And what is that?" asked my father.

"A mask from Arcainus, Your Highness," answered Churchill.

"Perhaps Elexi knows where it is," said my father.

"I'm sure I don't, Your Highness, but I will set the servants to the task of finding it right away. "Page!" said Elexi sharply, clapping his hands. A page approached him swiftly. "Tell all the maids and groundskeepers to watch for a plain white mask."

"I'm sorry," said Churchill as he raised a suspicious eyebrow. "I didn't say what it looked like."

There was a moment of awkward silence, and then Elexi retaliated with, "Any chancellor worth his salt will take the time to familiarize himself with the objects of state." Elexi's face turned red with fury.

I remember thinking, *This is one of the few times his face has had any color to it.*

"Now go!" he snapped at the page.

For the rest of that day, there was nowhere my father could go to get away from that pale scarecrow of a man. That night, though, I noticed Elexi was strangely missing while we ate dinner. I hurried through my meal and asked to be excused. I knew he was up to something, and I had every intention of finding out just what that something was.

I moved through the palace as quietly as I could. I checked the war room first, but found nothing, so I checked the throne room, and then the library. Finally, I checked our private quarters. As I turned the corner toward my father's room, I saw Elexi entering his chamber, carrying something under his arm.

It was the mask. I saw the ominous, sorrowful face with its deeply furrowed brow clearly as he opened the door.

It wasn't long after he went in that my father came upstairs. "Hi, honeyB," he said to me in a weary voice. "Turning in early, too, I see."

"Yeah," I said, as I moved to the door of my room.

"Yeah," he said. "It's been a long, long day."

I slipped into my room quietly and left the door ajar, so I could watch my father enter his room, which was across the hall and down from mine. As soon as he disappeared into his room, I slipped back into the hall and crept up to his door.

"Elexi," I heard my father say, "what are you doing here in my private chamber? Won't you leave me in peace?"

"I'm only turning down your bed, sire."

"Oh," said my father. "I'm sorry, Elexi, I'm very tired and a little grouchy."

"I understand," said Elexi. "Oh, by the way, a servant found the mask."

"The what?" my father asked.

"The mask, sire, the gift from Arcainus."

"Oh, oh yes, that," he said.

"Yes, sire. See, I have it right here. And there is a strange inscription on the inside. It reads: *The face of a king is a powerful tool, wear this face to empower your rule.*"

"That is strange, isn't it?" inquired my father. "Maybe that's what I need, Elexi."

"I'm sorry, sire, I'm sure I don't know what you mean."

"To make me feel more like a king," said my father. "I may be a king to you, but inside, I'm just a small town schoolteacher."

"Perhaps it is just what you need, sire," Elexi said with a certain glee in his voice. "I'll just leave it in your room for now. Should you decide to try it on in the morning, it will be here."

I was left with a strong feeling that he was trying to get my father to put the mask on for some strange reason. The doorknob turned slightly and I began to panic, as I was still standing outside with my ear pressed to the door.

It made a *click* as the latch fell out of place. I backed away from the door, expecting Elexi to catch me eavesdropping.

As the door began to creep open, I heard my father say, "Oh, by the way."

"Yes, Your Highness?" said Elexi.

"Which servant was it that recovered the mask?"

Elexi stammered a bit before spitting out, "Maribelle, Your Grace."

His hesitation gave me just enough time to escape to my room and silently close the door. I heard their muffled voices coming from the hall.

"Make sure she is properly rewarded."

"Yes, Your Highness. I will see to it that she is taken care of."

These final words did not rest well on my mind. With all the events of that day spinning in my head, it took quite a while before I could find enough peace of mind to fall asleep. But it eventually came, and night slipped quietly past like the space between the pages of my life.

"Are you going to sleep all day, Miss Emily?" said Maribelle, as she opened the curtains wide.

I remember stirring slightly as the light from the window struck me in the face. "Good morning, Maribelle," I said, rubbing my eyes. "Have you brought breakfast?"

"Breakfast, Princess? Breakfast is sitting stone cold on a tray beside your bed, I'm afraid. You must mean lunch," she smirked.

"Lunch?" I exclaimed. "Is it that late already?"

"Yes, Miss Emily. You must have had a late night."

"I couldn't sleep," I said plainly. "Maribelle?"

"Yes, Princess?" she answered in her usual cheerful fashion.

"Did you find the mask that was missing?"

"Goodness, no," she said. "No one has yet, Princess."

"What do you mean?" I asked.

"Well, all the palace servants eat at the same time in the servants' galley in the kitchen. And, well, that was the scuttlebutt of the morning. No one has yet seen or heard anything about it," said Maribelle with a puzzled look.

"Nothing at all?" I asked.

"No, Princess. That's what we were worried about. We were trying to guess what Elexi will do if it isn't recovered."

"Now, that really worries me!" I said.

"Why is that, Your Highness?"

"Because last I night saw Elexi enter my father's room carrying the mask, and what's worse, he seemed anxious for my father to try it on."

"That doesn't sound good at all, Princess," said Maribelle plainly.

"And what's even stranger is that I overheard him telling my father that you were the one who found it," I said, gesturing to her.

"Me?' Maribelle yelped. "I most certainly did not. I would have remembered a thing like that."

"He is up to something, Maribelle, and I'm going to find out what that something is," I said with determination.

"Be careful, Miss Emily. Elexi can be a treacherous sort. There is no telling what that man is capable of."

"So I've noticed," I said as I rolled out of bed.

I got dressed as fast as I could and rushed downstairs. I had told Maribelle to find Churchill or Greenwald and tell them what I had seen and heard. I was going to find my father and warn him, but when I caught up with him in the throne room, I was in for a shock. He was different somehow. His usual compassionate face was replaced with a pale, sickly one and his brow was furrowed.

Elexi stood close to his left side with his hand on my father's shoulder.

"Are you all right, Papa?" I asked as I approached.

"Of course, daughter, I have never felt better," he said sternly.

Daughter? I thought. *He has never called me that before. When he is upset with me, he usually calls me by my full name, but never daughter!* "It's just that you don't look like you're feeling well," I said, concerned.

"Nonsense! I am on top of the world today," he said with confidence. "In fact, this is the first time I have truly felt like a king."

Elexi watched him closely. I looked deep into my father's eyes for some sign of compassion, which was his trademark, but all I saw was a cold, pale face. The lines of his face were hard and unforgiving, as if they were chiseled from stone.

"Where's Mother?" I asked.

"I have sent her back to live with your grandmother."

"You did what?" I shouted in shock.

"Don't worry, daughter, I will send for her when..." He paused as Elexi tightened his grip on my father's shoulder. "When the time is right," he said, finishing his sentence. Elexi smiled slyly. "Now if you don't mind, I am far too busy for this conversation."

My eyes fell to the floor, as it was the first time that my father had ever said he didn't have time for me.

At that moment, the palace guards brought in a man with his hands and feet shackled. His arms were lashed to a pole, and the wounds on his back and face made it perfectly clear that he had been treated very badly.

"Who is this man?" my father demanded.

"He says he is a merchant from Kongwana, Your Highness," said one of the guards.

"These Kongwanee people are not like us. Are they all dark like this man?"

"Some are even darker, sire," Elexi whispered in his ear.

"Are these Kongwanee well educated?" asked my father.

"I have heard it said, sire, that they are ignorant and unwashed people of a violent nature," Elexi answered with almost a wicked pleasure.

"How do you know this to be true, Father?" I asked, questioning Elexi's intent.

"Elexi is a worldly man, I trust his advice," my father answered.

I could feel the hairs on the back of my neck stand up at the thought of my father trusting that wicked specter of a man.

"How can we trust one so different from ourselves?" said Elexi softly.

"True, true," answered my father, scratching his chin. "What is his name?"

Elexi approached the man and looked into his sorrowful eyes. "What is your name?" he demanded. The man just stared up at him, puzzling over what was being said. "Name! Name! What is your name?" shouted Elexi. Turning to my father, he said, "It is no use, sire, these Kongwanee people are a stubborn lot."

Just then, a page entered the room and presented a piece of paper to Elexi.

"What does it say?" asked my father.

"Ah," said Elexi. "Apparently, Your Highness, he is a seaman on a merchant ship that has recently made port, a midshipman and a carpenter by trade. His name is Marlow Basseti."

The stranger smiled faintly and repeated, "Marlow Basseti," as he pointed to himself.

"It says carpenter, sire, but really, can anyone so savage be that accomplished? I tell you, something sounds suspicious…truly," said Elexi, his eyes beaming with an unholy light.

"Suspicious, you say? Hmm," my father pondered." To the dungeon with him!" ordered my father. "Notify the executioner that we may have need of his services."

"Father, no!" I shouted.

"He could be a spy," snapped my father.

"You mean you would kill him, even if you did not know for sure?" I exclaimed with a scowl.

"No! Please!" the prisoner cried. "Mercy, Sontar."

"Did you hear what he called me?" screamed my father.

"He obviously doesn't know our language!" I argued in his defense. "At least hold him until you can prove he is a spy."

"That shouldn't be hard to do, Your Highness," chirped Elexi.

"Very well then, throw him in the dungeon until I figure out what to do with him!" ordered my father.

I glared at Elexi, then turned and followed the guards as they led the man away. I wanted to make sure the guards didn't mistreat the man left in their charge.

On the way down the grand stairs, I heard a voice calling out, "Princess Emily! Princess Emily!" I looked around to find it was Maribelle, calling from the base of the stairs. I slowed my pace a little to put some space between the guards and us as I reached the bottom of the stairs.

"Did you find Churchill?" I asked frantically.

"No, Miss, nor did I find Mr. Greenwald. They're gone."

"What do you mean by *gone?*" I asked.

"I mean, no one has seen them since last night."

"I bet Elexi is behind this as well," I fumed.

"More than likely, Miss," said Maribelle. "And what of your father, did you talk to him?"

"No. I found him in the throne room, or at least I think it was him," I said, still puzzled at my father's behavior.

"Don't you recognize your own father?" she asked in amazement.

"Well, he looked a little like my father, but he sure didn't act like him. He was in the process of dispensing Elexi's version of justice. That's why I'm going to the dungeon right now, to ensure that a certain prisoner gets treated well. Will you come with me? I really don't want to go alone."

"Certainly, Miss Emily," said Maribelle.

We followed the guards through narrowing halls that led to the very pit of the palace. The dark, damp, stench-ridden shadows of the ever-deepening stairs gave credence to the infamous tales of the bloodthirsty, false King Dorauch. The smell of human sorrow seemed to grow stronger with every echoing footstep. Chilling sounds, like the turning of an ancient lock on a creaking door, whispered doom to any soul unfortunate enough to be led this way. I found it hard not to let my imagination get the best of me.

Finally the guards stopped at a large door. One of them retrieved a key from his belt and unlocked the door. We all crossed the threshold into a hall of cells—dark, cold, and rife with decay. A cell was selected and the prisoner was relieved of the yoke across his shoulders. The guards held him fast by the arms and dragged him into the room. Thrusting him against the wall, they prepared to shackle him to the cold, moss-ridden wall.

"That won't be necessary," I said sharply.

"But, Princess," a guard began to argue.

"I said, it won't be necessary!"

They dropped the shackles and released him into the dark loneliness of this neglected cell. There was a bed of sorts, but it was covered with rotting straw.

Turning to the guard closest to me, I said, "I want clothes and blankets provided for this man, do you hear me?"

"Yes, Your Highness," he answered somberly.

"And he shall be fed no less than twice a day from the servants' kitchen, understand?"

"Yes, Your Highness," was all he said.

"I shall be checking in on him, and I shouldn't like to think that anything unfortunate would befall him while he is here."

The guards exited the room and locked the cell behind them. I peered in at the man; his dispirited brown eyes filled me with such remorse I could hardly contain my frustration. The faint outline of his frail black face and gray hair was all I could make out in the all-consuming shadows of his cell. In the awkward moments of silence that followed, I could hear whispered voices from another cell further down the hall.

"Who else is being held down here?" I asked.

"I don't know, Your Highness," one of the guards answered.

"Very well, leave us," I said sternly.

After they left the hall, I leaned in to Maribelle and whispered, "I think I'm finally getting the hang of this royalty thing." She smiled and put her arm around me, then we wandered down the hall following the sounds of the hushed voices. "Who is there?" I called out.

"Princess, is that you?"

"Greenwald! What on earth are you doing down here?" I said in astonishment.

"I was stolen out of my bed, Your Highness. Eldon is here, too."

"Elexi had us thrown into the dungeon in the middle of the night," said Churchill. "Princess, I fear for your life," he added.

"Yes, Princess," said Greenwald. "You must get yourself away from the palace."

"But what about you? I can't leave you here. Perhaps I can get through to my father," I said as I drew closer to the door.

Looking in, I could see them faintly against the far wall. There was a window above their heads that shone light on the opposite wall too high to be of any use to anyone. They were shackled to the wall in a painful condition. Greenwald's portly shape left no room for comfort of motion with his arms in the air.

"Please, Princess," he said, "try not to worry about us. Talk to your father. You must reason with him."

"I'll try, but it won't be easy. He's not himself since—" I stopped short as I recalled the mask.

"Since when, Princess?" asked Greenwald.

"Well, I think it has something to do with the mask," I said.

"The mask?" asked Churchill.

"Yes. Look, I'll see what I can do. At the very least, I can make sure the conditions are better for you." I called, "Guards! Guards!"

"Yes, Your Highness?" they answered as they burst back into the hall.

"I want these men released, right now!"

"I'm sorry, Princess. We are under strict orders not to move these men. Only your father can change that."

"We shall see about that. At least unchain them from the wall and give them proper bedding at once!"

"Yes, Your Highness, we will do that immediately," one stammered, and they frantically set to the task.

I winked at Maribelle and flashed a quick smile. "Now, let's go see my father. I hope, for your sake, he is in an amiable mood," I said to the guards.

Once we had made our way out of the forsaken bowels of the palace, Maribelle asked, "What are you going to do now?"

"I don't know. I suppose I'll try and talk to my father."

"Will he listen?" she asked.

"I am not sure, but I have to try something. Look," I said, "I want you to go to the kitchen and see to the preparation of the meals for Churchill, Greenwald, and our guest, Mr. Basseti."

"Certainly, Miss Emily. I must say, you're handling this very well," she remarked.

"Thank you, Maribelle, I'm doing my best," I said with a smile. Then I made my way back to the throne room.

When I arrived there, I found my father had gone. *Where would he go?* I thought to myself. I was stumped at first, until I remembered who was shadowing his every move, that dark cloud that always seemed to be looming over his shoulder. *The war room*, I thought with confidence. *It is most certain that Elexi has led him off to the war room.*

Sure enough, I found them hovering over the large table, plotting the next step of Elexi's evil plan, whatever that was. As I entered the room, their backs were turned to me, so I stood motionless for a few minutes and listened.

"I want the rebellion crushed!" ordered my father. "If it is a king they want, they shall have me! Send the regiment of my best troops into that area to enforce peace, and set up a governor that answers solely to me!"

"Brilliant, Your Highness!" cackled Elexi.

"Now, about these treacherous Kongwanee people. I wish to—" My father stopped short, having turned around and found me standing there. His face grew very stern. "What are you doing here?" he demanded.

"I have come to ask why Greenwald and Churchill are being held in the dungeon," I snapped in defiance.

"I do not answer to you, child. I am king!" he bellowed. "They were caught conspiring with our enemies."

"What enemies? When did we get enemies?" I scoffed. "Two days ago we were a peaceful nation. Now we suddenly have enemies!"

"This is the business of the king and should not be discussed with her, Your Highness," Elexi said softly into my father's ear.

"Quite right!" snapped my father. "Remove yourself from my presence, young lady!"

"No! I will not," I said with a scowl. "Not until I find out what Greenwald and Churchill have done wrong, and why they are being held." I stared at my father's face, hardened and white like marble, enraged and full of madness.

Elexi leaned in and whispered, "She could be a liability to your plans, Your Highness. Perhaps we should restrain her."

"You leave me no choice, daughter. Guards! Guards!" he shouted, slamming his long scepter on the table.

Four guards immediately entered the room.

"Take the princess to her quarters and see to it that she does not leave until I say so! Two guards shall be posted outside her door at all times," he commanded.

The two guards closest to me took hold of my arms and began to lead me away. "I can walk on my own, thank you very much!" I scolded, snatching my arms from their grip. They led me away like a common criminal. *Me! His only daughter!* I steamed in silence.

Straight to my room we went, marching as if I was to be executed. Once we were there, a guard cordially opened the door for me and I responded by slamming it in his face. Enraged by my confinement, I began hurling things at the door, starting with abusive words and working my way up to combs, brushes, perfume bottles, and finally, my own shoes. One shoe missed its target and shattered the long oval mirror in my room. Having run out of things to throw, I flung myself across my bed and sank into a fit of tears.

Around evening, I heard voices in the hall. It was Maribelle giving the guards what for, as they were showing her some resistance about entering the room.

"Step aside, you big oaf. I have the princess's dinner here and it's getting cold," barked Maribelle.

"I'm sorry, mum, but we'll have to check with our superiors," said one of the guards.

"Oh, don't be ridiculous. You don't think the king would sentence his own daughter to death by starvation, do you? Who do you think ordered the meal to be brought? She hasn't eaten all day. I'm sure she's famished," retorted Maribelle.

"All right, mum, but we'll have to check that tray."

"Suit yourself," said Maribelle. There was a moment of silence, then the door opened wide and Maribelle entered the room. "My goodness!" she exclaimed. "What natural disaster passed this way?" She carefully stepped through the shards of broken glass and objects lying about my room.

"I guess I went a bit overboard," I said, as I straightened my hair and dress.

"It's quite all right, Princess. It's perfectly understandable after all you've been put through," she said in that gentle voice of hers. "I don't need to ask how the meeting with your father went."

"He's not my father!" I exclaimed. "I don't know who would claim him, but I most certainly do not."

"Here, eat something and you'll feel better," she said, placing the tray next to my bed.

"I'm not hungry," I said, pouting.

Maribelle quietly stepped to the door and closed it. Then, returning to my bedside, she spoke in a hushed voice. "You must eat, Princess. I don't know when you will get another chance."

"What do you mean?" I asked.

"Shhhh," she said. "We have to get you out of here. Your father—I mean, the king—is planning on going to war with Kongwana, and Elexi is making plans for your execution."

"What?" I said, struggling to stifle my voice.

"Shhhh!" urged Maribelle.

"Why are we at war with Kongwana?" I asked.

"I don't know," said Maribelle. "Some foolishness about color and mistrust."

"How am I going to leave? There are guards at the door night and day."

"There is a hidden corridor, behind the headboard of your bed. Someone will lead you through the passageways and beyond the palace gardens to safety. But first, you must eat."

She pulled away the silver shell that covered my meal and reached for the folded napkin that contained my silverware. From it, she pulled out a pair of scissors and a comb.

"What are you going to do with those?" I asked, concerned.

"I'm going to cut your hair."

"But why?" I asked.

"You can't leave out of here looking like that. You'll be recognized in an instant. First, we're going to have to make you look like a boy," she said.

"A boy?"

"Shhhh," she said again. "It's ok, I've raised three sons and have given them haircuts many times," she said, as she snatched up a lock of my hair and snipped it off.

I ate heartily as she cut away. Large clumps of my shiny brown hair fell about me on my bed, and before I knew it, I was staring at my reflection in the silver dome that had covered my dinner plate and a fair-faced young man was staring back at me. I had all the looks of a young man of seventeen.

After I had finished my dinner, Maribelle lifted her dress and removed from her person a set of men's clothes that were strapped to her thigh by a belt. I snickered and fought back a laugh at the sight of her unconventional hiding place.

"Here, put these on, and leave your dress on the bed when you're done." She immediately went to the fireplace and lit a fire. It took a few minutes for the flames to reach their fullness, but once they had, she rolled up the bedsheets, with my hair and dress inside, and cast them on the flames.

"Charlotte, the maid, usually leaves an extra set of bed linens above your closet so she doesn't have to make the long trip to the linen closet," said Maribelle. Sure enough, there was an extra set of sheets, which she promptly put on the bed. Then, turning to the vision of me fully dressed in a groundskeeper's pants, shirt, and cap, she said, "This just won't do. Take off the shirt."

"What's wrong?" I asked.

"There's a little too much of...of...of you standing out," she said. She moved to the window, taking her scissors, and cut a long, wide strip of the satin lining away from the back of the curtain. "Here, hold this," she said, putting the wide satin sash under my arm. Then she wrapped it around my chest once, twice, three times, pulled it tight, and tucked it in.

"Ouch!" I squirmed.

"Shhhh! Do you want us to get caught?" she scolded.

"Of course not," I said. "But I'm not used to being suppressed."

She helped me on with my shirt and cap, and then said, "There, that should do it. Now, let's call your escort." Maribelle opened the doors that led to my balcony overlooking the garden. She lit a lamp and set in on the ledge of the balcony. "I had better go," she said. "If I am with you for too long, the guards will grow suspicious."

She gave me a great big hug and looked at me one last time. Her face looked as if I was her own child who was leaving home for the first time. Then she quickly left, making sure that the guards were afforded only the smallest view of my room. I heard her say to them as she was leaving, "Just turning down her bed, gents, no need to sound the alarm."

Standing in the silence, I gazed at the flickering flame of the lamp, poised upon the ledge. *I wonder what will become of me now*, I thought. The trip to the palace had in no way turned out like I thought it would. I began to feel a little sorry for myself.

Then I heard a sound, a faint tapping that brought me back to my senses and sent me searching for the source. Wandering about the room, I listened, and the tapping led me straight back to my bed.

I leaned next to the headboard and whispered, "Who's there?"

A voice whispered back, "Help me push the bed away from the wall."

I climbed off the bed, placed a foot firmly on the wall, and then, taking hold of the bedpost, pulled with all my might. The grand old bed moved ever so slowly away from the wall. Finally, the familiar face of that young boy peered out of the darkness of the small opening in the wall. He carried a candle in his hand and had a bundle tied with a strap slung over his back.

"Good evening, Princess," he said cheerfully. He reached out his hand and said, "I know you have many questions, but they will all have to wait. There is a wagon just beyond the garden gate, so please, for your own safety, say nothing and move as swiftly as you can."

I nodded my head in acceptance, and stepped into the darkness of the passage in the wall.

He set the candle down momentarily, and we pulled and strained to move the bed firmly back against the wall. I took hold of his thick leather sleeve as he led me into the dark, narrow passage—down darkened corridors and through passages so forgotten that the creatures of the shadows had taken them over with well-spun citadels of silken webs. The dusty floor bore the tracks of rats and mice. I heard laughter coming from the other side of the wall. I remember thinking, *We must be near the guards' barracks. They sound like they are in a drunken state.* The echoes of their laughter sent chills down my spine.

The boy burned away swaths of web with the candle, and sent the crawling things fleeing back into the cracks and holes in the ancient mortar and stone. We moved as swiftly as we could until we arrived at a place where the passage split in two directions. We stopped for a moment and stared at the two empty corridors.

"Which one is it?" I asked in a hushed voice.

"Just a moment," he answered, holding the candle out before his squinting eyes.

"You mean you don't know?" I gasped.

"It has been so long," he said, peering into the black. He began feeling along the walls with his fingers, first the left, then the right. He took a few more steps and the light of his candle revealed a cross carved into one of the granite stones on the right wall. "This way," he said, motioning to me with his hand. The narrow walk seemed to go on forever, winding this way and that and back again. I was thoroughly turned around when finally, the path opened into an old part of the palace.

Hanging ivy draped down the east wall of the castle, covering an ancient doorway from a forgotten time in its history. The burnt stumps of torches still rested in their stanchions on the walls.

"This is where it gets a bit dodgy," he said to me. "We will have to make our way through the garden to the southern gate."

"We'll be spotted for sure," I said.

"Not necessarily," he answered. "But you will have to carry this for me." He slid the bundle off his back and over his shoulder, then handed it to me. It was as long as my arm and at least twice as heavy. It was completely shrouded in black cloth and tied with a strap. I must say it piqued my curiosity.

"What is it?" I asked.

"I will show you later, but first we must get a safe distance from the palace," he said, staring through a parting in the ivy. "For now, I want you to stay close to me and keep a keen eye out for guards."

He reached into a satchel he carried around his waist and pulled from it the long black cape I had seen him in before. He draped it over his shoulders and tied it around his neck. Using his arm, he pulled back the hanging ivy, giving us a view of the moonlit garden. Aside from the movement of the guards upon the wall, the garden was still.

It was a cold, cloudless night, and the brilliance of the full moon left us little in the way of shadows to cling to. We began to creep along the wall within the borders of light and dark. We watched the guards pace along the wall in the distance. Having run out of shadow, we were forced to cross the brightly lit path in the open.

We crouched down low and waited for an opportunity. The two guards atop the wall stopped for a moment to talk, so we scampered across the path and ducked beneath a low bush beside the path. We couldn't stay there long or we would be found, so from there we moved to some larger shrubs and on to a line of trees.

Once we passed the aviary, I felt a little better. I could see the garden gate in the wall. We moved once more to the darkness along the garden maze. As we did, a call came from the palace.

"Secure the perimeter! The royal scepter has been stolen! Secure the perimeter! Secure the perimeter!" The words echoed along the wall.

"Oh, damn!" said the boy, as he watched two guards march toward the gate. We ducked into the maze until they passed.

"What now?" I asked.

"Stay here," he said. "I will try to lead them away. When I do, you make your way past the gate. I will meet you on the other side."

"But what are you going to—" I had to stop short when I realized he was already gone; vanished like before. Watching the guards at the gate, I heard a sound come from the bushes at the other end of the maze.

"What was that?" said one of the guards.

"I heard it, too," said the other guard.

Suddenly, the boy appeared; he was going into one of the many other openings to the maze. "Hey, you! Stop!" yelled one of the guards, and chased after him into the maze. The other guard remained at the gate, still alert to any sound. Once again, the boy appeared out of nowhere, going into the aviary. "Stop where you are, boy!" shouted the other guard, and pursued him into the aviary.

The gate was left unguarded, so I shot like an arrow straight to it, but as I reached it, the first guard returned. "Stop, you!" he shouted at me. I slowly turned to face him, but as

I did, the boy suddenly appeared behind me. He threw his arms around me and whispered, "Don't move, he can't see you."

The guard ran to where we stood and poked around with his sword as if we weren't standing right in front of him. I could smell his foul breath in my face, as he passed unbelievably close. Then, as if we had planned it, a great din rose out of the aviary. It was the other guard. In his zeal to find the boy he disturbed all the birds in the aviary. Squawks of every kind rose from that direction. This alerted the guard, still puzzled by our disappearance. He took up his sword and ran, calling out, "Did you find him? Did you find the boy?" As soon as his back was turned, we bolted through the gate, letting it slam shut as we ran.

Once out of sight of any guards on the wall, he led me to a wagon hitched to a horse. "Climb in the back and cover up with those blankets. Try to get some sleep, while I take us someplace safe."

"This thing is heavy," I said, as I threw the bundle I was carrying into the back of the wagon.

"Careful with that, Princess. You will need it where you are going," he said.

"Where are we going?" I asked.

"Tomorrow," he said. "I will explain everything tomorrow. For now, get some sleep."

I crawled into the back of the wagon and nestled between the sacks of grain and seeds. I covered myself with the warm goodness of a thick wool blanket, and soon the movement of the wagon gently rocked me to sleep.

CHAPTER SIX

PORTS UNKNOWN

I was awakened early the next morning by the boy gently shaking my shoulder. "Wake up, Princess, it's time for us to go," he said. Slowly opening my eyes, I saw the thick ceiling of a dense forest.

"Where are we?" I asked.

"All right, I'll answer all your questions now, Princess," he said.

"How else am I supposed to find out what is going on?" I grumbled.

"True enough," he said, handing me a cup of hot tea, which, by the way, I was all too happy to accept. "We are in the woods north of the Port of Daymond."

"How did you know you could get me out of the palace?"

"I didn't," he said. "It was much easier with your father. Of course, he was just a baby when I smuggled him out." I gave him a look of skepticism as if he were crazy. He just smiled and refilled his cup. "To answer your question from last night, we are on our way to the country of Kongwana."

"Why Kongwana?" I asked.

"To prevent a war," he said plainly.

"But how can I—"

"Do you want your father back or not?" he snapped.

"Of course I do," I replied.

"Then trust me, you are the only one who can set things right. Only you have the vision, Princess," he said, staring into my eyes.

"What vision?" I demanded.

"That's another thing," he said. "Hmm. From now on, I cannot call you Princess Emily."

"Thank goodness," I said. "I am quite sick of all these royal titles."

"From this point on, you should answer to Francis."

"Francis?" I scoffed.

"Yes, Francis Timonds," he said, laughing.

"Couldn't you do any better than that?" I retorted. "That's not a very manly name. And while we're at it, I don't know yours."

"That is because I haven't revealed it to you yet," he said with a beaming smile. "You don't know who I am because I haven't shown you."

"Shown me what? Look, I am getting tired of all this deception. Who are you?" I snapped.

"I can't show up to Daymond looking like this," he said. "I will have to change first."

The boy stepped behind the wagon to change his clothes, while I continued to nurse my hot tea. When he stepped back out, I had to laugh.

"Those clothes are twice your size," I said, snickering.

"But I'm not finished yet," said the boy with a grand smile on his face.

Then he reached into a small velvet pouch he had on a leather cord around his neck and drew from it a slender gold necklace looped through a bright ruby ring. The ruby of the ring shone like wildfire in the morning light. He seemed to enjoy the suspense as I waited to see what was going to happen.

He clasped the ring tightly with his left hand, and soon a rushing sound raced throughout the forest. A sudden blast of air burst forth from the woods, blowing from all directions and circling around him in a whirlwind. The wind whipped at his skin, hair, and clothes, twisting and distorting his features. With a strange magic, he aged right before my eyes. The years fell on him like so many drops of rain, until at last the wind died down and I saw before me the same old man that had started it all—the man who gave me the key.

"Lynquest," I said in amazement.

He had aged so much that I scarcely recognized him. Were it not for the unmistakable steel gray eyes beaming over that wild impish grin, I would not have known that he and the boy were one and the same.

The look of astonishment I wore must have tickled him a little, because he chuckled and said, "What's the matter, lass? You look as if you have never seen me."

"But...but...but how? I mean, why? I mean, what do you have to do with all this?" I stammered.

"Did your father not tell you the stories about me?"

"Of course," I said. "But that was so long ago."

"Think back to when you were young and the stories were new. In your heart of hearts, did you believe them?"

I paused a moment as I searched my memory. "Yes," I said. "Yes, I did. Somehow, I just knew they were true."

"Then why doubt the stories now? Because of time?" he asked. "But you yourself have seen that time is just the breath of life that blows on our bodies. The heart, if strong, remains as young as your dreams."

I shook my head in disbelief and pulled myself to my feet. "Then it's all true? The stories, I mean," I said, scratching my head.

"Well, you will come to understand it all in time," he said. "For now, we'd best be off. Our ship sets sail with the morning tide."

We climbed onto the buckboard and sat down. He took up the reins, gave them a sharp snap, and we were on our way, a seventeen-year-old girl pretending to be a boy and Tiny Lynquest pretending to be her grandfather. I felt ridiculous.

He passed me a basket with a small loaf of bread, a block of cheese, and some grapes. "It's not much," he said. "But you're welcome to anything I have. You're family now." He smiled at me warmly. I could see he was sincere.

"That's good," I said. "Right now, it seems I'm in need of family."

In the distance, a ship sat moored in the harbor, waiting to set sail. "Is that our ship?" I asked.

"Yes," he said with a nod. "The *Swiftly Gale*. Let's hope she's as good as her name. As far as anyone is concerned, we are merchants on our way to the Port of Waltzberg."

"Hey," I said, recalling the events of previous night, "did you hear that guard last night? Someone stole the royal scepter."

"I heard," he said softly.

"I wonder who it was?" I said, pondering the question.

"There is no need to wonder. It was you," he said in a matter-of-fact sort of fashion.

"Me?" I said, startled.

"Yes, you. What do think is in that black bundle I had you carry for me?"

"What? You sneaky old man!" I smirked.

"I look at it this way," he added. "The scepter is the property of the house of Millstaff, and, well, you are a member of that house. So, if you see it my way, it's not really stolen, is it? Besides, the scepter was made for someone with your talents. It really belongs to you."

"I doubt I shall ever understand all this," I said with disgust.

He chuckled and shook his head. "Don't worry, before this is all over, you will understand everything," he said.

"I certainly hope so," I remarked.

As we rolled cautiously through town, the streets became more active the closer we got to the harbor. The crystal-clear morning and the smell of salty sea air greeted us, and filled me with the bittersweet longing for the horizon. A sense of tomorrow came over me. A wonderment of what lies in places where the clouds stretch to meet the sun.

We arrived at the docks and Tiny pulled the wagon to a stop next to the place where the cargo was being loaded. Sailors hurried about the ship making ready to set sail; loading cargo, securing sails, and tending to the livestock that was going to be our dinner while aboard the good ship *Swiftly Gale*. I watched as the men carefully hoisted the heavily laden cargo net amidships and lowered it into the hull.

"Wait here," said Tiny. "I'll speak to the captain about making room for us aboard his ship." He climbed down from the wagon much like any elderly person would have, with both hands firmly planted on the holds provided. It seemed remarkable to me that he would even consider a journey at his time of life.

He strolled up to one of the sailors and asked a question. The man pointed to the helm of the ship. Tiny slowly made his way to where the captain stood and spoke to him. He seemed reluctant to take us aboard at first. They haggled a bit, and then Tiny reached into the leather pouch tied to his waist and offered him something. After a moment of hesitation, the captain took the offering. Calling to his men, he pointed to our wagon full of grain and me sitting conspicuously still.

Tiny ambled down the gangplank as they lowered the cargo net to where the wagon stood. He looked up to me and said, "This is where you play the part of Francis. You have to load the sacks of grain and seed into the net."

"What? Me?"

"Of course, you. They wouldn't expect an old man like me to do it, when I have a young, strong grandson." I climbed into the back of the wagon and began to slowly lift the heavy sacks and throw them into the net, grunting as I did. "Try to make it look easy."

"What do you mean by that?"

"Don't struggle so much," he said. "Remember, you're a strong young man. Nothing or no one intimidates you, least of all some overstuffed sacks of grain."

I lifted my eyes to the man standing on deck, watching me. I looked back with a cold stare, spat on the ground, wiped my chin with one sleeve, then rolled both up and began throwing the sacks with a force that surprised even me, although my back was not so easily fooled. There were ten sacks in all when the last had landed squarely in the net. I reached up, cocked my cap a little to the left, wiped my hand across my nose, and leaped to the ground beside the wagon.

"Good enough?" I asked with confidence.

"Impressive," answered Tiny with a smile.

I followed him up the gangplank and swaggered as I went. I knew I was in for a long trip as we boarded the ship and the crew began making me the focus of all their fun.

"Hey, Bo!" one called out. "Looks like we got us a new lackey, eh?"

"Ha!" another chimed in. "I've been needin' a new boy since we lost the last one to the sharks."

"What about you, Duffy? You need a new boot buffer, eh?"

Duffy was a scraggly, crooked-nosed man with a mop for hair, no shirt, and tattered pants. By the looks of his twisted, calloused bare feet, he hadn't worn shoes since he was old enough to walk. He gave a semi-toothless grin at the comment.

"Hey, mate!" someone called from amidships. "A shoe nare seen his foot, but he is a mite lonely."

"Yeah, mate, be careful he don't try to show you his tattoo."

The ship roared with laughter. I shot Tiny a worried look. He just shook his head.

"Enough!" a voice shouted from the helm.

It was the captain. A tall, straight man who stood at least three hands higher than any man aboard. His face was weathered and hardened by the sea. His eyes were cold and dark, like some furious ocean storm.

"I am Captain Stalwart and this is my ship," he said. "And if you two want passage, you will have to work like the rest." Turning to me, he added, "Since your grandfather is so old, you will have to do the work of two. While you are on this ship, I am law. Do as I say, and you will be allowed to remain on board. Don't, and you'll be tossed overboard with the garbage." My throat grew tight with fear. "Listen up, you swabs. Only the first mate, Stone, and myself will be allowed to go below to check the cargo. Is that clear?"

I looked around to see if any dared answer him. It was dead silent, except for the low creaking of the ship's masts as they gently rocked to and fro. The captain looked around slowly and then turned his eyes to the gulls in the sky, as if they had signaled him.

"Cast off all lines, men, the maiden calls!" he said.

"Maiden? What maiden?" I asked.

"The sea, lad, the sea," said Duffy, as he climbed his way up to the crow's nest.

A short, stout man approached me and said in a gruff voice, "Here, put this to work," and he handed me a mop. The feel of the ship rolling beneath my feet was a new and wonderful sensation. Once we were far enough from shore, the mainsails were unfurled, and with a loud *swoosh*, they filled with the midday breeze. Like a great flag before the sun, they billowed white and bent beneath the ship's weight. I marveled for a moment at the ship's movement, how wind and wave could carry us ever onward to ports unknown.

Turning back to face the fleeting sight of land, I felt a little like I was set adrift on the seas of fate, hoping against hope that I wasn't seeing my home for the last time.

"Hey, boy, get back to work!" The gruff voice of my taskmaster startled me out of my daze. Without a word, I returned to my mop.

Over the next three weeks, the crew took turns making me their lackey. Once, I thought Bo and Grunt were going to fight it out over who was going to order me about. Eventually, they cast lots for me and I became Grunt's for the day. I spent a major part of that afternoon wiping down the ship with linseed oil. My hands had become dry and sore from work. The many blisters I had at the beginning of our journey had long since become hard calluses.

Although I had learned a lot about the life of these men, I still felt somewhat of a lamb among wolves. Bo taught me the topper's job of scaling the masts and securing the rigging. He also taught me how to tie a sheepshank knot when I secured the sails. I even spent some time in the crow's nest as a lookout in place of Duffy. The ship's cook, a man by the name of Catfish, thought I made a good galley boy. Scrubbing pans and tin plates and cleaning the galley had become my job in the evenings after mess.

Another really big drawback that I could see to this way of life was the fact that I was never alone. We ate with the men, we worked with them, and we slept where the men slept. It was a large room directly below the bridge at the stern of the ship.

I had been Francis Timonds for so long that I was beginning to wonder who I really was. The discomfort of the wrap that concealed my secret was becoming increasingly hard to bear. *What I wouldn't give for one day of unrestrained womanhood*, I thought. The wrap made it hard to breathe and was almost impossible to sleep in.

One night, as I struggled to find a comfortable position in which to sleep, I heard the captain and the first mate, Stone, talking on the bridge.

"Evenin', Captain," said Stone.

"We pass the cape tomorrow," said the captain.

"Aye, Captain," said Stone.

"Steer southwest of it. We will give it a wide berth," said the captain.

"Yes, Captain," answered Stone.

"I'll not find my end in the boneyard," said the captain.

These were not comforting words to hear. They made the search for sleep all the more challenging.

The next morning on deck, Tiny pulled me aside. "There is something suspicious about this ship," he said. "They keep constant watch over the cargo hatch. I think the ship is smuggling something, but I don't know what." Then he looked into my tired eyes and whispered, "What's the matter, child? You look weary."

"Thanks," I said. "The way I feel right now, that's a compliment. I didn't sleep last night. This cursed wrap is killing me."

"Well, our journey is almost at its end. There are four more days, perhaps, that's all," he said.

"I may not last that long," I replied. "I have been suppressing these things for three weeks straight. If I don't find some alone time to let my hair down, so to speak, I'll go crazy." My voice resounded with urgency.

"Well, I suppose I could arrange for some time below in the ship's hold," said Tiny.

"But no one is allowed down there," I said.

"Precisely why you will be alone," he answered. "While you are there, I want you to look around and find out exactly what this ship is carrying. I don't believe it is really a merchant ship."

"Tiny?"

"Yes?"

"What's the boneyard?"

"Why, that's a strange question," he answered.

"I heard the captain and first mate, Stone, talking about a place called the boneyard last night. It's just another reason why I didn't get any peace of mind last night."

"The boneyard is a stretch of sea past the Cape of Misfortune. A thousand years ago, it was called the Sea of Fear. The coast along that stretch is rocky, with steep cliffs. It is said that a siren lives among the cliffs and she calls to those ships that are foolish enough to steer too close. The rocks are littered with the skeletons of ships that have fallen victim to her song."

"Look!" I said. "I can see the cape in the distance." I could make out a line of land on the eastern horizon. "Do you think we'll get close enough to see it?" I asked.

"I should hope not," he answered. "At least not while we're aboard. I'll see what I can do about your...eh-hmm...problem."

I went on with my chores, but I kept my eye on the coast as we passed.

A few hours later, Tiny returned bearing a key. He placed it in my hand and said, "Here is the key to the ship's hold where the cargo is kept. I will cause a distraction at the stern. When I do, you go below and have a look around. There you will be safe and alone, for a little while at least."

"Where did you get it?" I asked.

"I 'borrowed' it from Stone," he said. "He just doesn't know it yet. Now, remember, wait for my distraction."

His attention was drawn momentarily from our conversation to the sounds of the sails flapping sporadically in the failing winds. "Hmm," he said. "A calm, that can't be good." Returning his attention to me, he said, "No matter what you hear, don't worry, I will not leave you."

"I don't like the sound of that," I remarked.

"Just go below when you see the coast is clear, understand?"

"Yes," I answered.

I watched as his demeanor changed to that of a feeble old man and he made his way to the stern. He climbed the stairs with such an effort that it started to concern me. At the top, he stood just behind the captain and first mate. Suddenly, he clasped his chest with a gasp and fell against the rail.

"Are you ok, old man?" asked Stone.

The captain rushed to catch him before he hit the deck, but Tiny just waved them off and regained his stance, clutching the rail tightly. The captain and Stone hesitated a moment; then, seeing that everything was all right, they once again turned their backs to him and continued their conversation.

I surveyed the ship to find that not a single man aboard concerned himself with Tiny's antics. As I looked around, I heard a great splash come from the stern, and from the crow's nest came a shout of, "Man overboard!"

What? I thought. I spun around to see what had happened, and Tiny was gone. The captain and Stone were leaning over the rail to search the sea. "Tiny! Um...Grandpa!" I yelled. Bo gave me a strange look as he was rushing to the stern.

Every man aboard was scurrying about the ship, looking over the rail. At that moment, no one was watching me. I made my way carefully to the cargo hatch, bent down, unlocked the gigantic padlock, and quietly slipped below.

There was a lantern hanging from a crossbeam just below the hatch. The flame and oil were carefully maintained by the first mate's inspections. I took the lantern and descended into the belly of the ship. At the base of the stairs was the great space of the hull. The lantern pierced the black with its limited light.

Moving forward only a few steps afforded me the view of many crates shrouded with thick blankets. I pulled one away and uncovered an open crate. I peered in to find scads of swords. I moved on to the next crate and uncovered a myriad of shields, armor, lances, morning stars, and battle-axes. There were enough weapons to supply a small army. Along with these were the odds and ends parts for making catapults, giant crossbows, trebuchets, and other weapons of destruction.

I was so puzzled by the prospect of a merchant ship carrying weapons that I almost forgot why I had come down to this dark, dank, murky realm. I set my light on the floor and unbuttoned my shirt. Tugging at the wrap, I released the grip it had on my chest. *Ohhhh, freedom, what a wonderful feeling,* I thought. I reveled in that feeling, which I had not felt in weeks.

After buttoning up my shirt, I continued my search of the hull. In the bow of the ship I found the sacks of grain that we had brought aboard. I knew one of them contained the scepter. Checking the sacks, I came across one that had been re-stitched. *This one must have the scepter in it,* I thought. I pulled the stitching loose, opened the sack, and drew from it the glistening scepter.

It was captivating. The huge hand at the top of the scepter was at least twice the size of my hand. Two fingers wore the rings that my father had told me about, the white diamond of wisdom and the black stone of strength. The hand itself had all the form and line of my own. The gold was soft to the touch and had the texture of real skin.

I held the fingers against my face and immediately thought of my father. How he used to hold my cheeks in his hands as he kissed my forehead. *Oh, how I miss him.* A tear rolled slowly down my cheek. I had my eyes closed, of course, but I could have sworn that the great thumb of the scepter brushed my tear away.

The ship was motionless in the water. The lack of movement left me feeling uneasy. Staring into the darkness, the grim surroundings seeped into me, filling my soul with sadness. *What am I doing here?* I thought. *Can I ever go back?* The bleakness of my plight seemed insurmountable.

The silence was cut short by a loud crash of the cargo door being thrown open.

"The boy is nowhere on deck, sir," shouted one of the men.

"Then search below," said the captain.

"Aye, Captain," said Stone. "Bring a lantern, this one's gone missing."

I blew out my lantern and hid behind a crate. Barely breathing, I knelt, motionless, clutching the scepter tightly. I watched as the lantern cast a soft glow on the rafters of the hold.

"We know you're down here, Francis. Come on out now and no harm will come to you."

I looked down at the scepter. *Oh no, my wrap.* I had left it on the floor by the sacks of grain.

"Gotcha!" Bo exclaimed, as he clasped his hands tightly around my arms. "Over here!" he called out. "I got him."

As Stone turned the corner his eyes fell on me. Being held with both arms behind me, my true gender was made all too apparent.

"By all the winds that blow, he's a girl!" said Stone.

"And quite a handsome sight, I might add," said Bo.

I looked over my shoulder to see an evil gleam fill Bo's eyes.

"Bring her topside," said Stone, as he snatched the scepter from my hands.

I was brought up on deck where I had the immediate unwanted attention of every man aboard.

"It's a girl, Captain," said Stone.

"I can see that, Stone," quipped the captain.

"Well, what should we do with her?" asked Bo.

"Ya mean ya don't know?" chuckled Duffy. "I've got some idears myself," he added, his cold eyes moving up and down my body.

"Belay that, you dog," said the captain. "It will be me that decides the lady's fate."

"She was carrying this," said Stone, as he handed him the scepter.

"Blimey!" exclaimed Duffy. "It's the royal scepter."

"Well, well," said the captain smugly as he took the scepter. "And I'll wager you a gold piece that you're the missing princess."

"That's right!" I snapped. "My father is the king, so you had better be careful how you treat me!"

"Listen here, missy. Out here, I'm the king. I'll do what I will and damn the consequences. But I already have plans for you. Tie her to the mainmast topside, so I can keep an eye on her. If her father is willing to pay five hundred gold pieces to ready his army against Kongwana, then just think what he will pay for his own daughter!" He laughed heartily as he walked away.

I was taken to the mainmast and lashed tightly to it, hands and feet. My eyes searched the ship for any sign of Tiny.

"If you're looking for Grandpa, you won't find him. He's food for the fish by now, lass," said Bo, as he set the last knot in place.

As the knot was pulled tight, a strange gust of wind blew hard to port. The ship reeled hard to the left, and the call came from the crow's nest, "Storm head comin' in hard, off the starboard side."

"Batten down the hatches!" The captain's voice rang out over the scurrying men. "Secure the rigging! Helmsman, hard to starboard."

"Aye, Captain," said the helmsman.

"No matter what," screamed the captain, "don't let the storm blow us toward the shore! Keep us out of the boneyard."

The wind picked up speed and the waves began crashing over the deck. I struggled in my bindings, to no avail. I was utterly helpless and at the mercy of the tempest.

It was then that I heard it. It began as a soft moan, lost somewhere in the wind. It increased until the wind itself sang, loud and clear above the din of the storm. Strapped to the mast, I could feel it bend to and fro with the force of the wind and the lurching of the ship. Waves crashed high over the deck and pounded me against the mast. I gasped for breath between each wave, and felt the ship falter and sway hard to port.

I turned my eyes to the helm and saw the helmsman standing motionless, his arms at his sides, while the wheel spun wildly out of control. I tried to call out, "Hard to starboard!" But the sound of the thunder and crashing waves stifled my voice.

The next turn of events dumbfounded me completely. I watched in amazement as, one by one, the men leapt into the swirling sea. The men securing the rigging leaped first, as if they were jumping in to save someone. Then, the men on the forward deck; finally, the helmsman himself turned toward the rail and was swept overboard.

The ship's massive sail ripped above my head and flailed wildly in the gale. My body pitched violently with the ship's every movement. Straining to free my hands, I pulled with all my might, and to my amazement, they broke free. I looked down and suddenly felt the rope around my feet fall away. I turned to see Tiny, with his dagger in one hand and the loose end of the rope in the other. I threw my arms around him in a tight hug.

"Now, there's no time for hugs, Princess. We have to be going. Quick, quick, to the galley!" he cried.

We stumbled across the rolling deck and down the stairs. He quickly found two barrels, and hastily emptied of their contents. He took the lids and sealed them tight. Suddenly, the ship rolled hard to port and an avalanche of pots and pans fell out of the cupboards and pummeled us. The seconds turned to hours as I waited to see if the ship would right herself. If we got caught below deck when the ship went down, death would be certain. Slowly the ship raised back up; water rushed down the stairs like a river. Struggling to our feet, we each grabbed a barrel and ascended the stairs.

Once on deck, we lashed the barrels into a cargo net and dragged them to the rail. "On the count of three, we both go over, ok?" yelled Tiny. I nodded my compliance. "One!" he yelled.

Lighting flashed as I stared over his shoulder, and in that flash, I saw huge rocks and the skeletons of other ships lodged on them, dead ahead of our bow.

"Two, three, go!" I screamed. We hurled the net over and plunged into the deep black sea. "Swim! Swim for your life!" I yelled. As the words left my lips, the loud crash of the *Swiftly Gale*'s hull against the rocks sent a wave of fear through me.

I began beating the water with my hands and feet with a vigor that can only be inspired by mortal fear. Tiny, too, was busy clutching the cargo net and thrashing about in the water. An enormous crack split the sound of wind and waves as the forward mast snapped in two from the weight of the mainsail. Huge waves tossed us about, pitching back and forth. We paddled and paddled, until my limbs were numb and weary. The swirling current ushered us onward to the rocky coast, until at last our makeshift float was cast upon the rocks. The force of the impact shattered one of the wooden barrels.

"Where to now?" I asked loudly.

"Up there," he said, pointing to the towering cliff face.

"In this wind?" I asked.

"We have to," he said, "we can't stay here."

I looked back at the crippled *Swiftly Gale*, still rolling in the mighty surf. Half submerged, you could still see her bow and one great mast pitching hard against her rocky grave.

"How do we get up there?" I asked.

Tiny reached for the strap he had slung over his shoulder under his cape. He slid it around his body and small brass horn emerged under his arm. It looked like a ram's horn, only made from polished brass. He placed it to his lips and blew. I strained to hear a sound, but nothing came out. He blew it again, and once again I heard nothing.

"It's not working," I said. "I can't hear anything." He blew it a third time with the same results. "What are you doing? There is nothing coming out!"

"Wait," he said. "Sometimes it takes a moment."

The relentless waves crashed down on our backs and threatened to sweep us up and carry us back out to sea. The sky filled with a rash of lightning and a bolt struck the mast of our floundering ship, setting what was left of her sail on fire. It was in that light that I saw a wave two or three times larger than any other—a wave like no other. A giant mound of water piled up on itself, racing toward us.

"Tiny! Do you see it? It's headed straight for us!" I said, panicking.

"Yes, I know. Get ready to let go of the net!" he yelled.

"What? Are you crazy? We'll be smashed into the cliffs!" I shrieked.

The wall of water broke through the other oncoming waves and surged toward us, a mountainous wall of foam and spray threatening to swallow us up.

"Here he comes!" yelled Tiny.

Just as the wave crested and towered above our little rock, the head of an enormous dragon burst out of the wave. Its claws snatched us from the cargo net, and it soared straight up the side of the cliff face. Into the sky it flew, twisting and turning as it stretched for the clouds, and all the while Tiny and I dangled from its two massive front talons.

Like a ribbon through the sky, it twirled and dove until at last we touched down, light as a feather, on the red mossy ground above the cliffs. The dragon released his delicate grip and Tiny fell to the ground, laughing and rolling around.

"Subakai, you old rascal. You do love your dramatic entrances, don't you?" said Tiny as he laughed.

"I could not resist scaring the young one," said the dragon in a deep, rumbling voice.

I lay on the ground staring at the sky, hearing my heart pounding in my chest and struggling to catch my breath.

Tiny looked over at me and noted, "Success. I believe she is thoroughly frightened, my friend. Once again, I thank you for my life, and for the life of the princess."

The dragon peered down at me. His two gold eyes with slits of black twitched and flexed, trying to bring me into focus. "You are the princess?" he inquired, as his nostrils blasted me with hot dragon breath.

"Yes," I said, staring up at him. "A rather beleaguered princess in exile, but a princess nonetheless."

"I am honored to make your acquaintance, Princess," said Subakai.

"And I am honored to make your acquaintance, Subakai. I have heard many tales of you and Tiny, but never thought…umm." I stumbled a moment to find the words. "Well, you have always been my favorite tale."

He gave a gentle nod of his massive head and backed away. "I suppose," he said, glancing down at Tiny, "I should be going. I shall await you at journey's end."

"But what if we need you?" I asked.

"You needn't worry, Princess, I am never far from the sound of that horn." His eyes smiled as he spoke the words.

"Thank you again, my friend," said Tiny, as he reached up and stroked the dragon's thick white mane.

Subakai turned with a jolt and charged across the vast moss-covered plain, his long body writhing along the ground as his short legs stretched to keep up with his speed. Then, in one motion, he thrust his wings out, lunged off the cliff face, and disappeared into the low-hanging clouds.

We lay on the ground for a moment in the wind and rain, then, in a mysterious turn of fortune, the wind died down and the rain came to an abrupt end. That incessant sound that seemed to screech above the storm also faded with the dying of the wind.

I looked at Tiny and saw that he, too, was puzzled by the weather. That's when I noticed something in his ear, something white and small.

"There's something in your ear, Tiny," I said.

"What?" he asked.

"Your ear, your ear, there is something in it," I said, pointing my finger at his head.

"Oh," he said with a laugh. "It's candle wax. I put it there."

"Why on earth would you put candle wax in your ears?" I asked.

"To protect against the siren's song, of course. If I hadn't done that, I would have ended up in the sea, like the captain and his unfortunate crew."

"Why was I not affected by the siren's song?" I asked.

"The siren Salina is a woman, her song only works on men. You can thank your lucky stars you're a woman, lass," he said.

"Oh, I do," I said. "Believe me, I do."

He pulled the wax from his ears and threw it away.

I tried to stand up, but my hands sank into the deep bloodred moss that covered the ground. Pulling my hands from the muck, I stood and looked around as my boots sank into the mud. I was immediately struck by the vastness of the plain. It seemed to stretch on and on, and it was studded with stagnant pools of dark, still water reflecting the low-hanging clouds.

In the distance, due east, stood two tall bone-white spires set a ways apart from each other. Like two long swords they rose out of the field of blood. Twisted to their points and weathered by time, they stood staunch and stern, threatening the somber sky.

Tiny finally got to his feet and sniffed the air as if he was checking for some fragrant smell.

"Well," I said, "which way now?"

With a raised eyebrow, he flashed an impish grin my way. "We shall see," he said, reaching once again beneath his long black cape. To my surprise, he held out the royal scepter.

"But how?" I asked. "I thought Captain Stalwart had it with him when he jumped overboard."

"You know, he didn't even seem to notice me nicking it while he was listening to the siren's song," Tiny said, chuckling to himself.

Taking the scepter by the hand as if it were a walking stick, he stood it in front of himself, balancing it gently by one finger, and then he let it fall. Oddly enough, when I looked down at the scepter, it was pointing to the southeast. I don't mean it was just lying in that direction, I mean the hand at the top of the scepter was literally pointing its index finger in that direction. My jaw dropped in amazement.

"D-d-did that hand just move?" I asked, shuddering.

He just said, "That way," and smiled at me as he stooped to pick up the scepter.

We crossed the mucky ground; the soil was dark and rich. Each footstep plowed into the mud and uncovered bones, armor, shields, and discarded weapons as we walked. I couldn't explain it, but I could feel a presence in that place, something watching us, something evil overshadowing each step of our awkward trail across the vast plateau of crimson earth.

The reflection of a dark specter flashed across one of the stagnant pools. I turned to look, but it was gone. I saw something out of the corner of my eye in yet another pool as we passed, but each time I looked, there was nothing.

"This is a strange place, Tiny. I feel something evil here," I said. "It makes me uneasy."

"This is the site of many battles of old," he said. "A place where men fought out of fear and ignorance. It was here that an ancient evil drove men to kill each other for the most heinous of reasons."

"What was that?" I asked.

"The color of their skin," he said with a sigh.

My thoughts turned to Marlow Basseti, the dark-skinned man my father had sentenced to the bleak, cold loneliness of the dungeon. I was ashamed of my father for the first time.

"Yes, Princess, you were right to say that your father's behavior was not of his choosing," said Tiny. "This ancient evil has returned and your father is one of its first victims. Even now, your father prepares for war with Kongwana."

"War? But why?" I asked.

"Salina has returned, and she has found a new way to control the hearts of men. We will have to restore the balance to Bonangi."

"How?" I asked.

"With the scepter," he said plainly.

I scanned the horizon, searching for any sign of life; there were only the two spires to the east and a large mound directly in front of us. The mound was approximately the height of two men and the length of five. There were deep gashes in the earth at its base where something very large had piled the earth to make the mound. As we approached this hill, Tiny grew silent. I noticed a change in his demeanor.

"What is wrong, Tiny?" I inquired. "You seem sad."

"You are walking on sacred ground," he answered.

I looked at the deep scars at the base of the mound. "I wonder what made these deep scars in the ground?" I asked.

"It was Subakai. This is where we buried him."

"Him who?" I asked quietly.

Tiny just lowered his head and started up the hill. We slowly made our way to the top of the mound. Tiny knelt down and, with his hand, brushed away the moss from a stone at the top of mound. The stone had but a single man's name etched into it: *Lucias Merriweather*.

"This is where it all started, with a promise. A promise I made a thousand years ago to a friend and mentor. It was Lucias who sent me on my quest to reunite the four rings with the scepter, and that is where you come in," he said.

"Me?" I asked.

"Yes, you," he said. "The scepter was given to your family line. You are the one who has to seal the doorway to the netherworld and restore the balance in men's hearts."

"I'm afraid I still don't completely understand, but whatever I have to do, I will do, to get my father back. I have come this far. There is no turning back now, whatever the consequences," I said with a stern conviction.

"Good, good," he said. "That is what I like to hear. We are far from the end of our journey. It will take the heart of a warrior to see it to its end." Tiny looked down at the headstone with fondness and said, "I have brought her, old friend, just like I said I would. It has been a long road and many journeys traveled, but I will keep my word. I will see the day when Salina can no longer interfere with our world. Emily will put an end to her dark magic and there will be peace." He hesitated a moment, as if he were waiting for an answer, and then rose to his feet and brushed the dirt from his hands. "We best be off. I'd like to find some dry ground to sleep on tonight."

CHAPTER SEVEN

THE TIGER'S EYE

The southern horizon loomed far in the distance, but there could be seen a faint outline of a forest.

"That looks like a forest up ahead," I said.

"Yes. We will camp there for the night, as soon as we find some dry ground," he answered.

As we walked, I began to notice all the old pieces of armor and weapons hidden beneath the crimson moss. "Hey, it's an old battle-ax," I exclaimed, bending over to pick it up.

"Good," he said. "We can probably find a use for that."

It was a little rusted, but still had a fair edge to it. When we finally reached the woods and the red moss gave way to dry ground, we found a decent clearing and I set about gathering wood for a fire. I found a rock to provide a sharper edge on my ax, and in no time, we had more than enough wood to keep a fire lit all night.

Somehow, Tiny had trapped some grouse and we settled in for a fine dinner. It was during our dinner that I noticed a peculiar habit Tiny had. Before he began to eat, he would carefully set out a handkerchief and small shakers of salt and pepper. The salt he would put on his food and the pepper he would sprinkle on himself. He literally shook the pepper over his head and shoulders. When he noticed me watching, he simply asked if I wanted any for my grouse. I politely declined his offer, shrugged my shoulders, and returned to my meal.

As we picked the bones of our supper, Tiny said, "I haven't told you where we are going, have I?"

"Aren't we going to Kongwana?" I asked.

"Not exactly," he said. "We are going to see an old shaman woman that lives outside the small town of Safora. Her name is Morzia Finautwa."

"Why are we going to see her?" I asked.

"She has a gift for you, something I gave her for safekeeping. It's the fourth and final ring. The Tiger's eye, the ring of truth."

The words fell like music on my ears, full of mystery and magic. "Another ring?" I said, surprised.

"This one is yours," he said. "Only you can use it. One of your ancestors gave it to me."

"Which one?" I asked.

"Queen Aleana," he said warmly. Then he smiled and said, "You have her eyes, you know."

"Really? Do I look like her?" I asked eagerly.

"It's not how your eyes look, but what they see, that reminds me of her." A far-off look settled in his eyes, like someone who had just crossed over the boundaries of time and had been smitten by the memory of some melancholy ghost.

"You loved her very much, didn't you?" I pried.

"You see? You do have her eyes. I could never hide anything from her, either," he said, blushing.

"Did you ever tell her?"

"There was nothing to tell, really. She was a queen, and I, a faithful servant to the Crown. A love was impossible, not to mention highly unacceptable. Besides, I have devoted my life to the knighthood of the scepter. I have a promise to keep."

I gazed up at the night sky, searching for a star. Tiny watched as I stared up through the trees and clouds. When I turned my attention back to him, the firelight showed all too well the scars that the years had left on his face—in particular, the one beneath his right eye. It was deep and ran the length of his cheek.

"That's a nasty scar, Tiny. Would you mind if I asked you how it happened?" I knew I shouldn't have asked, but I felt sure it was a story I hadn't heard yet.

"Well, Princess, this is a story that I don't like to tell. Just thinking about it makes my blood run cold. Actually, it was on my quest for the ring of truth in the Far East that I met up with the ugliest, meanest, nastiest creature that had ever crawled from the darkest corner of the underworld. A creature I called the Blackheart."

"The what?" I asked, repulsed by the name. "The Blackheart?" As the words left my lips, I watched the look of true fear appear in his eyes. It was the first time I had seen it there, and the hair on the back of my neck tingled with suspense.

"There are many legends and tales, Princess, that lend themselves to the imagination, but none come close to the dark, horrid, drooling creature whose black blood courses through the veins beneath its transparent skin. This was a beast so gruesome, one could see its dark heart beat within it. As I said, I was in the Far East, searching for the final ring, when I came across an old friend."

"It was Subakai, wasn't it?" I blurted out.

Tiny just looked at me with a smile, and began his tale.

Subakai once told me about a place where the ground trembled constantly, and about a river that disappeared into the ground at the foot of a mighty mountain. So, I packed my possessions and he took me to that place. It was just as he had said. The ground shook beneath our feet as we stood on the bank of a slow-moving river that disappeared into a gaping hole in the mountainside.

As I had done in the past, I fashioned a raft out of large bamboo stalks, loaded my provisions, said good-bye to Subakai, and prepared to embark on the journey into the cavernous unknown. I had brought a small buckler made of iron, and with it four fair-sized stones. With these things, I made a place on my raft to light a fire. Being that the current was slow, I saw no need for a paddle, but I did take a long pole with which to push myself along.

I took one last look at my dear friend as I slipped into the darkness. I neither hoped nor despaired in the moment. I have found that life is like an hourglass; moments like these are easier to take one grain at a time.

The water was too deep for the pole I had brought, but the ceiling was low enough that I could push off it. I had floated along for some time and had lost all sense of direction when the ceiling slanted upward and I was adrift.

There was nothing to push against. There was no ceiling, no walls, and not so much as a breeze to help me along. I squinted my eyes into the murky black. The only sounds the void gave up were those of drops of water falling into the now seemingly motionless river and the still low, constant rumble of the trembling mountain. It felt like being suspended in time, nothing but my tiny raft floating on a sea of darkness.

I stood there, puzzling for a moment what to do next, as I searched the darkness. I heard some flapping of wings. *A bat, perhaps,* I thought. The sound grew nearer and nearer until it seemingly dropped out of the darkness, knocking me down on my raft. I jumped to my feet with my pole in hand and began swinging at the air, but it was too late. Whatever it was had disappeared back into the cave. Once again, I could hear it coming at me from my left side. I set my feet beneath me, raised my bamboo pole, and at the first sight of its silhouette, I swung.

Snap! went my pole as it connected with the beast. It let out a screech and plunged into the water beside my raft. It flailed about violently and then descended into the depths of the river, leaving no trace of what it was or where it went. I looked around frantically and clutched the two halves of my once long pole in anticipation of it resurfacing. But it never came.

Then I saw the warm, familiar flicker of a distant fire. It was so far away that it looked like a speck in the distance. Were it not for the slight smell of smoke, I would not have believed my own eyes. I cursed myself for not bringing a paddle, and then I knelt down and began using my hands to move my tiny raft through the water.

After what seemed like an eternity, I reached a white sandy beach. From the shore, I could see that the cave continued on dry land to the left. To my right was a sight that completely baffled me—a great door flanked by two large urns, with a fire burning in each. The door was hanging off its hinges and was set ajar across the threshold. There were strange claw marks etched deep into it by some animal of which I had no knowledge. I pulled my puny raft onto the soft sand of the beach before turning to examine the urns closer.

The urns burned with an unusual light. Looking into the flames, I could see no wood. A thick black liquid fell in a steady drip from the ceiling of the cave. Both urns were supplied with a constant source of this odd liquid in this way. *They must have been burning for years*, I thought to myself.

When I moved to inspect the door more closely, I accidentally kicked something in the sand. I bent over to pick it up and was completely dumbfounded when I saw a dagger—not just any dagger, but none other than my own. It was the very dagger I had given to the old hag that lived in Kautchitzar while on my quest for the Heart of Mater. It is a family heirloom given to me by my father. I was so ecstatic that I almost forgot where I was.

Looking back at the urns that burned for no one, in a place where no one ever went, and finding my grandfather's dagger in the deepest, darkest corner of nowhere I had ever been, left me more than a little uneasy. My suspicion was that the old hag in Kautchitzar and the siren Salina were somehow connected. I would have to be very mindful of this place and all its dangers.

The door was resting awkwardly against the threshold. The hinges had come loose from the frame and the door sat crooked. There was a fairly large crack between the bottom of the door and the wall of the cave, though I would have to crawl a bit to get through it. I stooped down and peeked in, but once again, I was met with the bleak vision of darkness. Still, I could sense no movement in the dark. So, I retrieved a piece of my broken pole from the raft and tied my handkerchief to one end of it. Dipping it into one of the urns, the soaked handkerchief provided a nice torch.

Returning to the door, I crouched down, lay on my back, and slithered through the opening. When I stood up and turned around, I was faced with a chamber of horrors. The flickering light of my torch revealed a vast room of carcasses hanging from the ceiling—those of cattle, sheep, goats, and dogs. Obviously, I had stumbled on the feeding chamber of some hideous creature.

Among these was also the corpse of a young man. He was dressed like a thief, in dark clothing, and wore gloves and a long, flowing black cape like my own. His face was painted black, like one would do if he were trying to hide in the shadows. All the grisly corpses had part of their necks torn away and it looked as if their flesh had literally been drained from them. Their dry skin clung tightly to their fragile bones.

I looked at the young man's face. A look of tortured misery still showed on his features. Though his eyes were long gone, it was as if he were still crying out for help. I felt quite sick and sorrowful at the sight. Surely, his was a horrific and lonely death.

I noticed his hands and arms were stretched downward toward the ground. At first glance, I thought that was the way they should hang, but it looked like his fingers were reaching for something. Then, I caught a glimpse of that something half glistening in layers of dust below his hands. I knelt down and sifted through the dirt.

There, amid the sand discolored by the young man's blood, was the final piece to the puzzle, the prize I had been searching so many years for—the ring of truth.

How it had come into his possession, and what had brought him to this horrible place, were both a mystery, but I felt sure it was the ring that sealed his fate.

Somehow, I knew, at the bottom of all this was that subterranean soul stealer, Salina. My determination to restore the balance to the spirit of the scepter and seal the doorway to the netherworld forever was forged in stone. More than ever, I wanted to set things right.

I peered down at the ring in my hand. The ring of truth is a single jade tiger's's eye stone set in a band of white gold. I knew nothing of its powers, only its name and of the connection it had with the other three rings of old.

Still clutching the ring in my hand, I cautiously freed the man's feet from the low ceiling. He seemed to be stuck there by some strange white clay that had hardened around his feet. I carefully chipped it away with my dagger and gently lowered his body to the floor. Looking around the chamber, I found some rubble in a corner. I buried him there beneath a pile of rocks. Standing in the silence of that cold, dark emptiness, I couldn't help but feel the loss.

I looked at the stone set in the ring once more and began to wonder what truths it was meant to reveal about the human heart. I must say, I was reluctant to put it on my finger.

Suddenly, I heard a sound outside the door. There was a *whoosh* as something rushed past the door. Clasping the ring tightly in my hand, I quickly snatched up the torch I had stuck in the ground and watched the door. *Whoosh*—once again the sound came, and a shadow swept past the threshold. Then *whoosh*, and with that, the soft glow of the urns outside the door was gone. My torch was the only source of light.

There was a sound of scratching on the door that fell upon my ears like the etchings of doom—the sound of something trying to claw its way through the door. Then, a deep creaking noise that led to a long groan as the big door began to move against its frame. *Crash!* The door finally gave way and landed flat on the floor.

A great blast of air threatened to extinguish my light and a cloud of dust filled the room. I had to protect the flame from the blast with my arm to keep it from going out. Without the light of the urns outside, the doorway was dark and obscured by dust, but I heard something enter the chamber.

Cautiously, I moved toward an ominous shadow in the doorway. I held the torch out in front of me, and there before me was a creature huddled into a ball. It was short and stout, and its back was covered in sparse tufts of stringy black hair.

"Without any warning, it spun around and flung open its enormous bat-like wings. I was thrown to the ground and the torch was knocked from my hand, but I stubbornly held on to the ring as tightly as I could. The torch landed a few steps away. My only light began to flicker as I scrambled to reach it before it went out.

The beast overshadowed me like death itself with its gaping jaws and protruding spiky teeth. White foaming drool oozed from between its jagged teeth. The drool dripped on the floor and immediately hardened into white clay. It was the same white clay that had bound the dead man's feet to the ceiling.

It wasn't hard to figure out—if I didn't do something soon, that young man's fate would be my own.

Like a lightning flash, I moved. Snatching up the torch, I swung it through the air. It flickered a bit and then regained a healthy glow. Holding the flame between the creature and myself, I examined the hideous thing more closely. It tried to shelter its face from the glow of the torch for a moment, but then, it spread its wings and began weaving and bobbing its body back and forth. To and fro, side to side, it moved closer to me as I backed away slowly. It seemed to be looking for a way to get at me without getting too close to the fire.

The underbelly of the animal was thin, pale skin. I could see black twining veins running the length of its enormous wings. Black twisted veins ran all the way out to its bony hook-like claws and covered its long, sinuous, muscular arms. I could even see its big dark heart beating wildly within its sunken rib cage beneath that transparent skin. Two large ears stuck out of either side of its crested skull. The nostrils on the thing were two long slits on what looked to be its forehead. They opened and closed with every foul breath the beast took. The creature's eyes almost seemed useless, as they were merely small black buttons on either side of its head, just above its jaws.

"*Graggik*," it muttered in the dark as it bobbed back and forth. "*Graggik, graggik*." I slowly pulled my grandfather's dagger from my belt. When I did, the demon raised its head, arched its back, and let out a cry that chilled me to the bone. "*Scwuaaaeeek!*" The echoes left my whole body covered in goose bumps, and the hairs on my arms tingled with fear.

I seized the moment with quickness and lunged at the demon, my dagger gleaming. But, as quick as I was, the creature was quicker. It blocked my thrust with a swipe of its claw, so without hesitation, I kicked it as hard as I could in the chest. The beast lost its balance and tumbled backward across the ground. At that moment, I bolted past it through the door and headed to my waiting raft.

Thinking the light might lead it away from me, I set my torch adrift on the raft, pulled the hood of my cape of whispers over my head so I could not be seen, and watched from the mouth of the ever-deepening cave.

The creature emerged from the doorway, puzzled at first by the fire floating on the water. I could see it standing there in the slowly fading light of the torch upon my raft. It stared at the raft out of one side of its head as the river's current slowly pulled the raft away. I felt sure it would follow, but no. Instead, its ears began to twist on both sides of its head, turning this way and that. I came to realize that it couldn't see the raft at all. The demon was listening for something. I held my breath, so as not to make a sound. Still the ears moved frantically back and forth.

Then I heard it. It was soft at first. *Thump, thump…thump, thump*. It was the sound of my own heart throbbing in my ears.

Thump, thump…thump, thump. The sound grew louder with every movement of the creature's large ears. *Thump, thump…thump, thump*.

The beast's ears began to twitch in rhythm, *thump, thump*…twitch, twitch, first the left, then the right. *Thump, thump*…twitch, twitch. *Thump, thump*…twitch, twitch.

It became all too apparent that I was being betrayed by the beating of my own heart. The demon turned its face in my direction, sniffed the air, and grinned a wicked smile. *Time to run for my life*, I thought to myself, and I began to run into the black unknown of that dark tunnel.

Down the tunnel I flew, with the beast just steps behind me. I could hear it screeching in wild rage as it raced along. I stumbled on a rock and my feet floundered as I flew through the air, landing with a thud. The ring I was clutching flew out of my hand.

My fingers scrambled to find the ring in the dirt. Fumbling about in the darkness, I could hear the beast bearing down on me as it methodically lurched toward me. The animal's footsteps rang out clearly over my shoulder, though I didn't bother to look back.

Then, my finger struck upon the ring in the sand. I quickly plucked it from the dirt and slipped it on my finger. Suddenly, I could see. There was no light, but no need for fire—I could see every detail in the dark. Looking back, I saw that it was only steps behind. It lunged for me as I placed my feet in the air.

The demon's full weight came down on my legs and it jaws snapped at me, just beyond my nose. I thrust my legs over my head and rolled across the ground. The creature flew forward and tumbled head over claws. Quickly, I jumped up and ran off down the tunnel.

As I ran frantically through the tunnel, I noticed that the rumblings of the mountain were growing stronger and louder. *Even better*, I thought. *If the beast can't hear me, perhaps I can lose it in the maze of caves.*

As the rumbling grew stronger, I followed all passages that led toward the sound. Soon, the ranting of the creature behind me faded into the more constant roar of the mountain. Not knowing whether I was putting distance between that thing and myself, or whether the mountain was merely drowning it out, I pressed on.

The ring I wore gave off no light and had no apparent sign that it was anything but a nice-looking gem set in white gold, though my sight in the dark was amazing. Even the tracks of various small animals in the sand seemed easy to make out in the utter darkness.

As I drew nearer to the source of the mountain's now thundering rumblings, I began to understand just what made the mountain shake. Then I turned another corner and saw light at the end. I raced to the opening and stood in front of the only thing that could shake a mountain from the inside. "Of course," I said, as I stood in an enormous cavern where the great river cascaded over a tremendous waterfall. *Surely, that demon can't hear me now*, I thought.

The waterfall was so powerful and the ground shook so much that parts of the roof of the cave had fallen into the river. Light streamed in from the crest of the mountain, showering the mist of the falls in a rainbow veil.

Unfortunately for me, this was where my road ended. There was no other way out but the way I came. I saw only a precipice that rose beside the towering falls. I walked to the edge and looked down. A torrent of swirling foam and spray, with not so much as a ledge to step down on, lay before me.

Turning my attention back to the open cave that had led me to my predicament, I hoped that I had lost that hideous thing in the labyrinth of tunnels. It was quite some time before my racing heart calmed down. Though resting in the idea of the Blackheart wandering aimlessly through the maze of caverns, I did not take my eyes off the deepening darkness of that passage.

Soon, my curiosity got the best of me, and I made my way back down the slope to the cave's entrance. As I cautiously approached the tunnel, a bony hook-like claw reached out from the darkness. *How on earth did it find me?* I asked myself, as a wave of fear swept over my body.

The wretched thing crawled along the ground with its nostrils flaring as fast as they could. As of yet, I didn't think it could tell I was but a few steps away from it. It certainly couldn't hear me—the roar of the falls made that impossible—and I don't think it saw me, either. I still had the hood of my cape of whispers pulled over my head.

I slowly backed away as it crawled into the light. The mere sight of the creature in the full light of the sun sent me into a panic. *What do I do? Where do I go?* My mind raced in time with my heart.

Step-by-step it followed me back to the ledge that loomed over the turbulent water. In a quick look over my shoulder, I saw my tiny raft plunge over the falls and shatter on the rocks below. My fate seemed all too clear.

The Blackheart was sniffing the ground near my feet. Then it reached my feet and sniffed its way up the length of my body slowly. As it neared my face, I literally began to tremble. Its huge nostrils burst open, and with each foul breath there was the distinct smell of rotting flesh. You couldn't have slipped a knife's blade between its nose and mine. That's how close we were.

Then it slowly drew back its ugly head and grinned an evil grin that is still the subject of my nightmares to this day. Somehow, it knew I had nowhere to go. Without warning, the sharp claw of its left wing swiped across my face in a downward motion, slicing open the skin beneath my right eye. I clapped my hand over my face as the blood began to trickle down. The beast drew the bloody claw close to its mouth, sniffed it slightly, and licked it clean with long strokes of its slimy blue tongue.

I looked down at the churning water below and thought about the tormented face of the young man I had found. *If I am going to die, I would rather die quickly. At least I will cheat that demon out of dinner,* I thought.

Without hesitation, I leaped to what I thought was my certain death. I remember falling with my eyes closed and waiting for the bottom.

The cold, wet mist of the falls washed over me as I plummeted downward. Just when my rocky doom seemed imminent, I felt a jolt. Something snatched hold of my leg and carried me over the raging river. I opened my eyes and looked up. The Blackheart had swooped down and caught me by one leg. It soared downstream, just above the rolling current, to search for a nice place to feast, no doubt.

I struggled—flailing my limbs about in a desperate attempt to break free. But the cursed animal's hold was too strong. Once again, I reached for my grandfather's blade and sliced at the Blackheart's bony grip. I cut its ankle just above the claw and it let out a horrendous screech, releasing me into the river to be swept away downstream.

Swiftly, the current moved me, bobbing up and down as I went. The water would pull me under and then toss me in the air. I violently kicked my feet and used my arms, working against fate to keep my head above water. The river seemed to be gaining speed as the tunnel in which it flowed closed in around me. I was sent cascading down a number of smaller falls. Time after time, I was plunged into the icy water. Suddenly, the ceiling sloped down and there was almost no room left to breathe, so I took one final deep breath and submerged.

Like an arrow from a bow, the water forced me through a small passage in the side of the mountain. I burst into daylight and shot out of a sheer cliff face. "Aaaahhhh!" I screamed, as I was hurled over the vastness of a calm dark lake. It felt as if I was floating through the clear blue sky for just the shortest of time—then, of course, came my landing.

After that, my story gets a little fuzzy. From what I was told, I made a terrible sound when I hit the water. And the splash was enormous.

Unbeknownst to me, this large dark lake supported several fishing villages. As a matter of my good fortune, there was a boat nearby and the people on it saw my rather ungraceful descent into the water.

When I opened my eyes, the world was a blur. There was someone hovering over me, but I couldn't make out any details.

Then, a young voice called out, "Papa, he wakes."

A deeper voice answered, "Go, bring some *voya*, quickly."

I didn't know what *voya* was, but it tasted like fish soup. My eyes began to focus after a short time and the world once again took shape.

The young voice belonged to Ying Mou, the daughter of Hi-Ko, a fisherman. In fact, his whole family lived on the boat. They fished the lake for their living, and every ten days they would visit one of the villages on the shore to sell their catch. For the first few days while I recovered, Ying Mou was my savior. She cared for me while her father and two older brothers tended their nets.

Hi-Ko was a modest man, to be sure. His family lived a meager life, but there was always an abundance of laughter and good-hearted conversation. To my recollection, I could not remember a more content group of people. Hi-Ko asked me how it was that I should fall from the mountain. I told him about my experience in the mountain, and about the creature and the young man I had found. I told him how I barely escaped with my life.

Hi-Ko told me the young man was a thief who had stolen a ring from a young girl known as the Keeper of Truth. This girl lived among the villages on the lake. If there were any disputes between the people of the villages, the parties involved would be brought to her and she would bear witness to the truth. This thief took shelter in the mountain, knowing the people of the village would not follow.

The Blackheart that I spoke of, he told me, always soars in the night sky, searching for prey. He saw the deep scar under my eye and asked how it came to be. I told him and watched as a grim look came over his face. Then he told me something that set my nightmares in motion.

He said, "Once the Blackheart tastes of your blood, it will not rest until it has consumed your flesh. You must not sleep on deck anymore."

For the remainder with my stay with the good Mou family, I slept in the hold with all the salted fish. Though the accommodations were horribly aromatic, I didn't have to worry about the Blackheart catching my scent. Everything I owned smelled like fish.

As soon as I was well enough, I bid them a fond farewell, called for my good friend Subakai, and returned home to my precious Queen Aleana. The journey was long and tedious, even for a dragon.

When I arrived at Ironcrest Castle, I found Sarah, the queen's handmaiden, waiting at the garden gate.

"Oh joy!" she said as I approached. "I didn't think you would return in time."

"Time for what?" I asked.

"You have been gone so long and Her Majesty fell ill. So quickly, quickly with you, go to her. Even now, she clings to life. She awaits you in the throne room!"

I sped off toward the palace. Arriving in the throne room, my heart sank, as I saw her feeble face from across the room. Her bed had been moved to the throne room and they were currently gathered around her—family, friends, and subjects—all in a sad communion of helpless moral support.

The master of the guard presented me to the queen. At the sound of my name, her face lit up ever so slightly. I approached her, knelt down on one knee next to the bed, and took her frail hand. I heard someone whisper, "That's the first time I've seen her smile in weeks."

"My Queen," I said.

She motioned for her handmaiden to draw near. Then she whispered in her ear.

"Yes, my lady," the woman answered.

She then ushered everyone out of the room rather abruptly. In just moments, I was left with the vastness of the throne room and the frailty of her condition.

"I am sorry for my absence, my Queen," I said, with my head cast down in shame. "I did not mean to tarry so long."

Her trembling finger caught my chin and gently raised my face to meet her crystal-blue gaze. "We are alone now, Tiny. You may use my name," she said softly.

"As you wish, Aleana," I answered.

"Look at you," she said. 'How is it that time has no power over you? You look as if you are not yet thirty."

I smiled, blushing slightly.

"Have you some magic for this old matriarch?" she asked. She paused a moment, just looking into my face.

Keeping the right side of my face turned away from her, I said nothing, for fear of weeping.

"No matter," she said. "It's only vanity. Queen or peasant, we all see our end."

"Please don't talk of such things," I said. "I can save you from this end."

"For what reason, that I might die some other, less honorable way? No. I can think of no better way to part than with those that I love. And you are among the dearest to me. My dear sweet Tiny Lynquest. You shall never know what measure of joy you have brought me over the years. But your youthful face has made you conspicuous, so you should not remain where you are known, lest feeble minds think you evil and seek to do you harm. Before you go, I have a charge for you. I know there has always been an air of enchantment about you. I implore you, as a friend and as your queen, to watch over the house of Millstaff, as long as you are empowered by that wonderful magic that makes you, you. Please secure the throne for an heir with a good and honest heart."

"Yes, my Queen. As long as I have breath, there will be a Millstaff on the throne," I said, lowering my head to meet her hand.

She pulled her hand away and slowly stroked my hair with her trembling fingers. "I can see you are vexed by my condition. I do not wish to see such sadness in your face," she said.

"I cannot help it. I shall miss you very, very much," I murmured.

"Then you should go. You need only know that I have loved you my entire life, and now I carry that same love into the everlasting sleep," she said in a whisper.

Unable to bear the pain any longer, I begged the leave she granted and fled into the wilderness surrounding the palace. There I stayed until her passing, only three days later.

The fire crackling in the night air became conspicuously loud after Tiny's story ended and he fell silent. His enchanting elf-like smile had vanished from his face. Suddenly, I felt ashamed for having brought up his scar.

"I'm sorry if I opened old wounds," I said, feeling awkward.

He regained a half-helpless grin and said, "You know, Emily, I have not spoken with anyone about these things in literally hundreds of years." He gently touched the scar upon his face with his right hand and said, "There are some scars that even time cannot heal." Then he quietly lay down, turning his back to the fire, and said, "Good night, Princess."

I snuggled down close to the fire and stared up at the glimmering stars, contemplating the strange little man's life and what kind of love could transcend so much time. As I began to feel the effects of a full stomach and a warm fire, I rolled over to face the flickering light, nestled my head into his rolled-up cape, and drifted off to meet the morning.

CHAPTER EIGHT

A HOME AWAY

When I awoke, the gentle light of day seemed to chase away all the shadows of the previous night's conversation. Tiny had once again changed into that youthful little sprite I had come to admire.

"It's so much easier for me to travel like this," he exclaimed.

I have to admit, it always amazed me how such a wrinkled-up old man could be so transformed. Even his scar had disappeared.

"Is that the way you looked as a boy?" I asked.

"The same," he said delightedly.

"I don't know which I like more, having a doughty old grandfather, or an energetic younger brother," I said, snickering.

Tiny just laughed and we started out on the remainder of our journey. As we traveled, Tiny began telling me about the scepter, where it came from and its purpose. He told me of the powers of each of the four rings: wisdom, strength, compassion, and truth. He also told me how the rings imbued the scepter with the power to unite all the people's hearts in peace.

"There has been a change in the spirit of man," he said. "This change couldn't have come at a worse time. The first full moon of the great convergence is only days away."

"What is the great convergence?" I asked.

"Every thousand years, between the first full moon of spring and the second, the netherworld and our own align themselves. At that moment, a doorway between the two worlds can be opened. No one knows where the doorway is, but it is at this time that the scepter is at its greatest risk. Were Salina to get her hands on it, mankind would be at eternal war." His face grew very grim at the thought.

"Why would we be at war?" I asked.

"Because Salina is one of the ancient maidens of the netherworld, and gains her power from chaos. There is never more chaos in man's heart than when he is at war. Wherever there is a conflict arising from greed, fear, or hatred, her dark magic is at work, clouding the weaker minds and bending their wills. You will have to put things right," he said.

"How do I do that?" I asked.

"Well, Salina cannot be killed," he said. "So you will have to find some way to seal the doorway, perhaps from the other side."

"But, won't I be trapped in the netherworld?" I asked nervously.

"We will just have to work our way around that," he said.

"I don't think I like the sound of that," I said, glaring at him.

"Don't worry," he said. "You will not be alone. I go where you go." Then he smiled and patted me on the back.

We traveled all day, resting only a few times in the woods. By nightfall we had made our way through the forest and to the village of Sazway.

Tiny amazed me when he spoke the language fluently. He and I were the only people of, shall we say, a lighter persuasion. I felt quite out of place, though the natives seemed friendly enough.

It didn't affect Tiny, though. He haggled with an old man about the price of two horses, until finally the old man gave up and sold him the horses at Tiny's price. I snickered a bit at the way the man scratched his head and rambled on at this boy who spoke the language so well, and who beat him at his own game.

Tiny turned to me afterward and said, "I would have paid him what he asked, but it's all we have."

We spent the night camping outside the village of Sazway, and then rode the rest of the way to Safora the next day. Safora was a modest town on the banks of the shallow, slow-moving River Topaz. It reminded me a little of my own small town of Summers Glen. It was nestled in the rolling hills of the countryside, and there stood a sod house of sorts on the tallest hill.

"Do you see that hut?" asked Tiny, as he pointed to the house.

"What? The one on the hill?" I asked.

"That is where we are going," he said. "It belongs to a shaman woman named Morzia Finautwa. She is a descendant of the shaman that created the scepter. Her family has been waiting for you for a long, long time."

There was an old woman standing in front of the house with, of all things, a large monkey holding her hand. She was partially hunched over, with frizzy white hair and a soft, sweet smile that reminded me of home. She wore a modest tan dress and a woolen shawl draped over her shoulders. She waved to us as we rode up to the house.

"*Somgalli!*" she yelled. "*Somgalli mojhow banauki.*"

"Ha, ha, ha. *Magato polaky ezzusoo,*" Tiny replied. "Remember," he said. "*Agalli eck o magpelle.*"

They both laughed heartily as we dismounted, then Tiny hugged her in a warm embrace and introduced me.

"Morzia, *tuban ono byutome*, Princess Emily."

"Forgive me, child. Where are my manners? I am not used to speaking in your tongue. My humble house is honored by your presence," she said as she took my hand.

I was struck by her beautiful green eyes, unlike any green eyes I had ever seen. They were the color of fine jade, a brilliant pale green that beamed as bright as her smile against her dark brown skin.

"What a nice thing to say," was my response to her warm welcome.

"Not at all, Princess," she said. "The whole of our village welcomes you with open arms." Then she embraced me as if she had known me her entire life.

"Look," said Tiny. "Beyond that river is the land of Kongwana. The people of Safora are a free people. They govern themselves by the spirit of Bonangi, the spirit of the scepter."

Morzia nodded her head in agreement, and then said, "Come, you must be hungry. Meeka and I will make you something to eat."

"Is that the name of your monkey?" I asked. "Meeka?"

"Yes, Meeka has been with me for a long time. I have been training her to help me do things around the house," she said.

The monkey led Morzia into the hut by the hand and fetched things such as plates, cups, and even her cooking pot from the cupboard. Even though Morzia was capable of doing all these things on her own, she would have Meeka do them for her.

"Meeka must be extremely helpful," I said.

"Yes, she is," said Morzia. "But soon she will be absolutely necessary."

Morzia prepared a soup of vegetables in a broth of some sort, with some flat bread. She explained that the bread was made for dipping, so I needn't worry about manners.

"Just dig right in," she said. As Tiny and I ate, she timidly asked, "Did you bring it?"

"Of course," said Tiny.

"May I see it? Please?" Morzia's face was filled with reverence.

Tiny stood up, crossed the room, and retrieved his cape. Carefully reaching into the bundle, he slid the scepter from its hiding place. Her eyes lit up with a radiant light as he gently placed the scepter in her hands.

"Ohhh, it is beautiful," she said. "Look at it. Stories about this scepter have been told in my family for thousands of years, but look at it. Is it really as powerful as I have heard?"

"Even more powerful than you could possibly imagine," said Tiny.

"Look at the hand," said Morzia. "Just as it was the day it was joined."

"I know," I said. "It looks real, doesn't it?"

Morzia looked at me in astonishment. "It is real," she said.

"What?" I choked on my soup.

"It was a sacrifice my ancestor made for the sake of peace."

Her answer was firm and resolute. Tiny looked at me and raised his eyebrows.

"You mean," I stammered.

"What I mean is, the hand on this scepter is the right hand of Showhaun Finautwa, my ancestor and the only shaman powerful enough to create such a work of art."

I was struck dumb, my mouth agape.

"You will understand more after we perform the ceremony of the stones," said Morzia. She patted my cheek with the palm of her hand and handed the scepter back to Tiny. "For now, you should rest. You have had a long journey and it is far from over."

Tiny and I ate our fill and then he took me on a tour of Safora while we collected some things for Morzia at the market. She had made a list, but that didn't help me, it was written in Kongwanee. The strange language, customs, food, and animals all led to an overwhelming feeling of awkwardness. I was a stranger in their town, and as such, felt the differences between us, in leaps and bounds. Tiny tried to keep me focused on our task by calling out to me the items on the list.

"One crocodile tooth," he said.

"A what? A crocodile tooth?" I exclaimed.

"That is what it says. One crocodile tooth, the left ear of a dingo, two sand lizards, four dried scorpions, and a *zaba* fruit." He smiled when he realized how ridiculous the list sounded.

"I hope we are not shopping for dinner," I said. "If we are, I'm eating the *zaba* fruit. It's the only thing that sounds edible." Tiny just laughed and shook his head.

When we returned, we found Morzia and Meeka on their way to the well to draw water. I watched as Meeka led Morzia to the well by the hand, and even handed her the rope with which to draw the water skin from the well. It seemed there was nothing Morzia did that Meeka didn't help with. I realized everything about this place was foreign to me.

I spent the rest of that day pondering my predicament with a heavy heart. I had never felt so alone. I was a princess without a kingdom.

All my pondering led me to a place on the hillside overlooking the town. I sat down in the tall grass and watched as the people of the town scurried around like ants on a mound. It wasn't long before Meeka and Morzia sought me out and found me hiding in the grass.

"What's the matter, child? Have you no place to call your own?" she asked.

"What? Oh, I just needed some time to myself," I said.

Morzia approached and knelt down next to me. She brushed the hair from my face like my mother used to do, which only made me miss home all the more.

"Feeling out of place, are we?" she inquired.

"Well...I mean no disrespect, but everything about this land is strange to me. I miss my home, my family, and all the people of my own little town," I said.

"Are we so different?" she asked.

"Of course you are," I said. "Look at me. The color of my skin, my hair, the way I talk, the things I wear, they all make me different. I want to understand. I want to belong."

"Look at the town,' she said. "Tell me what you see. And be honest."

"OK," I said. "I see a marketplace selling things I would never dream of eating in a town where I don't speak the language. I feel so out of place. I mean, I couldn't even get lost in Safora, even if I were standing in a crowd of people." My words reflected my frustration.

"We are all different, my dear, and yet we are all the same," she said, as she slid a ring off her finger. "Give me your hand." I held out my hand and she slipped the ring on my finger. "Now, look at the town once more, and again tell me what you see. Be honest."

I stared down at the town again; my eyes were filled with all the activities of the people of the town. "Well, let's see," I said. "I see a woman fighting the wind as she hangs out her laundry on the branches of a dead tree."

"Yes, go on," said Morzia.

"I see another woman scolding one of her many children for playing in the mud of the river," I said. "Hey, she reminds me of Mrs. Jennings back home. She even caught the child by the ear like Mrs. Jennings used to do."

"Good, good, keep going," said Morzia.

"There is a man watering his cattle like Mr. Tomory, and his wife is sweeping out their home upwind from him, leaving him in a cloud of dust. That's just like Summers Glen," I said.

"You see, we are not so different, are we?"

"How did you do that?" I asked.

"You have to look beyond the obvious," she said. "Of course, it helps if you are wearing the ring of truth."

I looked down at my hand, and sure enough, there was the most beautiful Tiger's eye gem set in a band of white gold. The stone was a magnificent shade of green, like pale jade. It reminded me of Morzia's eyes.

"Do you like it?" she asked.

"It's beautiful," I said.

"It is yours now," she said, clasping my hand.

I looked into her face to thank her—her eyes had turned milky white.

"Morzia, your eyes! What happened to your beautiful eyes?" I was mortified.

"I was born blind, Emily," she said plainly. "Tiny brought me the ring for safekeeping. When I put it on, it not only gave me my sight, but the ability to understand things I was seeing and recognize the people I saw."

"But you are blind now. How can I take your sight from you?" I asked.

"You did not take my sight, I gave it to you. If you are going to do any great thing, it is going to take some measure of sacrifice. My ancestor, Showhaun Finautwa, understood this."

Her words rang clear and true in my heart. Then a thought came to me, and slowly sank in; that was why she had Meeka help her with all the chores. She was training her for just this moment.

"Tell me now, Princess, what are the people of the town doing?"

"They are breaking down and clearing away the stalls of the market in the center," I said.

"They are preparing for the ceremony of the stones. It is taking place tonight," she said.

"Tonight?" I exclaimed. "But, I'm not ready. I'm, I'm, unsure."

"Unsure of what?" she asked.

"I don't know…of where I am going, of what I am doing, even of who I am anymore," I said sadly.

"You are in transition," she said.

"I am so far away from my childhood, so far away from who I once was. I am so scared, Morzia."

"Sometimes, child, in order to become who we truly are, we must leave behind who we once were." Then she reached out her hand and said, "*Konicha*, Meeka. Come, Meeka, we must prepare dinner."

I called out to her as she left. "I will have the *zaba* fruit, if it's all right with you?"

"Nonsense," she said. "That is for Meeka. We shall all have chicken."

That's a relief, I thought to myself. Letting her words sink in, I lay down in the tall grass and stared up at the sky. *Isn't it funny*, I thought. *That is the same bright blue sky that looks down on my small town back home. Perhaps, we are not so different after all.*

I sat up and again gazed out over the town, and the vast expanse of the horizon that lay beyond it. The amazing blue sky stretched on and on before me. *And we all live under it*, I thought. "I guess it helps if I think about it that way," I said to myself. "Goodness, what a wonderful world it would be if—"

"Emily!" Tiny called out to me. "Come help me with the horses and we will wash up for dinner."

"Coming!" I yelled back, as I jumped up and dusted myself off.

When I arrived to help with the horses, I found that Tiny had changed back into his old self again. He seemed to be cleaned up a bit as well. Not dressed up, by any means, but his hair was combed and his clothes were clean.

"How is it that your clothes are clean, Tiny?" I asked with a smile.

"Oh, these," he said nervously. "I keep a set of clean clothes here for when I come to visit."

"I see," I said. "Morzia is pretty special, isn't she?"

He flashed a big smile and replied, "Yes, she is, Princess. Yes, she is."

Tiny and I fed and watered the horses, tied them on a long tether behind the house, and then we washed for dinner.

Once inside, we found Morzia merrily chattering away at Meeka as if she weren't a monkey at all. It seemed strange to me, to see the monkey fetching whatever she asked for, and Morzia seemed to move through the hut just as she always had. When we sat down to eat, Morzia gave the *zaba* fruit to Meeka, who took it to a corner where she could eat it in peace.

"I guess she would rather eat alone," I said.

"I don't think she wants to share," said Tiny, smiling. Then he noticed the ring on my finger and looked up at Morzia. "Oh," he said. "I see you gave it to her already."

"Yes," said Morzia. "It was time. The ring has finally found its true home. I am grateful that I got the chance to see the scepter with my own eyes. That is something that even my father did not get. Thank you, Tiny, for the time I had."

Tiny said nothing. He just reached across the table and gently squeezed her hand. Then he returned to that unusual ritual of salting his food and sprinkling pepper over himself. I shot him an awkward glance.

"What's the matter, lass?" he said, laughing. "Do you want some pepper as well?"

"Do you mean for me, or for my food?" I asked jokingly.

"Either," he said, smiling.

"You know, someday you are going to have to explain that peculiar behavior to me," I said, shaking my head.

"It is more of a precaution than anything else," he said.

"OK," I said. "Don't tell me."

As we ate, I noticed the ring glistening green and black, like some flirtatious eye winking at me. That's when it occurred to me: tigereye gems aren't green. They're golden brown.

"This is an extraordinary gem," I said. "I have never seen a green tigereye stone before."

"Oh, it's not a tigereye stone, Princess," said Morzia.

"No," said Tiny. "It is one of the eyes of a sacred statue of a tiger."

"Yes," Morzia continued. "The statue was a golden tiger that watched over the Chain Lee temple in the Far East. The monks of that temple guarded three sacred truths passed on to them by the Hung Wu priests of the Bakalou dynasty."

"Those three truths were said to be engraved on the backs of the two jade eyes of the tiger," said Tiny.

"So, what happened?" I asked. "How did it end up set in a ring?"

"Well, the Magong warriors from the north swept down on the temple and burned it to the ground," said Tiny.

"They killed the monks and carried away all the gold, including the tiger," said Morzia. "They plucked the eyes from the statue and melted it down to make gold coins."

"As soon as they did," said Tiny, "strange things began to happen."

"Yes," said Morzia. "One of the eyes was lost when the man carrying it fell through the ice of a cold, deep lake."

"Then," said Tiny, "a terrible plague ravaged the Magong people. It was a strange plague that left the people in agony. Their eyes burned and long welts appeared all over their bodies like stripes."

"You mean stripes like a tiger?" I asked in astonishment.

"Precisely, like a tiger," said Tiny.

"Then what?" I asked.

"They knew they had angered the spirit of the temple," said Morzia. "They sent their finest warrior back to the temple to place the eye on the pedestal that the statue had rested on."

"And that's where it sat until Showhaun helped the Chain Lee people rebuild the temple," said Tiny.

"They were so grateful," said Morzia, "that the priests gave the eye to him as a gift."

"After they had engraved the three sacred truths onto an enormous granite statue of the tiger, of course," said Tiny.

"My ancestor, Showhaun Finautwa, set the jade stone in the ring when he forged the scepter," said Morzia.

"And what about the Magong people?" I asked. "What happened to them?"

"They disappeared," said Morzia.

"Disappeared?" I shrieked.

"Yes, lass," remarked Tiny, "disappeared. But you can find snow-white tigers roaming the woods and mountains if you travel north of that temple today."

I looked down at the ring on my finger. "It looks so innocent now," I said. "One would have never guessed it had such a sinister past."

"Don't be fooled, Princess," said Morzia. "The truth can be a very powerful thing."

"Provided," said Tiny, "one is willing to accept the truth." We ate in silence for a moment, and then Tiny said, "I am sure your father, the king, would agree, Princess."

"Perhaps he would, if he were still my father," I said.

"What do you mean?" asked Morzia. "Did you disown him? He is still your father, is he not?"

"No," I said. "I didn't disown him. I just don't recognize him anymore. He looks different, he acts different."

"My dear, what do you mean by 'he looks different'?" asked Morzia.

"Well, let us just say, he has had a change of disposition," I said.

Tiny looked at me and said, "I think he is enchanted."

"Well, I don't find him enchanting," I said.

"No, not enchanting," said Tiny. "Enchanted. He is bewitched, under a spell of some sort."

"Now that you mention it," I said, "there was a strange white mask that Elexi wanted him to put on. It was a gift from some unknown country."

"What?" exclaimed Tiny. "Why did you not tell me about this, lass?"

"I didn't think about it until now," I said.

"Then he is most certainly bewitched," said Tiny.

"This is most unfortunate," said Morzia.

"I am sure, were it not for that mask, my father would not want war with Kongwana," I stated.

Morzia choked on those words. "War!" she blurted out. "With Kongwana?"

"Yes," I said bluntly. "I overheard him and Elexi discussing it in the war room of the palace. I tried to stop him, but he had me locked in my room."

"Yes," said Tiny. "We fled the palace after dark."

"It is Elexi," I said. "He has some strange power over my father. Maribelle told me that Elexi was plotting to have me executed."

"Is this Maribelle an honest person?" asked Morzia.

"She helped me escape," I said. "I owe her my life."

"I will attest to Maribelle's honesty as well," said Tiny. "She has been at the palace since she was just a wee lass. She served under Malcolm when she was young."

"Well," said Morzia, "it is a good thing that our good King Azutoo detests war. He has ruled over Kongwana for many years and is well thought of by nearly everyone."

"That's a relief," I said.

"Yes, Princess, he is a man who is slow to anger. He will find peace with your father," said Morzia. "So," she added, "tell me about your journey. After you fled the palace, what happened? Was it exciting? I get so little excitement in my small town."

As we finished our meal, we told Morzia about our journey from Salizar and all its perils.

After supper, Tiny retrieved his pipe from a box on a shelf beside the door. He left it there, no doubt, on an earlier visit. When he lit it, the whole room filled with the smell of jasmine and cinnamon.

"Ah," said Morzia. "That is a smell I have not smelled in quite a while."

Tiny sauntered over to her, put his arm around her, and gave her a gentle squeeze.

"You two make a cute couple," I said, chuckling.

Morzia just waved me off with her hand. "We are too old to be a couple," she said. "We are more like a pair than a couple. Ha, ha, ha," she laughed.

Just then, a sound rose up from the village, soft at first, but constant. *Boom…boom, boom…boom, boom…boom, boom…boom.*

Both Tiny and Morzia stopped in their tracks. Morzia turned to me and said, "It is time. The village elders are beating the ceremonial drums. They are calling people from all around to join the celebration. You know, those drums can be heard all the way in Marzadune, the capital of Kongwana."

"It's a celebration?" I asked.

"It is a time for remembering the history of the scepter," she said. Morzia called to Meeka, "Meeka, *casa na italli ga*." The monkey quickly crossed the room and retrieved a fair-sized wooden box. She brought it to Morzia and set it before her on the table, then, without missing a step, returned to her *zaba* fruit in the corner. Morzia opened the box, saying, "These are the four memory stones."

"They look like plain flat stones from the river to me," I said.

"They are stones from the river," she said. "But these stones contain the collective memories of Showhaun and Kahutma Finautwa, from the time before the scepter until the founding of the knighthood. They are all here in these four stones."

"So, what do I do?" I asked.

Morzia smiled and said, "You are the guest of honor. You get to ride in the Showhaun chair and share the Bonangi cup. Come, Tiny," she said with enthusiasm. "We will need the things you bought in the market today."

"Just exactly what am I supposed to drink out of the Bonangi cup?" I asked rather nervously.

Tiny simply raised his eyebrows and puffed his pipe delightedly as he gathered up all the things she needed. When we stepped outside Morzia's modest home, I was taken aback by the beauty of the moment. Twilight had fallen, the drums were calling, and the people were all carrying small torches into the town. Out of every home, from every hilltop, and from across the river they came, bearing fire. Streams of light flowed into the town and converged in what was the marketplace.

They had built a large bonfire in the center of the town, like the one we had in Summers Glen when I was a little girl. One by one, the people added their torches to the bonfire once they had reached the center.

Tiny, Morzia, and I descended the hillside in the faded light of the evening. Tiny and Morzia carried a big cooking pot by the handle, while I lagged behind them.

I couldn't really put it into words, but there was something magical about that night. The drums not only called the people, but awakened some ancient slumbering spirit from the depths of my being. I was alive with the sound of the drums, burning with the mystery of the evening, and tingling with the excitement of the fellowship of man. I felt a strange kinship, not just to these people, but to all beneath the stars as we slowly made our way down the hill and into the town.

CHAPTER NINE

Carried Away

When we arrived at the edge of the town, I found myself surrounded by the women and was separated from Tiny and Morzia. The women painted my face, arms, and hands with colors of red, white, black, and yellow; they streaked my hair with white and yellow. The women then lifted me up and passed me along above their heads, directing me toward the enormous fire in the center of town.

"Tiny!" I yelled in desperation. "They're going to throw me in the fire!"

Across the flames, I saw Tiny and Morzia standing opposite me. They laughed at my situation and thoroughly enjoyed themselves at my expense. Closer and closer to the fire I was passed along; then, just before the raging flames, I was spun around, flipped on my back with my face to the sky, and plopped down in a large chair. It was a chair made out of reeds from the river. The arms hooked upward, not down, a point which I thought was rather strange. Two long poles were connected by brass rings to the arms of the chair. They stuck out like the tusks of an elephant, front and back.

The women that had seated me turned and began to sing and dance in a circle around the fire. That is when four large men dressed in ceremonial garb approached the chair in front of me and behind. They took hold of the poles and raised me high into the air by placing the poles on their shoulders, and then they joined in the dance around the fire.

Once, twice, three times we went around as the flames reached into the night sky. More drums and clapping of hands were added to the fray. Their song and rhythm moved through me in waves of excitement, and I threw my hands in the air. I couldn't help myself; I was overcome with joy, clapping and singing along as best I could. And all the time, the drums got louder and louder. The sound of the people's voices rang out as one great heart in the night air. Then, just when my jubilation reached its peak and I was singing at the top of my lungs, they abruptly stopped.

I was left babbling to myself in the silence. Looking around and noticing that I was alone in my celebrating, I put my hands down and my singing trailed off to a mumble. "Oops," I said. "I'm sorry if I don't know the words."

They set me down in front of Morzia. The four men lined up in front of me with their faces to the ground. Morzia spoke before the crowd. Tiny stood beside her and translated for me.

"These are the elders of our town. They welcome you to the fellowship of Bonangi. So that you will know the purpose and will of the scepter, they offer you the memories of Showhaun Finautwa, the maker of the scepter and embodiment of the spirit. Do you accept this responsibility?"

I looked at Tiny with a gesture of uncertainty. He smiled back at me and gently nodded in agreement.

"Yes," I said. "I accept the responsibility."

"Good," said Morzia. "Tiny, the scepter, please."

Tiny reached beneath his cape and produced the scepter. A wave of astonishment moved through the crowd as he handed the scepter to Morzia. Then, he snapped loose the small velvet pouch he had tied around his neck and handed it to her as well.

Morzia reached into the velvet bag and pulled the ruby ring from its depths. She slid the ring off the gold chain it dangled from and gently placed it on the scepter. The scepter now had three of the four rings on it and a light began to glow in the palm of the hand on the scepter's top.

Turning to me, she said, "It is time for all four rings to be united, Princess."

I slid the Tiger's eye off my finger and placed it in her hand. She slipped the ring on the scepter and it began to hum in a harmonious, low-pitched melody that split the silence and resonated in my chest. *I wonder if anyone else can feel it churning within their chest, as I can,* I pondered. A light blue and brilliant that rivaled the bonfire beamed forth from the palm of the scepter's hand.

Morzia held the scepter high in the air for all the inhabitants to see. "Look," she said. "Look upon the spirit of the shaman Showhaun."

The people backed away and sheltered their eyes from the intense light. Morzia placed the scepter across the arms of my chair; the beam of light shot into the sky, piercing the heavens above my head.

She then called for the cup of Bonangi. A child of the town brought the cup. The chalice of bronze rested on a modest wooden tray the boy was carrying. Once she had the cup in her hands, she instructed some women close by to bring her the big cooking pot she and Tiny had brought. They placed it before me and returned to the crowd.

I looked down at the pot filled with a blue foamy liquid. The thought of a crocodile's tooth and a dingo's ear popped into my head. *Oh no,* I thought. *I am going to have to drink that.*

Morzia dipped the cup into the pot and swept the foam off the top. She turned to the four men standing before me, dipped her finger into the cup, and placed a drop on each man's forehead. She then turned to me.

"Hold out your hands," she said.

I held my hands out in front of me. She placed the chalice in my left hand and clasped my right hand around it so that it was cradled in both hands. I looked down at the disgusting blue foam sloshing around in the cup and felt my stomach start to turn on me. I peered down at my violently rebelling gut. "You coward!" I muttered to myself, then I closed my eyes. *Two sand lizards and four dried scorpions?* I thought. *This is going to taste terrible.* I took a deep breath and committed myself to the task.

"Oh well," I said loudly. "Here I go!"

I placed the chalice to my lips, but just as that nasty foam crested the rim of the cup, Tiny yelled, "Stop!" I froze and my eyes popped open.

Tiny quietly stepped forward and whispered something into Morzia's ear.

She tilted her head slightly and laughed. "You don't drink it, child," she said, shaking her head. She then clasped her hands around mine, raised the cup in the air, and dumped the contents on my head. I felt the noxious ooze seeping into my hair and streaming down my forehead. Tiny smiled at me and snickered. I must have looked ridiculous and pathetic in my paint and blue lather. I saw him holding back his laughter at my humiliation.

"You knew about this, didn't you?" I said, and then I scowled at him.

Morzia took the cup from my hands and handed it to Tiny. She then placed my hands on the scepter that lay across the arms of the chair. Immediately, I felt the energy surge up my arms and enter my heart. It passed through me like waves at the seashore.

"You are going to see some terrible things," Morzia said to me. "You must not be afraid, you must endure. You must."

Morzia turned to the elders and called for the first stone, the stone known as the war stone. The man standing farthest to my left stepped forward, knelt down on one knee, and held out the flat river stone in the palm of his hand. Morzia took the stone, spat on it, and pressed it to my forehead.

Suddenly, I was transformed and transported to a battlefield where two great armies of the ancient world fought in a pitched battle against each other on the Plain of Sorrows. I was Showhaun Finautwa, a powerful shaman and a strong military leader. I wore a body shield and light armor, and carried a small spear. As the enemy advanced, I blocked the blows with my shield and stabbed with my spear. Blood poured forth from their wounds and their cries echoed through the air, along with the sorrowful cries of the dying.

Arms and legs flailing, I stabbed, kicked, slashed, and beat my way to the mound at the center of the field. I took the high ground slowly, one enemy at a time, until I stood above the fray. But wait—I was searching for someone in the midst of all the chaos. There, among the living, was a young dark warrior still fighting a pale soldier from the north.

"Bauchaton!" I yelled. "Bauchaton, behind you!"

As the young man's lance penetrated the armor of the white soldier, another cut him down from behind.

"No!" I screamed at the top of my voice.

Overcome with rage, the blood ran with anger in my veins and I cried out for vengeance. Blind with fury, I slaughtered the first man I saw. It no longer mattered what crest he wore or why he fought. I felt only the madness of the moment and the pure desire for more death, for the sake of it.

Fighting my way to the young man's body, I protected it from any who would defile the ground on which he lay. The battle raged on for the rest of that day. The once light green moss that covered the plateau was forever stained red with the blood of the fallen heroes.

By dusk, the few who were still standing were too tired to fight any longer. I fell to my knees beside the body of the young man and wept bitterly.

"Bauchaton! Bauchaton, my son, forgive me, forgive me," I cried. "I was lost in battle and I was not there. Forgive me, forgive me."

The limp body of my son lay cradled in my trembling arms as I pressed my forehead to his and let my tears wash across his sleeping face.

When I could cry no more, I stood and looked around. I began to notice the faces of the dead. They were all young. They were all sons or fathers. *Have we been at war for so long?* I thought. *How many sons have died, and how many more must die before the Plain of Sorrows is satisfied? And worst of all, the question remains unanswered: why do they hate us?*

I heard something. There was a sound rising into the air close by. It was a cry for help. Someone lay buried beneath the bodies of the fallen. I searched among the carnage until I came across a white soldier pinned down and wounded, his body half covered by his fallen comrades. I stared down at him with pity at first, and then I felt that anger again crawling its way up from the pit of my soul. The young man's face filled with fear as I raised my spear and plunged it deep into the ground beside him.

"Not this one," I said. "You will not have this one!"

I rolled the bodies off the man and helped him to his feet. I tended to his wounds in the shelter of the forest until he was well. His name was Gorlland. He told me he had lost his father and two younger brothers to the war. I showed him the body of my son, and later, we both took Bauchaton's body back to Safora to be buried in the hills. After that, I said good-bye to Gorlland and he returned home to his wife and children a wiser man. *I have lost a son, but I have gained a friend*, I thought.

When I returned to my home, I called out to my two remaining sons. "Illutoo, Kahutma, I am home," I said. "I am finally home." But to my dismay, only my youngest answered. "Kahutma, where is your brother?" I asked.

"The soldiers came and took him away. They said it was his duty to fight for the king of Kongwana," he said in trepidation.

"No!" I cried. "Not him, too!"

"What is wrong, Father? Where is Bauchaton?" he asked.

"He is dead, my son. He is dead," I said, my head hung in shame. "I could not save him."

"Will Illutoo come back?" he asked.

"I do not know," I said. "But this war has gone on too long. I have lost count of the years, and the years of my father before me. We will have to bring peace, you and I."

"Me, Father?" Kahutma asked.

"Yes, son. Before I lose you, too, something has to be done. Come," I said, "we cannot stop this war with war. We will try some wisdom, courage, compassion, and truth instead."

Morzia pulled the stone from my forehead and my body collapsed back into the wicker chair. Panting, I tried to cope with the vision. Morzia placed the stone back in the hand of the man still poised on one knee. She then called for the second stone, and as the first man stood up, the man next to him took his place.

Once again, a stone rested in his outstretched palm. Once again, she took the stone and spat on it. "This is the memory of the first scepter. The failing stone," she said, and then she pressed the stone against my forehead.

Another vision came to me, as vivid as the first. I was once again transformed into Showhaun Finautwa.

This time, I was preparing for a journey to the distant mountain of Kajacon. With my young son Kahutma, the four sacred gems, and all the books and magic tomes of the ages, we disappeared into the eastern wilderness.

When we arrived at the top of the mountain, I cast a spell upon the calm waters of a deep dark lake that lay below. I watched reflections—no, images—on the water. They were images of the battle on the Plain of Sorrows, images of Illutoo, my son. He had become a great warrior for Kongwana.

I spent the next five years on that mountain, setting the gems in bands of purest gold and forging the scepter. I wore the rings while I made the mold for the scepter. The gems were gifts from shamans and sages from around the world. Their powers were given to them by the most powerful sorcerers. Everything I did was imbued with their power. I used only acacia wood and baby's breath for the fire to melt the gold, and the sphere at the top was an opal mined from the mountain itself. A hole I drilled through the stone provided a mount for a golden spike that jutted out from the top of the scepter. I carefully hammered the base of that spike back down on the opal to hold it in place.

When the scepter was finished, we returned to Safora to find all the young men gone. There were only old men, women, and children left in the town. In the evenings, the drums would sound, pounding out the names of the fallen. I would listen very carefully every evening with bated breath, until I could not take any more. I prepared to join the battle, this time with the scepter in my left hand and the rings on my right.

I said good-bye to my son Kahutma and left before the sun rose the next morning. I reached the edge of the forest and cast my eyes upon the dead and the battling hordes. This was to be my moment of truth. I realized that, other than the scepter, I was completely unprotected, but my desire for peace was so great that I stepped out on the battlefield and touched the shoulders of two men who were fighting. Immediately, they dropped their weapons.

"Go home," I said. "Friends do not fight. Go home to your families."

The two men looked at each other and, without saying a word, shed their armor and disappeared into the woods surrounding the Plain of Sorrows. This was how the magic worked, one man at a time. One fight at a time, I made my way across the field and back to the mound at the heart of it all. One by one, they left, each man to his home, until at last I stood above the fray once more. I look down at the rift that was my path to the hill; it was then that I saw a massive warrior fighting his way through the crowd to the west. From the point of the two great spires, he cut his way through the throng of men, leaving the dead and dying in his wake. He stormed toward the mound where I stood and finally reached its base. Looking up at me with burning eyes of rage, he caught sight of the rings of gold upon my hand.

Ascending the hill, he caught me by the throat and swung his ax. "Aaaahhhh!" I screamed, as the ax severed my right hand below the wrist. Throwing me to the ground, he reached down and picked up my limp, bloody right hand. It still bore the four magic rings. He then turned around and held it high in the air, declaring himself the victor. But when he turned back around, the scepter in my left hand lunged upward. It was as if it had a will of its own.

The scepter stabbed the hand and the golden spike sank deep into the wrist at its base. My blood covered the large round opal that made up the sphere on the scepter, and to both our amazement, was absorbed by the stone.

We marveled as the hand fused with the golden spike and the massive opal, turning to gold and then coming to life. I could feel the power of the warrior's rage flow through me as I held on to the scepter and he held on to the hand. I could feel his poison bleeding into my heart, filling me with anger and resentment.

Suddenly, the hand on the scepter lurched forward and grabbed hold of the man's throat. Our internal rage fed the magic of the rings. Our anger focused on the scepter, causing it to constrict around his neck until his breathing became shallow. I could not stop it. This dark magic was too strong. *Where is this magic coming from?* I thought. *How is it that it is more powerful than my own?*

Finally, against my own will, the great warrior expired right before my eyes. The light of life that shone in his face flickered and faded away. He collapsed to the ground and rolled down the hill. His lifeless body was piled up at the bottom with the rest of the dead.

Weak and bleeding, I stumbled down the hill and tried to make my way across the Plain of Sorrows amid the still battling armies. At one point, I faltered and tumbled to the ground before one of the many dark pools that covered the plain. I saw my reflection, just before the blood of my wound spilled into the water, turning it red. As it did, my reflection changed. It took the shape of a raven-haired beauty, pale and seductive, with eyes like burning embers of black and red.

She laughed and mocked me from the pool of water tainted by my blood. "What is this?" she said. "The mighty Showhaun crawling away defeated, like some dog licking his wounds? What is the matter, Showhaun? Am I too powerful for you and your puny scepter?" Her words resonated with contempt and malevolence. "You foolish mortals have been feeding my lust for blood and chaos for far too long. I am much too strong for you now. So I will leave you to die with this one question: What would you give for peace? Ha, ha, ha."

Her image faded as a shadow appeared on the ground beside the pool. Shaken by the vision, it took me a moment to realize that someone was standing behind me. I jerked around, throwing my handless arm up in defense as a tall slender Kongwanee soldier loomed over me. It was Illutoo, my son. He had found me and was staring down at me in disbelief. He wept when he saw my condition. Without saying a word, he bound my wrist, threw my arm over his shoulder, and carried me home.

My vision blurred as Morzia pulled the memory stone from my forehead, and I sank back into the chair, drained by Showhaun's experience.

Exhausted by the ordeal, I looked up at Morzia. "I don't know if I can take much more of this," I said, catching my breath. "The bloodshed is too great, the tragedy so complete. I have never seen such suffering."

"You must endure, my dear," she said. "You must."

She called for the third stone and retrieved it from the third man's open palm. "These are the memories of Kahutma Finautwa, son of Showhaun and founder of the knights of Bonangi," she said. And then, just as before, she spat on the stone and pressed it to my head.

Once again, I felt the power of the scepter surge through me, and the image of Showhaun slowly bled into my eyes.

He was sitting up in bed, his wrist bandaged, and he stared across the room at the scepter resting in the corner.

"What is the matter, Father?" I asked.

"The scepter was not strong enough," he said. "We are dealing with an ancient magic, perhaps as old as time itself."

"The Kongwana soldiers came for Illutoo while you were sleeping," I said.

He hung his head in frustration. "With only one hand, I can neither fight nor stop the war," he said.

"You must rest first," I said. "Illutoo is a strong warrior. You will see. The war will end and he will come home."

At that moment the drums rang out in the town, as they did every evening, pounding out the names of the dead. My father fell silent as he listened closely, then he released a deep sigh of relief; Illutoo's name was not among them.

"Bring me the scrolls from my chest of spells," he said. "Perhaps there is something I have missed."

He told me of his vision in the pool at the battle and how he felt sure that he had overlooked something. Day after day, he would search the scrolls and ancient tomes in his collection and read them to me aloud. Hour after hour he would sit, frustrated, scouring the ancient writings and making notes. Then one day, he came across a legend so old, it no longer occupied the consciousness of man.

It was a story about the foundation of the world and the five maidens of old, or spirits, which inhabited the netherworld. There were two spirits in particular that were in constant struggle: Salina, the spirit of chaos and destruction, and Bonangi, the spirit of balance and harmony.

"We can see Bonangi, the spirit of balance, in nature," he said. "There is only enough death to sustain life."

"But what of man?" I asked. "Why is there so much death?"

"The balance in men's hearts has been disturbed. They have put their trust in the wrong spirit. They do not believe in peace," he explained.

"What can be done?" I asked. "Is there no way to awaken the spirit of Bonangi in the hearts of men?"

My father told me the scepter was a talisman for the two maidens; it could serve either spirit. "As it is, Bonangi is too weak to stand against Salina," he said. "But, I shall find a way." His hardened face reflected his fierce determination.

But then came the evening that changed everything for me. As the drum sounded in the town, an old man riding in a horse-drawn wagon brought something to our door. It was the body of my brother Illutoo.

My father ran to the wagon, crying out, "No! No! Not again. Not Illutoo." He took my brother's body in his arms and cradled him in tears.

I just stood in silent mourning, numb to the world and stunned by the loss. I watched from a distance as he begged forgiveness from my brother, over and over. We buried his body beside Bauchaton's on the family land in the hills above Safora.

That night, my father stood in the doorway and looked across the river in the direction of Marzadune. "They will be coming for you next," he said to me.

"Should I go?" I asked.

"I cannot stop them," he answered. "The scepter is still too weak. It needs something to strengthen Bonangi, something I am not sure I am strong enough to give."

"Perhaps, Father, I could give it what it needs," I said.

"If you did," he said, looking into my eyes, "I would have nothing left to live for." He then smiled a feeble smile and patted me on the back as he turned away from the door.

It was only three days later that my father's words came true. Soldiers from the capital of Marzadune came for me. I went without a fight, saying good-bye to my father for the last time. He hugged me and then turned away, as he couldn't bear to see me leave. It was a long, lonely night's ride to Marzadune, and my heart hung heavy in my chest all the way there.

Once we arrived in Kongwana, I learned how to fight. I learned how to hate the pale ones. I knew if I were going to survive, it would be out of pure hatred and revenge for the death of my brothers. I soon became a strong warrior and found my first day in battle.

It was a morning in spring, though the sun never shines on the Plain of Sorrows. Our army was lined up on the southernmost edge of the field and my eyes were fixed on the enemy to the north.

Patiently we waited in the morning mist for the battle horn to sound. A nervous, uneasy silence pervaded the ranks of the line. Then a clanking noise, as one man began to beat the butt of his sword against his shield in protest of the delay. "Let's get on with the killing!" he proclaimed. A roar broke out, and then a blast of the horn, and we charged the field, screaming our bloodlust to the sky.

With a crash, we collided with our enemy, slashing and stabbing. My heart filled with unbridled rage at the death of my two brothers. I grew more empowered by the cries of every man who fell to my spear or dagger. Completely consumed by the moment and my own rage, I tore through the flesh of these pale ones like paper in the wind.

Then, a familiar face distracted me. I saw him out of the corner of my eye. He walked calmly and quietly through the chaos and carnage, unaffected by the death all around him. He crossed the plain untouched and ascended the hill at the heart of the great plateau. There, he stood proud and unharmed at the top of that mound.

Raising the scepter high into the air, he called out, "I have come for you, Salina! In the name of Bonangi, this ends today!"

Suddenly, a pale warrior broke through the ranks and ascended the mound. He charged my father with his sword bloodied from the fight. My father never moved. Instead, he buried the point of the scepter in the ground at his feet and knelt down before it with his arms outstretched.

Baring his chest to the warrior, he cried, "Bonangi! I believe in peace!"

"Father, no!" I cried as I ran.

The soldier's blade pierced his chest and my father's spirit rose as a bright blue light, like a beacon above his head, and it disappeared into the scepter before him. Then, he collapsed on the ground.

When the pale blue light of his spirit sank into the hand upon the sphere, a huge blast of air exploded out in all directions. Every man fell to the ground and a beam of pure white light shot out of the scepter into the sky. The beam of light was set against the clouds and they began to part. The crystal-blue mantle of the endless beyond peeked through the somber gray clouds for the first time in anyone's memory.

Every man there marveled at the sight of the burgeoning sky. They were all on the ground in the place where they had fallen, dumbstruck by the silence. It was a sound that hadn't been heard on that plateau for almost a hundred years.

Slowly, one by one, they got to their feet and looked around. In the light of day, they saw the bodies of their friends, fathers, sons, and brothers. The field shone bright red with the blood of the ages, and the sound of men shedding their armor, one by one, echoed across the land. A hand of friendship was held out for any who were in need, no matter what shade. They simply dropped their weapons and returned home.

When I got to my father body, I looked down. His lifeless body lay curled on the ground with the scepter's shaft still in his left hand. Kneeling down, I held his face in my arms. I finally understood what it meant to believe in peace. I took his body home to rest beside my brothers. All three fought the same battle in their own way.

As Kahutma's vision came to its end, I saw his face before me, his eyes staring into mine he spoke. "It was I, Emily, who created the knights of Bonangi. I was the one who hid the rings in four corners of the world, and I gave the scepter to the king of Salizar, a strong and wise ruler. I did it to protect it until the world was ready for the one who could heal it. Now the scepter is yours. May the spirit of Bonangi empower your steps and guide your hands. My father readied the soil and Tiny planted the seed," he said. "But you must speak its name." His words echoed in my head as Morzia pulled the stone away.

I looked around as I came to my senses. The four men still stood before me, and the good people of Safora were silent and somber in their attendance. I had no idea how much time had passed while the visions were playing in my head.

Morzia called for the fourth stone. The fourth and final man dropped to one knee and held it before her. She took the stone, saying, "This is the destiny stone. It speaks of the shadows of your future and the secrets of the door to the netherworld. Only a truly honest heart may know these things." She spat on the stone and pressed it to my head.

As I slipped away into the deeper awakening of my thoughts, I saw only flashes of an unsettled mind. All the visions of the stone appeared to be fractured, disconnected, and in no particular order in time. A myriad of floating thoughts seemed to ascend out of the darkness of my inner self and drift past me.

A sound began to enter my awareness and it tracked me like a hound on the hunt. It grew in range and intensity. Before I knew it, I was standing on the Plain of Sorrows once more in the midst of a raging storm. The siren's song called out above the wind, rain, and thunder.

There was a maiden standing on the edge of the cliffs overlooking the sea. She was completely naked, with her back to me, her long black hair flowing wildly in the wind. She held her hands to the sky and did not seem to notice that I was approaching from behind. Her song was a single wretched voice of three dissonant notes formed into one that sliced through the sounds of wind, wave, thunder, and rain. I came within arm's length of her, and gently rested my hand on her shoulder.

Her concentration broken now, she turned to face me. My curiosity became horror when I saw no face at all, only a gaping hole in the center of her head. Her shimmering black hair turned to kelp from the sea, and her arms faded from a radiant pale white skin to the gray-blue opaque flesh of some creature from the unknown depths of the sea.

I felt the cold touch of her tentacle arms as they wrapped tightly around my neck and constricted my throat. The hole that made up her entire face stretched wide, as if she was going to consume me. She lifted me off the ground with no effort and dangled me above the rocks and the raging surf below. Another tentacle with a giant eyeball at its end floated in front of me. She used it to look me over with great care, and then she cast me in the air from the cliffs.

As soon as she let go, I saw nothing, but felt my body tumbling through the void. I fell through the deep, dark, unknown realms of the destiny stone. Suddenly, my body hit the ground with a thud and I felt the solid form of a damp, cold stone floor. The limited light that streamed in between the bars of a small opening close to the ceiling left me with the perception of being in chains in some dank dungeon underground. I heard the restless sound of chains echoing through a vast chamber of shadows.

Whispered voices murmured whimsical words in the night. "The king is not well. All is not right. Where the brothers dwell, the siren feeds the fight."

I also heard a young man's voice muttering in the shadows, "Father, where are you? You seem so unkind. The face you wear deceives you, this face has made you blind."

Getting to my feet, I slowly moved toward the sound of the young man's voice. I stretched my steps as far as my shackles would allow and made my way, feeling in the dark. Suddenly, bats flew out of the darkness and fluttered about my head, screeching. I panicked and screamed, flailing my arms in wild desperation. The bats flew off in all directions, leaving me with my hands covering my face in horror.

When I regained my senses and opened my eyes, I realized I no longer wore shackles and was outside in the courtyard of an enormous castle. Instead of groping in the dark, I stood beside a beautiful pale brown horse. I ran my fingers over its short soft coat.

Tiny was in the distance, in his child form. He was running from the Kongwanee soldiers along the palace wall. He was calling out to me.

"Ride!" he yelled. "Ride to Morzia's and I will meet you there!"

With quickness, I leaped atop the horse's back. Snatching up the long braided reins, I gave a kick and yelled, "Hyah!" The horse broke into a gallop and bolted across the courtyard.

I heard the call from the towers, "Lower the gates! Seal the courtyard!"

I dug my heels into the horse's sides and lowered my head. With my eyes forward and a tight grip on the reins, I charged the gate as five soldiers crossed my path, attempting to stop me. The horse reared up and I was thrown to the ground.

I quickly jumped to my feet, but I was no longer in Kongwana, but back on the Plain of Sorrows. Tiny and I were standing right between the two towering spires. I held the scepter in my hand, but I did not know what to do with it.

"Well, lass, what are you waiting for?" he said to me. "Say the word."

"I don't know what I am supposed to say," I told him.

"The name of he who became the seed of hope," he said, staring back at me as if I was supposed to know.

"But who was that?" I asked. I gazed out beyond the spires at the gently sloping hills that seem to end at their feet.

"Here we are at the gate to the netherworld on the day of the great convergence, and you don't know his name?" Tiny scoffed at me.

"I don't know," I snapped. "I don't know!" I shook the scepter at the sky in anger. "I don't know!" I screamed.

Then I threw it at the ground and it stuck deep into the dark, damp soil. The ground itself began to rumble beneath our feet. It slowly grew louder and louder, until I recognized its source.

"It's the sound of charging horses," Tiny said. "An army of horses, Emily. They are coming. They are coming for you. Run!" he cried.

There was a scream and Morzia dropped the destiny stone. "Run, Emily!" she yelled. "The soldiers are crossing the river. They are coming for you! Run! Hide!"

Tiny snatched the scepter from the arms of the chair, pulled the hood of his cape over his head, and disappeared. Morzia grabbed my arm and pulled me to my feet, urging me, "Run! Run!"

The soldiers on horseback sacked the town as the infantrymen searched each house, one by one, turning them inside out. I darted behind one of the huts, only to be chased out again by a horseman.

No longer under the influence of the memory stones, their words and commands fell on my ears like babbling and squawking. The only word I could make out was "Bonangi!" They feverishly and methodically tore the town apart looking for something. The houses that were searched and found to be empty were burned to the ground. Women and children cried and screamed in the chaos as everyone fled the streets.

A young boy, separated from his mother, wandered aimlessly in the street as the horses and men charged about. I ran to save the child before he was trampled to death in the mayhem. Snatching him up, I ran to place him in his mother's waiting arms. Just as I did, two soldiers caught hold of me and threw me to the ground.

They quickly shackled my wrists and slid a pole through my arms behind my back, then they used the pole to drag me backward across the ground. "Aaaahhhh!" I screamed, when my shoulders felt the full weight of my own body. They were nearly pulled from their sockets.

Morzia pleaded with them, begged for my life, as they took me away to their commander. But they shoved her to the ground and stepped over her as if she were a pile of rubbish beneath their feet. They took me to a decorated soldier on horseback. He barked out an order and pointed to a wagon with a yoke for the pole I now bore and shackles for my feet.

I called out to Morzia. "Don't worry, Morzia! I know where the door is! I know!" I yelled. "Did you hear me? I know where the netherworld is! Tiny will come for me! Don't worry!"

As I spoke those final words, a soldier stepped forward and slapped my face. He glared at me with his hand poised to deliver a second blow. I held my tongue as they loaded me onto the wagon like common livestock. I was left to my fate as the wagon proceeded to cross the river into Kongwana. My last view of Safora was one of a town in flames and utter destruction. My heart filled with despair.

CHAPTER TEN

FACE TO FACE

The wagon plodded and jostled along as it approached the slow-moving waters of the river. The cold water rose beneath the wagon wheels and above. It swept past my legs and then my waist. Finally, it stopped rising when it reached my neck. *It's a good thing the river isn't any deeper*, I thought.

Still, I could not take my eyes off Safora burning in the distance. Though the water washed over me, it could not cleanse that vision from my mind.

Looking into the night sky, I saw the first full moon of spring. If Tiny was correct about the great convergence, then we only had four weeks until the second full moon and the last day. I was in no position to argue with my hosts about that point.

The visions of the memory stones haunted me throughout the rest of that long, lonely ride to Marzadune. The shadow they had cast upon the past could quite easily fall upon our future as well. The destiny stone in particular plagued my mind. The fractured thoughts and broken dreams left me with more questions than answers. *Who was the maiden I saw, and what is the name of the seed of hope?* Little did I know, I was to have plenty of time to ponder these questions in the days to come. That night passed slowly for someone hanging from a pole stretched between two yokes and chained to the bed of a wagon.

The shimmering sun crept above the eastern horizon, piercing my weary eyes with light. As I looked at the fields surrounding Marzadune, I noticed some of them had been cleared and were full of tents set up in camps. Looking closer, I saw men busy fashioning spears, swords, and axes. There were corrals of horses, some of them wearing armor. Targets were set in a row for practicing archery just outside the encampment. *If I didn't know better, I would swear Kongwana is preparing for war*, I thought to myself.

It was only a short while later that our little caravan of misery entered the gates of Marzadune proper. It was a sprawling city, comparable to Salizar in almost every way. The people of the city lined the streets with faces of astonishment. Some were getting on with the business of life, but some gawked at me as I passed as if they could not make out what I was.

We wound our way through the streets and finally came to the towering walls of the palace. There was but one large gate and beyond that a courtyard; a courtyard that looked strikingly familiar. Inside the courtyard, several craftsmen worked feverishly on different objects carved from the trunks of trees. One didn't need to be a general in order to see that they were making catapults—lots of them—and the catapults were of an immense size.

I now believed Tiny's fears of war were well justified. The wagon stopped with a jerk in front of a set of steps. At the top, stood four giant pillars that held up a buttress of gleaming white limestone. Two guards from the palace unshackled the yokes that held the pole I was lashed to. They dragged me from the cart and we ascended the steps. I tried to keep up, but with my feet in chains, I stumbled, and the tops of my feet dragged across the steps.

They carried me through the many halls and corridors of the palace until we reached a towering archway that led to a massive room—the throne room, no doubt. There, perched in an elaborate chair of gold and green velvet, was Morzia's good King Azutoo. A flock of dignitaries and advisers stood by nervously as I was dragged before him and cast to the ground.

I twisted my neck to look up at this so-called "good king." He was a man of considerable size. His skin was a deep shade of brown, the color of a walnut, but his face had an unnatural glow. It was a dark face with deep, tortured eyes of rage and discontent. He had every bit the madness in his face that my father had the day I left Salizar. He wore a long flowing robe of green and gold, and a stately crown beset with emeralds.

"*Onomatee!*" he shouted, as he looked down on me in disgust. "*Onomatee cassito gui!*"

"*Omnamie*, Azutoo," said a voice that rose out of the gaggle of men standing close by. "*Omnamie ocko agatti.*"

Then a man stepped forward and I got the shock of my life. He was a man with all the gaunt features and malevolent charm that the memory of Elexi could evoke. Though Elexi was as pale as a bloodless corpse and this man was as dark as a burnt coffin, they could have been twins. He was skinny and frail, with straight jet-black hair, and looked sickly. His eyes were sinister black caverns of emptiness that consumed all hope in their void. I was immediately filled with contempt and mistrust.

He motioned to the guards to pull me from the floor and set me on my knees. Then he circled me in silence for a moment at first. I watched the way he moved. He had all the pompous arrogance and cunning of the man who controlled my father. I could have sworn he was Elexi.

He stopped pacing and stood in front of me. Then, he smiled a devious smile. It was a smile I felt sure I recognized.

"Elexi?" I queried. "Is that you?"

Suddenly, his eyes filled with rage and he slapped my face with the back of his hand. "How dare you speak my brother's name in my presence?" he scolded. "I am Argose, chief adviser to his eminence, King Azutoo. His Majesty does not want to soil his tongue speaking your foul language, so I will translate."

I slowly turned my face to meet his indignant stare. His cutting gaze glared down the length of his long crooked nose at me.

"You are an intruder here. What is your name?" he asked.

"Emily," I answered. "My name is Emily."

"Why were you found so close to our borders?" he asked, as he began to pace back and forth in front of me.

"I was visiting a friend in Safora. That is all," I said calmly.

"Ha!" he scoffed. "*Azacki ni bagato gee!*" he shouted as he turned toward the king. "Is it not true you were taking part in a festival in Safora? There is no use in lying, we all heard the drums."

"I was," I said plainly.

"So you admit you were sowing the seeds of discontent in the hearts of the good people of Safora," he said with a devious grin.

"No!" I snapped.

"You!" he said, waving his finger in my face. "You treacherous, pale-skinned little vermin. You came to our land to breed rebellion against our good King Azutoo."

"No!" I protested. "I was only attending the festival." I turned to the king and said, "It was your soldiers who burned Safora to the ground."

Argose waved to the guards and pointed to the floor. They promptly shoved me down to the ground and placed their feet upon the pole across my back. My face was pressed firmly to the floor.

Argose knelt down to speak directly to me. "You will only address me at this assembly. Is that clear?" Then he leaned in close and whispered in my ear. "Careful, Princess, you don't want to lose your head...yet." He rose to his feet and waved the guards back to their positions.

How does he know who I am? What else could he know about me? The thoughts raced through my head.

"*Awnati, agqwa tolemy* Bonangi," said the king.

"King Azutoo wants to know what you have done with Bonangi," said Argose.

"Bonangi?" I said cautiously.

"The scepter! What have you done with the scepter?" shouted the King.

"I...I...I don't know where it is," I said nervously.

"She has hidden it, Your Highness, *somatti backloval arasome* Safora," said Argose.

"*Nomani copgalli zoa?*" asked King Azutoo.

"The king wants to know where you are from," Argose said with a smile and a raised eyebrow.

I knew that the answer to this question would not sit well with the king, but to be caught lying would only make matters worse. "Salizar," I answered softly.

"Salizar?" scoffed Argose. "You might as well just admit it, you're a spy!"

"No! I am not a spy!" I retorted.

"Did you know, Emily, we will soon be at war with your beloved Salizar?" said Argose with a twisted delight.

"What? War? You can't, you shouldn't…I mean, what reason could you possibly have to make you want to go to war with Salizar?" I said with my fists clenched in rage. The chains upon my hands rattled out my frustration.

"Do you see, Your Majesty? These people, these traitorous pale ones from the north," said Argose, pointing his disparaging finger in my face. "She claims to know nothing of the war, yet I have it from reliable sources that she gained passage to our country on a warship." His eyes literally glowed with the prospect of proving my guilt. He then turned and looked deep into my face. "All the more reason that she should be exterminated, Your Highness." His voice rumbled with the reassurance of a malcontent.

I was helpless in my chains. Questions were sparked in my mind. *How does he know about the* Swiftly Gale*? I didn't even know it was a warship until the day of her sinking.*

"*Ana otto aunumatzi?*" said the king.

"Why, yes, Your Highness, I do," said Argose. "I recommend that you lock her in the dungeon until such time as you see fit to execute her."

The king rose to his feet, stepped down from his throne, and drew close to me. He looked upon me as one would a warthog waiting for slaughter. His face was unnaturally dark and chiseled, and his eyes were deep, furrowed pits of radiant malevolence. It was like looking into the face of my father the day I left Salizar.

"Take her away," he said to the guards softly. "She is fouling the air with her presence. Take her to the dungeon."

The guards quickly jerked me off the floor. Argose seemed thoroughly pleased with himself and folded his hands in contentment.

The guards carried me briskly away, but as they did, I caught a gleam of light reflected by some object in the corner. It was a large full-length mirror, identical to the one I shattered in my bedchamber in Salizar.

As they dragged me through the palace, I saw more and more—there were mirrors all over the palace. They were in every room and in some of the halls. They were exactly like the ones Elexi had brought to Ironcrest Castle.

The guards took me down a dimly lit spiral staircase. Down, down into the pit of the palace's core. My thoughts flashed back to poor Marlow Basseti and the deep, dark, lonely despair he was left to. *Is that to be my fate? What kind of misery do they have in store for me?* I wondered.

We reached the end of that long spiral staircase and entered a vast chamber, with many shadowy and ominous corners. The dungeon was not divided into separate cells, but rather two long cells on either side of a corridor of bars. These bars were as thick as my wrists, and there was but a single door in both of these barred walls.

The guards chose the door to the left, unlocking it and marching me through. They had to enter the cell sideways; the threshold was too narrow for the pole I bore. They finally freed me from that cursed pole and chained the shackles around my hands to a long thick chain mounted on the floor. I was able to walk around some, albeit only in a circle. I was still grateful for that.

Once the guards had finished, they took their leave by that one door, slamming and locking it. I could hear the tumblers of the lock rattle and roll until they fell into place. It gave a sense of permanence to my predicament.

I looked around as my eyesight adjusted to my new surroundings. A pile of straw that was to be my bed lay loose in the corner. A small barred opening close to the ceiling was the only source of light during the day. It was too high for me to reach and too small for me to fit through. It was put there, no doubt, simply to let the noxious smell escape—and, unfortunately, to let the rain in. Massive pillars fortified the foundation of the palace and they, too, were decorated with the ornaments of shackles and chains.

The guards had taken their place just outside the door. Since it was an open chamber of bars, they could see me and I could see them, though they did not seem too interested in my movements as I rattled around in my chains. The light would be nearly gone from that small opening before I would receive my first visitor.

Argose emerged from the base of the stairs and approached the two guards. "*Socanall bauctumazu ozm gui*," he said.

One guard handed him the keys to the cell and then both guards disappeared up the stairs. Argose calmly unlocked the door, entered the cell, and stood just out of reach of my hands.

"They have gone to fetch your rations for the day," he said. "It is more than you deserve."

"Get to the point," I snapped. "What do you want? Why are you here?"

"You used my brother's name. How I detest that name. He has been a thorn in my side since the day we were born." His words echoed with contempt. "So, you are one of his spies. I should have known he would sink to treachery of this nature."

"I am no spy, but if I have my way, your war will never happen," I said, shaking my fist at him.

"Well then," he said smugly, "we must take special precautions to make sure that you don't get your way." He looked around the cell. "I think we have done rather well to be certain that doesn't happen, don't you?"

"Rest assured, Argose, you will have your day," I growled.

"Oh, I intend to, Princess, a day when I and King Azutoo crush my brother and his puppet King Tobias, your father. Ha, ha, ha." His laughter rang throughout the dungeon, adding fuel to his already overextended ego. He seemed to revel in the sound of his own voice. "Don't worry, Princess," he added. "We will find the scepter and your alleged grandfather, Tiny Lynquest. Then, backed by all the powers of the netherworld, I will finally grind Elexi into the dust, along with the rest of you pale-skinned vermin."

Just then, the two guards returned with some bread and water. Argose stood to one side as they entered the cell, placed the food just within my grasp, and returned to their posts.

"Tiny will bring me the scepter, Emily. He will bring it, or you will be executed. He has three weeks," he said. And then he departed, leaving me with that parting thought as a morsel to go with my rations.

That night, the guards spoke among themselves as I listened. "I wish I spoke Kongwanee," I said aloud to myself. Then I heard a voice I understood coming from the shadows of one of the giant pillars. It was a soft, kind voice of a young man. I stretched my chains in that direction. "What?" I muttered softly. "What was it that you said? I didn't hear you."

A young Kongwanee man leaned into the flickering light of the oil lamps that were lit. He was chained to the back side of the pillar in the dark. "I said they are talking about the king," he said softly.

"You mean your so-called good King Azutoo," I grumbled. "What are they saying about him?"

"They are saying the king is not well. Something is not right. They are saying there are rumors that Argose is actually controlling the king somehow."

"What about you?" I asked. "What do you think?"

"Me?" he asked. "I know the rumors are true."

"How do you know?" I asked.

"I am his son, Prince Cahogway. My father had me locked up down here, so I didn't interfere with his plans for war." The young man's face reflected the futility of his situation.

Good grief, my father just sent me to my room, I thought to myself. "But how do you know Argose is the reason?" I whispered back.

"My father is a man of peace. He has always detested war," he said.

"Maybe he has had a change of heart," I said.

"It was more like a change of face," he answered.

"What?" I asked loudly.

The guards fell silent and looked into the cell. I tried to look like I was talking to myself, which, with all I had been through lately, would have made perfect sense. After a moment or two of watching me, they went back to their conversation, and we returned to ours.

Slowly, I leaned into the shadows toward the young man. "What do you mean by 'a change of face'?" I asked.

"Several weeks ago," he said, "a gift came to the palace from some strange country."

"Wait," I said, "don't tell me. It was a mask, wasn't it?"

"Yes, how did you know?" he asked in astonishment.

"Was it white, with a menacing look of anger?" I asked.

"No, it was black, but it had all the evil expression that you speak of," he said. "I saw Argose talking to his reflection in a mirror and telling someone he would, as he put it, 'See to it that the king tries the mask on.'"

"After that, your father was different, wasn't he?" I said.

"Yes. The very next day he began to speak of war with Salizar, some strange talk about returning the scepter to its origin, to the 'honorable people,' to use his words."

"I spoke out against war with my father and he had me locked in my room," I said.

"Argose made sure I was out of the way. That is how I ended up down here." His head sank in a quiet, reluctant surrender. "But, how is it that you know of these things?" he asked.

"Because Argose has a brother," I said. "His name is Elexi, and he has some strange spell on my father. And just like yours, it all began with a gift: a white mask from a country that no one had heard of."

"Then you and I are connected by these two masks, these two faces," he said.

"I guess we are," I said. "Here, have some of my bread. We have to keep up our strength."

"Why is that so urgent? We are not going anywhere."

"Because Tiny will come for me, and when he does, I want you ready to leave," I said.

"How are you so sure this Tiny is going to be able to get past all the guards? Is he really capable of such a feat?" he asked in skepticism.

"Oh, Tiny will come," I said. "You can be sure of that. He will never give up the scepter to Argose, and I must accomplish a task before the next full moon."

"A task? What kind of task?" he asked.

"I have to seal the door to the netherworld from the other side," I said.

His mouth fell open and a look of complete bewilderment came across his face. "You do realize that you are talking like a crazy woman, don't you?" he remarked.

"Look," I said plainly, "it is far too complicated to explain and still appear sane. Just trust me. Tiny will come for me and we will get out of here."

"I guess a morsel of hope is better than no hope at all," he said.

"Besides," I added with a smile, "who else can you trust at this particular time? Shut up and eat the bread."

We would share my rations for the next two and a half weeks. Argose came and threatened me with execution three more times, and each time it ended with him storming out in a huff.

Cahogway and I became fast friends in those dark days, and he told me how his father had made sure he was educated in many languages and cultures. That is how we could speak so freely. It gave the mask his father wore an even more cruel and ironic twist. Talking with Cahogway, I came to know his father as he used to be, a kind and gentle man of peace.

I felt committed to Cahogway; he had lost his father to the magic of the masks, too. Though the pieces of this puzzle were beginning to fit, I still did not know what Salina's part was in all this. Somehow, I knew she was behind it, feeding the madness of war once again.

Eventually, there were only three days left until my scheduled execution, and still no sign of Tiny. Cahogway had heard the guards discussing an increase of guards around the palace.

"Argose must be expecting Tiny to come for me," I said.

"Do you really think he will?" he asked eagerly.

"Oh, he'll come all right," I said. "I don't know how, but he will definitely come. We just have to be patient."

The following day came and went, but still no Tiny. My execution was scheduled for the next afternoon, and I was stubbornly rebelling against any thoughts of that dismal prospect, especially when the punishment for being a spy was to be hanged from a mast above the palace rampart. I lay my head down on that pile of straw that night, listening for any sound that could be interpreted as a sign of rescue.

"Pssst." Cahogway was trying to get my attention. "Pssst, pssst. Emily…he will come, won't he?"

"He'll come. I don't know when, but he will come. The great convergence is tomorrow night. He will come or all will be lost," I said, burying my head in the straw.

Cahogway sank back into the silent shadows and quietly waited out the passing of the night. I, too, lay still, impatient and restless in that sleepless night.

The rooster crowed early the next morning, as if I really needed waking. I stared up at the opening near the ceiling. The morning light streamed in and showered its brilliance in a pool on the floor. I took my place in that pool and bathed in the light, drinking it in as it fell upon my face. *Oh, what I wouldn't give to see out that window right now,* I thought. Letting this pure light wash me clean, I prepared for the worst. *I've done the best I could.* I thought. *And now?*

"*Zumogwee! Doka zumogwee!*" A cry rang out from the staircase. "*Mallagitu sombyani obigatie!*"

The guards said nothing, but took up their arms and ran out. As they ascended the stairs, a curious thing happened—the keys that hung on one guard's belt just fell to the floor. He didn't seem to notice in his urgency to leave.

"What is happening?" I yelled. Turning to Cahogway, I asked, "What does it mean? The word *zumogwee*, what does *zumogwee* mean?"

He looked at me as if he could not believe what he was about to say. "Dragon," he said. "It means dragon attack."

My heart jumped in my chest at the sound of those words. "He is coming!" I said in excitement. "Tiny is coming to get us!" I turned once again to see where the keys had fallen, but they were gone. "What?" I shrieked in disbelief. "No! What happened to the keys? How are we going to get out of here now?"

Then, there was a most peculiar sound. It was the sound of someone whistling; whistling like he didn't have a care in the world. I looked around, but no one was there. Just the sound of someone whistling a tune could be heard, and a merry little tune at that. Suddenly, the tumblers of our cell door lock were disturbed. Someone was unlocking the door.

As pretty as you please, the door swung wide open, as did my mouth. Then my shackles fell off my wrists and I was set free.

"Tiny, is that you?" I asked as I groped around.

At that, he materialized right before my eyes. "You were expecting your valet, perhaps?" he said with a smile.

I threw my arms around him and kissed his boyish face. "Oh, what a grand sight you are," I said. "And just in time, too. What took you so long? They are going to execute me today," I scolded.

"Over my dead body," he said sharply. Tiny took off his cape and placed it over my shoulders. He tied it good and tight around my neck. "Come, Princess, we must be going," he said.

"Wait!" I said. "We have to take Cahogway."

"Who is Cahogway?" he asked.

I pointed into the shadows as Cahogway's frail, dark, emaciated face peered back at me. "He is the prince, King Azutoo's son," I said. "His father suffers from the same madness as my own. We can't just leave him behind."

"I see," said Tiny. "Well, this does change everything." Tiny quickly unchained Cahogway from the pillar.

"This is him?" scoffed Cahogway. "This is your great Lynquest? He is but a child himself, how can he free us?"

"He made it past the guards, didn't he? And you are standing there with no chains on you, aren't you?" I remarked.

"It's all right lass," said Tiny. "I have always found that being underestimated was one of my greatest advantages."

"How are we going to get past all those guards, anyway?" I asked.

"Someone scattered all the army's horses to the four winds and started a fire in the stables," he said nonchalantly. "Currently, Subakai is engaging the army to give us more time." Tiny then turned to Cahogway. "Can you run?" he asked.

"Can I? You just try and stop me," Cahogway answered.

"Good," said Tiny. "Where is the highest tower in the palace?"

"It is the north tower. It is used by my father's mages for stargazing and overseeing Marzadune," he said.

"Excellent," said Tiny. "Run for that tower and I will meet you there. Emily, keep the hood of my cape over your head. If you do, no one will see you. You will find a horse tied up in the courtyard. It has a bridle, but no saddle. Take the horse and ride to Morzia's. Cahogway and I will meet you there."

"But, what will you do?" I asked.

"I will lead the guards away from you and Cahogway," he said.

"How will you get away?" I asked.

"Don't worry, lass, I still have my horn and a friend in the sky," he assured me.

I smiled and hugged him before pulling the hood of his cape over my head.

"Where did she go?" asked Cahogway.

"She is still here, lad, you just can't see her. She will be following right behind me until we get to the top of the stairs. You just get yourself to the tower," said Tiny.

Tiny led the way up the spiral stairs cautiously. Reaching the top, he stepped out into the light.

"*Valmot!*" someone shouted. "You, boy! Stop right where you are!" It was Argose; he was on his way to check the dungeon and had cut us off at the top of the stairs. He snapped Tiny up by the arms below the shoulders. "Who are you?" he said, shaking him violently. "What are you doing in the palace?"

Tiny's feet dangled beneath him as Argose held him off the ground. I froze in my tracks. At least, until I remembered, *Oh yeah, he can't see me.* Then, I took the opportunity and kicked Argose as hard as I could in the shin.

"Oh!" he yelled, dropping Tiny and grabbing his leg.

Tiny wasted no time; he sped off down the hall as Argose limped behind, calling for the guards.

I stepped out into the hall and checked to see if anyone was coming. "Come on," I whispered. "Now is your chance. It is all clear. Go. Go, and I will see you in Safora."

Cahogway took off like a flash for the north tower and I carefully made my way toward the palace courtyard, giving Tiny a good head start. As I neared the giant columns at the palace entrance, I could hear the commotion Tiny was causing with the guards. I slipped outside completely unnoticed and found the horse Tiny had spoken of. It was a tall light brown horse with a blond mane. I ran my fingers over its shiny coat.

Tiny burst through a door at the top of the horseshoe-shaped wall that made up the courtyard and ran along the length. Two guards were chasing him and two guards blocked his way. Then, he leaped atop the buttress and jumped over the archer's nests one by one. The guards frantically tried to grab his ankles, but he was much too quick, they never had a chance. Tiny had succeeded in drawing the attention of all the guards on the wall. They all chased him like a chicken on a weasel farm. Even the guards on the ground followed him with their eyes.

I looked at the horse and remembered the vision of the destiny stone. *I have been here before,* I thought. *And I know what to do.*

Untying the horse, I jumped onto its back. Unfortunately, when I did, a breeze caught the hood of the cape and blew it off my head.

"*Amacha!*" someone yelled. "*Amacha gamboni!*" he repeated. I had been spotted.

Tiny called out to me as he ran, "Ride, Emily! Ride to Morzia's! Ride like the wind!"

Just then, Argose cried out from the balcony above the courtyard, "*Zavodumati!* Lower the gate! *Zavodumati! Zavodumati!*"

I snatched up the reins and charged across the yard. Lowering my head and digging my heels into the horse's sides, I charged the gate, but five guards barred my way with spears held high. The gate slowly closed behind them and left me trapped within the walls of the yard.

Presented with the points of five spears, the horse reared up and I nearly fell off. I threw my arms around the horse's neck and dangled until it dropped back down on all fours.

Pulling hard to the left, I brought the beast around and faced the palace once more. As I did, I looked up—and that is when I saw him. He was descending from the sky above the palace like some massive dark green crescent moon. His eyes gleamed gold and black, and plumes of smoke and fire belched from his nostrils.

"Subakai!" Tiny yelled. "The gate!"

Subakai landed upon the bone-white buttress resting on the pillars, took a deep breath, and released a huge ball of fire toward the gate. The men standing in the way ran for their lives to escape the blast. The ball of fire collided with the thick wooden gate and it exploded in a shower of slivers and flying lumber.

Through the smoke of the scorched earth, I saw the streets of Marzadune, so once again I pulled the hood of my cape over my head and charged toward the gate and freedom. Though the streets of the city were bustling, the only thing the good people of Marzadune saw was a riderless horse bolting for the open fields and beyond.

Meanwhile, Tiny had jumped down from the wall onto a craftsman's roof and again to the ground, as he tried to make his way around the palace's east side. The archers on the wall took their aim, but as they did, Subakai leaped down from the buttress above the pillars and whipped his tail around, smashing the catapults and wagons against the wall. The archers quickly took cover when he blew fire at them. Subakai took care not to hurt them, just scare them, giving Tiny time to get away.

Tiny darted through a small gate in the wall that led to the gardens on the eastern side of the palace. It was in front of the fountain that lay before the steps of the eastern entrance to the palace that Argose caught Tiny by the arm. He dragged him along, calling for the guards. Tiny struggled, but he had grown tired from running.

Out of breath and weary, he dug his heels in and forced Argose to drag him. Suddenly, someone darted out of a nearby bush and shoved Argose headlong into the fountain. It was Cahogway; he had been watching from the north tower and had seen Argose enter the garden.

"It was a lucky thing you were watching," said Tiny. "He nearly had me."

"Well, I wasn't going to let you have all the fun," Cahogway replied.

Argose floundered around in the water, still trying to call out to the guards. "*Amacha! Outimal osaca!*" he screamed.

"The guards are coming," said Cahogway. "Quick, follow me."

Cahogway led Tiny to a stairway that rose the full height of the north tower along the outside. Archers lined up at the bottom and began firing volleys of arrows at them, while Argose led another group of guards up the stairway after them. Up, up, up they raced, until they arrived at the top, tired and with nowhere else to run.

Tiny ran to the buttress and climbed into the archer's nest. "Come on," he said. "They are coming!"

"What are you going to do, jump?" exclaimed Cahogway.

"Yes," said Tiny. "We both are. Now come on!"

Cahogway reluctantly climbed into the archer's nest next to Tiny just as Argose arrived with his gaggle of guards. The guards raised their weapons, but Argose held them back.

"Well," he chirped happily, "if it isn't the king's treasonous son. Go ahead, Cahogway, jump. It will be easier to explain to your father than death by the sword." Argose smiled wide, knowing that he had them trapped.

Cahogway looked over the side at the towers' dizzying height and then smiled back at Argose. Tiny looked down and said, "Are you ready? You grab the left one, I grab the right." Tiny gave a slight bow to Argose and they both jumped over the side.

Argose waited and listened for the thud, but it never came. Slowly, he approached the ledge from which they jumped. His eyes grew wide and his face flushed with fear as Subakai's giant head rose above the tower. Tiny and Cahogway were hanging from his enormous horns.

"Run!" screamed Argose. "*Asachee, asachee!*"

The group of men stumbled and tripped over each other, desperately trying to get down the stairs first. Argose threw two guards in front of himself, saying, "*Palipow, palipow!* Protect me, protect me!"

"*Umatwa zanoti gui*, Argose," said Cahogway, as he climbed up on Subakai's head. "I will return for my father's soul," he added.

Subakai released a roar that left no doubt; there would be no man who would dare attack or follow. Then he turned and flew off toward Safora.

CHAPTER ELEVEN

SEED OF HOPE

As Tiny and Cahogway soared above the soldiers scrambling to gather up their horses and put out the burning stables, I was charging across the open fields toward the River Topaz. I arrived at the river under a high midday sun. The cool water caressed my legs as I made my way across just downstream from the town. Then, strolling into the town slowly, I wandered among the burned-out wreckage and charred skeletons of what once were people's homes.

Some people had already begun to rebuild, with fresh stacks of sod neatly piled one on top of the other. The women of Safora were busy sifting through the remains of their belongings, searching for anything still of use. One or two of them looked up as I strolled by; of course, all they saw was a stray light brown horse aimlessly wandering the streets.

As I looked down into the eyes of one lonely old woman, I noticed a shadow pass rapidly over the ground. It quickly moved along the street out of town and up the hillside toward Morzia's home. When I reached the heights of her modest little house, I saw the unmistakable shock of Subakai's whiplike tail disappearing behind the hills beyond. Lightly pulling on the reins of my horse, I made my way out of town, leaving the good people of Safora to sift through the shards of their shattered lives. I couldn't help feeling it was all because of me.

When I had arrived at Morzia's, I left the horse tied up outside, pulled the hood off my head, and went in unannounced. "Morzia," I called out. "I am free. Hello? Is anybody here?" The silence left me baffled. *Where could they be?* I thought. I looked around at her simple dwelling. *Everything is still in order. The kitchen looks tidy and everything is put away. Surely, the soldiers would have come here, too. But where is the scepter?*

Going back outside, I went around the house. It was then that I noticed that the horses Tiny and I had tethered were gone.

"Emily!" Morzia's sweet voice called to me. "Emily! Up here! Look up here!"

I lifted my eyes to the top of the hill that rose behind her house. She was standing with the reins of both our horses in her hand. They were saddled and ready to ride.

I ran to the top of the hill and threw my arms around her. "Morzia, I'm free, I'm free," I said. "They were going to hang me today. Can you believe it?"

"No, child. We would not let that happen," she said, holding me tightly.

"Where are Tiny and Cahogway?" I asked.

She pointed down the other side of the hill, and there at the bottom was Subakai, a very old Tiny Lynquest, and a very, very bewildered Cahogway.

"I see you have witnessed Tiny's transformation," I said, chuckling. Cahogway just stood there with his mouth agape, staring at Tiny. "Close your mouth," I said. "You're drawing flies."

"Ha, ha, ha," Tiny laughed, and then said, "that is but a small sample of the power the scepter holds, lad."

"If that is true, we must make sure Argose never gets hold of it," said Cahogway. "He would surely abuse its power."

"Where is the scepter, anyway?" I asked.

"Don't worry, lass, it is truly safe," Tiny replied.

"Yes, but where?" I asked insistently.

"As you wish, Princess," he answered with a bow. Turning to Subakai, he said, "Subakai, if you would be so kind?"

The massive dragon bent low to the ground and bowed his head before me, as if he was paying me homage. There on his long thick bronze horn was the scepter. It had been lashed to the back of it.

"You strapped it to his head?" I exclaimed.

"Can you think of a safer place?" retorted Tiny.

"As a matter of fact, I can't," I said, laughing.

Tiny untied the scepter from Subakai's horn and slipped the ruby ring on its hand. Then Morzia once again removed the Tiger's eye from her finger and consigned herself to darkness as she handed the ring of truth to Tiny. He held her hand for a moment before taking it from her. I could see it was much harder for him to take the ring than it was for her to give it up.

He slid the final ring onto the pinky of the scepter and marveled at the sight of the four rings together. "There they are," he said. "The white diamond of wisdom, the black onyx of courage, the red ruby of compassion, and the green eye of truth." He handed the scepter to me and said, "It is yours now. It will be yours to carry from now on."

He then gave me a small quiver to keep it in. Sliding the quiver over my shoulder and head, I slipped the scepter into it.

"We must be going," said Tiny. "Wherever the door to the netherworld is, we must reach it before midnight tonight."

"It is on the Plain of Sorrows. That wretched place where death is always present," I said. "The two giant spires mark its place in our world."

"Huh," said Morzia. "It seems so obvious, does it not? Only Salina would put a grave-yard at her doorstep."

Tiny turned to Morzia, saying, "I will say a proper good-bye, then, my dear, for I do not know whether I will return." Then he kissed her ever so softly on the lips and gave her hand a squeeze.

A single tear rolled down Morzia's face. "You had better return," she said. "I would be lost without you."

I mounted my horse while they said their good-byes. Looking down at Cahogway, I said, "I will be looking forward to your friendship in a more peaceful time."

He smiled up at me. "As will I," he said.

"Come, Tiny, we must be on our way," I said.

Tiny released Morzia's hand and mounted his horse. "Keep a memory stone for me, Morzia," he exclaimed, "for today we are living the stuff of legends!"

We turned our horses and charged up the hill. Safora lay below us, tattered and somber, but still full of hope. Making our way down to the road that led to Sazway, we headed in that direction and rode our horses as fast as they would run.

Once we reached Sazway, we rode into the hills around the village, so as not to be seen. There were soldiers in the village posted as guards on all the roads leading in. We watched from our vantage point upon the hills. In the distance behind us, I could see a long ribbon-like caravan marching on the road to Sazway.

"Look," I said to Tiny. "Is that the Kongwanee army?"

"It is," said Tiny. "We must have left Safora just in time."

"If I was to venture a guess," I said, "I would say those big covered wagons are the cata-pults I saw them making in Marzadune."

"I would wager you're right, lass. And they are probably heading to the Plain of Sorrow as well. We best be off," said Tiny. "We should try to put some space between us and that army."

From the heights of those hills, we tore off toward the forest that surrounds that dismal plateau. In no time at all, we had reached it and entered the woods in the easternmost end. We moved as quickly as the dense, dark forest would allow, leaping fallen trees and forg-ing lesser gorges as we went. Finally we arrived at the plain. We dismounted and tied our horses to a low-hanging tree branch at the forest's edge.

We knew we had reached the Plain of Sorrows when we felt the cold stare of an ever-present shadow hanging over us. It was like a thousand jealous eyes were watching our every move as we trod the muddy earth. We slowly approached the enormous spires on foot. They towered high into the sky, at least as high as twenty men.

At the base, they were as big around as a water wheel turned on its side, with tops narrowed to a point, and the sides, though round and smooth, were pitted with deep grooves that twined their way to the top. The appearance of rust in these grooves gave the bone-white stone the look of fresh blood. We stood between the two great spires, looking up.

"Well, lass," said Tiny, "we are here. What now?"

I pulled the scepter from my quiver and held it up, but nothing happened.

"Are you sure this is the place?" he asked.

"I am positive," I said. "But wait—I was supposed to call out a name."

"A name?" he questioned.

"Yes, the name of he who became the seed of hope," I said.

"Yes, yes," said Tiny eagerly. "And what is that name?"

"I don't know," I said.

"You don't know?" he snapped. "Here we are at the doorway to the netherworld on the last day of the great convergence, and you don't know?"

"The destiny stone didn't reveal what his name was," I barked back in my own defense.

I looked down in frustration. *Think, Emily, think!* I struggled in silent contemplation for a moment. *Who would have been the seed of hope, and what do you do with a seed?*

I looked around at the plateau that stretched out from the two giant spires toward the cliffs and the boneyard beyond. And then, I noticed the burial mound of Lucias in that entire vast expanse.

"Tiny?" I asked. "What possessed you to bury Lucias here on the Plain of Sorrows? It seems such an unlikely spot for his final resting place."

"I did not make that decision, lass, it was the scepter that chose that spot," he said. "As Subakai and I were flying him back to Safora, the scepter jumped out of my quiver and stuck itself into the ground on that very spot. I could not pull it from the earth until I had planted his body there."

"Then I know who is the seed of hope," I said with a smile. I held the scepter high in the air and yelled with confidence, "I evoke the name of he who is the seed of hope, Lucias Merriweather!"

Suddenly, a beam of blue-white light shot straight into the sky and then split into two distinct lights—one blue and the other white. The blue light struck the top of the spire to my left and the white light to my right. The ground began to rumble just like in my vision, but differed somehow. The low rolling hills that lay beyond the spires to the east seemed to move, as if they were a restless giant waking from his sleep. The hills themselves began to rise up, growing taller and taller. The ground at the base of the spires swelled and became a bog of black mud and earth.

Just behind each spire a mound appeared. Like two large bubbles, they swelled to the point of popping, and then they suddenly rolled over to reveal that they were the eyes of some gargantuan creature that had been submerged in an ancient bog beneath the ground. Higher and higher it rose, until the entire head was above the ground. It was the head of an enormous ancient lizard. Gills and webbed feet made it look like a salamander. Its slimy skin carried the mud of thousands of years. It looked down on Tiny and me as if we were but ants under its feet. We stepped backward and watched in amazement as it continued to grow. Finally, it rested its gigantic head on the ground between the spires, swallowed deeply, and belched a clear bubble formed by its gaping mouth.

I looked at Tiny in astonishment and said, "This is the doorway to the netherworld, a belching lizard?"

"Never question what you do not understand, lass. Just be glad you're not going in there alone," he said, staring down the throat of the ugly reptile.

At that moment, the scepter came to life and pointed directly into the darkness of the lizard's open throat. I felt the scepter pulling at my arm, drawing me into the giant's mouth.

"The scepter is urging us on," I said.

"Then we should go," said Tiny. "I have been on many adventures, Emily, but never down the gob of an ancient lizard. This should be interesting."

We slowly stepped through the cold, slimy mucus that made up the bubble and onto the creature's soft, spongy tongue. When we made our way back toward the innards of this bog-dwelling lizard, we heard the mouth close behind us.

"We have no choice now," said Tiny. "We have to go on."

Still the scepter called me forward, dragging me ever deeper into the murky depths of the underworld. I felt the ground beneath my feet harden and become firmer to walk on. A strange fog enveloped us and the scepter began to glow in that beautiful blue-white light, cutting through the dense mist and darkness.

Somehow, we were no longer in the belly of that beast, but had crossed over into a realm without boundaries as I knew them. We saw no ground, nor any walls, or any sign of ceiling or sky; just a black as thick as mud and glowing pale amber mist that seemed to swirl around us.

Giant white crystal shards, jutting upward in all directions, stuck out of the ground like trees of a forest in discord with the sky. Some lay in piles one on top of the other. In this forest of angled glass there were many dark and forbidding corners that would lay siege to our courage, if we let them. Then suddenly, around one of these lost corners, I saw a figure of a man appear out of nowhere. My heart jumped up into my throat. There, in the midst of the white crystals and fog, was a statue. It was the exact height and likeness of Captain Stalwart of the *Swiftly Gale*.

"Emily!" Tiny yelled to me. "I have found something!"

"What is it?" I asked.

"It is a statue," he said.

"Yes, I found one, too," I said. "This one looks like Captain Stalwart."

"This one looks just like the old hag I met in Kautchitzar," he said. "Here is another!" he exclaimed. "This one looks like Dorauch, the man who stole your father's throne."

As I turned a corner to see the statue of Dorauch, I saw yet another statue staring me in the face. It was Elexi—his precise likeness captured in every detail, right down to the arrogant malevolence on his face. Across from that statue stood the statue of Argose, his brother.

For the first time I was able to compare the two of them with my own eyes. They were mirrored opposites of each other. They had the same gaunt features and the same cold stare, their hair was exactly alike, and even their clothes were identical, though one was as dark as night and the other white as a ghost.

"Tiny!" I called out. "You have to come see this."

"Ah!" A woman's voice echoed through the cavernous underworld. "I see you have found my collection."

"Your collection?" I answered. "Just what kind of collection is it?"

"I collect souls, my dear." The voice seemed to come from every shadowy corner at the same time, resonating throughout. "Any unwary soul that is unfortunate enough to sail into my waters."

"Your waters? Who made them your waters?" I shouted back in indignation.

"They have been my waters since the foundation of the world, you impertinent little girl!" she raged. "Most of the souls I collect are pathetic, weak, insignificant spirits that lack the cruelty I find so desirable. I keep those souls in the pools that dot my beloved garden, my plateau of woe, my field of blood." Her voice bristled with malice and self-satisfaction.

"Have you no soul of your own, Salina? Have you no compassion, you miserable wretch?" I scowled.

"Once in a while, I come across a soul so bitter with indifference toward its fellow man, that I forge its likeness here in the netherworld and cast it back into the world of the living to do my bidding," she cackled.

"Then Elexi and Argose—"

"That's right, Emily, I control them both. So the puppeteers have their kings, but I am their master, ha, ha, ha. I am the true puppet master, ha, ha, ha, ha!" Her laughter rang out from every corner and resounded from every crystal. "Of course, they don't know that they are already dead. Where is the fun in that?"

"Tiny," I called frantically. "Tiny, where are you?" The scepter I held above my head shone light into the murky black void as I darted this way and that, desperately calling his name.

"You know, Emily," said Salina calmly, "not all things are dead here in my world. There are certain…creatures I have kept down here for my amusement. I like to think of them as pets, ha, ha, ha."

"Tiny, answer me!" I shouted. "Answer me!"

Then, as I turned another corner, I found him. He stood stock-still, motionless, staring at yet another statue. This one was the truly hideous Blackheart. A more gruesome animal I have never seen. Its large round head curdled with veins beneath the transparent skin. A gaping lipless mouth was made worse by the presence of long needlelike teeth. It stood on two legs, hunched over, and its back was covered with sparse patches of long hair. Its bat-like wings hung down on both sides and its enormous ears stuck out on either side of its head. I could literally feel fear trickle down my spine.

"Tiny," I said calmly, placing my hand on his shoulder. "It's just a statue. Don't let it scare you."

He slowly reached for the pouch he kept at his waist. Reaching in, he pulled the pepper shaker from its depths and began dumping its contents over his body.

"What are you doing? It is just a statue!" I exclaimed.

"Run, Emily," he said quietly. "Run, lass. You must find her inner sanctum, the place where Salina casts her spells. Quickly now, go, go."

"But it is just a stat—"

Just then, the Blackheart moved. My blood ran cold and chills raced across my skin.

Tiny started backing away from the wretched thing as it sniffed the air. It actually had a faint smile on its upturned face, as if it had just found something it had lost.

"Run, Emily, I will handle the Blackheart. Now go," he said, pulling the dagger from his belt.

"But I can't just leave you," I protested.

"Don't argue with me, lass!" he snapped. "Just go!"

Suddenly, the Blackheart leaped down from its pedestal and began to sniff the ground in my direction. Tiny jumped in front of me and pushed me away. At that moment, I felt a tug from the scepter. It was calling me away. My hand felt as if it had become part of the scepter as it dragged me deeper into the netherworld, leaving Tiny to fend for himself.

I heard them scuffling in the darkness. The Blackheart squawked and screamed terribly. "*Kasitzgeg, kasitzgeg,*" was the strange sound I heard as the scepter dragged me away. "*Kasitzgeg, kasitzgeg.*" Then Tiny screamed, and the beast made a horrifying screech, and then…silence. I felt my own heart sink in my chest.

Nevertheless, the scepter did not rest. It dragged me deeper and deeper into the land of the dead. It carried me along the ledges of pits that plummeted into black and across bridges of bones, and all the while, the muffled whisperings and mutterings of lost souls filled my ears with their loneliness. The despair of the ages echoed through the ramblings of their ghosts.

Finally, I reached a place I recognized. It was the bone-white face of the hideous maiden I had seen in the destiny stone. The image of her, at least, was carved into what passed for rock in the realms of the dead. Just as in my vision, it was a face without eyes or nostrils, only a gaping mouth as big as a house. The scepter, undaunted by my struggling, dragged me into the mouth of that stone face. It led to a room surrounded on all sides by crystals, white and gleaming. The ceiling, too, was made up of giant crystals laid one on top of the other.

A glimmering pool of quicksilver was at the center of this room. A fair-sized pool, about the size of a small pond, its surface shimmered like a looking glass, but moved like water. I looked into its depths expecting to see my reflection, but instead, I found myself looking at Maribelle as she cleaned the palace in Salizar.

"Maribelle!" I called out. She stopped what she was doing and looked around, as if she had heard me. I watched as she searched for the source of my voice. With a shrug of her shoulders, she went back to her task of dusting the mantel of the fireplace in my father's quarters.

"Welcome, child," said that persistent voice. "Welcome to my inner sanctum. I see you have discovered my pool of sight. It is how I see into your world."

"How does it work?" I asked. "I can see Maribelle, but she can't see me. I think she can hear me, though."

"From that pool, I can see through any reflection in your world. Mirrors are my windows into your world and I use them to my benefit," she said.

"This is how you are manipulating Elexi and Argose!" I exclaimed.

"Mankind is such a foolish creature, so easily misled. Vanity and pride being their weakest character," she said calmly, reveling in her words.

"And what of Elexi and Argose? How did you turn them against each other?"

"That is the beautiful thing. They have been rivals since the day they were born, allowing their differences to dictate who they are. They were foolish enough to squabble over their father's fortune in a battle along my boneyard," she said.

"Then their hatred for each other is not of your doing?" I asked.

"No," she said. "Their hatred kept me from the forgotten place, the place where nothing dwells. You see, since that fateful day when Lucias kept me from reaching the scepter, I have been waning, simply fading into oblivion. There was no war to feed my passions, only the odd ship that ventured too close to my cliffs. Elexi and Argose kept me alive in their hearts."

"Alive, but in your place!" I mocked. "Kept in the depths of the land of the dead where you belong."

"I need war to make me strong again. So, I fashioned two masks from the same earth I made their likenesses from and cast them back into your world. The soul of Elexi is directly connected to the very mask your father wears, ha, ha, ha."

The ground beneath my feet trembled with her laughter and the netherworld resounded with her voice.

"The war you plan will never take place. I have come to stop it!" I barked with conviction.

"Stop it? Ha, ha, ha. My dear, it has already begun!" she cackled. "Look into the pool and I will show you!"

Turning my eyes to the pool, I saw the images of men trudging through the mud and blood on the Plain of Sorrows. They battled, man against man, and madness against madness, with no end in sight, and there, standing on the mound at the heart of it all, was my father with his stone white face of rage brandishing his sword.

"You see, time in the land of the dead moves quite fast, ha, ha, ha," she cackled.

"Then it is too late," I said.

"Yes, my dear. It is much too late. I grow stronger with every drop of blood that falls from the eternal hourglass of life." Her voice seemed to swell with confidence.

I looked into the pool once more and again saw the horrors of war. The image was stained red by all the loss. Then, as I watched the chaos, I found myself focused on a dot in the background of the image. It grew larger as it drew nearer to the surface of the pool. After only a moment, I saw her hideous face becoming clearer and clearer as she rose to the top of that war-torn vision, her tentacles stretched upward in a grievous attack.

Suddenly, a tentacle broke the surface and latched on to the scepter. Then another grabbed the edge of the pool, and a third tentacle holding one great eye slowly emerged. Finally, she rose from the pool, as she was a faceless horror with kelp for hair and pale rotting skin.

"Give it to me, girl! All is lost! Accept your defeat!" she raged at me.

"No!" I screamed. "You'll not have it!"

By now the scepter had firmly attached itself to my hand. I couldn't let go even if I had wanted to. Her body slithered out of the pool like an octopus on dry land. She lashed two more tentacles onto the scepter and tried to wrest it from my hands. As she did, the beautiful blue-white light turned an evil amber-red.

"Do you see, Emily? I control the scepter. It is mine now and there is no one left to help you. You are all alone!"

With every word she spoke, the light grew brighter and brighter and burned with a fiery intensity. A bitter rage raced within my soul, clawing its way up from the depths of my heart. An anger inspired by pure malice took hold of me as I clung to the scepter with both hands.

I closed my eyes and concentrated on Morzia's face, her dark skin and compassionate smile. Like a flash of lightning, a vision came to me. I saw the blue light of Showhaun's spirit as it entered the scepter, and then I realized…

"No!" I shouted back. "I am not alone!"

"What?" she exclaimed.

"I have brought someone with me," I said. "Someone stronger than you."

"What are you squawking about, child?" she railed.

"I have brought your sister, Bonangi, and Showhaun!" I cried out.

In that instant, the bright red light flashed a brilliant white and a beautiful blue orb rose out of the hand atop the scepter. The orb grew until the face of Showhaun appeared in its glow.

"No! I killed you!" she screamed.

"My soul was never yours, Salina!" said the orb. "Back to your hole, siren. Back to the pit from which you came!"

I began to chant as if the words were being pulled from my mouth. "*Shallimbye guya onotu, et* Bonangi. Restore the balance, free Bonangi."

Salina let go of the scepter and covered her face as the white light grew brighter and brighter. She slowly backed away; her formless body twisted and writhed backward toward the pool. I shoved the scepter at her and she flinched, reluctantly slithering halfway into the pool.

"No! No!" she cried. "Not in my sanctum! Not here, sister! Not in my house!"

The power of Bonangi surged through me and I stepped forward, forcing her even further into the pool.

"No, sister, no! Not the abyss!" she pleaded. "Not where nothing dwells!"

Finally, the white light swelled and outshined even Showhaun's blue orb, overtaking it in sheer brilliance. Suddenly, a flock of pure white doves burst forth from the light and fluttered about her now-glowing sanctum. The crystal walls began to pulsate in unison with the light emanating from the scepter. The doves swooped and lunged at her, relentlessly pecking at her faceless form and one great eye.

"Curse you, child," she ranted. "I will still have my share of blood before this day has ended!"

"Into the black of the shadows, siren!" I yelled. "Back to your hole!"

Before that wretched mouth slid beneath the surface of the pool, she cried, "Camille! Come do my biding and I will have their souls!"

Then she slipped below the shimmering silver pool and the scepter gently touched the surface, turning it to stone. In an instant, the doves were drawn back into the light and the light dwindled to a soft blue glow.

I stumbled backward, my arms fell to my sides, and the scepter slipped from my hand. Weak and beleaguered, I fell to my knees and cradled my talisman until I regained my strength. No longer was the sacred scepter leading me, yet that soft and beautiful blue light still blazed forth in the darkness of that place. *I suppose I will have to find my own way out*, I thought.

I picked myself up and endeavored to find a way back through this bleak and dismal realm. I traced my steps, as well as I could recollect, wandering aimlessly in search of Tiny or any sign of a way out, and all the while, the ceaseless murmurings of those lonely formless spirits fluttered about my ears. *My life must be a beacon to the restless ghosts of the boneyard*, I pondered.

Suddenly, I remembered the Blackheart and the chilling sound it made when I heard it last. Truly, I did not want to meet up with something like that in this sinister world. I struggled forward until I found myself amid the forest of giant crystals where I had left Tiny to his fate.

"Tiny!" I hollered in the dark. "Tiny, can you hear me?"

Holding the scepter above my head, I followed my heart whichever way I felt he would have gone. Small droplets of blood on the ground led me to a trail of blood that snaked its way through the maze of crystal towers. I followed the trail, not really being sure but knowing I must find who was at the end. Around the crystals and through the mist, I traced the blood, calling Tiny's name, hoping it would be him that answered and not the Blackheart.

Finally, in a twisted corridor of gleaming rock, I found the remains of something. It was piled up in a corner. Its pale transparent skin and sparse tufts of matted hair let me know it wasn't Tiny. I crept up to it carefully, holding the scepter in front of me. I used the scepter's end and slowly rolled it over to find the cold, dead stare of the Blackheart. I breathed a sigh of relief when I realized it was dead. *Thank goodness*, I thought. *Tiny is still alive. If I had found him, I wanted it to be alive and kicking.*

Tiny had beaten it, and in a morbid twist, something had taken its heart right out of its chest. *Perhaps it was Tiny, making sure the Blackheart would never haunt his dreams again*, I thought.

Once my curiosity with what I had found was satisfied, I continued my search for a way out of this forsaken bog. Finally, tired and frustrated, I fell to the ground exhausted. The ground felt moist and soft beneath my hands. *Have I found the mouth of that cursed lizard?*

My memory wandered back to the time before our journey; thoughts of home flooded my weary mind. Thoughts of my mother, my grandmother, and even Churchill and Greenwald filled me with an overwhelming yearning that I had never known; a longing for all the little things that I had come to take for granted. Things like fresh-baked bread, warm spring days, and the security of my mother's open arms. Oh, how I yearned for life in my own world. *I want to go home*, I thought. *This must be what it is like for Salina's lost souls. This must be their fate. But wait*, I pondered. *I don't belong down here. I am not one of Salina's doomed spirits.*

"I want to go home," I said loudly. "I want to go home right now!" And I slammed the point of the scepter into the ground.

My voice echoed through the netherworld. I listened as it grew fainter and fainter. Then I heard the sound of rushing water and a guttural groan coming from the depths of this primeval being. The water filled the space around me, and in a giant surge I was spat out in a bubble of clear liquid. The bubble slowly rose through the black mud and earth of that ancient bog.

Whatever it was that that oldest of lizards lived in surrounded me on all sides and I could feel myself gently rising through it. Then, all at once, a window opened and I saw a gloomy sky, but it was sky nonetheless. With a pop, the bubble burst and I found myself on the cold, damp ground of that plateau. Never was I so happy to see that dismal plain as I was at that moment.

I lifted my eyes to greet the world, but was met with the sights of the scourge that was Salina's magic. The spell she had unleashed upon the earth had taken hold of men's hearts, and now an ocean of soldiers waged a futile war against their fellow man. A hard rain fell and the air was filled with flashes of lightning and rumblings of thunder.

An enormous gray dragon swooped down and swallowed up men like stalks of wheat, its talons crushing them as it snatched men off the ground and broke them like dry twigs, their limp bodies fell back to earth. "Stop!" I screamed as I jumped to my feet, but the thunder and the dragon's booming roar swallowed up my voice. Snatching the scepter from the ground, I raced to where we had left our horses.

As I ran, the scepter resonated with the sound of Salina's voice. Through it, her chant rose above the storm, "Camille, Camille, my beautiful pet," she beckoned. "The time is nigh to harvest souls, the fruit is heavy on the vine. The bell will summon as it tolls, their souls will all be mine. Ha, ha, ha, ha."

When I reached the tree where Tiny and I had left our horses, I found the bridle to Tiny's horse hanging from the branch by its reins. His saddle had been folded up with the stirrups under it and left beneath the tree. There was no sign of Tiny or his horse, just his tack carelessly left behind.

I untied my horse, mounted, and tore off across the plateau, weaving my way through the battling hordes with my eyes firmly fixed on the mound at the center of it all. There, clasped in a mortal combat of their own, above the clamor of war, stood the two men responsible for this harvesting of souls. The two kings battled hand-to-hand, my father with shield and sword and Azutoo with a mighty battle-ax. Mere puppets in this deadly game, they raged against each other for the rights to their own madness, trapped in the foolish struggle for supremacy.

At the foot of the mound, perched proud as peacocks on their steeds, were the two vain pawns of Salina's bloody charade, Elexi and Argose. A garrison of soldiers surrounded each man as they jeered at each other and urged the kings on to fight.

The scepter shook wildly in my hand as Salina called out to her dragon once more, "The kings, Camille! Bring me the kings!"

As I neared the mound, I saw the great gray dragon in the distance. It turned in the sky and charged the ground, heading directly for the center on the field.

"Enough!" I cried. "This ends now!"

I hurled the scepter high in the air, straight at that cursed mound. It left my hand with a force I had never known. End over end it twirled, far above the dueling kings, and just as the dragon was but a breath away from my father, the scepter plunged into the earth between the two kings. It stuck straight up and that magnificent blue-white light shot toward the sky, catching the dragon in midair.

The dragon froze for a moment; it hung curiously, not falling or rising, not moving at all. Time itself seemed to stand still. I watched in amazement as the field of warring men fell silent. All stood motionless, and one by one they turned their faces to the sky. It was as if Showhaun was about to do something miraculous and he wanted the attention of every man there.

When every last man faced the clouds and the two kings cast their cruel masks sky-ward, the dragon suddenly exploded in midair. It shattered into thousands and thousands of little pieces that gently floated back to earth as slowly as the seeds of a dandelion. One to a man, each bit of this dragon fluff landed on the forehead of every upturned face.

Finally, when the kings received their portion of the dragon's remains, these seeds from the sky, they screamed in pain and fell to their knees. The masks on their faces cracked and fell to the ground, leaving them both broken, weak and trembling in the mud.

"Father!" I yelled. I leapt from my horse and ran to his side.

Looking down at his broken mask that lay side by side with Azutoo's, the scepter between them both, I knelt beside my father and clasped him in my arms. He looked deep into my eyes with a face filled with remorse.

"Oh, honey-B. What have I done? What have I done?" he said, weeping. "What good could possibly grow from the ashes of so much destruction?"

That is when it happened, like some emerging grace that dared to defy our imaginations and bless our presence despite our foolish hearts. From the dark soil of that mound where Lucias's body lay, a plant slowly began to grow next to the scepter. Ever so gently it made its way up the shaft, winding around it as it went. Beautiful full green leaves sprang to life from its stalk as it grew. When it reached the hand at the top, a bud appeared and slowly unfolded its petals outward to greet the sun. That's right, the sun. For the first time in a thousand years, the sun broke through the clouds that hung over that plateau and lighted upon the rose that bloomed in the scepter's palm. The light spread out from that point across the Plain of Sorrows, warming each man's heart as it went and sparking to life the seed that settled in his mind.

All of a sudden, two shouts broke the silence.

"No!" Elexi yelled.

"What is happening?" screamed Argose.

Silently, while we watched the flower blossom before our eyes, the wretched arms of death had slithered out of the pools next to Elexi and Argose. Their bodies hit the ground with a thud when they were pulled from their steeds. The two hands grasped their legs and dragged them back toward the pools to the land of the dead.

"No!" they screamed. "Help me! Help me!"

Each desperately clawed at the ground, trying to cling to life. Soldiers that were near grabbed hold of their arms, but they were no match for the bony hands of death that had come to reclaim their souls.

"Help us, Emily!" they cried. "Help us!"

"I cannot," I said sadly. "I cannot help you. For you are already dead. You belong to her now. I am truly sorry."

And with that, their frightened faces faded into the black water as they dipped below the surface of the dark pools that now lay beneath the infinite blue sky of that plateau.

The silence was broken once more, but by a different sound. It was the sound of metal hitting the ground. All around me were the sounds of weapons falling and armor being shed. The men had begun to leave the plain en masse, to return to their lives in peace. For the first time, I watched as hands were extended, man to man and black to white. No longer did Salina's magic hold sway over their hearts or minds. Bonangi had planted a seed where once only hatred dwelled—and that seed was hope.

I looked at my father as he marveled at the now full and radiant rose. He reached for it as if to claim it as his own, but was skewered by thorns that appeared beneath his hand. "Ouch," he said, pulling back. "I guess it doesn't belong to me anymore." As he held his bleeding hand, the thorns disappeared.

"It is a beautiful thing, isn't it?" I asked my father.

"Yes, honey, it is a magnificent flower," he answered.

"Oh, I wasn't speaking of the rose, Father," I said. "I was speaking of the peace. The spirit of Bonangi makes it so. You see, Father," I added, as I bent over to pluck the scepter from the ground, "in order for good things to grow, you must have peace."

I pulled the scepter from the cold, damp earth and was surprised to see the rose come as well. It released its roots, the blossom tenderly cradled in the palm of Showhaun's hand. His blue orb gave the red rose a purple hue and a magical glow of its own.

"Come, Father," I said, helping him to his feet. "I will have your men take you home."

"But what about you, Emily? Aren't you coming with me?" he asked.

"No, Father, not just yet," I said. "I would like to take King Azutoo home to his son Cahogway, who misses him very much."

"What will become of me?" asked Azutoo. "How can I return after what I have done?"

"The spirit of Bonangi does not live in our mistakes," I said, holding out my hand in peace. "She lives in the hope that we will learn from them. You shall return to Marzadune and rule as you did before the mask ever touched your face."

"But there is guilt, and as a king, I know where there is guilt, there should also be punishment," he said firmly.

"There is punishment," I retorted. "Your punishment is to live with that guilt the rest of your life. But don't let it stop you from helping me change our world." I thrust my hand in front of him once more.

He laughed as he reached for my hand. Smiling at my father, he said, "How did you come to have such a wise daughter?"

My father looked at me with eyes of admiration and caressed my cheek with his trembling hand. "I don't know," he said. "She seems so much stronger now. More like a queen than a princess."

Azutoo took my hand and I helped the big man rise to his feet. "I am already looking forward to a long and peaceful friendship with you and your people, Queen Emily," he said. Then he stood for a moment, staring at me as I held the scepter cradled in my right arm, the red blossom shimmering with life. "Queen Emily," he said again, smiling. "Queen of the Eternal Rose."

"You are a queen, Emily," said my father, reaching for my hand. "I am not fit to be king, nor do I want to be. I was happier as a teacher in Summers Glen than ever I was as a king. I shall return to your mother in our little part of the world and you can rule as queen in my place." Before I could even respond, he yelled, "All hail, Queen Emily! All hail, the Queen of the Eternal Rose!"

As one, their voices rang out across the plain, "Hail, Queen Emily! Hail, the rose of Salizar!"

Azutoo chimed in as well, and the entire assembly bowed low before the mound on which I stood. There was nothing I could do; I had to address them.

"Remember this day!" I yelled to the men. "Remember it not as a day of war, but as a day of peace! Tell your children and your children's children! Let the rose stand as a symbol of eternal hope! May the magic of wisdom, courage, compassion, and truth be continuously reborn in their hearts! Now, return to your homes and sow the seeds you have been given. These seeds of Bonangi are the seeds of peace!"

"Heed her words well!" Azutoo added. "Lest our souls be found among these wretched pools!"

I looked at my father as he stood with downcast eyes in the shameful shadow of his royal rule. Gently lifting his chin with my finger, I softly kissed his cheek and whispered, "You will always be king in my heart. There, you will always reign supreme."

He smiled and took my hand. "Thank you, Emily, for rescuing me from that mask of ignorance," he said. "Now, I think I will go home to your mother. I have a lot of explaining to do. You don't suppose she will believe me, do you?"

"Ha, ha, ha. I'm not sure I believe what I saw," I said. "But I do believe peace will work, if we always try to understand before we act. Let's hope she does the same."

I helped my father in his weakened state onto his horse and watched him ride off across the plateau, back to Salizar. Then, as I was about to mount my horse, something caught my eye. Made of bronze, it was half buried in the mud next to the stone marked with Lucias's name.

I bent over and scraped the dirt from its shiny surface. It was Tiny's small bronze horn, complete with the leather strap that he used to wear over his shoulder.

"Are you coming?" asked King Azutoo.

"No," I said. "I think I will stay here a little while and say good-bye to this place. I should never want to return."

"There is nothing out here but old ghosts," he said.

"Yes, but even old ghosts deserve a farewell," I said. "I will meet you in Safora. You will find Cahogway there, at the home of Morzia. You can't possibly miss her house—it is the only one left standing."

"I guess now is as good a time as any to start undoing the damage I have done," he said. "I have a lot to make up for."

"I will see you there. You'll see," I said.

"I will be waiting. We will share the cup of friendship, you and I," he said. He then turned his horse southward and led his men home.

I waited until the last stragglers left the plateau and then turned my attention to the little bronze horn. *What has become of Tiny?* I wondered. The smoothly polished horn beckoned my lips to try. *Do I dare? Would it work for me?*

Carefully pressing my lips to the horn, I blew softly. Of course, nothing happened, so I blew again, and still there was no sound. "Huh," I said to myself. "I will never understand how this thing works."

Longingly, I gazed into the dusky sky. The sun dipped low in the west and subtle traces of crimson hung on the horizon. A bird glided effortlessly on the breeze in that western light. It swooped and twirled as it drew nearer to me. *Surely, that is the happiest bird I have ever seen*, I thought. It seemed to delight in its frolicking so; I found myself more than just a little envious.

It wasn't until it got close enough that I realized it wasn't a bird at all. It was Subakai, and resting between his two massive horns, holding on for dear life but laughing his fool head off, was Tiny. I literally jumped for joy, waving to them as they descended before me. Subakai lowered his head and Tiny slid to the ground as smoothly as you please. Running up to him, I threw my arms around him and squeezed with all my might.

"You're alive!" I exclaimed.

"Not for long, lass, if you don't loosen your grip a little," he said, laughing.

"I thought I had lost you to the netherworld," I said as I straightened his coat. "How did you ever get away from the Blackheart?"

"Well, that creature likes to find its prey by smell, so I always keep a little pepper on my person. There is never a time when one is more vulnerable than when one is sneezing," he said with a smile.

"Ah, now I understand why you kept dousing yourself with pepper!" I exclaimed.

"I was never sure when I was going to meet up with that thing, so I made a habit of it," he said.

"And how did you get out of the netherworld?" I asked.

"Yeah, well, apparently that ancient lizard didn't like the taste of pepper much. It spat me right out. I flew a good ways, too, before I hit the ground," he said with a chuckle.

"Well," I said, "the doorway is sealed and your adventures are over. What will you do now?"

"Without the ruby, I am forced to act my age," he said with a smile. "So, though it may be a bit late in life, I thought I might try my hand at settling down. I know a little old shaman woman who suits me just fine."

"Funny," I said, "I was heading that way myself."

"Subakai and I can get you there quicker, or slower, depending on whether or not you like the ride," he said with a wink. "I myself prefer to fly, even after a thousand years. It never gets old, ha, ha, ha."

I removed my horse's bridle and saddle, and smacked it on the backside. That horse took off across the plain, as free and as happy as an old man and his dragon. I took one last look around me at the plateau. The numerous black pools that dotted the plain now reflected the bright blue and crimson sky, which brought a whole new perspective to my eyes.

"Good-bye, you lost souls of the boneyard!" I yelled. "I have learned well the lesson of your fate and it will not be forgotten! Good-bye! May Bonangi bring peace to where you are!"

After putting the scepter in the quiver Tiny had given me, I climbed up on Subakai's head and took my place behind the old storyteller.

"Hold on tight," said Tiny as Subakai rose up from the ground. "Sometimes he likes to go pretty fast."

That great eastern dragon charged across the field as fast as it could, his gargantuan body rising and falling. Then, without warning, his wings opened like giant sails and he leapt into the air, carrying us aloft.

"Eeeeek!" I screamed, as I clung tightly to Subakai's horns. Tiny just laughed at the sound of my panic-stricken voice. That is one thing I shall never forget about that old man. He always did know how to have fun.

From there, we flew to Morzia's and reunited Cahogway with his father. We all celebrated and vowed to keep the spirit of Bonangi strong in our hearts. When we were done, Subakai and Tiny flew me home to Salizar, and as they say, the rest was history.

CHAPTER TWELVE

MIND OF A CHILD

"And that ends my story for this year, children," said the kindly old queen, as she sank back into the comfort of her throne.

The abrupt end to her story left the children sitting about the grand throne room stunned and bewildered.

"But wait, Queen Emily!" one young boy called out. "What happened to Tiny? Is he still alive?"

"Yeah!" another said. "Did you ever see him again?"

"And Subakai, what about him?"

"And Morzia?"

"And Cahogway?"

The questions flew up from the crowd of young faces.

"Tut, tut, tut," said the queen. "I will only answer questions if your hand is raised." Then she noticed the same little child that had previously given her the rose. She sat quietly with one hand timidly above her head. "Yes, my dear," said the queen, singling her out. "I will answer your question."

The frail little girl stood and nervously cleared her throat. "Eh-hmm…my question is about you, Your Highness." The room suddenly fell silent as the girl spoke softly.

"Yes, my dear, what is your question?"

"Do you ever miss him? Tiny, I mean. He did at least say good-bye, didn't he?"

The sweet old matriarch pondered the girl's words for a moment. Her subtle smile sagged a bit as if she had been cut to the quick. But true to her word, she continued undaunted.

"Well…Holly, isn't it?" she asked politely.

"Yes, mum," the girl answered.

"Well, Holly, here are the answers to your questions."

As I said, Subakai and Tiny flew me back to Salizar. We landed in the woods just beyond this palace many years ago. There, in a clearing, Tiny and I said our last good-byes. I stood in the shadow of the trees as Tiny climbed down from his beloved dragon.

"Here, this belongs to you," I said, handing him the little bronze horn.

"Keep it," he said. "You never know when you will be in need of a good friend, and Subakai is the best."

I hugged him one last time and lost my struggle against the falling tears. They rolled down my cheeks and onto his collar.

"Now, now, lass," he said. "Let's not end in tears."

"Are queens not allowed to cry?" I protested.

"They are," he said, wiping the sides of my face. "As long as they are tears of love."

"They are," I replied, sniveling.

"I will miss you, too, lass, but I have finally earned my place in this world. And because I have done all that I have, I know what that is worth. Be happy for me," he said.

"But what if I need you? What if the Crown needs you?" I asked in desperation.

"You have the scepter, and that is all you need," he said. "I shall live out what little time I have left with Morzia. I, too, have earned my right to peace in this world."

"Then this really is good-bye," I said, wiping my tears again.

"I'm afraid so," said Tiny. "If you find yourself missing me, tell our story. As long as you do that, I will be there."

"Thank you, Tiny, for all you have done. You have done the house of Millstaff proud. Lucias is smiling on you from within the scepter, I can feel it. The hosts of the spirit scepter bid you blessings in all that you do," I said. "We are all in your debt."

Tiny slowly climbed back up on Subakai's head and patted his thick mane. "Come, my old friend, I am flying home for the last time," he said. "Good-bye, Emily, and remember, believe in peace and it will always reside in this world."

"I will," I called back to him. "I promise!"

He disappeared above the tall trees and I was left alone with my scepter. Looking down at the soft purple glow that sparkled around the petals, I said, "Come, Showhaun, we have a promise to keep."

Then I walked the short distance through the woods to Ironcrest Castle, where my father, Greenwald, and Churchill were waiting. Churchill had apparently posted lookouts in the palace towers to notify him of my approach. They were all waiting at the garden gate when I arrived.

"Queen Emily!" Churchill exclaimed excitedly as I walked up the path.

"Welcome home, honey-B," said my father, as he reached out to hug me.

"Well, Rupert, aren't you going to say hello?" I said with a smile. Churchill snickered a little at the fact that I still remembered Greenwald's middle name.

"Certainly, Queen Beatrice," he said with one raised eyebrow. "Eh-hmm." He cleared his throat defiantly. "That is what the B stands for, isn't it? Emily Beatrice of Millstaff?"

"Greenwald, I am surprised at you," I said firmly. "Talking to your queen in such a manner. Impertinence like that gives me grounds to punish you. In fact, I think I will punish you and Churchill both."

"Me?" cried Churchill. "What have I done?"

"From now on, you will both be forced to wear the title of chief adviser to the queen," I said with a devilish grin. "Now you can dote on me instead of my father." I then took my father's arm and said, "Come, Father, we must prepare for a long and prosperous peace." And we strolled toward the palace, leaving the two of them to figure out what just happened.

In the years that followed, my father went back to Summers Glen and lived the quiet life he chose. Greenwald and Churchill helped me in all my endeavors to unite the surrounding provinces into one strong country, which was called Salucia, after our beloved city of Salizar and he who became the seed of hope—Lucias.

Cahogway eventually took his father's place as king, and a treaty was written on a stone tablet that rests alongside Lucias's gravestone on the Plain of Sorrows. There it will ensure, for generations to come, that war will never again take place between our two countries.

Tiny, to the best of my knowledge, lived out a peaceful existence in Safora with Morzia until his passing. The story I have heard is that they were both laid to rest on a mountain to the north of Salizar called Abiding Mountain. It overlooks the small town of Eadenburrow, where he grew up.

Some say that late in spring, when the moon is full and the sky is clear, a dragon sleeps in a cave at the top of that mountain. They say a strange wreath of smoke can be seen circling the mountaintop on windless nights.

"At least that is what I have been told," said the queen.

"But some people say the stories about Lynquest aren't real," remarked one little boy in the fifth row. "They say that they are all made up."

"I guess that is for you to decide, isn't it?" said the queen. "I know there are skeptics among the adults, so I will present this as proof and let you decide for yourselves what to believe."

She waved to a young page that was standing close by, holding something on a large velvet pillow covered with a satin scarf. He briskly brought the pillow before the children and lifted the satin scarf to reveal a small bronze horn still laced in its leather strap and shining like new. "Ohhhh!" said the children collectively. *Oohs* and *ahs* filled the air as the page walked among the children displaying the bronze relic of the queen's past.

"So you see, children," said the queen, "whether the story is true, or make-believe, is simply a matter of opinion. I know I believe, and I hope you will, too, for as long as we believe together, the seeds of peace will continue to grow."

"I believe," Holly said with conviction.

"Me, too," said another child in the back of the room.

"And me, I believe," said yet another.

Soon the whole room echoed with the sound of young voices proclaiming their belief in her story.

"Good, good," said the queen. "I can see the spirit of Bonangi is strong in this group of children. Now comes the reason for my story. I am a very old woman and will not be around forever. I need people to continue telling my story. That way, Bonangi will always bring balance to our hearts and my dear friend, Tiny, will always be in an adventure somewhere. Can you do this for me?"

"Yes, Your Highness!" they all said.

"Do you promise?" she asked. "Do you promise to tell your children?"

"Yes, yes," they said. "We promise! We do! We do!"

Bong! Bong! Bong! The bells in the city chimed and the good queen smiled as she said, "Now, look at that. We have finished just in time." She then waved to Mr. Featherbee. "Now it is time for us to say good-bye," she said. "Mr. Featherbee will escort you to the waiting carriages that will take you all home. I want to personally thank you for being such a good group of children, and I have a gift for you before you go."

At that moment, the palace servants brought in baskets of seeds and gave each child one seed to take home and plant as a reminder of that day.

One little boy who received his seed felt the need to ask a question. "If I may, Your Highness," he said politely, "what kind of seed is this?"

"Why, it's a *zaba* fruit, of course," said the queen with a wink and a smile.

She watched as the children filed into line and marched off down the hall, following Mr. Featherbee. She enjoyed the sweet satisfaction that came from telling the story, even if it was followed by the bittersweet reality of its end.

Having fulfilled her promise for yet another year, she called for the master at arms and sent for her royal coach. "I will be journeying to Millstaff Manor on the west coast and I want to leave tonight," she said. "Ready the team for my departure as soon as possible."

She left within the hour on the two-week journey to Millstaff Manor. On the last day of her trip, her party encountered a terrible storm. The carriage was rocked by mighty winds and rain. Lightning splintered the dark and gloomy sky.

The master of the guard approached her coach on horseback. "My Queen," he yelled, "I fear for your life in such a storm. We should seek shelter at the inn in Hamleborn and overnight there. Perhaps the weather will be more suitable for travel on the morrow!"

"Nonsense!" she called back. "That old siren doesn't scare me. Tell the coachman to drive on. I want to be at the manor before morning, despite the ranting of that old crow."

"Yes, Your Majesty," said the guard. Then he called out to the coachman. "Driver, drive on! We must make journey's end before daybreak tomorrow!"

"Yes, sir!" said the coachman, and he cracked his whip in the air above the horses' heads, urging them on. "Hyah! Hyah!" he yelled, and the carriage sped off across the moors in the driving wind and rain.

Arrive she did, just before dawn. The storm had subsided as she stepped from her coach and made her way up the long stairs. Willford, her butler, was there to greet her at the door to the manor.

"I took the liberty of having your bed turned down for you, madam, assuming you would be weary from your journey," he said.

"Not just yet, Willford, I would like to take breakfast on the balcony off the setting room first, before I rest," she said.

"Certainly, madam," said Willford, as he took her long thick overcoat. "Shall I put the scepter in its case for safekeeping, Your Highness?"

"No, that's all right," she said. "I will hold on to it for a little while longer."

"As you wish, Your Majesty," he said with a nod.

"Are my lovelies awake yet?" asked the queen.

"I am sure they are, Your Highness. They always are when you are back from Ironcrest Castle. I shall tell them you are in the setting room and Cook can make three plates."

"Good, good…Willford, what would I ever do without you?" she said, placing her hand on his shoulder as she stepped past him.

"I should never like to find out, madam," he said. "I am too fond of your company."

"As I am yours," she said, and then she slowly made her way through the big house toward the setting room.

In the lavish setting room, she found Sarah, her handmaiden, tending the fire in the grand old fireplace. "Good morning, Sarah," she said as she entered. "Goodness, doesn't anyone sleep at Millstaff Manor anymore?"

"Good morning, Your Highness. I was just making sure the setting room was good and warm for you," said Sarah.

"How did you know I was going to be in the setting room this morning?" asked the queen.

"I have been in service to the Crown since Maribelle retired, mum. It must be going on twelve years. I think I have discovered your likes and dislikes by now."

"Well, you're very conscientious in your duties, Sarah. You are to be commended," said the queen.

"Maribelle taught me well, then, wouldn't you say, milady? I know that when you arrive in the morning, you like to take breakfast on the balcony with your grandchildren. In fact, I am rather surprised that they are not here yet," said Sarah with a smile.

"Yes, well, my two turtledoves are probably sleeping in this morning," said the queen.

"Not likely, mum. They are probably waiting to surprise you."

"At any rate," said the queen with a laugh, "I will be on the balcony, pretending I'm surprised when they arrive."

"As you wish, Your Majesty," said Sarah sweetly.

The weary matriarch sauntered out the double doors that led to the balcony overlooking the coastline and was immediately taken aback by the view. The morning light streamed in from the east, turning the cliffs and sand of the coast a brilliant white, while the dark and somber storm clouds hung over the turbulent sea. They cast a sinister shadow upon the churning ocean like an ever-present phantom, darkening its raging depths. The contrast between light and dark was played out in the form of a line that ended at the water's edge.

A breathtaking rainbow crested the gap between the malevolent, brooding clouds and the sterling white cliffs. The long grass that topped the cliffs shown emerald green in the morning sun, and as if all this was not enough to take in, a flock of glistening seagulls played in the rainbow like children in the rain.

The sonnets of a thousand poets could not sum up more eloquently the struggle of her life than the scene that now filled her eyes and warmed her heart. Somewhere in the dancing of the gulls, she found herself rejoicing with the spirits of the scepter in the victory over the retreating storm. There they were—Tiny, Morzia, Lucias, and Showhaun—frolicking in the magnificent colors as nature had always intended. A gentle tear pressed itself against her grateful eyes, but did not dare to fall. So lost in the vision was she, that she did not hear her two grandchildren sneaking up behind her.

"Surprise!" they yelled.

"Oh my goodness," said the queen. "You gave me a start!"

"Ha, ha, we scared you," they said, laughing.

"You most certainly did," said the queen. "I was just admiring the beautiful sunrise. Look children, do you see the rainbow?"

"Wow, Grandmama! That is beautiful!" exclaimed Tina, the older of the two children. "Have you returned from telling the children the story?"

"I have," said their grandmother. "It was better than last year. I do believe I am getting better at telling it every year."

"Will you tell it to us?" asked her little grandson.

"I will when you turn seven, my dear," said the queen, running her fingers through his hair.

"Did you hear that, sis? You get to go next year," the little boy said.

"Yep," said Tina. "I'm going to be old enough next year. I can't wait." As Tina said these words, a question popped into her head. "Grandmama, why do you tell the story to the children every year? If you have to be older, why not tell the grown-ups?"

"Yeah!" declared her younger brother. "Why do you tell the story only to children?"

Queen Emily paused a moment and looked back at the birds dancing in the sky, and then down at the beautiful rose that adorned her beloved scepter. She lightly touched the petals with the tips of her fingers, and, looking deep into her grandson's eyes, she said, "Because, my dear, sweet Tiny, hope blossoms eternally in the mind of a child."